THE SCOUT OF WOUNDED KNEE

michael@michaelamclellan.com

“If America had been twice the size it is, there still would not have been enough.”
— Tȟatȟáŋka Íyotake (Sitting Bull)

“The only good Indians I ever saw were dead.”
— Philip Sheridan

“Those Indians who go over to the white man can be nothing but beggars, for he respects only riches, and how can an Indian be a rich man? He cannot without ceasing to be an Indian. As for me, I have listened patiently to the promises of the Great Father, but his memory is short. I am now done with him. This is all I have to say.”
— Maȟpíya Lúta (Red Cloud)

History is almost always written in a light which favors the writers.

Chapter 1

February 25, 1929

Wyatt Earp is dead.

It was on the front page of the newspaper some weeks ago.

I met the man once, in Dodge City, Kansas. I can't say I cared for him much. The newspaper said he was eighty-years-old, which is a few years younger than I am. I suppose I could be sharing space in Hell with him before too long.

If there is such a place, it's where we both belong.

Down the page from the headline about Mister Earp's death, there was a story titled, *The Battle of Wounded Knee*, by one Miles Falmouth. An illustration accompanied the story. It depicted U.S. soldiers engaged in heavy combat with Indians. I didn't read it. The headline and the drawing were enough for me. You see, I've seen battles, more than I care to count, and I'm here to tell you that this wasn't one. So I figured I'd write a story of my own—my story. Perhaps I can set some things straight, and hopefully alleviate some of my nightmares in the process. I've had them nearly every night for thirty-nine years. There was a time I could stave them off by getting drunk, but I don't tolerate liquor too well these days. Most nights now I lie awake listening to the rafters creaking until well after midnight. Most mornings I'm up long before the sun. A guilty conscience is a heartless companion.

I'm not a writer, but I've read a thousand books if I've read one, and though my eyes aren't what they once were, I still have a decent enough memory. I ordered some good quality paper and a pair of fountain pens from the Sears, Roebuck, and it all arrived just yesterday. The paper is nice. This one here is the first sheet.

My name is Everett Ward. I was born in Missouri on Dec 1, 1845, on a little scrap of a farm near Osceola. My mother and father were both from Virginia. I don't know what would have made them want to relocate to the ramshackle house on that flood-prone twenty acres, and I never thought to ask them while they were alive. Looking back on it, I realize how little I knew of them. I know that my father used his small inheritance to buy the farm not long after my older brother Clyde was born in 1842. I also know they were both educated, a fact that makes the purchase of the spread even more curious.

My father was a poor farmer, in both senses of the word. His corn never grew worth a damn and his hogs were always sick. My mother tutored local children sometimes and took in mending when she could. Around Christmas time she'd sew quilts for extra money. Clyde and I never went to a school but our mother and father took turns teaching us. They had a fair collection of books they'd brought from back east, and in the evenings after supper all four of us would read to one another from of them. We never had a lot of money, and sometimes in the winter we only ate one meal a day, but there was happiness. It was a good life.

My brother and I joined the Confederacy in 1861. Not because of politics or slavery, but for the twenty-five dollars each we were given to sign on. My father was sorry to lose the labor—he didn't believe in keeping slaves, and couldn't have afforded any if he did—but he was grateful for the fifty dollars. Truth is, we would have joined the Union just as readily if we would have been offered a cash bounty from the boys in blue first. We just wanted to help our mother and father.

Clyde and I were issued our ill-fitting grays along with a couple of worn-out looking Springfield rifles and sent marching south. Two weeks later we were standing at the bottom of a hill with only three balls apiece for the old muzzleloaders, waiting for the order to charge the Union line on the south slope of the hill. Clyde made less than a dozen steps before he went down. It turned out there were union sharpshooters lying in the grass at the top of the hill. The ball took him in the knee. It shattered his kneecap along with some of his femur and tibia. The army sawbones attempted to take off his leg halfway between his hip and his knee that same night. My brother died screaming while I stood listening less than ten feet away. He was three days from being nineteen-years-old. Six weeks later my mother and father were dead too. They were dragged from the house in their bedclothes in the middle of the night by Unionist Jayhawkers, and shot dead in the dooryard where Clyde and I used to play jacks. The house and barn were burned to the ground. It was cold comfort they didn't have to grieve Clyde for long.

As for me, I spent the next four years fighting and never took a scratch.

One morning about a month before things ended, I leaned my rifle up against a tree where we were camped in the woods southeast of Kansas City and walked away. I wasn't the first. In the early months of 1865 men were deserting in droves, at least in Missouri they were. I wasn't a deserter, though. My commitment to the Confederate Army had ended six months prior. I stayed on because I had nowhere else to go. You would have been hard-pressed to find an officer who'd have given a tinker's damn if I was deserting like the rest of them anyway. The command in our regiment had long since crumbled and officers were deserting as well. By that time most of us were nothing but a bunch of sick and half-starved wraiths wielding empty rifles.

When I struck off through the woods toward home, I had the pistol I'd taken from a dead Union officer at Lone Jack in '62, the jackknife my father gave me for my tenth birthday, a speck of flint, a canteen that belonged to the Confederate Army, and one hardboiled egg. I didn't have anything else to my name. Even my clothes belonged to the Confederacy.

I made my way south, staying off the roads to avoid contact with troops of either side. It was early March and it was cold and there was still some snow. I didn't curse the snow because it was never very deep, and I could melt it for water. It took me a week to make the journey and that hardboiled egg was all I ate the entire seven days.

When I reached the farm I spent some time poking through the four-year-old ashes, but I was too weak to dig very deep and it appeared as if it had been sifted through many times before. Even the stones of the fireplace had been carried off. I was only hoping to find a photograph of my mother. She never consented to Clyde and I joining up. "Fifty dollars be damned," she said when we broke the news to her and my father. "It isn't worth your lives." It was the only occasion in my fifteen-years that I'd ever heard a curse pass my mother's lips.

I sat down against the big cottonwood which grew between the house and the barn and wept for a while. I woke up to someone kicking my foot. I opened my eyes; not kicking my foot, but tapping it with a walking stick.

"You're John Ward's boy, ain'tcha? Clyde.... No, that's not right, you're the other one, Everett."

I nodded. "Yes, ma'am, Missus Bishop."

"Well, if you ain't a sight...." She cocked her head toward the black rubble that was once my family's home. "You got word of what happened, I expect?"

"Yes, Ma'am. Not long afterward."

"Well, I'm sorry about your folks. It was a terrible thing what those men did.... Most everyone's gone now, 'cept me and the Sundersons and old Mac down by Lawson's Bend. There's a few up in town but there's nothing left but cinders, so God only knows why they're still there. You want to come up to the house, get yourself something to eat? I don't have much but I'll share what there is. I don't know if you remember Nathanial—*Mister Bishop*—but he's gone now. The consumption finally got the better of him. He passed two summers ago, God rest his soul. It's just me and a goat and a half-dozen chickens."

I stood up a little too sudden and staggered on account of the hunger. Missus Bishop grabbed my upper arm and steadied me. I remember how strong her grip felt, even through my wool coat. She was rail-thin and her hair had been as white and wispy as a summer cloud for as long as I could remember. Clyde and I thought both her and Mister Bishop as old as Methuselah, but she didn't seem old or frail to me that day.

I began to weep again.

"There now," she said. "You'll feel better once we get something hot into you. You want to see where they're buried 'fore we go?" She didn't wait for an answer. She only looked at me appraisingly for a moment, likely to see if I was going to faint or not. Seeming satisfied, she released my arm and started off toward the fenced area where my mother used to keep her garden.

"There weren't nobody to make a headstone," she said apologetically "The Hutchins brothers did all the other work, even said some words over 'em. Them two left for the east not long after."

I pulled the wooden bolt and opened the gate. The side-by-side graves of my mother and father were in the far corner. Someone—presumably the Hutchins brothers—had covered them with rock cairns. I walked over and kneeled down between them. I thought about what my mother said about mine and Clyde's lives being worth more than fifty-dollars. Now she and my father and Clyde were all dead. Clyde called me a damn fool when I first brought up enlisting. He came around, though, once I told him about the money. Sitting there by those graves I wondered if I didn't sell all three of their lives for fifty-dollars my mother didn't even want.

After several minutes I stood. I waited a moment for the faintness to pass and started toward the gate. Missus Bishop turned and started off without a word, leaning heavily on her walking stick. When she past the cottonwood she bent down stiffly and picked up a medium-sized burlap sack. "It's fortunate for you I chose today pick clover," she said over her shoulder as she made her way toward the road.

The Bishop house was a mile up the main road and then another mile on an overgrown one-lane track into the woods. It made sense that the Jayhawkers missed the place. The one-room house was situated in a cleared-out spot in a fairly thick mixed grove of trees. It was built of logs and the floor was dirt but it was well-oiled and not dusty, and the rest of the place was as neat as a pin. There was a bed in one corner and a kitchen along one wall with a large stone hearth not unlike the one I'd grown up with. The burned-down embers of the morning's fire were still glowing. There was a wooden rocker next to it. "You can sit over there while I put things together," Missus Bishop said, pointing to the chair.

"Can I help?" I asked.

"You just sit down before you fall down. Mayhap if you stay on for a few days and get your strength back you can cut some wood for me. I've been having to walk farther and farther to drag back pieces small enough for me to manage."

She built the fire up and I was soon asleep in the chair. I awoke a short time later to the maddening smell of chicken soup.

"I made some potato dumplings," she said, handing me a chipped enamel bowl with a small cloth underneath to protect my hands from being burned. "I haven't had any wheat flour for near a year, but corn binds 'em well enough in a pinch. You'll have to eat sittin' here. I busted up the dining table for firewood some time back."

I wolfed the food. I still hold it among the best meals I've ever eaten.

After supper she cleaned up the dishes and then hung a fresh kettle of water over the fire. She walked over to a large wooden trunk at the foot of the bed, rummaged through it for a moment, and came up with a stack of neatly folded clothes with a bottle resting on top.

"Nathanial bought the whiskey the last time our son William came out to visit from New York. This was in the summer of '57. He's dead now o'course. Horse threw him later that fall. Nathanial was never a drinker, so we just kept the bottle for guests." She handed me the clothes and the nearly full bottle.

"As you can see, we didn't have too many visitors. The clothes were Nathanial's. They'll probably fit loose until you fill out some, or can get some others. There's a pair of boots over there in the corner that might fit you. They ain't new, but they're in a sight better shape than the ones you got on. I'm going out for a walk. There's a wash cloth and hunk of soap over there on the cuttin' board. Water's about hot. You can clean yourself up."

When she was gone I took the water and the wash cloth out to the little back porch—just a couple of wide planks set atop some pine rounds—and washed up the best I could. She was right about her husband's clothes. He was both taller and wider than I was, even when I wasn't half-starved. The wool trousers weren't terrible, just long, but the heavy cotton shirt hung off me like a ship sail. I was grateful to have them regardless, because they were *civilian* clothes. I took the Confederate grays back into the house and threw them on the fire. I tried on the boots and they fit just fine.

Staying on for a few days turned out to be two weeks, but the time gave me a chance to regain my strength and take care of some chores Missus Bishop couldn't do for herself. I worked most of those days cutting what dead trees I could find within a quarter mile of the homestead and dragging sections back and cutting them up into even smaller sections I could split for her fires. In the end I must have put by two cords. In the evenings I would take Nathanial Bishop's old rifle—which was even older than the ones Clyde and I were issued by the Confederacy—and go out into the woods looking for game. There wasn't much to be found, but I did manage to shoot a small doe on an outing.

One day I carved out a scrap of wood plank with my parent's names and walked back to the old place, drove a stake into the ground and then nailed the plank to it. It didn't look like much, but at least they were marked.

Most evenings after supper Missus Bishop would have me read to her from her Bible on account of her eyes not being good and then I'd excuse myself to her woodshed to sleep for the night. Most nights I'd dream about the war. It took a long time before I dreamed about anything else.

We were standing in her dooryard, saying our goodbyes, when she offered me Nathaniel's rifle. At first I declined to accept, but she insisted that even though she could still heft it, she couldn't see well enough to shoot anything with it. I thought it over for a moment and said I'd accept the rifle if she'd take the pistol I'd lifted off of that dead Union officer. That was if she didn't have any misgivings about where I got it.

"I reckon he don't need it wherever he is now," she said.

"No," I agreed, removing the pistol from the waistband of the trousers she'd given me and holding it out to her. "There's only four balls in it."

"I don't expect I'll need a one. You certain you don't want to keep it?"

"I'd like you to have it."

She took the pistol and looked down at it thoughtfully. It looked impossibly large in her hands. After a time she lifted her head. "Your brother, Clyde …"

I nodded.

"It's been a terrible time.... Go on. Go up and get the rifle, and make sure you take the powder and shot. And there's a flour sack on the cuttin' board with a little food in it for your journey."

I walked back to the house and took the rifle from the iron hooks on the wall, as well as the powder-horn and the leather pouch of balls that hung next to it, and then I fetched the flour sack as well.

When I returned she looked like she'd been weeping.

"God be with you, Everett," she said. "I'll be praying for you."

I made my way south, down to Texas, over the next two and a half months. It was a tough trip, and outside of a handful of short wagon rides, I walked the whole way. Though I was grateful to have it, the food Missus Bishop packed for me, and the surprise seven dollars she'd stuffed down in the bottom of the flour sack wrapped up in a scrap of cloth, didn't last long. I took work when I could find it, but the war had taken its toll on folks and money was scarce. Mostly I'd trade work for meals: plowing fields, running fence, repairing roof shakes and cleaning out horse stalls. I was hungry most of the time, but eventually I made it down to a town named Sherman where I took a job at a hotel called The Englebright. The proprietor, a tiny, fussy man in his middle forties, was named Calvin Englebright. Englebright was a born and bred Texan, though his mother and father were first generation Americans. His father got into the cattle business long before Texas statehood, and Calvin still kept a finger in the business though he hadn't spent a single day in the saddle himself since his father died a decade earlier.

The Englebright boasted a saloon as well as a restaurant and a stable. It was a profitable business in a town that had a slew of empty storefronts. My job was cleaning up around the saloon and occasionally helping out in both the kitchen and the stable. At the beginning, Mister Englebright provided me with an empty stable stall to sleep in, since I didn't have any money or a place to stay. I appreciated it even if it wasn't out of charity. He was a smart man and as shrewd as I've ever met. If you gave him a jar of dust he'd manage to squeeze a nickel out of it. Silus, one of the Englebright's bartenders, told me later there had been someone sneaking in the stable at night and stealing feed, tack, and lanterns and the like, and that Calvin Englebright had been thinking about hiring a boy to keep a night watch. It explained why Mister Englebright told me to keep my ears open for anything unusual in the stable.

After two weeks sleeping in a pile of hay, I found an opening at one of the boarding-houses at the end of town. The woman who ran it—Marylyn Hardy was her name—only charged me twenty cents more a week than I was paying Mister Englebright for the stable stall, and she laundered the sheets once a week.

I fell into a routine. The hours were long and I often had to work late into the night—this was when the millers or cowboys got paid, and there was a silver mine nearby and the miners would come in a couple of times a month to blow off steam. The saloon was smoky, loud, and there were a lot of fights and not a few shootings. There was so much hate and animosity directly after the war that it always seemed to come spilling out of folks when they were in their cups. The town must have had around a thousand people in it that year and sentiments were about evenly split—as far as I could tell—between pro-Union and pro-Confederacy. I kept my head down and tried to avoid trouble, but sometimes it found me anyway. Once, I had a near full spittoon dumped on my head for accidently spilling a man's drink, and another time a man shot at me for staring too long at a whore who'd been paying attention to him. If I *was* staring, I didn't realize I was doing it, and thankfully he missed. I suppose if I looked a little too long it's because I was curious. She was beautiful and not wearing much of anything and I was nineteen and had never even kissed a woman before, let alone had one sitting in my lap, whispering in my ear like she was with that fella. On that occasion Mister Englebright docked my pay two dollars for the damage done to the bar by the man's bullet.

After a couple of months I started thinking about leaving. It was like the war was still going on in Sherman. It was all people seemed to want to talk about. There were two newspapers in town and you could get the sort of propaganda you wanted from one or the other based on what side you were on. The pro-Confederacy paper was writing stories about how the Confederate army was being rebuilt down in Mexico and would soon be returning to resume the war. I was ready for the war to be over.

One day near the end of July I was pitching fresh hay into the stalls at the stable like I did every week, when Mister Englebright came up behind me. As usual, he looked flustered and in a hurry.

"I'm tired of not being able to send you on errands. You need a horse. Ed McBain's got a mare; she's getting old, but he claims she's still a good saddle horse. He needs post and rails run for two new corrals and his hands are too busy with the new herd he just brought in. I recommended you. Old or not, the horse is worth a lot more than the amount of work you'll be doing, but he owes me a favor or two. You do the work, he'll give you the horse, though you'll have to do it on your off time because I can't spare you." He started off without waiting for a reply. When he reached the stable door he stopped and turned. "That Mexican boy, Carlos, delivers eggs out there every Saturday morning. He'll drive you out in his wagon. Getting back you'll be on your own."

Two days later I was up with the sun and heading west out of town on Carlos the chicken farmer's wagon. The McBain ranch was five miles out, near a bend in Little Creek. A man not a whole lot older than me met us near a cluster of outbuildings adjacent to the house.

"Buenos dios, Carlos," he said, approaching the wagon.

"Buenos dios, Michael," Carlos returned, hopping from the wagon and trotting around to the back.

Michael turned to me. "You must be Everett."

"Yes, sir," I said, stepping down from the wagon.

"Pleased to meet you, Everett. I'm Michael McBain. Give us a hand, then I'll introduce you around before I show you where you'll be working."

We unloaded the crates of eggs and walked them around to the back of the main house, a sprawling one-story adobe with a clay tiled roof. A door opened as we approached and a girl of about my age stepped out and held it open for us. I can't say I was immediately smitten, exactly, but I can't say

I wasn't, either. I was young, and she was dark-skinned and beautiful, even in the frayed and faded blue housedress she wore. I nodded as I passed, feeling flushed and gangly. She smiled at me and my heart sped up.

"Thank you, Rebecca," Michael said.

Inside was a kitchen nearly as large as the one at The Englebright and just as busy. An old man with a sunburned and craggy face pointed to a table in the corner. "Mornin' Mister McBain. You can put those over there," he said, wiping his hands on his white smock.

We set the crates where we were instructed and Michael cocked his head toward the opposite end of the kitchen. "This way, Everett," he said. "I'll introduce you to my father before I take you out to meet the boys. See you next week, Carlos."

"Adios, Michael."

I thanked Carlos for driving me in and then followed Michael through the busy kitchen. The girl, Rebecca, had moved away from the back door and was standing over a cast-iron stove where she was tending to something on the cook-top. I watched her as I walked by and remember feeling disappointed when she didn't turn from her work.

I followed Michael down a short L-shaped hallway and did my best not to gape as we entered a high ceilinged and spacious drawing-room furnished with richly upholstered chairs the color of Burgundy wine. There were tables decorated with beautiful lamps and figurines, and ornately carved wood moldings around the windows, doors, and fireplace mantle. The Englebright Hotel had been the nicest place I'd ever been inside of up until that moment, and it appeared a pauper's shanty in comparison to the McBain house.

A stout, balding man sat at a roll-top desk in front of a picture window facing the open prairie. Michael stopped several feet away from the desk and waited. The man was writing something and didn't immediately acknowledge our presence. After some time he returned his pen to his inkwell, removed his spectacles and turned.

"This Everett Ward?" he asked, addressing Michael.

"It is, sir," Michael said.

The man nodded. "I'm pleased to meet you, Everett," he said warmly, "I'm Edward McBain, in case my son didn't tell you. Calvin Englebright speaks highly of you, which is rare for him. He claims you're as hardworking as they come. He also said you fought for our side in the war."

"Yes, sir," I said.

"In that case I'm happy to have you. Work hard and there might be a future in it—that is if you're meaning to stay around. I'm always looking for good help, and Calvin can always find himself another saloon boy." He paused and regarded me for a moment. "Well, better get to it then," he said, and turned back to his desk.

I spent the next hour following Michael around and meeting the hands. After the first few stops—the tack-house, the bull corral, and the number one stable—I stopped trying to keep the names straight. There were a lot of head nods, hand-shakes, and *pleased to meet you's.* I met the foreman—John Delaney, his name was— at the number two stable, and he and Michael showed me the mare I'd be working for.

"She's eighteen, almost as old as you and me," Michael said. "But she's still got some trail left in her."

She was a big bay with a little S-shaped patch of gray on her muzzle. I approached her stall and cooed a little and stroked her cheek and neck, taking pleasure in her coarse but silky hair. I'd been around horses in the war and almost every day at Englebright's, but for some reason this one made me homesick. I asked what her name was and the foreman shook his head and laughed like it was the funniest thing he'd ever heard. He was still laughing as he moseyed down the aisle to another stall.

"You can name her whatever you want," Michael said, putting a hand on my shoulder. 'C'mon, I'll show you the tool-shed and you can get to work."

The work was hard. I was set to digging postholes a hundred feet or so from the working corrals, while another man, James, dropped posts and rails on the ground at ten-foot intervals. The holes had to be two-foot deep and big enough around for a good-sized split post. The ground was as stony as a hanging judge's stare and it was Texas-summer hot. The going was slow, but I just kept thinking about that beautiful bay horse. I decided I'd name her Evelyn. It was my mother's name.

Michael came up in the mid-afternoon and said if I was hungry there was a table set up outside the kitchen with beefsteaks and biscuits.

Back at the house I washed up in the galvanized pan they had set up next to the well pump with a cake of lye soap. Twenty-five or so men were either lined up at the wood plank table dishing up or already sitting around with their tin plates in their laps shoveling food.

"Don't be shy, Everett," John, the foreman who'd laughed at me, called out from where he was standing at one of the tables. "Grab yourself a plate over there and get some of this before these jackasses eat all of it."

I walked over to the end of the table and picked up a plate, fork and cup. There were steaks piled on a big platter, beans, biscuits, and corn, as well as pots of coffee. I was ravenous but was careful not to take too much. Partially because I didn't want a full stomach to slow me down when I went back to work, but mostly because I was raised to not take advantage of a host's generosity.

I took my food and coffee and sat down off by myself with my back against the wall of the house. The eave provided some shade and I was happy to be out of the sun for a while. When I was finished eating, I drank down the last of my coffee and put the cup on top of the empty plate and put the whole works aside. I put my head back against the cool mud wall and closed my eyes, figuring I'd rest for another few minutes before I went back to work.

"I'll take your plate if you're finished."

I opened my eyes and Rebecca was standing over me with a stack of plates in her hands. I picked up my plate and stood. "I am, thank you," I said, carefully setting my plate on top of the others.

She nodded primly and turned toward the kitchen door. I walked over, opened it, and held it for her. She afforded me a brief, almost reproachful smile and then glanced over her shoulder before hurrying past me into the kitchen. I let the door close, feeling discomfited, as if I'd broken some sort of convention.

The sun was low in the west when I finally called it a day. I said goodbye to Michael and Ed McBain before I started my walk back into Sherman. They both thanked me and wished me well. Once on the road I realized how tired I was and the dusty five miles seemed like ten. The coyotes were already bickering and howling, and I was dead on my feet by the time I reached the boarding-house. I didn't even stop by the kitchen to see if there were supper leftovers. In my room I flopped down on the bed fully-clothed and was asleep in an instant.

Thoughts of Rebecca grew in my mind over the next few days while I was working my shifts at the Englebright. In these daydreams she was always in some sort of trouble. In the course of several days, I rescued her from a pack of wolves, a wild boar, and a gang of bandits. Afterward we always ended up kissing under the shade of a big cottonwood on a sandy bank of Little Creek.

On Friday I was working in the saloon, scrubbing down tables, when Silus, the bartender, came on shift. It was around four in the afternoon and the place was slow. A couple of regulars were at the bar, and a lone four-handed poker game that was still running from the previous night went on quietly in the corner by the shuttered piano.

I set my wash-brush down on the table I'd been cleaning, took a deep breath, and walked over to the bar on the opposite end of the drinkers. Silus nodded to me and sauntered over.

"Afternoon, Reb. What can I get you?" Silus always called me Reb. He didn't fight in the war and I never heard him take a side on it, he just liked to give everyone nicknames. I didn't really like when he called me that because I preferred strangers didn't know which side I served on. It saved getting dragged into too many arguments, or worse.

"I don't need anything to drink," I said. "I was just hoping I could talk with you for a minute."

"So long as Englebright don't come walking in." He pulled a dirty looking cloth out of his belt and started wiping the bar between us with it.

"Do you know anything about … courting?" I said.

"You mean like a woman? Sure, I reckon I know enough. As much as the next man anyway. I been married twice haven't I?"

"I didn't know that," I said. "Well, I met this girl—*woman*—at the McBain ranch and I was wondering … you know … how I'd go about courting her."

"A woman out at the McBain ranch," he said, musingly. "I wasn't aware there was any women out there. Old lady McBain's been dead since Hector was a pup, and far as I know Michael was their only child. Old man McBain, now he's got a sister comes out from California and visits from time to time. She stays here at the hotel when she comes. Not sure why she don't stay out there…."

"She's not in the McBain family. At least I don't believe she is. She's an Indian … I mean, I *think* she's an Indian—I've only seen one other in my life. Her name is Rebecca. She works in the kitchen."

"An Indian, huh? An Indian named Rebecca. Well, I haven't never courted no Indian woman and don't know what you'd want with one truth be told, but seeing how most women I've known are all the same, I suppose an Indian woman can't be much different. Might be even easier considering she ain't likely to be too spoiled like some white women. Anyways, it's gifts, Reb. Women want gifts. Shiny gifts, mostly: hairpins, hatpins, broaches, bracelets … and flowers. Women love when a man gives them flowers."

"There's not much blooming this time of year," I said.

Silus laughed. "You don't want to give them *picked* flowers. You want to give them *bought* flowers." Suddenly he snapped the fingers of one hand and then pointed at me. "A new dress," he said exuberantly. Every woman wants a new dress. It don't even matter how many they already have."

"That may be nice," I said.

"You know I don't recall ever seeing no Indian woman around Sherman, 'cept for that one old Shithouse Ned Johnson married. She died of the wet lung back in 58 or 59."

I didn't ask Silus why he called the man Shithouse.

"May be she lives at the ranch," I said.

"Could be, could be."

The light brightened briefly in the saloon as the batwing doors swung open. Three men entered and approached the bar.

"Anyhoo, Reb," Silus said, stuffing the cloth he'd been using to wipe the bar back into his belt. "Best of luck to you. Just buy her something pretty and speak politely to her and smile a lot. You'll do fine."

The following morning I hitched out to the McBain ranch with Carlos again. Calvin Englebright allowed me to have Sunday off from work at the saloon so I'd have two days in a row to work on the McBain corrals. That Saturday morning went by as slow as molasses in a Missouri winter because all I could think about was whether or not I'd get to see Rebecca at the afternoon meal. On top of that, I'd went and bought some new trousers, a red work-shirt, and a new hat at the mercantile, and the canvas trousers were so stiff I could scarcely move in them and they chafed something fierce.

Though the time seemed to move slowly that morning, the work didn't. With the help of a steel breaker-bar I finally figured out the quickest way to get the holes dug and I was moving along twice as fast as I had the previous week. Eventually John Delaney came around and told me chow was on. I hadn't seen Michael that morning. I picked up my saddlebags—another purchase I'd made at the mercantile—and started toward the house.

"You pick a name for your horse yet?" John called from behind me and started laughing fit to split.

A few of the men nodded at me when I reached the rear of the house but most didn't pay me any mind. I wasn't a regular hand, after all. I fixed myself a plate and sat off by myself in the same spot by the kitchen door I had the previous week. I ate my meal and set my plate aside just like the last time except this time I set it on top of a small brown paper package tied up tightly with string that I'd taken from my new saddlebags. Rebecca soon came around collecting plates, and when she neared I stood and set the package along with my plate on top of the stack she was carrying. She looked down at the package and then at me. At the time I couldn't read her expression, but in retrospect I know it was fear.

"It's a gift … for you," I said. I wanted to go on but I suddenly found myself too tongue-tied to speak. It was too late anyway. She turned so abruptly she nearly lost the stack of plates. She headed toward the kitchen door. I started forward but stopped myself. She balanced the plates against one arm so she could free up a hand to open the door, which slowly swung shut behind her as she disappeared into the kitchen.

As I returned to work on the corral fencing, I couldn't shake the feeling that I'd made a terrible mistake. I chided myself as a foolish, ignorant farm boy. I don't recall exactly how I thought things would go when I presented the gift to Rebecca, but that certainly hadn't been it.

About an hour before sundown Michael McBain came striding up. Butterflies started up in my stomach because I felt sure this had something to do with Rebecca. I set my shovel aside and waited.

"You're moving right along," he said, stopping and looking down the row of fence posts. "At this rate you'll be finished in a few weeks."

"That's about what I figured," I said.

"Why don't you quit for the day. I got something I want to talk with you about. Walk with me back to the stables."

"All right," I said, and began gathering up the tools so I could return them to the McBain's tool-shed.

We walked in silence and Michael waited outside while I returned the tools to their places along the wall of the shed. When I was finished I followed him over to the number two stable. The bay mare, Evelyn, as I'd come to think of her, was standing outside of the stable doors tied to a hitching rail.

She was saddled.

My father and I didn't see the point in you wearing yourself out walking to and from town. We wanted you to go ahead and take the horse. You can keep the saddle and bridle as well. They're as old as the horse but in good shape just like she is. I see you already got some saddlebags...those from Milton Watt's store?"

I was so moved by the gesture that I was all but speechless. "Yes," I answered finally, approaching the mare. "I bought them earlier this week.... I don't know how to thank you."

"Those are good quality bags. I have some myself… and you're very welcome. Your work is good and my father likes to help folks who fought for the South. We're hoping that you decide to stay on."

"I think I might like that."

"Good enough. You enjoy her. And we'll talk later about you quitting over at the Englebright and coming to work out here. I have to be getting inside. When will you be back?"

"Tomorrow."

"I'll see you tomorrow, then."

Evelyn was eager to please and she had a fine gait for one her age. When I reached Sherman, I bypassed the boarding-house and went straight to the Englebright. I found Calvin behind the front desk at the hotel and after he looked me up and down like he thought I was dirtying up the place, he agreed to rent a stall out to me for the same fifty cents a week he'd charged me when I'd been sleeping in one.

Chapter 2

My destiny was shaped on Sunday, July 30th, 1865. At least that's the way I've always seen it. That morning I saddled up Evelyn and headed out to the McBain ranch just as the sun was creeping up in the east. I still felt foolish about the previous day and I was so anxious about the possibility of seeing Rebecca that I packed away a couple of plums and a biscuit in my saddlebags so I could skip the afternoon meal behind the house.

I tied Evelyn to one of the hitching posts outside stable number two and started for the tool-shed. As I was collecting tools I caught movement from the corner of my eye. I turned to the doorway and Michael was standing there.

"Morning, Michael," I said.

"Good morning, Everett. If you could take a minute, my father wants to see you in the house."

I set the armful of digging implements aside and stepped out of the shadowy shed. Michael's face was red, either with anger or shame, I couldn't tell which. He turned and started off toward the house without a word and I kept my mouth shut and followed. He opened the front door and stood aside and I entered into a small foyer. The foyer opened into the big sitting room where I'd first met Ed McBain. The drapes were pulled shut and the room was dimly lit with lamplight. Ed McBain was sitting in a large, upholstered armchair next to the cold fireplace, smoking a cigar. Rebecca stood next to him, staring at the floor. She was wearing the white and purple dress I'd given her.

I stopped a few steps into the room and waited. Michael walked past me and sat on a Chesterfield across from his father.

"Good morning, Everett," Ed McBain said pleasantly. "Come in and sit down. How do you like the horse?"

"I like her just fine, thank you," I said. I took a few more steps into the room but didn't sit. I glanced at Rebecca, then back to McBain.

"I see you've taken an interest in Rebecca," he said, waving his cigar toward her. "I can't say I blame you, young man like you are. And she's about the finest example of an Indian woman I've ever seen. Step forward, Rebecca, and show Everett what you look like in that pretty dress he bought for you. That's right, turn around. See there, it fits just about perfect. I have to say though, son, for the price you paid for that dress you could have gotten yourself a white woman in town, and as pretty as she is, she's still just an Indian."

He puffed his cigar and regarded me. Finally, he leaned forward in his chair. "You seem like a decent young man, Everett, but I can see you don't know much so I'm going to let this go." He turned to Rebecca. "Rebecca, I don't believe it would be right to keep that dress, do you?"

Rebecca shook her head, still staring at the floor.

"Well, then, you best take it off and return it to Everett."

She nodded, then turned and started away.

"No, no." McBain said, standing and putting out an arm to block her way. "You can take it off right here."

She didn't move.

"You do as I say," McBain said, all amiability gone from his voice.

She slowly started unbuttoning the housedress.

"Turn around and face him," McBain said.

Rebecca did as she was bidden, her wet eyes flicked to mine before she lowered them and continued releasing buttons.

"This isn't necessary," I said. "It wasn't my intention to offend you, sir, or the young lady. Please accept my apologies and do what you will with the dress." I turned and stormed from the house.

Dismayed is the word that comes to me when I think about how I felt immediately afterward. I was *dismayed,* and for more than one reason. I tried to push Rebecca from my mind and keep my attention on what was pressing. I stood for a moment on the front porch and thought things over. The McBain's already gave me Evelyn—an advance, more or less—so I was obligated to finish the job I was hired to do.

I walked to the tool-shed, collected the what I needed, and I went back to work. An hour or so later Michael rode up on a big roan. "I'm happy you stayed, Everett. My father only wanted to teach you a lesson. Seems like it was one you needed to learn. I don't know why you didn't ask around or something if you'd taken a liking to Rebecca. You could have come to me. For all you knew she could have been someone's wife." He took off his hat, beat the dust off of it against his leg and then put it back on. "Well, no real harm done and he won't hold it against you. I have to ride out and look at the herd. Corral's coming along nice."

That night after I stabled and fed Evelyn, I went to the saloon and asked Silus to fill me a bottle of beer—I didn't mention what happened at the McBain ranch— and I walked up the street to the boarding-house. Upstairs in my room I lit a candle instead of the lamp. I carried the single rickety chair that was furnished with the room over to the window. The window overlooked a small plum orchard. I found the view relaxing. I sipped the beer and tried to forget about the day.

I must have dozed off because I was still sitting in that old chair when I was startled awake by a knock at the door. Unmindful of the still half-full bottle of beer between my legs, it hit the bare wood floor with a clunk as I stood and stumbled in the dark to answer.

I opened the door and Layton, the boarding-house's caretaker, was standing on the other side holding a lamp and wearing a nightshirt and a scowl.

"There's an old man outside who wants to see you. I told him it was hours past visiting but he insisted it's an urgent matter."

"Do you know who he is?" I said.

"No, I don't. Do you want me to send him away?"

"No. I'll be right down. Thank you, Layton."

"Ms. Hardy has rules here, and the house is always full, with some waiting in line. You might want to make certain folks aren't knocking at all hours." He started away, muttering. "Suppose I'll make some tea, only way I'll get back to sleep now..."

I hurried downstairs, a little more than curious as to who it could be. The only old man I knew better than just a face passing on the street was Walter Watt, who was the father of Milton Watt, owner of the mercantile. Walter was originally from Missouri and we spoke of home now and then when I was in the store.

The lantern Layton burned at night on the front porch cast a meager glow, and I didn't immediately recognize the man standing near the bottom of the porch stairs. He took a step forward as I started down, and I saw that he was the man from the kitchen at the McBain ranch.

"Mister Everett … my apologies, but I don't know your surname—"

"Ward," I said, stopping on the last step.

"Thank you, Mister Ward," he said and began to cough. The fit doubled him over but he recovered after a moment, pulling a handkerchief from his back pocket and wiping his mouth with it. "Pardon me. My name is Jonathan Peckham. I oversee the kitchen for Edward McBain. I have Rebecca with me, in a wagon up the street. She wants to talk with you, if you will."

To this day I'm uncertain of what I felt most at that moment. Fear, I suppose, but there was more: excitement, for one, fed by the vague romantic notions of an unworldly young man.

"Where?" I said.

He cocked his head. "At the end of town, before the boneyard."

"All right," I said.

He stepped forward and gripped my arm. "Are you a good man, Mister Ward? Because she needs some help. For some reason she believes you're the one who'll give it to her. I should have done something myself when Edward brought her here ten years ago, but I'm a coward, and now I'm an old coward, and if God doesn't strike me down on judgment day then there is no justice to be found in him."

I didn't understand what he was talking about. "I'll do what I can," I said.

When we neared the end of town I could make out the buckboard not far from the last of the Sherman's buildings. It was a silhouette; only slightly darker than the nighttime plains backdrop it sat against. A horse tethered to the rear stamped restlessly at the ground. Rebecca was sitting on top and she turned as we approached. I could see she was wrapped in a blanket though the night wasn't cold. It was over her head and she held it tightly around her face with both hands. It was too dark to make out her features.

"I brought a horse. It's mine … well, it *was* mine. It belongs to her now," Jonathan said, while he fussed with some things in the back of the wagon. "She hasn't ridden in ten years or better and even then she was just a child …"

I only stood there, bemused and unsure of the situation. Rebecca was looking down at me. I couldn't see her eyes but I felt them. Finally, I asked, "What do you want me to do?"

She didn't reply.

"You have to tell this man what you want of him, Rebecca. If you want his help," Jonathon said.

"My name isn't Rebecca," she said. Her voice was small and there was no rancor in the statement. "My name is Wačhiwi. I'm Lakota, and I wish to go home."

"Where's home?" I asked.

When she didn't immediately answer, Jonathon did: "She doesn't exactly know, Mister Ward—"

"Everett," I said.

"Like I said, Everett, she doesn't exactly know.… She's Sioux. Sioux Indians are up north of Kansas, so I'd suppose it would be somewhere up in Nebraska or Dakota Territory. She says her family's camp was attacked by soldiers and near everyone was killed, including her mother and father. There was some ruckus with the Sioux up near the Platte River back in fifty-five. It made the papers. It might have been that—probably was that. Edward McBain brought her here in the spring of fifty-six. He said he found her at a trading post near Fort Kearny … I don't know the particulars of how she ended up there and she doesn't talk about it. I wouldn't want to know anyway. I know enough of what's gone on since she's been at the ranch to last me what little life I have left. Anyhow, she doesn't expect you'll find any of her kin. She just needs help finding other Sioux. They'll take her in."

"Indian Territory … I'll have to think this through some," I said, knowing full-well I was going to do what was asked of me.

"I wish I could say take all the time you need, but I can't. Edward is going to be looking for her come—" He began coughing again and leaned on the wagon for support.

"Damn, don't that hurt," he mumbled as he regained himself. "He won't be happy when he finds out she's gone. You need to go, right now, tonight."

"I haven't finished paying for my horse yet. That would make me a horse thief."

"*Please,*" Wačhiwi said, pleading.

"Here," Jonathon said, coming around the wagon to stand in front of me. "I have two, twenty-dollar gold pieces. I was going to give you both of them for your provisions but I'll keep one and pay a couple of men to finish the work you were hired to do. Either that or I'll pay Edward. That mare was a good one in her day but she's old and isn't worth more than twenty-five dollars anyway."

"All right," I said. "I have to go and gather up my things and then go by the hotel and tell Mister Englebright I'm leaving."

"You shouldn't tell that man anything, but if you must, don't tell him where you're going or who with."

"I won't. I'll see you back here in an hour."

I settled up with Layton—who took pains to appear inconvenienced—at the boarding-house after I packed my few belongings into my saddlebags. I didn't have any traveling gear, but I did have fifteen dollars I'd saved from working at the Englebright and I hoped to obtain what I needed in Gainsville. Calvin Englebright was asleep so I left him a brief note at the front desk thanking him for employing me before going to the stable to saddle Evelyn.

There was a lantern hanging from the side of the buckboard when I returned and it cast a dim glow. Jonathon was busying himself tying some items to the horse he'd brought for Wačhiwi. Wačhiwi was sitting on the horse, looking out into darkness. She was prepared for travel, wearing a pair of wool trousers and a man's work shirt. Her hair was pulled back tightly into two braids.

"She's got some beans and a pot to cook them in, a couple plates and cups, along with some corn biscuits I made up this morning, a little horse feed … a few other things," Jonathon said. "You'll have to get most of the necessaries you'll need along the way. I gave her a pistol and showed her how it works. It's old, but it fires."

He finished what he was doing, patted the horse on the flank and looked up at Wačhiwi. "Farewell, child. I pray the rest of your life is better than the one you've had so far." He turned to me: "Goodbye Everett. God bless you. I would have like to have known you." Then, in a whisper, "Don't ever come back here."

We left him sitting atop his buckboard and headed west out of Sherman. The main road would have taken us right past the McBain ranch so we rode out along the creek until we were well beyond it and then cut back to the road.

There was only a quarter moon and Wačhiwi didn't ride with confidence so the going was slow. I made a couple of attempts at conversation but she didn't seem inclined to talk. I gave it up and we rode in silence for the rest of the night. The sun was still a few hours from noon when we reached Gainsville. The town was smaller than Sherman, dusty, and it reeked of cattle. But it was busier than Sherman. We took some looks riding down the short main street and it didn't occur to me right away that it wasn't only because we were strangers. The store was midway through town and a sight larger than the Sherman mercantile. Gainsville was a hub of sorts for cattle being driven north to Kansas and beyond. The trails were long and it made sense that the men would have to be well-supplied.

The store was bustling and the plank porch running the length of the building was stacked high with wooden crates and burlap sacks of goods. The windows were soaped with the prices of dry goods and signs hung here and there advertising cookware and textiles. We tied the horses and were starting up the steps when a voice came from behind us:

"You can go in but the squaw has to stay outside."

I turned and there was a man in a sweat-stained felt hat standing at the bottom of the steps with a stack of fabric bolts in his arms. He brushed past us and up the stairs. "Indians ain't allowed," he said as he opened the door with his foot and disappeared inside. I could feel all of the eyes on us as well as I could see them. I turned my eyes to Wačhiwi and then back to the door. Just then she saved me having to decide whether or not to argue the point.

"I'll stay with the horses," she said, turning and walking back down the steps. She didn't look angry, or sad, only … resigned.

I walked the rest of the steps and entered the store. The inside was stocked to the rafters with goods and it smelled like tobacco and cinnamon. Patrons milled about the shelves. The man from outside was standing behind a counter with glass display cases underneath that ran the entire length of the building. He was measuring and cutting lengths of fabric while eying me suspiciously. I looked around for a few minutes to see what they had before approaching him. I didn't have the faintest idea how to supply for a journey like this one so I mostly stuck to what I knew from the war.

"Morning," I said when he didn't acknowledge me.

The man set aside his scissors and nodded once, curtly. "Help you?"

"I'd like five pounds of beef jerky, a pound of that biscuit flour, a pound of coffee, and three pounds of dried apricots. Also, one of those canteens hanging there behind you … the larger one, and may I look at this compass?"

I pointed at a Drayton compass in the display case. It was the old kind with the sundial in it.

The man didn't move right away. "We don't extend credit here."

"I'm not asking you to," I said, beginning to feel nettled.

He opened the cabinet, removed the compass, and set it in front of me. I opened the turned walnut wood case and examined the works; it was clear it was used, but it looked to be in decent condition.

"I'll take this. Do you have any maps?"

"Only the one on the wall over there." The man pointed to a large map pinned to the wall by the door. "That be all?"

"I believe so," I said, moving over to the map.

"You want your coffee raw or roasted and ground? It's ten cents more if you want it ground."

"Ground."

"Four dollars, and I'll take payment before I pack it up."

The price seemed high but I decided to let it go. I walked back to the counter and set the twenty-dollar piece in front of him. He picked it up with a scowl and disappeared through an opening in the floor-to-ceiling shelf that spanned the wall behind the counter. A minute later he returned and dropped the sixteen dollars change on the counter. "Be a few minutes," he said.

I examined the map while I waited. It was a passing fair map for the time and was dated 1860. I figured if we kept due north we'd get up to Kansas, and I could start asking questions about where I might find the Sioux. The plan seemed sensible in the mind of an artless young man with only nineteen years behind him.

I filled the new canteen at a pump in front of the store while Wačhiwi loaded the supplies onto our horses. We headed north out of town. It was only a handful of miles before we were in Indian Territory—what is Oklahoma now—but it wasn't the right Indian Territory. I estimated it would be two weeks give or take before we reached Kansas. That was if we didn't run into any trouble.

We made about twenty miles that day, mostly in silence. I was never much of a talker myself but I'd be lying if I didn't say I was about half-mad with it by the time we set camp by a little creek early that evening. I gathered wood and started a fire going while Wačhiwi silently prepared a pot of beans to cook for our supper. Once the fire was burning I saw to the horses and set my bedroll out on one side of it and

Wačhiwi's on the other. I knew the beans would take two or three hours, so I was considering taking the rifle off into the scrub to see if I could hunt up some meat when she said: "Thank you for helping me."

"I'm happy to do it … I have been wondering why you chose me …" I trailed off.

She regarded me from across the fire for a moment and then lowered her eyes.

"Well, I'll go see if there's any game … I'll be back before dark."

I took my rifle and walked down to the summer-low creek that was more stones than water and headed downstream. The area was mostly barren outside of scrub but I could see a good-sized stand of trees about a mile off and thought it would be a likely spot to chase up something if there was anything to be chased up. The muzzleloader wasn't much good for small game but it was all I had.

When I neared the trees I slowed up and crept forward in a crouch the last hundred feet or so. I might as well have ran to the stand of oaks waving my arms and shouting for all the good stealth did. The only living things I saw were a few crows and a lone lizard sprawled on a rock trying to make good use of the last few rays of the westering sun.

Resigned to a supper of beans—which I didn't care for then and don't care for now—I shouldered Nathanial Bishop's old rifle and started back. I was still a ways off when I heard the shouts. I slid the rifle back around infantry fashion and set off at a run. I saw Wačhiwi; she was running along the creek bank in my direction. There was a man on foot chasing her and another on horseback coming on a diagonal from the direction of the camp. The horseman was on a course to cut her off. The man chasing Wačhiwi on foot saw me first; he slowed down a little, unsure, and began shouting. I dropped to one knee, aimed the rifle, and fired. The ball took him in the neck and he fell in a heap. I don't think Wačhiwi even realized he was down. She turned westward, splashing across the creek and up the bank on the other side. The horseman veered toward me. I attempted to reload the rifle but I was prepared for hunting, not battle and had my shot and powder slung over my back. The horseman was on me in an instant, he reined in his horse, pulled a big revolver and fired.

That's all I remember of that day.

The sun was high when I awoke the first time, and I was in more pain than I previously would've thought it possible for a man to endure. I'd witnessed men suffering; my own brother for one. I'd seen men with limbs torn off by cannon, and I'd seen men trying to hold in their own innards so they wouldn't drag on the ground. Seeing it was one thing; you could feel sympathy but not much more. I finally learned for myself what all those men went through.

The second time I came around it was night. Blue fire exploded in my chest with every breath I took, and I could hear a faint whistling sound as I exhaled. The pain was unbearable. Wačhiwi was hunkered next to me. She was holding my hand in both of hers. Her look was grave. I recognized that look. I begged her to shoot me.

It was midday again. The pain wasn't quite as bad but it was a near thing. Soon Wačhiwi came and knelt beside me. She lifted my head and put a canteen to my lips. The water was magnificent and I tried to quaff it but she pulled the canteen away.

"It's good you're thirsty," she said. "We have to move from here. Tomorrow morning. Edward will send more men when those two don't return."

The pain made it difficult to think straight and to concentrate on anything else but how bad it hurt. "I don't know that I can ride … how bad is it?"

"You may die if we leave here. You *will* die if we stay. They will kill you and take me back to that place."

I lifted my head with some effort and looked down at myself. I was shirtless and there was a poultice on the left side of my chest.

"It went all the way through," she said.

My eyes opened; the sun was coming up. Wačhiwi was patting my cheek and speaking to me. "… have to leave now." She held a cup out to me. I could smell the coffee.

"Can you sit up?"

I tried but only made it halfway before falling back down. My chest hurt fierce when I put pressure on my left arm and bright pain flared in my upper back from the exit wound. She set the cup aside and put out a hand. I took it with my right one and she pulled with a grunt. The pain was terrible but she got me up straight and I worked my legs in and crossed them so I wouldn't fall backwards again. I felt weak and light in the head, and the pain, which had been bad but tolerable when I first woke, was a great deal worse. She handed me the cup and strode off toward where the horses were tethered.

I sipped the coffee, which was strong and sweet. I didn't buy any sugar so she must have brought it. I looked after her, she was cinching down her bedroll on her horse.

Even through my own suffering I remember thinking about how beautiful she was.

The coffee and sugar invigorated me some, and I even felt a little hungry. As if she could see my thoughts Wačhiwi walked over and handed me a corn biscuit. It was stale but I dipped it in what remained of my coffee and it softened up. I only got through half of it before I felt full and I thought to ask how long it was since the man on the horse shot me.

"Three days," Wačhiwi said, kneeling in front of me. She had the shirt I'd been wearing when I was shot, along with the only spare I owned. She set the spare aside and started carefully slipping my arms into the sleeves of the one I was shot in.

"I washed it in the creek," she said, buttoning the shirt. "It's ruined but it might help to keep blood off the other one if you start up again."

I looked down and saw the hole in the shirt just below the left breast. I wondered if any of the fabric was pushed into the wound by the ball. I'd met a doctor in the war who claimed such things caused more death than the wound itself. He said men would rot from the inside out, just like a corpse.

"Are you ready?" Wačhiwi said.

I said I was.

Wačhiwi walked Evelyn over and stood waiting. I knew she wasn't offering to help me rise because she knew that if I couldn't stand on my own, there was no way that I was going to get mounted on Evelyn, even with her help. I readied myself, leaning heavily on my right arm, and then stood. I was weak, but not as bad I thought. Evelyn was a good horse. Wačhiwi dropped the reins and Evelyn stayed steady while she helped me get my left boot into the stirrup. I reached up and grabbed the saddle-horn with both hands and Wačhiwi pushed me from my backside as I swung me right leg over. It hurt like holy hell but I got into the saddle without falling.

That's about all that went well.

I began bleeding again almost immediately. Not too much, but it started blossoming on the front of my shirt after an hour or so of riding. The pain was bad and I was having trouble rolling with Evelyn's gait, so every one of her hoof-falls felt like a fist-cuff. On top of that I guided us down the middle of the creek for some time to hide our back-trail. The cantaloupe-sized stones of the creek bed made the riding tough. As we passed the partially eaten body of the man I killed, it occurred to me for the first time to ask Wačhiwi about the horseman who shot me.

"He's there," She said, keeping her eyes forward and pointing a ways off across the creek.

I waited for more. When there was none I asked her what happened. She seemed not to have heard and I was about to ask a second time when she turned toward me and answered.

"He came after me," she said. "I was hiding behind … those little trees … I don't have the English word … for Lakota it is *čhaŋȟáka* . He saw me there. He left his horse and ran toward me. I killed him with Mister Peckham's pistol."

She began to weep then, softly.

"Don't feel sorry for him," I said.

After a moment she nodded, and wiped at her eyes. I felt ashamed. I should have said something to comfort her.

As the morning progressed my pain grew worse and by noon I didn't think I could continue. By mid-afternoon I was sure of it. The day was hot and beyond the pain I was beginning to feel fevered and out-of-sorts.

"I have to stop," I said. "We need to look for a place to camp,"

She looked me over and nodded.

We chose the shade of a lone oak that sat atop a low rise. Wačhiwi wordlessly untied my bedroll and prepared it over the thin duff of fallen leaves that surrounded the oak. The day had taken its toll on me and I was too weak to get a leg swung over so I could dismount. In the end, Wačhiwi had to grab my boot and push my leg over Evelyn's haunches.

Through the night the fever grew worse. One moment I'd be burning up and the next I'd be shivering so violently I'd shake the blanket right off and be unable to control my hand enough to pull it back over me. I remember Wačhiwi sitting with me, wetting a piece of cloth from the canteen and laying it on my forehead. She spoke to me softly for hours. Even through my delirium I remembered a lot of what she said:

"I chose you because you didn't look at me how other white men look at me. White men see me as they see something that crawls. Some look at me wanting what men want from a woman, but with them too, the other look is still there. I've met white men who are kind—men like Mister Peckham—but most are weak. You're both kind and strong. Though it's been many years since I've prayed in the Lakota way, I prayed to Wakan Tanka. I prayed for you to remain here in this world." Then she whispered in my ear: "*Quiet White Man*," and brushed my hair back from my forehead.

"When I was a child, my home was on a great river. I don't remember its name. One day the blue soldiers came—white men; army men. My father sent me to hide with my mother and my brother. We hid inside … I don't have the word … rocks … *oȟlóka,* with other women and children. The soldiers shouted words we didn't know. They used their guns. My mother and the other women who hid with us were killed. Soon only my brother and I remained. He sent me to run, and then he went out to fight … perhaps he died with the others. After the fighting most of the men and many of the women and children were dead. The soldiers walked us somewhere far away …"

And then she was gone.

I awoke nonplussed and thirsty but my head felt clearer. I was lying in some sort of lean-to fashioned from branches and sagebrush. I couldn't recall being moved from underneath the oak. A young woman in an animal skin dress stood over me. She spoke to me in a language I couldn't understand. The words sounded similar to some of the Indian words Wačhiwi used. It could have been the same language for all I knew. Much later I surmised she was Chickasaw, not Sioux.

"Where's Wačhiwi?" I said.

She shook her head and kneeled down, placing her hand on my forehead.

"Where's Wačhiwi?" I repeated, trying to shout. What came out was more of a dry croak. She recoiled slightly and shook her head again. Her eyes were wide and full of confusion. It was clear she didn't understand.

"I'm sorry," I said.

She seemed to relax a little at my tone. After a moment she stood and left the lean-to.

My clothes were in a heap next to me. I lifted the blanket and saw I was naked. There was a foul smell and I wasn't certain whether it was the wound or the muddy-looking poultice that was placed over it. Soon a man entered; he wore only a loincloth. His skin was as dark and dry as old leather and his face was so deeply lined that his eyes nearly disappeared into the caverns made by the folds. He spoke some words to the woman that sounded like scolding. The woman scolded back and left the lean-to. She returned a moment later with a water skin. The man kneeled down beside me and gently lifted my head. The women knelt on the opposite side of me and crooned softly while she poured water into my mouth.

I asked the man about Wačhiwi as well, but like the woman, it was obvious he didn't understand.

The pair cared for me for the next sixteen days. I marked the days by scratching the bottom of one of my boots with a stone. I have no way of knowing how long they'd been administering to me before I'd come around. Those first days I slept most of the time, and either the old man or the woman would wake me to feed me some dried meat or have me drink a bitter tea from a dented and leaking tin cup. Once I awoke to the woman cleaning my private parts and shortly afterward the old man came into the lean-to and lifted his loincloth and mimed urinating. He could have made his point without removing his covering but I understood in any event. I felt ashamed that I'd been pissing—and probably something else as well—all over myself. He offered me his hand and helped me up. I was weak but could hold my weight and he guided me outside. The lean-to was built in a small stand of trees bordering a muddy and shallow pond. I walked out to the far edge of the stand behind one of the trees and did my business.

I made it nearly all the way back to the lean-to before I needed the old man's assistance.

Every day after that either the woman or the old man would awaken me at sunrise and walk with me. At first I could only walk forty or fifty feet out and forty or fifty feet back. They were both patient and the old man would exclaim and nod his head encouragingly. I regained my strength quickly, so quickly I had to resist the urge to depart and begin searching for Wačhiwi. Fearing a relapse of the fever, though, I stayed. After a week I was walking all the way around the pond. The woman changed the poultice every few days and I was relieved to find out that the smell was coming from it and not the wound. I couldn't see the exit hole but the entrance wound on my chest looked better each time. On the twelfth day she removed the poultice and didn't put on a fresh one. Instead she sprinkled the wound back and front with what looked like crumbled dry grass but was probably some herb.

On the morning of the sixteenth day, the old man woke me up and handed me a water skin and a fist-sized bundle of dried meat tied together with prairie grass. I knew what this meant so I nodded and said thank you. The man nodded in return and exited the lean-to. I wished I could thank the woman, even if it was only with a smile and a nod, but she was already gone.

Long since restless to leave, I immediately gathered up my belongings: the compass I'd purchased in Gainsville was still in the pocket of my trousers, along with thirty-one dollars and my father's jackknife. It looked like there was enough of the dried meat to last ten days if I was sparing. It wasn't a difficult choice, where to go first. The idea that Wačhiwi took my horse, my rifle and my other belongings and left me to die under that oak didn't ring true with me.

More likely we were tracked by men working for Edward McBain, she was taken, and they left me to die. I supposed it was possible someone else took her—Indians perhaps—but that made less sense. In the end I decided the only way to be certain was to go back to Sherman.

I struck off an hour after the old man. I didn't know where I was but figured the two hadn't carried—or dragged—me very far. Not much before noon I came to what I thought must be the creek Wačhiwi and I had first camped on. The creek ran east to west, I chose to follow it west because the view looked similar to when I walked down the stream to hunt. Sure enough two hours later I was looking down at the remains of our campfire.

I rested up the remainder of the afternoon and set out again at dawn. Eleven days later I walked into Sherman, hungry, thirsty, and ragged in my blood-stained shirt and brush torn trousers.

I walked straight to the saloon at the Englebright. Silus was behind the bar, talking with two men. He looked up when I came through the doors and he stared at me, mouth agape, as if I were Marley's ghost. I sat at the bar and he came over, still wearing that stupefied look.

"Christ-a-mighty, what are you doing here, Everett?" he said in a near whisper.

"A pitcher of water, please Silus," I said.

"Are you trying to get hanged? County sheriffs got a warrant for you. Says you stole a horse from old Ed McBain … Lord, Everett, is that blood all over you? Have you been *shot?*"

"I didn't steal—" I began, but then closed my mouth. I thought about the old man, Jonathan Peckham. I'd left town on his word he'd settle up for the horse. It was a fool thing to do. It wasn't Jonathon Peckham's affair. My business in regards to Evelyn was with Edward McBain and no one else. Stealing a horse was exactly what I did and I knew it when I did it. Often times a man—especially a young one—sees things how he wants to see them at any given moment. Horse thief. That's the way the eyes of the law would see it for certain.

"The water please, Silus," I said. "And a bowl of those peanuts, if you wouldn't mind."

Silus nodded and then shook his head, bemused. He brought the pitcher of water and a glass and then filled a bowl of peanuts from the barrel under the bar.

"You might want to go see Richard Flood. Maybe get this thing straightened out before …" he trailed off.

Richard Flood was the town marshal. a bear of a man who was nonetheless quite soft-spoken. He often supped at the Englebright and I'd exchanged a few words with him during my time there. He was well-liked and considered a fair man. I downed the pitcher of water and dumped the bowl of peanuts into my pocket. "Thank you, Silus," I said, and left the saloon.

I ate the peanuts while I walked to the marshal's office. I hadn't noticed so much when I'd come into town—likely because all I could think about was getting some water—but people were either stopping what they were doing to stare at me or eyeballing me warily and moving out of my way.

Sherman's marshal's office was a tiny building near the east end of town. The front portion acted as the office, just large enough to house a woodstove and a single desk. The rest was taken up by three eight-foot by ten-foot steel-barred cells. Bob Woodward, the deputy marshal was sitting at the desk eating when I entered.

"Help you with something?" he said, barely glancing up from his biscuits and gravy.

"I'd like to see the marshal."

"Marshal ain't here—" he began, finally turning his attention from his food. He set down his fork and took a long look at me. "What the hell happened to you? You're that boy from the Englebright—Ward. We got an arrest warrant for you."

"That's why I'm here," I said.

He stood. "The marshal's down at the livery getting his horse re-shod. I'll go get him … I, uhhh … I'm going to have to lock you up first."

I turned to the cells. They were all empty. "Which one?"

"It don't matter. Take your pick, they're all unlocked. I'll need you to turn out your pockets first, and take off your boots so I can see you're not carrying anything."

I turned my pockets and handed him the contents.

"You can keep your money. I'll need to hold onto the knife and the compass … you'll get them back if and when the judge lets you out." He looked me up and down. "You need a doctor?"

I said I didn't. He nodded toward the cells.

I chose the one furthest from the desk. The un-oiled hinges screeched as I swung open the door. There was a metal cot bolted to the wall and I sat down on it. It was the cell's only furnishing. Woodward removed a key ring from a hook on the wall and locked me in. I remember the sound the tumblers made as he turned the lock home. I imagined it might be what the mechanism of the gallows sounded like when the floor dropped from under you.

I was lying on the cot's thin and lumpy mattress when Woodward returned with Marshal Flood. The marshal's heavy footfalls shook the cot as he approached the cell and peered through the bars at me.

"McBain's cook told me what happened. I believe he gave me the straight of it. The man's about ten breaths from the grave so I don't see any reason he'd lie. Won't make a bit of difference in a court of law anyhow. Ed McBain intends to see you hang. You really put yourself in it. Over some squaw no less." He lowered his head and shook it. "Reckless and foolhardy."

"I suppose that's true," I said. "Do you know where she is?"

His eyes darted away, just for a moment, and he suddenly appeared discomfited.

"That's none of your concern, now," he said. "You have more important worries. I'll wire the judge, though I'd wager it'll be ten days before he gets here. It's Marcus Lane. He's as fair as they come … could be he'll see the whole picture. Until he arrives and sets a date, I'll make you as comfortable as I can. Bob says you don't want the doctor—"

"No," I said. "It's mostly healed up now.

"All right. You'd know best I suppose. I have some clothes at the house I can give you. They were my son's. He was about your size. Took after his mother … anyway, mayhap you'd look better at your trial."

"I'd be grateful," I said.

That evening I was sitting on the cot reading out of a book Marshal Flood had loaned me, when Calvin Englebright showed up with a plate of food. He had red blotches high on his cheeks and he appeared flustered. Bob Woodward opened the door and let him in the cell and then stood there and waited. Calvin held out the plate, his hand was shaking visibly. I set the book aside and took it.

"No charge for the food. The marshal's office is paying for it."

"Thank you, Mister Englebright," I said.

"This is terrible—"

"I'm going to have to ask you to step outside the cell now, Mister Englebright. You can talk to him from out here," Woodward said.

"Of course." Calvin patted me once on the shoulder and did as he was asked. Woodward locked the door after him and went back to the desk.

"Edward McBain wants you to hang," Calvin said conspiratorially. "And it has nothing to do with that old mare. Edward's been a friend, but he's a hard man. I'll do what I can for you."

Three long days passed. I remember thinking about something a boy we called Dutch said to me during the war. He said I'd survive because I wasn't afraid of dying. He also predicted that he wouldn't make it because he was. He was right about the latter. He died a month later. Me and another boy whose name I can't remember were each holding one of his hands when he went. As to what Dutch said about me; he couldn't have been more wrong.

The door to the office opened and Wačhiwi walked through, followed by Edward McBain, Michael McBain, John Delaney (the McBain's foreman), Marshal Flood, and two other men I didn't recognize. They all crowded into the tiny room and stared at me. The first thought I had was that they were there to lynch me and they were going to make

Wačhiwi watch. I steeled myself to make a charge for the door as soon as the marshal unlocked the cell, but instead of unlocking the door, Marshal Flood turned and stepped over to the window where he stood looking out at the street. I could hear his sigh from across the room. "Let's get this done, Ed," he said without turning.

"I heard you were dead," Edward McBain said with a smile that didn't reach his eyes. "Ambushed by Indians and killed up there in Oklahoma Territory. But somehow here you are. Goes to show you can't always trust hearsay." He turned to Wačhiwi. "Rebecca, I believe you have something to say to this man?"

Wačhiwi moved up to the bars. I stood and met her. She held my eyes but I couldn't read her expression. It could have been anger.

"Ómakiya ye, Iníla Ská Wičhášá," she said softly. Then she spit in my face.

The act was met with gales of laughter from the men. I took a step back wiping my face with my hand. I don't know what I was expecting but it wasn't that. She turned and walked to where Edward McBain was standing. He was smiling wryly. He put a hand on her shoulder and led her to the door. The other men followed. Then it was just me and Marshal Flood, who was still staring out the window. I sat back down on the cot and waited for what was next.

After several minutes the door opened again. Marshal Flood still hadn't moved from the window. Michael McBain stepped through the door and said: "He's satisfied, Marshal."

Marshal Flood turned from the window and retrieved the keys from the hook on the wall and unlocked the cell door. "Charges have been dropped," he said, swinging open the door. "You can go, Mister Ward … I have your effects over here. You can keep the clothes. My son stopped needing them in sixty-six."

"Am I going to be lynched when I walk out the door?" I said.

"No one is going to do anything to you," Michael said. "It's over. You can thank Calvin Englebright."

I walked out of the cell and over to the desk where the marshal handed me my compass and jackknife.

"Good luck to you," he said.

I nodded and started for the door.

"Your horse is outside, along with the saddle and everything else you had on her," Michael said. He held out a folded sheet of paper. Here's her bill-of-sale. She's yours, legal now. Calvin Englebright gave my father two hundred acres of grazing land and the last of the Englebright interest in the cattle trade. You own the most expensive horse in Texas now, Everett.... I hope she was worth it." He reached out and gripped my arm. "And you know I don't mean the horse."

I shook my arm loose and took the bill-of-sale. I met his eyes, the open friendliness I saw in them when I'd first met him was nowhere to be found. He nodded toward the door. "You should consider yourself fortunate. Don't come back."

Evelyn was tethered to the hitching rail outside, just like Michael said she would be, and no one was waiting with a hanging rope. I stroked her cheek and then untied her. Instead of riding I walked her up the street to the Englebright under the interested eyes of the townsfolk. I found Calvin seated in the Hotel's dining room. He had both of the town's newspapers in front of him along with a cup of coffee. He looked up as I approached.

"Would you like some coffee?" he said, gesturing to the chair across from him.

"Thank you," I said.

He tapped the newspapers with his finger. "You made both papers. They'll be disappointed you're not going to be paraded to the end of town and hanged as a horse thief."

"Michael McBain told me what you—" I began, but Englebright shook his head.

"I've been looking for a way out of the cattle business for years. It was my mother and father's enterprise, not mine.… You're a good young man, Everett, but I suggest you find some sort of a purpose for your life, and find it far away from here."

I nodded, stood, and extended my hand. "I reckon I'll forgo the coffee. Thank you for what you did for me."

Calvin Englebright stood and took my hand. "Farewell, Everett."

Chapter 3

I could have stayed. I knew it was likely that McBain compelled Wačhiwi to do what she did at the jail. The knowledge was cold comfort, because there was nothing I could do for her. If I stayed in Sherman, McBain would likely make her life harder than it already was, and chances were good I'd take a ball in my skull some night in my sleep, or get ambushed somewhere outside of town and end up carrion far out in the Texas scrub.

So I rode out of town that very day. I rode north, not because I had a particular destination in mind, but because I hoped to see the old man and young woman who saved my life. I wanted to thank them properly. I stopped at Milton Watt's store and purchased supplies before I left. I noted that Milton wasn't so friendly to me as he'd been previously. He wasn't hostile, but it was clear mine wasn't a welcome face.

Along with things I needed for the trail, I bought some hard candy and some strawberry preserves, special in case I saw my saviors. I even camped by the little pond for two days, but they weren't there. I never did see them again.

I reflected a fair amount on that journey. I began to question whether or not I had an unsound sense of right and wrong. I thought about my mother and father, and Clyde, and the war, but mostly I thought about Wačhiwi. I wondered if I left her to torment. The whole affair began to seem almost unearthly, and I had trouble making sense of it.

I ended up in Lawrence, Kansas and found work at James "Red" Macklin's ranch a few miles outside of town. Macklin was a tower of a man, just beginning to show the first signs of old age when I took on with him. He was as straight a shooter as I'd ever met, and if he had something to say he came right out and said it. He was wealthy but never made a show of it and was the first to throw a hand in when a neighbor needed help. People respected James Macklin, not because he demanded it, but because he earned it. His wasn't the biggest spread in the area but it was a close thing. He kept a bunkhouse that was free of charge to the hands and there was plenty of year-round work. I spent most of my time in the stables, but I mended fences and chased down livestock when an extra man was needed. Evelyn was getting too old to be a good cow horse but Macklin had three stables full of ones that were and I could use them whenever I needed to. Macklin was in the horse business as well as the cow business and I was fortunate enough to have Oliver Belle, Macklin's stable foremen, take a liking to me. One morning I was slopping out a pen of hogs when he came up and leaned on the fence.

"I've seen that you're pretty good with horses," he said. "Red and I were thinking you might like to learn to break 'em. You're the right age; your bones don't splinter up too easy when you're young."

I picked up the empty slop buckets and tossed them over the fence to the outside of the pen and then let myself out through the gate. "I'd appreciate that," I said, hardly able to contain my excitement.

"Good. We have fifty head coming in tomorrow or the next day. We'll start you then, see how you do."

I took to it like I was born for it and over the next six months I went from spending most of my working hours cleaning stables to saddle-breaking James Macklin's horses full-time. The place began to feel like home to me; the hands all got along well—some I could even call friends—and no one argued about the war. Macklin made it clear before he took anyone on that he didn't want to know what side they were on and he wouldn't abide men who continually felt the desire to discuss it. "The war is over," he'd say. "We all get on with our lives."

I understand why he didn't want men dwelling on it. Macklin had a lot of men working for him and conversations could turn violent pretty fast when it came to the subject of the war, but James Macklin didn't fight in it, either. I'm not saying he didn't suffer any loss from it, he never talked about it so I can't say. I do know that some men—likely most men—never wholly got over the things they saw and did during those four years.

One evening near the end of June, I was lying on my bunk reading the Lawrence Daily Journal when James Macklin entered the bunkhouse. He waited there by the door for everyone to finish nudging each other to quiet down, or pause whatever they were engaged in.

"Is there any man here who doesn't feel that he can work, eat, and sleep side by side with a negro and treat him as an equal?" he said.

There was some foot shuffling and a few subdued murmurs to this but no one spoke up.

"Not one, huh?" Well, I thought I'd give you a chance to pack up and head out before he got here. I hired a new man, a carpenter, though he says he good with horses as well. His name's Henry, and as long as he can perform the work he claims he can, he stays. If I find any of you not treating Henry with the respect you'd afford a white hand, you're gone. Any questions?"

"We're all just here to work," Oliver Belle, said. "Isn't that right, boys?"

There were words of assent and the men began getting back to oiling their boots, playing cards or mending their clothes. Red Macklin donned his hat and left the bunkhouse.

An hour later I met Henry.

The first thing that struck me as he walked by and dropped his saddlebags and other belongings on the bunk next to mine, was his limp. The second was the thick scar on the left side of his face, which began just below the hairline near his temple and cut a path through his short beard, stopping an inch before his mouth. And then there was the way he carried himself. To this day I have trouble putting a finger on just what it was. He seemed possessed of a calm and deliberate surety that I'd never seen in someone so young, let alone a negro. He didn't appear much older than I was—maybe three or four years—but he *seemed* much older somehow. He caught me looking at him and nodded to me. "Evening," he said.

"Evening," I returned, setting my paper aside as I threw my legs over the side of my bunk and sat up. I extended my hand.

"Everett Ward," I said.

He took my hand and shook it. "Henry."

"I'm pleased to meet you, Henry."

"Pleased to meet you, Everett."

"You from Kansas?"

"Missouri."

"I'm from Missouri," I said. "Osceola."

"Well, I reckon the world isn't as big as it seems. I lived near Osceola, for a time."

Over the coming weeks Henry and I became friends. I was taken by his quiet but sure aspect and how he was somehow wise well beyond his twenty-four years. I also admired the way he seemed, outwardly at least, unaffected by prejudice. Most of the ranch hands did exactly as Macklin asked and treated Henry as they would any other man, but a handful, though not outright hostile, made it a point to try to make Henry feel unwelcome in as surreptitious of a manner as possible. Some of these men, who'd been genial to me before, cooled quite a bit after I befriended Henry. As for me, I'd never been on first-name terms with a negro before Henry. I'd been around them some, both in Osceola and during the war, but Henry was the first one who I saw as man the same as I was. I'm ashamed of that, but there it is. I learned through Henry that almost everything I'd picked up about negroes over the years was fallacious.

There were other reasons Henry and I got on well. Little things, mostly. We were both as comfortable with silence as we were with conversation, we read books and periodicals whenever we got the chance, and we'd survived nearly identical gunshot wounds—both in the left side of the chest, and both going all the way through and out our backs at almost the exact same spot. And, like most new friendships, stories are exchanged. We didn't work together often; I worked with the horses and Henry was busied building a second bunkhouse for the ranch. He and I sat together at supper in the evenings, though, and as I mentioned before we bunked next to each other. I told Henry about my life on the farm with my mother and father and Clyde. I told him how

Clyde and I joined the Confederacy for the bounty money—something he never passed judgment on me for, though many with his history would have—and how my mother and father were murdered by Jayhawkers the night they pillaged and burned Osceola. Henry told me how he met James Macklin; how Macklin showed him kindness on a Missouri roadside at the beginning of the war with a canteen full of water and a few thoughtful words. He fought tears as he spoke of how he and his wife Eliza were freed at the onset of the war, and how he was hanged and she was murdered only a week later by Missouri bushwhackers.

"I was saved by a length of rotted rope," Henry said as we sat with our suppers in our laps in the newly framed skeleton of James Macklin's second bunkhouse. "Eliza wasn't so fortunate.... Was there ever anyone special to you?"

"Yes, though I can't claim I was special to her," I said. "I would've liked to have been."

While we ate our suppers I told Henry about Wačhiwi and everything that transpired after I first met her. When I was finished, Henry was silent for a time. He looked thoughtful, as if he were working something out in his head. I was sitting there appreciating my coffee and the fragrance of freshly milled lumber, figuring that if he had something to say, he'd say it. Finally, he spoke, nearly under his breath, "I'm sorry, Quiet White Man."

"Come again?" I said.

"It's what she said to you before she spit on you, if you're remembering it right. *I'm sorry, Quiet White Man* ... she spoke in Sioux."

"Quiet White Man," I repeated. "I remember. She called me that once, when she was tending my gunshot wound. I was sick with fever, but I remember clear enough."

"Sounds like you meant something to her, to me. Do you ever think about going back?"

"Yes. But I don't see how any good could come of it."

"Can I interrupt you boys a minute?" James Macklin said, stepping into the bunkhouse through two wall studs.

"Henry and I both stood."

Macklin looked at me levelly. "It's actually Henry I need to speak with."

"All right," I said. "Hand me your plate and cup, Henry. I'll take them back to the kitchen."

"Won't trouble me any if Everett stays, Mister Macklin."

Macklin nodded as if it was no matter to him. "County sheriff's up at the house. He received a wire this morning from an army colonel who's looking for a negro with a scar on his face. A negro who goes by the name of Henry."

"Is that right?" Henry said.

Macklin removed a folded sheet of paper from his shirt pocket and handed it to Henry. "See for yourself."

The telegram form was filled out in a shaky but legible script. It read:

Sender: Colonel William Meecham

To: Douglas County Sheriff

Seeking whereabouts of negro known as Henry. Scar on left cheek. Former army scout. Do not detain.

"I've known Sheriff Goode since he was a boy," Macklin said. "His father and I rode together before either of you two were born. He'll do as I ask, if you don't want your whereabouts known."

"I'm obliged, Mister Macklin," Henry said, handing the telegram back to rancher. "I'm finished with the army. But I'm not running from them or anyone else."

"About what I expected. You boys have a good night.... The bunkhouse is coming along real nice, Henry."

We heard nothing else of Meecham or the sheriff for a week. But then, early one afternoon, a small army detail arrived at the ranch. An hour or so after that, James Macklin walked past the corral where I was working with a fresh batch of horses and out toward the new bunkhouse. After a few minutes he walked by again. He never lifted his head. At quitting time Henry strode up and hopped onto the fence. He sat there in silence and watched while I finished up.

"Well?" I said.

"The army colonel who sent out the telegram is here. Mister Macklin invited him and me to supper. Mister Macklin doesn't trust in the army. I can't say I do either. He thought you and Oliver might want to come along. That way the colonel can state his business in front of witnesses."

"I wouldn't miss it," I said.

We cleaned up for supper and walked up to the big house along with Oliver Belle. It was only the second time I'd been inside the sprawling brick and wood home, the other time being when Macklin first interviewed me for the ranch work. Outside of some hired help, Macklin lived in the house alone. His wife caught a fever and died ten years earlier, and he never spoke of whether or not there were children. June, his housemaid, answered the door and led us to the dining room.

Macklin was seated at the head of the huge polished oak table and was engaged in conversation with a man in a blue army officer's uniform who was sitting to his right. My first impression of the portly colonel with his neatly trimmed moustache was that he was a dandy, a toy soldier. Other than he and Macklin, the table was empty. There was no sign of the other men from the army detail.

"Come sit down, boys," Macklin said as we entered. "June, please pour these men a drink—that new brandy—and another for me and the colonel."

We all three sat on Macklin's left, across from the military man.

"Colonel Meecham," Macklin said, "this is Oliver Belle, my foreman, that's Everett Ward, and of course Henry, the man you rode all this way to meet."

Colonel Meecham stood and reached across the table, shaking our hands in turn. "It's a pleasure to meet you all," he said as he returned to his seat.

"The colonel was telling me about the Indian problems the army's having up north," Macklin said, "but now that you're here, Henry, we can talk about what brought him down here to Kansas."

"Of course," the colonel said. His eyes darted briefly to me and Oliver but he continued.

"Henry, I'll get right to it. Indians are harassing soldiers and civilians on the Bozeman Road. Sioux, Cheyenne, and Arapahos have joined together in sizeable mixed bands and are attacking supply caravans, settlers, and miners. They've killed soldiers, and they're stealing horses and supplies meant for Fort Reno and Fort Phil Kearny."

"Fort Reno and Fort Phil Kearny? These are on the Bozeman Trail?" Henry said.

"That's right. Fort Reno was completed last year and Fort Phil Kearny is being constructed as we speak."

"Two more forts … in the Powder River country. I don't know what you expected."

"Our treaty with the Indians provides for us to build posts on their land as we see fit to protect the road and supply those who travel on it."

Henry barked a short laugh. There was no humor in it. "You mean the Horse Creek Treaty? The men in charge broke that one years ago."

"The men in charge don't see it that way."

"Of course they don't. What do you want from me, Colonel?"

"Brigadier General Fitchner and Major Wynkoop, as well as some others have spoken well of you, and I'm told you speak and understand the languages as if you were a Native yourself. We need your skills as an interpreter. The treaty commission would like to secure new treaties with the big chiefs. The move would essentially reaffirm the particulars of the Fort Laramie Treaty of fifty-one—the documents you referred to as the Horse Creek Treaty—though Washington is under no obligation to do so. It appears that over the last fifteen years the Indians have forgotten what they agreed to. Nevertheless, the Department of the Interior is prepared to once again compensate the chiefs who sign, if it will ensure peace and the safety of our soldiers and civilians who use the road.… It's no secret you're sympathetic to them, Henry. This would be a way you could help them."

June arrived with a tray of brandies. The colonel paused while she passed them around. "Supper will be ready shortly," she said.

"Thank you, June," Macklin said.

"It pays one hundred dollars a month," Colonel Meecham said proudly after June departed. "That's an officer's wage, and unheard of for a negro."

Oliver whistled, impressed, but Henry didn't even appear to consider it. "I'm obliged, but I reckon I'm happy enough here," he said.

"Henry, there's an Indian named Standing Elk—not the Sioux chief, but a Cheyenne. An influential medicine man, I'm told. He was captured two months ago along with several other renegades for being in possession of branded army steers. He's in the stockade at Fort Laramie. There's been talk of hanging them, to set an example. I believe it would be accurate to say he's a friend of yours?"

"Now what's this, Colonel?" Macklin interjected. "The man respectfully declines your offer so you produce a hole-card to strong-arm him with? I'd have expected better manners from a guest in my house, particularly one of your upbringing and education."

"I beg your pardon, Mister Macklin. It wasn't my intention to appear unseemly. I only wanted to point out that if Henry could see his way clear to assist his country with this matter, that I'd personally return the favor by doing what I can for his Native friend. Possibly even obtain his release, though ultimately it's not up to me."

"That seems —" Macklin began, not sounding mollified.

"I'll do it," Henry said. "I'll need a week to finish up my work on Mister Macklin's bunkhouse and I want Standing

Elk's release to be more than a possibility. I want your pledge, right here in front of these men, that he and the others that were jailed with him will be released. You can take the beef you say they were found with out of my wage, along with whatever the army feels is a fair reparation."

"I'll pay for it out of my own pocket," Macklin said, "Or I'll cut out however many head you claim these Indians stole out of my own stock and have them delivered to you. I'm confident my beef will be of a better quality than what you lost."

"That's all well and good, gentlemen, but as I stated, in the end it isn't up to me. I'll use all of my influence, but I'm not certain I can guarantee—"

"Well then you best get James Beckwourth or Jim Bridger, and I can't speak of Bridger but I don't expect Beckwourth will help you gain any trust with the Cheyenne … or the Sioux."

The colonel raised his hands. "I'll find some way to arrange it. In the event I fail, I'll see you're paid a full month's wages and expenses for your travel time to Fort Laramie."

Henry nodded. "Fair enough.… There's one more thing; I'll interpret your treaty and say whatever else you want me to say, but I won't be party to any trickery."

"And you won't be asked to," said the colonel.

Back at the bunkhouse, after an unrelaxed meal with the colonel, we took our ribbing from the hands who were still friendly with us. They all wanted to know what made us so special that we were invited to the big house for supper.

Henry's mood was brooding but to his credit he tried not to show it. I did my best to carry the load and made a few jokes about how Henry struck gold digging out the piers for the new bunkhouse, and that Macklin wanted to negotiate Henry's lay.

Later, I was just beginning to doze off when Henry spoke softly from the bunk next to me.

"Everett, I was thinking you might want to come with me up north."

"It's a nice thought, and I appreciate the offer, but I've been considering moving on, heading back down to Texas … I've been meaning to tell you, I wanted to be certain of my decision first."

"You going after Wačhiwi?"

"Yes."

"You believe she's a captive down there? Even after what she did at the jail?"

"I do."

"Well then, I can't say I wouldn't do the same, if I was in your place. How about we go together? You come along while I settle this business with army, and when we're finished, I'll do whatever I can to help you return her to her people, if that's what she wants. Might be we can find out where she's from when we're up north. Ten years is a long time, but mayhap one of the Sioux fathers or mothers knows of her. Could be we can get the army involved if we find out where she belongs. The rancher might be compelled to let her go."

"I hadn't thought about something like that. I was thinking I'd try to sneak her out in the middle of the night …"

"Mayhap it'll come to that, but better to try the path that won't involve gunfire or getting locked up or being hanged, if we can."

"I suppose you don't want to get hanged a third time. I accept your offer, with thanks."

"You'd be supposing right. Goodnight, Everett."

"Night, Henry."

We rode out two days later. James Macklin wasn't happy about losing both Henry and I, but he understood the reasons why. James "Red" Macklin was a truly good man. A rarity in men of his kind of means. I was fortunate enough to know two of them in my life. I'll be telling you about the other one, later.

Macklin loaned me a horse for the journey. At first I argued that Evelyn was in fine shape, but he convinced me that I wasn't doing a horse her age any favors by taking her on such a long trip. Oliver promised to care for her and take her out regular. In the end I agreed and with thanks.

The horse Macklin entrusted me with was a five-year-old roan named Rose. Oliver Belle named her when she first arrived at the ranch due to her reddish-pink mane and tail. Henry was riding his long-time companion, Harriet. He told me the mare had been shot in the same battle he had, and that if it hadn't been for Standing Elk, Both Henry and the mare would have died in a rocky Dakota Territory creek bed.

We met Colonel Meecham around eight a.m. in Lawrence. We rode up to the livery and found him in heated conversation with a soldier. They were standing in front of a fully loaded supply wagon. The soldier was clearly discomposed and appeared relieved when the colonel's attention was redirected to us.

"What's this?" he said, eyeing me and Rose for a moment before turning to Henry.

"Everett and I have affairs to attend to once this business is done." Henry said. "He'll pull his weight and I'll be paying him half of what the army is paying me."

Colonel Meecham opened his mouth as if he was going to protest and then appeared to think better of it. "The supply wagons should be ready in one hour. Once we reach Fort Laramie, you'll have a day or three to rest up while arrangements are made for our departure to Fort Phil Kearny."

"An hour then," Henry said.

Henry and I left the horses and walked deeper into town to a general store. Henry bought twenty pounds of beef jerky, twenty pounds of flour, and two pounds of tobacco. On a whim I bought a half dozen cigars. I'd never smoked one but always thought they smelled good when someone else did.

While we were waiting for the elderly storekeeper to fill our order, we looked over the firearms in a wall-to-wall glass display case.

"How well do you shoot?" he said, conversationally.

"Better than most, if I was to be honest," I said.

The shopkeeper returned and set Henry's bundles on the counter.

"Will that do it for you?"

Henry turned to me and then pointed to a Spencer rifle in the display case, identical to the one he carried.

"I reckon you'd shoot a lot better with that," he said.

Without waiting for a response, he turned back to the storekeeper.

"I'd like this Spencer and two boxes of cartridges."

The storekeeper looked doubtful. "That's a fifty-dollar rifle, son."

"I reckon I'd like it a sight better for forty-five," Henry said, removing a small leather drawstring sack from his pocket. "But I'll pay your price."

Henry paid the man, who then took the rifle from the case and set it next to Henry's other purchases. Henry picked it up and then turned back to me. "I suppose we should have brought the horses. You think you can you carry your new rifle and cartridges *and* that sack of jerky?"

I started to protest but he held the Spencer out for me. "If there's trouble, you'll be more help if you're shooting this. You can trade me that old Whitworth of yours, if you're not too attached to it. It's a good rifle, it's just not suited for what we're doing."

I took the Spencer, smiling ear to ear. "I can carry it all," I said. "Thank you, Henry."

Henry nodded. "We best get back."

Back at the livery I removed the muzzleloader from its scabbard and put the Spencer in its place. Henry tied the old rifle to Harriet along with the rest of his gear. When we were finished we waited on the boardwalk in front of the livery office, where we'd be out of the way of the soldiers who were still loading the supply wagons. One hour turned out to be two, and we finally mounted up and fell in behind the fourteen-wagon caravan as it made its slow way out of town.

"How long will it take us to get there?" I said.

"Inside of three weeks if the wagons hold up and we don't run into any trouble."

"Then after that?"

"I can't say. Colonel Meecham hasn't been all that conversational as far as telling me exactly what they're planning to do. I reckon we'll have a council once we arrive. We should know more then."

Our work wasn't to begin until after we reached Fort Phil Kearny so there wasn't much for us to do. The fifty or so soldiers took care of their own business and Henry and I spent a lot of time hunting, though there wasn't a great amount of game to be found. I found the plains striking—this was in the days before the reticulated farms and fences that you'd see out there now—with its grasses that grew for as far as the eye could see. I felt as if I could be at home there.

We kept ourselves busy; Henry taught me how to make snares that actually worked and at night we'd sit at our own fire and he would teach me some Indian hand signs and useful Sioux and Cheyenne words. He told me more about his time living with the Cheyenne and scouting for the army, and I told him more about the war because he seemed genuinely interested, even though some of it was difficult for me to talk about.

Colonel Meecham rode in the wagon most days and retired early to his tent at night. When he was about in camp, he didn't seem inclined to talk with us. He gave the run of things over to a young lieutenant whose name I can't recall now.

Some nights a sergeant named John Church would sit with us. Henry knew him from some expeditions during the war years and was friendly with him.

"Word was, you quit scouting for the army, Henry. What brought you back?" sergeant Church asked that first night out.

"I wasn't afforded much of a choice in the matter," Henry said.

"How's that?"

Henry nodded across the camp toward colonel Meecham's tent. "I probably shouldn't discuss the particulars. Army needs an interpreter and it seems they're set on it being me."

"Well, that's not so curious. The brass knows you're friendly with the Cheyenne and they been having the most trouble with them and the Sioux ever since they opened up the north Bozeman and started building on it. You ain't been around as long as some others but when it comes to the Cheyenne, Arapaho and Sioux, Beckwourth ain't any good because he's too cozy with the Crow. Jim Bridger's getting old—not that Beckwourth ain't … there's a couple more, but who knows? Seems like trouble's brewing everywhere and we're spread pretty thin. How long has it been since you've been out this way?"

"More than a year."

"A lot has changed."

"Doesn't sound like it," Henry said.

Our journey took nineteen days.

"Fort Laramie, up ahead," Henry said, pointing.

It was early afternoon and Henry and I were riding vanguard a mile or so ahead of the caravan. At first I didn't see anything except more prairie. Henry's eyes were keener than mine. A short time later, when I did finally see something breaking up the monotone distance, I didn't see a fort. What I saw were tepees—a lot of them. I knew what they were, but they were the first I'd ever seen outside of some drawings. They were a sight.

"A lot of lodges near the fort," Henry said. "More than usual."

"Does that mean something?"

"Could."

I pointed to a weathered platform thirty yards or so off. "Looks like a hanging scaffold out there."

"That's what it is. Army made a show of hanging two Sioux chiefs last year. They hung them with artillery chain and then left them out there for days."

"That's grisly. What did they do?"

"That's the question. Army said they kidnapped a white girl and her mother; the chiefs said they bargained for her from the men who really took her and were bringing her here as a sign of peace. The commander here—a colonel by the name of Moonlight—didn't believe them. The word was that the white woman corroborated the chief's account … I wasn't there, so I can't say either way. I can say that I trust Colonel Moonlight about as far as I could throw him."

I stared at the scaffold until it was behind us, imagining men being hanged with chain.

The Indian camp was staged near the Laramie River a half mile from the fort. There were many more women and children than men, and most of the men I did see were old. The place had a disconcerting air of desperation; the prairie grass had been mostly cut—probably to feed the three sickly looking steers that were housed in a makeshift lodge pole pen—and what was left had been beaten down into the dust.

Women poked their heads from tepees and looked up from their cook-fires, their faces at once despondent and expectant. Some stopped what they were doing and started walking toward us. Five boys in animal skin loincloths ran past them smiling and shouting. Henry leaned over and handed the boys some beef jerky. I stopped and dug in my saddlebags and found the hard candy I'd purchased to give the man and woman who'd nursed me when I'd been shot. The boys were trotting alongside Henry but abandoned him and sprinted over to me when they spotted me reaching into the saddlebags. I handed off the small candy sack to the one who reached me first and the five of them ran off, grabbing and pawing at the boy with the candy. Henry stopped his horse and handed a bundle of beef jerky to one woman and a sack of flour to another before urging Harriet forward. The women were still waving at Henry and saying, "Piláymaya," as I passed.

When we reached the fort, we waited for the caravan. As we did so Colonel Meecham rode up on his horse in full dress. It was only the second time I'd seen him on the animal the entire journey.

"I'll arrange for your quarters," he said, reining in next to Henry.

"That won't be necessary, Colonel. We'll camp outside, back there apiece, just this side of the Indian camp."

The colonel appeared nettled but said only, "I'll send for you," before riding off.

Henry turned to me "Hungry?"

"As a bear."

"The woman at the sutler's bakes the best biscuits I've ever eaten," Henry said. "Let's see if there's any left."

We tied the horses in the shade of the porch and went inside. The place smelled of hot coffee.

"Well look who blew in," a bespectacled man with an English accent said from behind the counter.

"Afternoon, Mister Alden. It's been a good while." Henry said.

"That it has. Step up here, Henry. Who's that with you?"

"This is Everett Ward."

"Pleasure to meet you," he said, extending his hand across the polished plank counter.
"I'm Frederick Alden."

"Pleased to meet you," I said, taking the offered hand.

"*Ruby!*" he called out. "Come out here, will you? There's someone here you'll want to see."

I heard some shuffling coming from the other side of the store. Then a door opened on the far wall and a woman wearing a plain blue work dress strode out. When she saw Henry, she stopped short and put a hand to her neck. She let out a great breath and her face lit up.

"Oh, Henry, heavens, it's you in the flesh. There were terrible rumors … they said you were killed by Indians upriver. You and Ben Campbell. They brought Ben's body in, and they made a big fuss over it. That Captain—"

"Lange," Frederick Alden interrupted.

"Yes, Lange. He went so far as to make a speech, right there on the parade grounds. Then they buried poor Ben and didn't even mark the grave. That Captain Lange said he was a *deserter.* What with all of that, it had us believing you were … but here you are … Oh, I'm sorry. I forget myself. How have you been, Henry?"

"I've been just fine, Missus Alden. Just fine."

"Well, you look just fine." She moved forward to stand in front of Henry, giving him a brief pat on his shoulder before lifting a hinged portion of the counter and joining her husband behind it.

"Can we get you boys anything? Coffee?"

"Coffee would be nice and, well, I was talking up your biscuits to Everett here. I don't suppose you have any left this late in the day?"

"Of course I do. You two go have a seat and I'll bring you some.... Henry, we knew Ben and never believed what was said. Soldiers enjoy loose talk more than a women's tea club."

"That they do," Henry agreed.

The biscuits were every bit as good as Henry claimed they were and the coffee wasn't bad either. Frederick and Ruby Alden mined Henry for information about what happened to their mutual friend, Ben, the previous year, and what Henry had been doing for the last year, and why he wasn't scouting for the army anymore. Henry was vague about his parting with the army, and said he didn't know anything about what happened to Ben Campbell. He told me after we'd finished our biscuits and left the store how much he hated lying to them.

It was early evening and we were setting up camp by the river about halfway between the Indian lodges and the fort. I was feeding the horses and Henry was tending a pot of coffee when a man in hide trousers and a white linen shirt approached leading a horse behind him.

"Háu, Henry," he said from the edge of the camp.

"Háu, Itȟáŋka," Henry said, standing. "Everett, this would be a good time to share those cigars, if you're inclined."

"I am," I said, digging into my saddlebags for the cigars and matches. The man walked over and tied his horse to the stake I'd set for Harriet and Rose. He wasn't very tall or even particularly stout looking, but he was an imposing figure nonetheless. He nodded to me. His mouth was stern but his eyes were curious. I handed him a cigar and struck a match for him.

"Piláymaya," he said, puffing the cigar to life. He walked over to the fire and sat down with a satisfied grunt.

Henry and I joined him. I lit my cigar and coughed out the smoke. The man chuckled softly and mumbled something I didn't understand.

"This is Everett Ward," Henry said. "Everett, this is Chief Itȟáŋka. Chief Big Mouth, in English."

The chief raised his hand to me, "Wíyuškiŋyaŋ waŋčhíŋyaŋke ló," he said. Then: "Good cigar."

I smiled and nodded and raised my cigar to him.

He turned to Henry. "The White Chiefs sent for you to help them make peace." It wasn't a question.

"The White Chiefs want me to deliver their words to those chiefs who would listen," Henry said.

"The White Chiefs don't understand, and the White Father doesn't understand," he said in English. "Many of the Očhéthi Šakówiŋ will not give up any more land without fighting. The whites offer trinkets and lies for our land. If we say no they try to take what we will not give them. Red Cloud, Spotted Tail and others have promised war …" He smoked at the cigar and then waved his hand dismissively. "That is not the reason I've come; James Beckwourth has said he will kill you. If you go to the Powder River to parley for the whites. You may have to face him."

"I reckon that's true."

"I've spoken to Standing Elk, through his cage at the soldier's fort. They allowed me to bring him and the others food. He told me what you did for the Cheyenne village. It is known you are a man of honor. I am Lakota, not white—or Crow as James Beckwourth is want to ally himself with, but I will speak with him if I can."

"Piláymaya," Henry said, standing. "I have something for you."

Big Mouth also stood. Henry walked over to Harriet and removed the old rifle he'd asked me to give him in trade for the Spencer. He handed it to the chief without ceremony and then retrieved the sack containing the powder and balls and handed them over as well. The chief looked closely at the rifle, nodded, and then removed a knife in a beaded leather scabbard from the waistband of his trousers. This he handed to Henry before untying his horse's tether.

"Will they release Standing Elk and the others?" he asked.

"They'll release him …" Henry said. "Itȟáŋka, there's a young Sioux woman, down in Texas. Everett told me she was captured along with many other women and children after soldiers attacked her camp and killed all of the men … this was mayhap ten years ago. She would have been a child then. Her name is Wačhiwi. We were hoping to find some of her family."

Big Mouth appeared to think this over. "White soldiers attacked a camp during the Moon of the Brown Leaves. It could have been ten Cold Moons ago as you say. They murdered many Sičháŋǧu Oyáte that day. Most of them weren't warriors, but women, old men, and boys. Some of these women are with Red Cloud. You may find answers there."

Later, as we watched Chief Big Mouth ride off toward the Indian camp, a question occurred to me.

"Henry, he spoke English, better than some white southerners I knew in the war, So why did the army go out of their way to find you if there's Indians like that around who can speak English. Why don't they hire him?"

"The army uses Indians as scouts and interpreters," Henry said, poking at the fire with a stick. "Trouble is, Indians don't have much trust in the whites anymore, and it looks like it's getting worse. There's some Pawnee and Crow and Osage who speak fair English and work with the army pretty regular, but those nations are enemies of the Sioux and Cheyenne, so most often they scout, but don't interpret. There's white interpreters, but so many of them have lied to the Indians about what's written on government papers that they're not trusted either. Then there's men like Big Mouth and Standing Elk. They can speak English when they choose to, but they're not going to get caught between the United States government and their own and end up outcasts. Big Mouth walks the line, from time to time, for his own ends. He's a complex man. Anyway, there are Indians willing, but chances are good they never learned to read English when they learned to speak it. Pretty hard to interpret something you can't read yourself, and there's fewer and fewer of these people who will trust what a white military man from back east tells them is written on those sheets of paper."

He handed me the hunting knife Big Mouth had just given him. "I already have two of these, but it would have been impolite not to accept it. I expect you'll be able to make use of it."

I examined the knife. It had a plain bone handle and the blade was as sharp as a straight razor. The beadwork on the hide scabbard was simple, but somehow beautiful.

"Thank you, I said. "I expect I will."

They sent for us the next morning—well, sent for Henry, I was so much baggage at that point. A runner rode up on our camp in the midmorning and informed us that a meeting would be held at the adjutant's office at noon.

We broke camp and rode back to the fort and had a breakfast of Ruby Alden's biscuits and bacon. We left the horses there at the sutler's and walked across the yard to the adjutant's office. The sentry by the door let us in without a word.

The dim and smoky fore-room was occupied by three men: Colonel Meecham, a soldier with a wooly and unkempt beard, and a severe-looking man of middle-age who was dressed in a neatly pressed jacket and tie. Colonel Meecham stood and raised a hand. "Shall we get started, gentlemen?"

We joined them in the semi-circle of mismatched chairs placed in the center of the room. Colonel Meecham wasted no time.

"Henry this is Governor Edmunds—"

"*Former* Governor," the man in civilian attire interjected.

"*Former* Governor. My apologies, Newton." Colonel Meecham said before continuing. "Henry, I believe you've met Captain Lange?"

Henry nodded at the two men. "I have."

Captain Lange ran his hand through his prodigious beard. "Good to see you alive, Henry. You seem to be the only one accounted for after last year's misadventure—well, outside of Sergeant Campbell, that is. He's buried out there in the cemetery—in a deserter's grave."

Both Colonel Meecham and Newton Edmunds cast dark looks at the captain who didn't appear the least bit discomfited.

"And what is this young man's role in this?" Edmunds said, looking from me to Colonel Meecham.

"This is Henry's … protégé," Colonel Meecham said.

"Is that so?"

"I reckon that's right," Henry responded.

"Henry," Edmunds said. "By all accounts you are a trusted man. Both by the Indians and the army. Perhaps being a negro and therefore having no stake in the doings of either side makes you the perfect man to act as a broker for peace between us and the Indians. Thus far our efforts have yielded less than satisfactory results, and I—as well as others—have an interest in insuring that the Bozeman Road remains open and safe for travel. In the close future the new forts will be of the utmost importance to those interests. Most of the Indian chiefs have already signed new treaties—for which they received generously given gifts of blankets, powder, and food. They agreed not to hinder the construction of the forts or accost travelers on the road. We haven't asked them to relinquish any additional territory. We've only asked that they allow us fair use. Unfortunately, there are some chiefs—Red Cloud, Black Horse, and a handful of others—who have refused to sign the new treaties—"

"Which were only offered as appeasement," Colonel Meecham cut in. "The Indians signed agreements allowing the road through that territory years ago. The United States has no obligation to more."

"As the colonel says," Edmunds continued. "Regardless, we've reached this juncture and these warrior chiefs are attacking and murdering both soldiers and civilians—"

This time it was Henry who interrupted. "I'd be obliged if you'd just get to it and tell me just what it is you want me to do, Mister Edmunds."

"Of course. Simplicity is always best.... We want you to convince Red Cloud to sign the new treaty and leave off his attacks. If he signs, the others will follow."

"What makes you believe Chief Red Cloud will listen to me? I've never met him."

"We are only asking that you try. Colonel Meecham informed me that this Indian here in the stockade, this Standing Elk, is not only a friend of yours, but an influential man among his people. You've secured his freedom, perhaps he'll help you convince Red Cloud to sign the treaty, receive his gifts, and share this wide land."

"Standing Elk isn't Sioux," Henry said.

The former governor acted as if he didn't hear. Instead he leaned forward in his chair and added, "There is a substantial bounty on top of your scout's wage if you're successful. How does five thousand dollars sound, Henry? A remarkable negro like yourself could go far with that much money."

Henry nodded noncommittally. "Mister Edmunds, there's a Sioux woman in ..." He turned to me;

"Sherman," I said.

"Sherman, Texas. Everett can give you the particulars but it seems she's being held against her will on a ranch down there and we're hoping you might see fit to look into it."

Edmunds blanched. "Well, I don't see how I could be of much service to you in this matter. Were I still in office I'd have been happy to make some inquiries, though even then, I had no influence in Texas …"

Henry turned to Colonel Meecham. "Colonel?"

"Your list of demands is getting longer," Colonel Meecham said. He sighed, appearing put-upon. "If you do your part in this and your claim is credible, I'll ask some questions after we return. Now, if the govern—*Mister Edmunds,* is finished, Captain Lange and I will go over our departure."

"Yes, I've harried you more than enough," Edmunds said, standing. He brushed a crease from the breast of his suit. "I'll get out of the way so you men can discuss details." Good luck to you, Henry. It's been a pleasure to meet you—and you Mister Ward."

Once the Edmunds left the office, Colonel Meecham stood and moved to the room's only window and watched him walk across the parade grounds. Without turning, he began to speak.

"The *former* governor of the Dakota Territory has long been an advocate for peace with the Indians. In his shortsightedness he feels that propitiation serves the interests he seems so wont to speak of. His interests: railroads, mining, corrupt Indian agencies, are hindered when the Indians are angry. So his answer is to mollify the Indians with trifles that serve to sedate them while men like him profit from these interests. I say it's shortsighted because pacifying the Indians is becoming more and more ineffective as we encroach further and further onto what was once theirs. Men like the governor feel that open war paints a picture of instability in the territory and makes the public fearful. It obstructs their immediate monetary needs and so they choose the temporary illusion of empty treaties when the only two practicable solutions to the Indian predicament are containment or extermination. There are other men, powerful men—an ever-growing silent majority—who are sanctioning the latter. So as the war within continues, we're edging closer to that finality." He turned from the window, removed a cigar from his coat pocket, and pointed it at Henry and I. "I'm telling you this so you'll understand what's at stake here, and I beg you remember my words. This is the beginning of the end for the Indian way of life. You can help prolong that life, and perhaps ease their transition into a new one, by helping to convince Red Cloud to give up his war and sign this new treaty."

"Colonel?" I said.

"Yes?"

"Where do you stand on all of this?"

Colonel Meecham appeared to consider his answer carefully. He glanced briefly at Captain Lange before returning his eyes to me.

"My allegiance lies with the United States of America, Mister Ward.

He walked to the door, and then paused, his hand hovering over the knob. "You might want to ask yourself the same question," he said "Standing Elk will be released this afternoon. He'll be instructed as to your whereabouts. Captain Lange will see to your provisioning."

After Colonel Meecham left the office, Captain Lange stood. "Now that the muckety-mucks have gone and it's just us ordinary men, we can all speak plainly. I don't like you, Henry. I don't like you and I don't trust you. All that happened last year, with that Hanfield woman and Lieutenant

Elliot; Colonel Picton and Ben Campbell … and you, the nigger scout, right in the middle of it all."

Henry stood and moved toward the door. "We'll see to our own provisioning."

Captain Lange glared at Henry with barely concealed fury. "That Indian; I don't want to see him armed."

Henry turned and gazed levelly at the captain. "No, sir. You certainly don't."

A man entered our camp on foot shortly before sunset. Henry and I were busy packing a horse for Standing Elk along with the difficult and restless mule Captain Lange had requisitioned for us from the stable at Fort Laramie. Henry had purchased all of our provisions from the Alden's store on the army's account, and then we used our own money to buy extra dried beef and flour, which we delivered to the Indian camp that afternoon. Henry used the last of his money to purchase a bedroll and canteen for Standing Elk. I looked from the newcomer to Henry, who was smiling from ear to ear. He dropped the grain sack he'd been holding and hurried to meet him.

"Haáahe," the man said. His expression was solemn.

"Haáahe," Henry returned.

I finished tying off the bundle I was working on and started toward them. The man looked past Henry and regarded me curiously. He was tall, as tall as Henry, and his hair was long and black and streaked with gray. His hide trousers and shirt were soiled.

Henry followed the man's eyes and then stood aside. "This is Everett Ward." he said. "Everett, this is Mo'ohnee'ėstse. Standing Elk, in English.

"Haáahe," Standing Elk said.

I put out my hand; he regarded it for a moment and then took it in his. He gripped it tightly and looked me in the eyes. Finally, he nodded once and released it.

"It doesn't look as if they've taken very good care of you," Henry said, looking him over.

"They care for their mules better," Standing Elk said in English.

"You hungry?"

Standing Elk smiled and nodded.

"I'll start a fire," I said.

While Henry and I busied ourselves preparing supper, Standing Elk listened intently while Henry explained what Colonel Meecham was expecting.

Our meal consisted of biscuits, beef, and potatoes—all items we purchased at the Alden's store. Standing Elk ate heartily while he told us of his capture and imprisonment. He began his tale in Cheyenne but Henry asked him to speak English. He frowned briefly at this but nodded and started again.

"After you healed from your wounds, I traveled south, below the Arkansas River to visit with Black Kettle where he was sent to live by the whites. When I arrived, there was no food and they had no ponies. Little grows there and the hunting is poor. Many of The People were sick and I have no medicine to cure an empty stomach. The whites promised beef but never gave any. As you have seen, this is their way. Some of us went north, though Black Kettle did not approve, and we found a band of bluecoats pushing a large herd of cattle. We followed them that day. At night the soldiers left only two men to guard and we led six of the animals away while the rest of the soldiers were sleeping. When we returned to Black Kettle's camp there were bluecoats there, and White Whiskers Harney and others. We had hidden the beef before we came to the village but a bluecoat scout discovered them. The soldiers gathered all of The People and pointed rifles at us, demanding to be told who had stolen the animals. I told them I did. Little Mouth, Brave Bear, and Wild Wind stood with me. They took our rifles and our pistols and shot our horses, and then they took us to the fort and kept us there. William Bent, Big Mouth, and Owl Woman brought us food when the soldier chief allowed."

Standing Elk stared out across the river and sighed.

"The land is changing," he said.

I couldn't know just what he meant by that, but the sadness in his voice affected me. After a moment he turned his attention back to Henry and me.

"You will speak the white man's words but Red Cloud will not surrender the north hunting grounds to the whites, though he does not speak for all Očhéthi Šakówiŋ Chiefs."

"What about the Cheyenne?"

"We are also … divided."

For me, sleep was a long time coming that night. As I lay awake watching the coals from the night's fire fade slowly to black, I thought about Indians. Like negroes, I'd never known any, and outside of a few stories, I knew little about them. My father had mentioned once that all of the Indians who'd lived in Missouri were chased off long before we moved there from Virginia. Most of what I had heard through my short life had painted the Indians as primitive, unintelligent, and possessing a proclivity for violence.

On the journey to Fort Laramie, Henry told me about the incident at Big Sandy Creek and how it soured his taste for scouting for the army. That was the first time I'd heard the name Black Kettle. Henry told me how the army had attacked the chief's village with no cause and killed nearly everyone there. More than a hundred people—women and children among them—according to Henry. I had no doubt about the veracity of Henry's claim that the attack was unprovoked, but it still seemed fantastic. There was a great lot I didn't understand.

Like most nights I fell asleep thinking about Wačhiwi, though her face was becoming more difficult to recall.

We broke camp and departed the next morning from the fort along with Colonel Meecham, Captain Lange, and a mixed company of regular and galvanized soldiers—two hundred in all, I judged. Henry commented to Colonel Meecham that it was a large and overly-armed force for a peace party. The colonel replied that most of the men were reinforcements for Colonel Carrington's 18th Infantry Regiment. Colonel Carrington was charged with completing the Bozeman Road forts and protecting the road from the Indians who opposed the further settling of the Powder River country.

Henry, Standing Elk and I rode vanguard, though we weren't tasked to. The army had their own and they rode about a half mile behind us. The going was slow as the caravan had upwards of thirty heavily-laden wagons. We were to follow the Bozeman Road to Fort Phil Kearny in order to rendezvous with Colonel Carrington. From there we were to locate Red Cloud's camp and convince him to meet a delegation led by Colonel Meecham. Henry still hadn't been given an opportunity to read the treaty, which troubled him.

One evening, when Colonel Meecham was making an inspection of the camp, Henry waylaid him and brought it up.

"Colonel, the chiefs are going to want to know if the new treaties mean abandoning the forts along the Bozeman. Short of that, I reckon there isn't much of a chance they'll agree to meet you."

"I think you know the answer to that, Henry. Nonetheless, I trust you'll be persuasive," was Colonel Meecham's reply.

Two days out of Fort Laramie an army scout spotted a large group of Indians on horseback shadowing the column's eastern flank about a mile off. Captain Lange and a small detail caught up with us and asked us to investigate.

We rode northeast and found thirty or so riders in a natural depression which kept them hidden from the main body of the army caravan and the soldiers riding its flanks. We stopped at the top of the low rise overlooking them.

"Cheyenne," Henry said at the very same moment Standing Elk said, "Tsêhéstáno," and urged his army mount forward. Henry and I followed. The party of Cheyenne saw us and stopped their northward progress. Four riders broke away and headed to meet us.

We all reined in, stopping short and facing each other. The men were shirtless and they all wore animal-skin leggings. It was immediately apparent Standing Elk and Henry knew them. They spoke in Cheyenne and the greetings were friendly. I was briefly introduced, and I nodded and smiled. The conversation soon turned somber, though, and there was a good amount of hand gesturing and pointing in the direction of the army column. After several minutes the men took their leave and rejoined their party.

During our ride back Henry explained that the men came from Chief Black Kettle's village. They were heading north to join the chiefs Two Moon and Dull Knife in their alliance with Red Cloud against the whites, who they saw as invaders. They said that they could no longer abide Black Kettle's acquiescence to the demands of the Great Father and his soldiers.

"Black Kettle's way has always been peace with the whites," Standing Elk said. Now many of The People suffer."

We rode north and met the vanguard of the army column. Captain Lange was with them. Henry told him the Cheyenne were moving north to the Powder River and that they were no threat to the column. Captain Lange pressed him for more details but Henry only asked if this was going to turn out to be a punitive expedition. The captain got fairly puckered at that.

"Well if you aren't something," he said. "You might want to be careful and hold on to the friends you have, Henry. You're being afforded courtesies at present. When all of this with the Indians is over—and it *will* end—you'll be just another negro trying to make his way in a white man's world."

Standing Elk laughed at this and then pivoted his army mount and rode off ahead of the caravan. Henry followed. It looked as if Captain Lange was going to say something to me, but he appeared to think better of it. I nodded to him and went after Henry and Standing Elk.

A few evenings later we set our three-man camp at our usual half mile outside the perimeter of the army's camp. It made us less likely to be killed if any Indians decided to attack the soldiers.

We were sitting around our small fire, smoking the last of my cigars—Standing Elk thanked me for the cigar but lamented his pipe while smoking it—and I was thinking about our parley with the Cheyenne men. I found it maddening, being unable to understand what was being said, and as if Henry could hear my thoughts he said, "Standing Elk says he'll help you learn the languages. He's the one who taught me most of my Cheyenne and he knows Sioux as well as any Sioux. We talked about it while you were out fetching firewood. I told him about Wačhiwi so he knows Sioux is more important to you."

"Dancing Girl," Standing Elk said.

I looked at him, confused. When nothing more came I said, "Dancing Girl?"

Standing Elk turned to Henry and regarded him. Henry shrugged his shoulders and Standing Elk smiled ruefully, shaking his head. "Wačhiwi," he said, "means Dancing Girl in the language of her people."

He studied me from across the fire, holding my gaze. He nodded once. Up until that night, Standing Elk had mostly ignored me, and if I caught him looking at me at all it was plain that he was measuring me. To this day I've never met a man or woman who could say as much with a cock of the head or set of the mouth as he could. I knew for a certainty at that moment that he was offering his friendship.

"The whites will not help you free this woman," he said. "To them she has no meaning. I will help you speak the words of the Lakota, and also the words of the Cheyenne, though it will not be easy for you. Then perhaps I will travel with you and Henry to free this woman."

Chapter 4

Much like the trip to Fort Laramie, the twenty-day journey to Fort Phil Kearny was uneventful. The days were hot and long. We each took our turn leading the temperamental army mule, who was content as long as we were moving but had a penchant toward not wanting to start back up after an extended rest.

We had very little interaction with the army convoy outside of Captain Lange's occasional and perfunctory evening visits to our camp, and a glimpse of Colonel Meecham was a rarity. Most nights I went to sleep with my head spinning from the language lessons Standing Elk and Henry were giving me.

Riding day after day through the seemingly endless prairie, first to Fort Laramie and then to Fort Phil Kearny, educated me to just how vast the territory was. Vast, stark, and beautiful. At the time it was difficult for me to understand why there were clashes between the Indians and the United States government. It seemed to me that there was plenty of room for everyone with some to spare. I was guileless.

The first thing I noticed riding up on the fort was that there were no Indians camped nearby. The three of us eased off and waited for the column's vanguard. When they caught up with us Colonel Meecham was with them, along with Captain Lange. They called for a halt and we waited. Soon Colonel Carrington and a small detachment rode out to meet us. There were salutes all around.

"Colonel Meecham; gentlemen," Colonel Carrington said. "The scout you sent up this morning informed me that you encountered no hostiles on the road."

"A small hunting party, nothing more, Colonel."

"That's fortunate. They were as busy as a hive of bees here up until last week. I'd speculate they needed to resupply. They'll be back, and sooner than later I suspect. You may have to alter you plans." He nodded toward Henry. "Is this the scout?"

"Yes," Colonel Meecham said. "Henry will be interpreting for our delegation, that is if he can convince Red Cloud to speak with us."

"Is this Indian with him?"

Colonel Meecham shifted in his saddle. "Standing Elk is a respected Cheyenne. We believe he may be of some help."

"I see. Well, this is your party, Colonel but I'd send the scout and the Indian alone. If you take a delegation, you're all likely to be killed. If you take a force sizeable enough to discourage the Indians from attacking, they'll take it as aggression and disappear before you even see them. The slim chance you had at getting a treaty signed would disappear. I can't spare the men anyway, including the ones you brought with you. I have my own orders."

"And what would those be, Colonel?"

"Keeping this road open and making it safe, among other things."

Colonel Meecham's face darkened. He turned to Henry. "You and Mister Ward and Standing Elk will have to locate Red Cloud. I can't guarantee your safety."

"I reckon we're safer without you, Colonel."

"Your scout speaks the truth," Colonel Carrington said, before addressing a soldier in his detachment. "Corporal Rogers, Go find Jim Bridger, he's going to want to talk with this man."

We followed Carrington's detachment into the busy fort. There must have been close to eight hundred soldiers inside. Carrington left us with a sergeant who pointed us to the teamster's mess. "You can get yourself a meal there," he said. "Keep an eye on your Indian. Some of the men might not be so happy to see him in here."

The teamster's mess was a poorly-constructed and drafty oblong-shaped building with plank tables set upon molasses barrels. The makeshift dining room was deserted and no one was manning the open kitchen. There was a huge pot of some sort of watery stew on the stove so I took it upon myself to ladle some of it into bowls for us. There was coffee as well, several hours old by the taste but it was hot.

We were just digging into the overly salted stew when an elderly but hale looking man dressed in canvas trousers and an animal skin shirt walked through the door and came straight over. He glanced at me, nodded, then turned his attention to Henry and Standing Elk.

"Jim," Henry said.

"Hullo, Henry; Standing Elk," the man said, taking the seat next to me and across from Henry and Standing Elk. He turned to face me. "And who's this young man?" he said, as if he were speaking to someone else.

"Everett Ward," I said, dropping my spoon and putting out my hand.

"Pleased to make you acquaintance, Everett Ward. My name's Bridger. Jim Bridger," he said, taking the offered hand and shaking it once. "How did you manage to fall in with such an adventurous pair as these two?"

When I didn't answer right away, he said, "Well, doesn't matter," and turned back to face Henry and Standing Elk.

"James Beckwourth asked after you," Bridger said with what looked like a smirk on his face.

"Is that so?" Henry said, continuing to eat his stew.

"Yes, he did. You know I've wondered why you two don't get on better, you both being negroes and all … well, he's only half, but you know what I mean. Anyhow, care to share, seeing he isn't here?"

"I reckon not, Jim."

Bridger elbowed me and barked a laugh. "Of course not, you might have to string more than three words together to tell it…. Henry's the quietest man I've ever known … well, next to 'ol Cam Granger that is, but then Cam was deaf-n-dumb. Don't let that fool you, though. Henry's got more smarts than a Philadelphia lawyer. He just prefers to keep his own council. Anyhow, I didn't come in here to poke fun at you, Henry. Colonel Carrington thought I might have something useful to tell you about the going's on up here. I suppose I do, only I don't think it's the kind of useful he had in mind; in fact he'd probably have me shot …" He leaned forward then, his voice dropping to one of a conspirator. "Listen to me, son. The time for treaties is over, you understand? That colonel you came here with isn't here to get a treaty signed. He may think he is, but he isn't. He's here so that a year or two from now when congress holds all their pomp and fluff hearings about the Red Man to appease the bleeding-heart public, they can claim to have done all they could. They can claim to have been *magnanimous*. It's all cock and bull, after all. The way they see it the Indians signed away rights to keep us off of this land fifteen years ago, whether the Indians see it that way or not. Now let's say those big bugs with their fancy suits in congress are the left hand, and the War Department is the right hand … might be the left don't always know—or *want* to know—what designs the right hand is up to. It's an oddity that Colonel Carrington is all the sudden fired-to-the-feet to find out where Red Cloud and Black Horse and Dull Knife and the rest are camped. He has Pawnee and Crow scouts being paid infantry wages to crawl all over this country looking for them. Someone will find them, eventually, with or without you, and I'm not saying they're planning attacks, but it might come in handy if they knew where Red Cloud and the rest of them are, just in case. You remember Big Sandy Creek …" his eyes flicked to Standing Elk and then back to Henry. "If I were you, I might think twice about being the one to lead him right to them."

"You know the Indians didn't have the slightest notion what they were signing at Horse Creek," Henry said.

"I was there wasn't I?"

He stood up—a little painfully from the look. Arthritis I supposed.

"It's about time for me to hang up my fiddle. My contract will be up soon and I'll be going back to Missouri. I've had a foot on both sides of the fence for so long that I've gotten to where I can't see the truth of what's happening on either side. Mayhap I never could.… Take care of yourself, Henry. Good to meet you, Mister Ward … Standing Elk, *Marchez doucement. Un danger prévu est à moitié évité.*"

"Au revoir, Jim Bridger," Standing Elk said. It was the only time I ever heard him utter any sort of goodbye, though at the time I didn't know what au revoir meant.

He started away but stopped halfway to the door and turned around. "Henry, you remember that horseshoe-shaped lake in that little valley between the Tongue River and that creek?"

"Yes."

"I'd look there. You boys enjoy that stew."

"If I believe him, I reckon this complicates things," Henry said after Bridger was gone.

"He once told me he saw a bear with two heads," Standing Elk said.

"I heard that one. Do you believe him now?"

"Haáahe."

Henry drank down his coffee and stood. "I do too. I can't see him lying about something like this. And what Bridger said … I reckon it's about the same as what Colonel Meecham said back at Fort Laramie. Everyone wants something different. I think mayhap Colonel Meecham and Colonel Carrington have two different ends in mind."

"They desire the same end," Standing Elk said. "The end of the Indian. But they fight among themselves and cannot choose whether that end is death or putting all Indians in a corral."

"What are we going to do?" I said. "Now the whole affair seems meaningless."

Henry ran his hand absently over the rough surface of the plank table. "I reckon you're right about that. We'll have to think on it some."

Henry and I spent the rest of the afternoon coordinating with Captain Lange and a sergeant under Colonel Carrington's command to secure provisions. Standing Elk busied himself pitching a camp for us outside the fort. I got the sense that he grew tired of the suspicious looks and mumbled insults from the soldiers inside.

The next morning Colonel Meecham met us by the fort's northeast gate to see us off. The plan was for us to locate Red Cloud and convince him and any other chiefs who may be aligned with him to meet with what Colonel Meecham was calling his *Peace Delegation* at Fort Phil Kearny where they would be provided with gifts of blankets, food, shot, and powder if they touched the pen to the new treaty. "I'll even see that the chiefs who sign each get a new rifle," he added.

If the chiefs agreed to attend, Henry would be charged with reading the treaty to them and acting as interpreter between them and Colonel Meecham.

It was the consensus of the army leaders that Red Cloud was probably somewhere near the upper Powder River, so the three of us headed northeast with our three mounts, two spares, and one ornery mule. We were riding red-eyed as we spent most of the night talking things out. In the end we agreed that Colonel Meecham had so far been forthright with us and that in all likelihood the amassing of troops under Colonel Carrington was in preparation for the eventuality that Red Cloud and the other chiefs refuse to come in and sign the treaty. Both Standing Elk and Henry had seen firsthand that it was the army's way to strike preemptively when Indians rebuffed their demands.

Standing Elk was certain the Cheyenne chiefs Black Horse and Two Moon wouldn't sign the treaty, and he was equally certain that Red Cloud and some of the other young Sioux leaders would also refuse. Henry figured that Colonel

Carrington would have one or two scouts shadow us so he'd know Red Cloud's location. He also thought we could likely stay together and lose whoever Colonel Carrington sent to track us—the Indians had been able to harry work crews and troops in the area of Fort Phil Kearny and disappear without being found—but he didn't want to risk giving away Red Cloud's or any other Indian's position. So it was decided that we'd feign a heading toward the Powder for two days before Standing Elk and I set off on foot toward the Tongue and the lake valley Jim Bridger spoke of. We agreed it would be best if Henry was the one to act as the decoy for the scouts. As far as Indian country went, I was too green, and Standing Elk was likely to be shot if he was discovered alone on the prairie with army mounts and supplies. Henry was pretty sure any scouts would likely stay at least one day behind us so we wouldn't spot them, and that it would be easy enough for Standing Elk and I to slip away while he continued northeast along the Powder. We agreed on a meeting place that Henry and Standing Elk both knew of; an abandoned trapper's cabin twenty miles southeast of the lake. We were to meet in eighteen days, regardless of whether or not Standing Elk and I found Red Cloud's camp.

Before we parted company we filled some empty flour sacks with stones and tied them to Rose and Standing Elk's army horse so the animal's tracks would still appear as if they were carrying riders.

I wasn't particularly happy about what was decided but I kept to myself about it. Finding the camp on foot, if we found it at all, was going to take considerably longer than on horseback. I tried to understand the importance of what we were doing but it seemed to keep putting me further and further away from McBain's ranch and Wačhiwi. We were setting our watches by Jim Bridger's information about the location of the camp. I hoped to hell it was good.

Standing Elk and I struck out with what provisions we could easily carry, along with my Spencer rifle and Henry's Colt Navy revolver, which Standing Elk wore around his neck hung from a length of hide thong. The late summer weather was hot and the warm winds provided little relief. Trees were few and far between, and Standing Elk took to running the rolling hills. He was at least twice my age and carrying more than twenty pounds of pistol, canteens, and food, but I couldn't come close to keeping up. Once, during that first day on foot, he got so far ahead that I lost sight of him. I finally found him sitting in the shade of a lone cottonwood tree. "You run like a creek in the drying grass moon," he said, holding his hand out flat and moving it exaggeratedly slow.

I stood there, bent and winded, and blamed my boots. He laughed, stood, and took off running again.

That night we camped in a small grove of trees and ate a supper of beef jerky and dried apricots. I ate in silence with my stiff legs splayed and my swollen feet bared. Standing Elk gazed at me from across our small fire.

"My grandfather once told me to beware of the man who does not talk and the dog that does not bark." he said. "When I was young I thought this to be wisdom, but it is only something old men say. Henry is a man of few words but the words he speaks are not empty and are worthy of ears. The Great Spirit brought you and Henry together as Henry and I were brought together, and I see you are as he is in many ways. Sometimes his silence is in sadness and his thoughts are far away; they are in the past with one who no longer walks in this world. Your thoughts are also far away. They are with this Lakota woman."

"I don't know her," I said. "Something about her captivated me from the first time I saw her, but I don't *know* her, I never had the chance. I tried to help her but she was the one who ended up saving my life. Now so much time has passed I'm having trouble even recalling her face. I don't know what I feel. I suppose mostly I feel accountable for what happens to her."

Standing Elk appeared perplexed by this but soon his countenance changed to one of understanding. He grunted—it was a satisfied sound— and he nodded to himself.

"Why do you call Henry Nótaxemâhta'sóoma? I don't understand what it means."

He waved his hand. "You will learn this for yourself. Now we will speak the language of the Lakota … " He waited, looking at me questioningly.

"Sioux," I said.

"Yes, Sioux, as the whites say. This is a word of the French. It is used for all of the Očhéthi Šakówiŋ people."

"How did you learn to speak French?"

"In the time of my grandfather's father we traded with the French. This was long before the coming of the English speakers to this land. The French were peaceful traders and were held in high regard in the beginning, but soon their desire for more became too great. They turned Indians against each other and nations that were once friends became enemies. My grandfather's father taught him to speak the language of the French because he was a friend to the French. My grandfather too, taught my father for the same reason. My father taught me both French and English so that I would know my enemy's words. Now you must learn the language of the Lakota, so that when you again see Wačhiwi, you will speak to her the words of her people as a friend.

I learned later that Standing Elk spoke four Native languages. People call Indians savages, but here was a man who spoke six languages fluently, without ever having seen the inside of a school. To this day I count him among the wisest and most intelligent people I've ever known.

We spent the next several days alternating between running and walking during the daylight hours—this was dependent on the pace Standing Elk set—and two or three hours of language lessons at night. The soreness in my legs got worse before it got better but by the time we ran across the war party a week after parting company with Henry, they were finally starting to loosen up some.

One afternoon Standing Elk halted his relentless running at the top of a grassy rise and waited for me. When I reached him, he pointed roughly north, but I'd already spotted the dust cloud the riders were leaving in their wake. He gestured for my rifle, which I handed over, and when they got closer he held it over his head and cried out. At first they didn't appear to see him, but suddenly the lead riders shifted direction and headed our way. He handed me the rifle and told me to shoulder it, then started down the hill. We met the riders at the bottom; it was a mixed band of Cheyenne, Sioux and Arapaho. Standing Elk spoke in length with the leaders; a Sioux named Yellow Eagle and a Cheyenne named Three Fingers. I puzzled over the name of the latter some, because he possessed all five of his digits on both hands.

I felt some sense of accomplishment during the conversation because I understood pieces of it, though it was in both Sioux, and Cheyenne. There was some hand sign mixed in as well and I did fair with that also. The parts I didn't understand, Standing Elk explained to me afterward.

Standing Elk introduced me as his friend and a friend to The People. The men nodded to me solemnly and I saw no doubt in their eyes. He told them that we carried a message from the whites. He said the white's claim was that they desired peace, and that they would trade gifts if the chiefs would meet them at the soldier's fort and touch the pen over new treaties. He also told them that the whites had no intention to leave the land that belonged to the Indians and that he didn't believe the white's intentions were for peace unless it meant Indians living in a corral.

After that the conversation turned to whether or not the war party would continue forward to meet up with chief Two Moon and his warriors to make trouble for the whites on the Bozeman Road or travel back to the Indian camp with Standing Elk and I. There was a short debate between Yellow Eagle and Three Fingers wherein it was decided that though they agreed that Standing Elk spoke the truth, it changed nothing. They cut two horses from their string for us and told us where the camp could be found and bid us farewell.

Two days later, not long after sunup, we spotted three riders heading toward us from the northeast. They were lookouts, set to watch the area surrounding the camp. After brief words with Standing Elk one of them broke off and escorted us the rest of the way.

Some sights stick with you your entire life and riding up on the Indian camp in that little valley was one that I can still see as clearly as if it had happened this very morning. After joining the lookout we came to the top of a steep rise. The sun was still low in the east, low enough that its glow had just touched the western edge of the valley. I could see a thin layer of smoke and dust in the air below us. The size of the camp was staggering. There were lodges—tepees—as far as the eye could see; easily two thousands of them, staged out around the deep blue of a small egg-shaped lake. Smoke drifted from their conical tops. Thousands of horses grazed on the eastern outskirts of the camp and I could smell their comforting scent mingled with the smell of dust, wood smoke, and cooking meat.

We started down the hill and as we got closer I saw how busy the camp was. Outside of the tepees, it bore little resemblance to the Indian camp near Fort Laramie. I sensed no despair here, only an air of bustling purpose much as you would witness in any small city. Everyone was working: tepees were being constructed from stripped lodge poles, buffalo hides were being stretched over wood frames, meat was being butchered, clothes fashioned and cook fires tended. There was laughter everywhere, more than I'd heard since leaving home for the war. People stopped what they were doing and greeted us. All were friendly to Standing Elk and he was known by many. A few of the men eyed me with guarded expressions but most were convivial. We were guided—trailing a steadily-growing group of curious onlookers, mostly children—to a small circle of tepees set on a flat just above the high-water line of the lake.

We tied the horses to a lodge pole rail next to a few others. I stood aside quietly and smiled at curious children while waiting for Standing Elk as he had words with several people. I was happy to hear him speak to a woman of Wačhiwi. The woman nodded and waved her hands animatedly and then disappeared into the city of tepees. Soon we were invited into one of the lodges. The dimly lit interior was remarkably larger than it appeared to be from the outside.

It smelled of herbs and sweet wood smoke. The earth floor was covered with buffalo and deer hides and there was a small fire set in a stone ring in the center. What little smoke the fire put off rose to the top of the tepee and exited through a cleverly placed flap in the animal hide. Pieces of crockery were hung from a wooden rack against the wall along with utensils, a bough broom or duster, and other domestic trappings. An old woman offered us a slightly bitter but refreshing tea and chunks of seasoned buffalo meat on wood skewers. While we ate, several men and women began arriving. They sat in a rough circle around the fire. Most greeted Standing Elk as a friend, and outside of one stern-looking man who ignored me completely, they all smiled and nodded politely.

I was struck immediately when one particular man entered, and I recognized him at once as Red Cloud. As with most of the men present, he wore hide trousers and a hide shirt. Where the other men's shirts were largely plain, however, his was decorated with beaded tassels of animal hair and cunningly shaped and polished bits of metal. He was taller than most of the other men, and larger of bone, and like Standing Elk, his long black hair was streaked lightly with gray and his face was just beginning to show his years.

Standing Elk put his hand on my shoulder and said softly, "Mahpíya Lúta—*Red Cloud*" and nodded up at the man. Red Cloud nodded solemnly at Standing Elk and I in turn and then sat across from us. He looked around at the group; five men and four women, not counting Standing Elk and I. One of the men reached over and handed him a pipe, which he set in his lap but didn't light. "Standing Elk comes with a message from the whites," he said in Lakota. "But he is not their messenger." He nodded to Standing Elk and then picked up the pipe. As Standing Elk spoke, Red Cloud lit the pipe with a small stick he'd put into the embers of the fire.

Standing Elk told how Henry had been sought out by the whites to deliver the message that he now carried. He explained that by agreeing to carry the message, Henry had gained Standing Elk's freedom, and that he, Standing Elk was obligated to deliver the white's message in Henry's stead.

"The whites offer gifts if Red Cloud and the other Sioux chiefs and Two Moon and Black Horse of the Cheyenne and Black Bear of the Arapaho will meet the white soldier chief Meecham to hear him speak of new treaties."

The pipe came to me and I felt Red Cloud's and the other's eyes on me as I smoked and then passed the pipe to Standing Elk, who afforded me a look of approval before smoking himself.

When Red Cloud spoke again his tone was dismissive. "The white's treaties are meaningless. If we do not agree to give them all they want they will take it and make us beggars. I have spoken to the Little White Chief Carrington. I told him the whites must leave this land. He did not hear my words and the whites continue to cut the trees to build their forts. We will give no more. I cannot speak for the other chiefs who are not here but this is the message I would have you deliver. Now I would speak of this missing woman of the Lakota, and of this young white man you have brought."

Standing Elk turned to me with raised eyebrows. I gathered my thoughts and then spoke in English as Standing Elk translated. I told them how I'd met Wačhiwi at the McBain ranch and how she'd asked me to escort her back to her people. Red Cloud bid me lift my shirt when I said how I'd been shot by men looking to return Wačhiwi to Ed

McBain. I stood and did as he asked, turning so he and the others could see the scar left from the exit wound. There were some respectful murmurs and Red Cloud pointed at the wound and nodded reverently. I sat back down and continued. I explained how Wačhiwi tried to nurse me but had been taken away while I was in my delirium and that I was somehow found and saved by an old man and a young woman, who I assumed was his daughter.

The pipe made it back to Red Cloud and he puffed at it silently, appearing to relish the sweet tobacco smoke. After a moment he set the pipe in his lap and spoke to me directly.

"Long ago—you would have been only a boy, and I had no silver in my hair—the great Lakota chief Conquering Bear touched the pen to a treaty with the whites. In their treaty the whites promised much, but afterward gave little. The Očhéthi Šakówiŋ were to give up hunting on the land of their fathers and move their people near the soldier's fort where they would receive beef and flour and blankets from the whites. The promised food was rarely given and when it was, it was not enough, and the people were starving. One day a Lakota boy found a calf wandering on the prairie while he was out foraging for whatever he could find. He brought the calf back to the village, where it was killed and then eaten. Sometime later the blue soldiers came and said that the boy had stolen the calf. They wanted to take the boy away but Conquering Bear refused and the soldier chief was angry at this. One of the soldiers shot Conquering Bear in the back. We then attacked the soldiers. They were few and we were many and we killed them all. Many days later Conquering Bear went to the Spirit World.... I tell you this because this Lakota woman who is with the whites suffered from what happened that day."

Red Cloud turned to the woman on his left. She was around his age and her face was wet with tears. "This is Zitkala-ša—*Red Bird*—Wačhiwi's mother."

This revelation gave me a start because Wačhiwi told me her mother was killed in the attack. I was sick and fevered when she said it but I remember clear enough. I held my tongue and Red Cloud continued.

"After Conquering Bear was murdered by the whites, many of the Očhéthi Šakówiŋ returned to their old lands. This was true with the Lakota. Little Thunder became chief with the passing of Conquering Bear. He moved his people to their old home. Zitkala-ša and her daughter Wačhiwi were among them. The soldiers would not forget what happened on the day they shot Conquering Bear, and after twelve moons they found the Lakota village and attacked. I was not there. Zitkala-ša will tell you more."

The woman never once glanced my way. She stared across the room with distant eyes as if she were seeing something else. Could be she was. Standing Elk interpreted her words.

"It was morning. There had been a recent buffalo kill and the women were busy preparing the meat. We heard shouting and gunfire and then there were soldiers on horses in the village. They were shooting their guns and setting fire to the lodges. There was dust and smoke and people were running everywhere. I saw a mother carrying a child fall and her and the child were trampled by a soldier's horse. Wačhiwi and I and the other women and children ran. My husband and son found us and my husband sent us to the caves across the stream. We hid in the caves but the soldiers discovered us and fired at us from the outside."

She stood, still talking, and much as I had a few minutes before, she lifted her linen shirt and pointed to the puckered scars of two gunshot wounds; one in her shoulder and the second in her lower belly.

"After that, I knew no more," she said, and she began to cry. She finally looked at me, and then at Standing Elk. Her voice was pleading. "Please return Wačhiwi to us."

Red Cloud passed the pipe across the fire to me and began to speak. He put his hand up when Standing Elk began to translate. "You will do this?" he said.

I understood and returned in Lakota: "Háŋ."

The stern-looking man, who'd been gazing into to the fire expressionlessly since the conversation began, now spoke. He was younger than Red Cloud, possibly by ten years. His tone was severe though I'll stop short of saying his words were angry. I only understood a little of what he said, but with that the gist was clear. When he was finished he stared at me with his head up and chin out, his face was set, proud.

"This is Tȟatȟáŋka Íyotake—Sitting Bull," Standing Elk said. "He asked why he should trust a white man—any white man—simply because Standing Elk does. He said Standing Elk may possess great medicine for the Cheyenne, and he is a friend, but he is not Lakota. He also wants to know why a Lakota woman is important to you."

"I never asked you or anyone else to trust me," I said. "And I already told you, Wačhiwi means something to me … I'm not certain what that something is … she saved my life. I owe her for that, if nothing else. I'm going to do what I can for her. I'm ashamed I haven't already."

Standing Elk translated. Sitting Bull seemed to consider what I said for a moment, then he stood, and without a word, strode out of the lodge.

Red Cloud looked after him, his face was unreadable. He put another small stick into the fire. When it was alight, he handed it to me and then watched me smoke. I took a couple of draws and returned the pipe to him. He passed it to Standing Elk.

"Will you stay and fight the white soldiers or will you go with him?" Red Cloud said.

"I will go south with Henry and Everett Ward to find this woman, after we deliver your message to the white soldier chief Meecham."

"You will not be welcome in a village of white men."

"You speak the truth."

The conversation drifted to more mundane matters, and before the council was concluded we were offered lodges to rest in, but Standing Elk and I agreed that we should be on our way that very afternoon. I thanked Red Cloud for his hospitality and gave him a pouch of tobacco. He thanked me for it, stood, and started away. He stopped halfway to the buffalo hide that served as the lodge's door and turned and looked down at me.

"I would like cause to trust a white man," he said in Lakota. I didn't completely understand it so Standing Elk translated. Red Cloud exited the lodge without waiting for a reply.

A few moments later Standing Elk and I followed. There were a lot of children and not a few adults milling around outside. The same group of curious young boys was still there. One of them wanted to touch my several week's growth of beard; I let him. Standing Elk pointed to a cluster of lodges. He said they were Cheyenne, and that he wanted to make a short visit before we left the camp. We unpacked the horses we were given and turned them out to graze with the others before weaving our way through the maze of lodges. We hadn't walked far when Wačhiwi's mother hurried up to us. She held out a small doll, fashioned from buckskin and hair and beads. She said it belonged to Wačhiwi. Standing Elk turned to me and cocked his head toward the woman's outstretched hands. I took the doll and smiled reassuringly.

"Piláymaya," she said, "Piláymaya." *Thank you.*

Standing Elk found a family member in the Cheyenne portion of the camp; a young man named Okôhkęho'esta—*Fire Crow*. Nearest I could tell Fire Crow was his cousin. The reunion was fortuitous for both Fire Crow and Standing Elk; Fire Crow had stayed behind with his sick daughter when most of the other Cheyenne men struck out with Three Fingers to bedevil the whites on the Bozeman. The girl—only about seven-years-old—had been vomiting up anything she ate or drank for several days. Standing Elk spent the next two hours administering to the girl. He spoke words over her and then cooked up a foul-smelling concoction from herbs he asked Fire Crow to gather from his own pantry as well as from neighbors. The girl had regained a little of her color and was holding down water by the time we left late that afternoon. Standing Elk was a remarkable man.

Before we departed, Fire Crow outfitted Standing Elk with a new pair of buckskin trousers, moccasins, and an unadorned buckskin shirt. It was a big improvement over the soiled clothes he'd been wearing since his release from the stockade at Fort Laramie. Fire Crow also gifted him a beautiful antler-handle hunting knife and a plain wooden pipe.

We refilled our canteens and water skins in the trickle of a spring feeding the lake, then shouldered our makeshift flour-sack supply packs and walked out of the camp heading southeast. Standing Elk didn't run. I have to say I was appreciative of that.

Standing Elk seemed born to teach. He was patient and clever. If I didn't understand something the way he was explaining it, then he'd explain it in a different way. We continued the language lessons day after day, with Standing Elk often refusing to speak English for two or three hours at a time other than to give me the English meaning of a Cheyenne or Lakota word. The most difficult part for me was the switching between the languages. One day Standing Elk would awake speaking Cheyenne, and the next two, Lakota.

While we walked, he taught me how to read animal sign in ways I'd never thought of. He could count how many wolves were in a pack, even if the tracks were confused, and he knew how many of them were male and how many were female. This may seem outlandish to some, but I never doubted him. He also taught me how to tell if a deer was walking or hopping or galloping by subtleties in its tracks. He taught me how to locate small game by faint patterns in the prairie grass, and he showed me the best ways to find water on the prairie. He identified countless edible plants and herbs, and could navigate at night by the stars.

One night after a supper of dried meat and some bitter prairie greens he told me stories—in English—of the

Cheyenne, and of how they were once great farmers in the east before they migrated and became a people of the horse and the buffalo. He told me of the Cheyenne's ongoing war with the Crow, and how the increasing intrusion of the white settlers and soldiers caused him to ponder it more and more frequently.

"We fight the Crow and the Pawnee, and have even fought the Lakota. We fight each other for food, and hunting land, and horses. The whites came and gave us a common enemy, yet still we fight. It is our future that the whites will vanquish all of us, and then our wars will seem meaningless to any who are left."

I wanted to disagree with him at that moment. I wanted to tell him that eventually whites and Indians would find a way to share the land. But somehow I knew in my heart that it wasn't true. Through my whole life Indians were most often spoken of in the past tense: *There used to be Indians here. Sometimes you can find some of their tools or other leavings,* my father had said of Osceola, Missouri. A man I'd met in the war, Jarvis Hemsworth, his name was, once told me that his father had been a soldier—a major, and was charged with overseeing the removal of the Creeks from Alabama back in the thirties. *"Marched every last one of those savages outta 'bama, and shot the ones who didn't look happy about it,"* he'd said of his father.

We arrived at the earth and wood shack with three days to spare. There was no sign of Henry and we were troubled by the fact. Even at a leisurely pace, he should have been there well before us. Our only recourse was to wait, so that's what we did.

The one-room trapper's shack was built against a hillside in the shade of a cottonwood grove, on a sharp bend in a seasonal creek. It was well into summer so there wasn't much water, save for a few stagnant and foul-smelling pools that weren't fit for a horse, let alone a man. The shack itself had three log and mud walls, the fourth was the side of the hill. The roof was made of sods and there was a pitted and rusty stove pipe stuck up through a mud fire-block fashioned upon it. There was a rotting piece of canvas hung from the log lintel, which acted as a door, and one glassless window on the south wall. Inside there was ancient refuse scattered everywhere: food tins, rusted out pots, scraps of clothing and bits of leather. There was a pile of raccoon scat in the corner but it was old and there was no sign of the animals. A small plank table with a single chair were the only furnishings.

We set to cleaning up the place. Standing Elk surveyed the mess and muttered something derogatory about the poor habits of white men. Outside, he found an old piece of driftwood marooned on the rocky bank of the creek. He split it in half using his knife as a wedge and a rock as a hammer. The larger half made a makeshift shovel to scoop up the refuse and the raccoon scat, which he tossed into the grass well away from the shack. The fireplace was made from stones gathered from the creek and having no mortar, part of it had collapsed. I restacked the rocks the best I could and loaded the fireplace with wood for the evening fire. Once the place was as tidy as it could be we decided to take my Spencer and go for a hunt; but we didn't really hunt. Standing Elk picked up the tracks of a lone deer not far from the shack and we followed them for a while, but neither of our hearts were in it. So after an hour or so Standing Elk just stopped and turned back. Conversation between us had all but ceased. The busywork in the shack and the hunt were only diversions to keep us from discussing what we both feared. Henry was as reliable as a Swiss clock. Something had happened.

The next three days came and went with no sign of Henry, so we waited two more.

In the early morning hours of the sixth day, we packed up our supplies by firelight. With hardly a word between us, and before the sun was much more than a promise in the east, we were on our way.

We walked southwest toward Fort Phil Kearny. Standing Elk knew the route Henry was likely to take and we followed it hoping we might come across some sign. We found some, only not what we were looking for. In the early afternoon we began to smell the sickeningly sweet smell of decomposing flesh. A short time later we came upon a wide swath of trampled grass, littered with corpses and stained the dark maroon of dried blood. The air was heavy with death and the buzz of flies was louder than the ever-present prairie wind. There were horse trails branching from both the north and the south.

We counted nine bodies in all. Bruised and bloated. Seven were soldiers, two were Indians. Standing Elk said the Indians were Pawnee; probably hired as scouts. Most of the soldiers were stripped of their clothing, and all of them were scalped and mutilated. Not even in a war fueled by hate like the war between the states had I seen a man inflict such atrocities on another. Most of the soldiers had missing ears and two had had their genitals cut off and placed in their mouths. The Pawnee men were just as dead, but their bodies were left unmolested. Standing Elk stood over one of the soldiers and ran his hand over the fletching of the arrow in man's leg. "Crow," he said, gripping the arrow's shaft and giving it a tug. It held fast, likely embedded in the bone.

There were no arrows in any of the other men, though there were puncture wounds on all of them. Standing Elk told me that the warriors would have retrieved any arrows that would easily come free.

I stared at Standing Elk, speechless.

"Soldiers murdered my wife at the place the whites call Big Sandy Creek," he said in English. "They killed many others there: women, children, and old men who did nothing to provoke the attack. The soldiers took prizes and decorated their saddles with them. Do not weep for these men."

"My mother was fond of saying that two wrongs don't make a right."

"Your mother was not Indian."

We came across another trail left by several horses, less than a half mile from where we found the bodies of the soldiers and the Pawnee men.

"There," Standing Elk said in English. "Nótaxemâhta'sóoma."

"Are you certain it's him?" I said.

Standing Elk gave me a look that told me he didn't believe the question deserved an answer.

I studied the sign. The trail began at a large circle of trampled grass and headed south/southwest. Only it wasn't really the trail's beginning, it was the *end.*

"Assuming it was Henry," I said. "He traveled here, stopped, and then turned around. The best I can tell there's six animals, and that's how many Henry had with him when we left."

Standing Elk nodded his approval. We followed the trail another three miles before it terminated in another wide swath of trampled prairie grass. The sign said that twelve horsemen had come up on Henry from different points of the compass. The horses were small and unshod, so the riders were Indians. The terrain was all low rolling hills and there were few trees, so Henry would have seen them coming, but he didn't make a run. The eight horsemen, along with Henry's mounts and the mule, all headed northeast together. There was a pile of stones on the ground; the stones we'd used to weight the horses. I asked Standing Elk what he made of it all; he only shook his head. It was clear he shared my sense of foreboding.

I set my Spencer down, along with everything else I was packing, and sat down on the pile of stones. I took off my hat and stared out at the prairie. Soon, Standing Elk joined me. We sat in silence for quite some time. We hadn't kept the horses Three Fingers had given us, though we could have. Neither Standing Elk nor I thought it was necessary to take the mounts only to travel the short distance between the Indian camp and the trapper's shack. It would have meant two more extra mounts for us to feed and care for on our return trip to Fort Phil Kearny. I can't speak for Standing Elk because we didn't discuss it afterward, but it never once crossed my mind that Henry might not arrive to meet us. Those two horses would have made what I decided what to do next a whole lot easier.

The silence stretched out.

"I can't go after him," I said finally.

Standing Elk appeared to consider this. After a moment he removed his pipe from inside of his shirt and began to fill it. I found my battered box of matches and handed them over.

"Your shame for leaving the Lakota woman has become a sickness of your heart." He pointed at the trail heading northeast through the prairie. "This is my path. I will follow it and find Henry."

"Even if you run you might never catch them on foot."

He appeared unperturbed. He struck a match and touched it to the pipe's bowl. He smoked and then passed the pipe to me. When we'd smoked it out he knocked the ash from it by tapping the bowl against the palm of his hand. He looked it over for a moment, turning it this way and that. He nodded once and then held the pipe out to me.

He never did respond to what I said, and there were no goodbyes when we parted. We divided the food and water there on the trampled earth, and then he stood and slung his flour-sacks and water-skins over his shoulders. After that, he simply walked off. I stood there motionless and watched his back. Soon he began to run, and I continued to watch him as he grew smaller and smaller and his movements became indiscernible from the rhythmic motion of the windswept prairie grass.

One of the sentries at the gate took my name and sent someone to locate Colonel Meecham. I sat and waited with my back resting against the pine log wall. I knew returning to Fort Phil Kearny was a gamble, but if I didn't, I was putting both Standing Elk and Henry—if he was still alive—at risk of being arrested, or possibly even hanged for subversion. I figured I'd tell Colonel Meecham the truth and let the chips fall where they would. There was a part of me that held a small hope he'd be concerned with Henry's welfare and send a detachment out to look for him, but it was unlikely he'd put his soldiers in harm's way, given the situation with the Indians.

A short while later the gates opened and Colonel Meecham stepped out. He was hatless and wearing a white cotton shirt with his uniform trousers and military suspenders. It was the first time I'd seen him in less than full uniform. He appeared beyond weary as he stared down a me, rubbing at his balding head. "Come inside," he said.

I followed him to a tiny office near the commandant's quarters. He opened the door and ushered me in. The room was furnished with a single battered desk and two chairs. He strode past me and sat behind the desk. With an audible sigh he opened a drawer and removed a silver flask and two small glasses.

"Please sit," he said as he poured.

I set my effects in the corner by the door and did as he asked. He pushed one of the glasses across the desk before downing his own. I picked it up and sipped; brandy. I might have known.

"I'd offer you a cigar but currently there aren't any to be had," he said, pouring himself a second brandy. "My father told me when I was a boy that ill news was best given, *and taken,* like medicine. I've found that bit of wisdom to be of value in most instances, so why don't we get to it?"

I told him everything that happened from the day we departed the fort until the day Standing Elk set off to look for Henry. I left out what Jim Bridger said to us, and planted the decision to mislead anyone who may have tried to follow us squarely on me and Henry's shoulders.

"That's very unfortunate," he said. "Excluding Captain Lange's rather low, and I dare say questionable, opinion of Henry, I've been told nothing but good about the man and his abilities.... quite a remarkable negro. I hope he hasn't fallen victim to hostiles or some other foul players, though if such was his fate, I'm sorry to say it was of his own doing."

"Oh?" I said. "And how's that?"

"Henry was to be paid to facilitate a meeting between the Indian Chiefs and the U.S. government, not to be a decoy while his inexperienced protégé and his Cheyenne compatriot acted in his stead. We wanted Henry for reasons I won't go into with you. The entire affair revealed poor judgment on his part, and to some degree yours, though I must take into account both your inexperience in these matters and the fact that unlike Henry, you were never officially contracted in any capacity. I allowed you to accompany us only to indulge Henry. However, since he is not here, and quite possibly deceased, I'm going to have my aide draft an affidavit for you to sign in his stead, stating that Chief Red Cloud refused the offer of negotiations with representatives of the United States. Afterward, you can be on your way."

"What about Henry? Will you send out a detachment to look for him?"

"You already know the answer to that. Anything else?"

"Yes. The Sioux women Henry mentioned at our first meeting. Her name is Wačhiwi—they call her Rebecca—you said you'd look into—"

"I'll see that a letter is drafted to the local sheriff. Now if you'll pardon me…."

"If you don't mind me saying it, you don't seem overly distressed by any of this."

"Mister Ward, I traveled more than a thousand miles to this unpleasing bit of wasteland to perform a distasteful task for my country, which I can say I have done to the utmost of my ability, and that stands whether the outcome was the most desirable one. I will be happy to leave this situation with the Indians in the hands of others." He pushed his chair back and stood. If you'd care to wait here, I'll send Corporal Murphy right over."

Corporal Murphy, a fastidious man of around thirty, scurried in quite some time later with a leather case containing his pen and inkwell and other paraphernalia. He unloaded everything onto the desk with practiced deliberation, and gave me a perfunctory smile before setting to writing. He appeared to be copying at least a portion of what he was putting down from another document he'd placed neatly on the aged and stained blotter next to the one he was drafting. He was finished in ten minutes and then spent another ten painstakingly explaining the contents of the documents as if he were speaking to a child or a simpleton. Finally, he asked me to either sign or put my mark to the paper.

I signed the document, he thanked me, and I gathered my things and left the office while he was still packing up the tools of his trade. I caught movement to my left as I closed the door. Captain Lange was sitting there on the porch, smoking a pipe and eyeballing me.

"Captain," I said.

"Mister Ward."

"Everett, if it's all the same to you."

"Fair enough, Everett. Colonel Meecham wanted me to supply you with a horse and saddle. He thought it would be the right thing to do seeing that the road isn't exactly safe for a lone white man at present. As a matter of fact, I'm surprised you made it back here with your scalp still on your head without Henry and the Indian to give you credentials."

"I suppose Standing Elk thought I was safe enough."

He pitched his half-smoked cigarette into the fine, boot-beaten dust of the yard. "Or he didn't care one way or another.… Anyway, it took some doing but I secured you a civilian mount through one of the teamsters, at Colonel Meecham's expense."

"The army's just going to leave Henry out there?"

"Use your head, Everett. This part of the frontier is a powder keg with a lighted match sitting on it, and at any moment it's going to blow to high heaven. Colonel Carrington isn't even going to send a detachment to retrieve the men you say are lying out there on the prairie.… Let me give you some unsolicited advice: choose your friends more wisely. Henry plays reckless with these Indian affairs and he doesn't seem to know what side his bread is buttered on. You know he murdered a Cheyenne chief? That's right, and then he put himself in the middle of some other nonsense that was none of his business and it got a lot of men killed—*white men*. Most of them ex-soldiers like yourself. And that Indian, Standing Elk? I'd trust that cow-thieving savage not at all. Now listen to me; you get on that horse, keep at least a mile west of the road, and get the hell of here."

"Seems like everywhere I go someone's telling me that."

"Well, you might want to ask yourself why. How long did you fight in the war?"

"All of it," I said.

"Well, pardon me for saying so, but for someone who saw as much of that Christ-awful pile of horse-pucky as you did, you still seem damned green."

"I suppose you're right."

I departed that very afternoon after a hot meal in the teamster's mess. I took Captain Lange's advice and rode a mile or so west of the road before turning south. I was still fairly well provisioned with dried meat and apricots, and Captain Lange had given me a sack of day-old biscuits from the officer's mess before bidding me farewell at the gates. I also had three small pouches of tobacco.

The horse was as old as Evelyn but nowhere near as well cared for. She walked with an awkward gate which was magnified by the ancient saddle that came with her. My legs and back were sore after only a few hours of riding, but I was grateful to have her nonetheless.

I camped that night in a dry creek bed. The wind came up late in the afternoon and the creek's banks were high enough to provide somewhat of a break. I chose a spot on a bend where sand had accumulated enough to cover most of the rocks and provide a soft spot to rest my sore backside. I ate a few of the dry and flavorless biscuits for supper and then sat with my back to the bank and smoked the pipe Standing Elk had given me. I devised my plan while I smoked and watched the sky darken from a dusty blue to a twinkling, ice-flecked black.

The next morning I turned southeast and made for Kansas. It would lengthen my journey to Texas, but I could get Evelyn and possibly put in a week's work at James Macklin's ranch to earn some money to resupply. Then I could set out with an extra mount, which would come in handy in the event I was able to free Wačhiwi. Of course, that was if she indeed needed to be freed.

I was startled awake several mornings later by what I first mistook as thunder. I jumped up, jerking my head around blindly in the purple glow of the pre-dawn. The ground shook under my feet and the roar of the thunder continued to grow louder until it was near deafening. It occurred to me then what it was....

Buffalo.

I tied up my bedroll and packed up the nervous mare as quickly as I could. As I removed her tether from the rock I'd tied it to, the sound hit it's crescendo and began slowly receding into the west. I mounted the mare and rode in the direction of the sound, pushing the old girl harder than I should have. I came up over a rise, and then another, and there before me was the most exciting sight of my life; the entire prairie below, as far as I could see from east to west and north, was a cloud of rolling dust and the shifting mass of thousands of stampeding buffalo.

I sat atop the mare and watched the herd pass as the sun rose over the eastern horizon. When they were finally gone, the silence left behind was stark and somehow lonely.

The animals' backtrail of obliterated prairie marched off into the distance almost due east. I followed it for a time, fascinated by the contrast between the undisturbed grass and the buffalos' path of destruction.

Midmorning I came upon a party of about fifty Lakota who had set a camp in unmolested grass on the southeastern edge of the buffalos' path. They saw me at about the same time as I saw them. Four of the men mounted and rode to meet me, checking their horses when they were still several feet away. They all wore nothing but loincloths and their hands and forearms were stained with blood. I saw no hostility, only curiosity.

"Háu," I said, raising my hand.

The four men glanced at each other, seeming nonplussed. Finally one of them, a man of around Standing Elk's age, smiled and raised his hand in return.

"Háu," he said. "Táku eníčiyapi he?"

"Everett Ward," I said.

He nodded and smiled broadly and then introduced the other men. His name was Great Deer.

I reached into one of the flour sacks I had hanging from the saddle horn and removed a pouch of tobacco and a bundle of the muslin-wrapped apricots. I urged the mare forward and held them out to Great Deer. He took the offered items and, after examining them, he handed them off to the younger man next to him.

"Piláymaya," he said, and then added something else I didn't understand.

I shook my head and told him so, "Owákaȟniǧe šni."

He nodded and cocked his head toward the camp, then all four of them turned their horses and started off. After a moment he stopped and looked back at me. He nodded his head toward the camp again and waited.

I accepted his invitation.

I counted nine men at the camp, the rest were women and a handful of children. Much like the camp on the Powder

River, the place was a hive of activity. Some were working on butchering the remnants of five or six buffalo, others were packing the meat onto several travois, and still others were breaking down lodges and securing them to more travois. The subtle difference between this camp and the one on the Powder was that here there seemed to be more of an urgency about the tasks. Neither had possessed the air of raw desperation that I felt at the camp near Fort Laramie.

What I was able to work out in my brief conversation with Great Deer, using my improved but still broken Lakota, was that the buffalo at the camp were killed the previous afternoon by the nine men present. There were other men who didn't fare as well and they'd left the camp before sunrise to pursue the herd. I surmised they were probably the ones who caused the early morning stampede. Great Deer and the rest of the people at the camp were preparing to catch up with them.

Great Deer disappeared for several minutes. The men who'd accompanied him to meet me scattered and busied themselves around the camp. I tended to the mare under the curious eyes of three children who were obviously too young to work. When Great Deer returned he handed me two hide packages. I unwrapped the corner of each of them to have a look. One contained about ten pounds of raw buffalo meat, the other, smaller package, contained waxy-white chunks of bone marrow.

"Piláymaya," I said, closing the packages and stowing them in the flour sack with my other provisions. He nodded and signed *good,* and then turned abruptly and strode away. The action reminded me of when Standing Elk and I parted company and, much like with Standing Elk, I watched after him for several moments. I watched as he walked over to a boy in his early teens, who was tying lodge poles onto a travois. Great Deer spoke some words that sparked laughter in both of them and then he began helping the boy with the work. I climbed up on the mare, briefly consulted the Drayton compass, and struck off south.

Chapter 5

It was early September when I rode up to James Macklin's ranch one evening, soaked to the bone from an afternoon thunderstorm. Wet or not, I went straight for the big corral and there she was, with twenty or so others, looking hale and stout: Evelyn.

I tied up the mare that Colonel Meecham had so generously supplied me with—she'd turned out to be a sight heartier than she appeared—and stroked her neck while I called out to Evelyn. The old girl came at a trot and I climbed up and over the fence and patted her and cooed to her for a moment.

"Well, I'll be damned, if ain't Everett Ward in the flesh! I told you I'd take care of her."

I turned to see Macklin's foreman, Oliver Belle, striding toward me through the mud left behind from the storm.

"How have you been, Oliver?" I said, putting out my hand.

"Better than you, looks like. I thought you had enough sense to get out of the rain."

"Wasn't any shelter handy."

"Well, c'mon over to the new bunkhouse. We moved your chest over there. You got a change inside it?"

"I do."

"Let's go. We'll see to your mount afterwards.... She's an ugly one, ain't she?"

I looked back at the mare. "She certainly is."

Oliver made coffee while I pulled my chest out from beneath the shelf of spare bedding it was stored under. I dug out a pair of trousers, some wool socks, and a faded but unstained red cotton shirt. After I changed I hung my wet clothes in the mud room and joined Oliver in the small bunkhouse kitchen.

"So where's Henry?" Oliver asked while pouring me a cup.

"I don't know. We got separated."

"That's it? Is he in one piece?"

"I don't know that either.... It would take a while to tell you the whole of it."

"Well, you got a while, don't you? Caleb Thompson just delivered twenty new horses that need breaking."

"I can spare a few days, if Mister Macklin will have me. Truth is I need the money. Then I have to get down to Texas."

"Uh huh.... I can't speak for Red outright, but I expect he'll have you for whatever time you got to give."

"Is he up at the house?"

"Yuh. He's there."

"Thanks for the coffee. I'll just go up and see him."

"Good ... then come back and tell me what all you been into."

At the big house, James Macklin invited me in and offered me a drink, which I accepted. I told him what I wanted from him and he told me he'd gladly pay me for one day or one hundred. He wanted to know the details of everything that happened after the day Henry and I left with Colonel Macklin and his army detachment, and I agreed to tell him if he'd allow me to fetch Oliver Belle so I didn't have to tell it twice. He responded to that by inviting Oliver and me to supper.

Over a meal of fried chicken, potatoes and peas, I told them the whole story, including how I met Wačhiwi in Sherman and all that happened afterward. I'd never spoken of Wačhiwi to anyone at the ranch before, except for Henry. June had long since cleared the supper dishes and we were on our second cups of coffee when I finally finished.

There was silence for a time. Oliver sat fiddling with his cigarette makings and Macklin stared into his coffee cup. Finally, he looked up at me.

"Every man has to travel his own road, Everett," Macklin said. "But I'm inclined to advise you to reconsider the one you're on. You could make a life for yourself here. You can work for me as long as I'm around. Perhaps move out of the bunkhouse and get yourself a little house in town, or save your money and buy a little spread of your own, eventually …" he trailed off and regarded me gravely. For the first time since I'd come to work at the ranch it occurred to me wonder just how old James Macklin was, because at that moment, it seemed It seemed as if all the ages of the Earth were set in the lines of his face.

As if he could see my thoughts he said, "Never mind. I'm getting old, and I'm not as sharp as I once was. It's plain your mind is set. You spend the next few days on those new horses, and I'll see to it you're well supplied."

"What about Henry?" Oliver said. "You believe this Indian's going to find him?"

"If I ever went missing, he'd be the one I'd want doing the looking," I said.

The work on the new horses took four days. On the fifth, I rode into town and purchased dried meat and corn flour and cheese and tobacco. Macklin instructed me to buy whatever I needed on his account at the store, and if I went over the two dollars a day he normally paid me for my horse work, we could settle up, if and when I ever made it back. I thanked him for his generosity but bought within the wages I earned for the four days of horse breaking.

I packed everything up on Missus Trimble—I decided the previous evening that the mare Colonel Meecham provided me with needed a name other than *The Mare*. Missus Trimble was a neighbor of ours back in Missouri. She was as old as all the hills but she still managed to chop her own wood and plant and harvest corn and beans every season for the twenty some-odd years Mister Trimble had been in the ground. She was as hardy as they come. The mare reminded me of her.

I put the old saddle that Missus Trimble had come with on Evelyn because my saddle was on Rose—the horse James Macklin loaned me for the trip to Indian country. I'd offered to stay and work off the price of the horse but Macklin responded by saying, "There's no way of knowing whether or not I'm going to get the horse back, so let's not worry about paying for anything just yet." It was a kind gesture from a kind man. We both knew things didn't look good for Henry, and that went for anything he had with him. Macklin even insisted on supplying me with feed for the horses. His argument being he bought if for the half the price I'd pay in town.

On the journey to Texas I made a stop at the pond where the old man and young woman had nursed my pistol shot wound. There was no sign anyone had been there for a long time.

I passed by Sherman on the morning of September twentieth. I avoided the town and went straight for the McBain ranch. I spent the day in the shade of a low bluff about three miles from the house. I grew more and more anxious as the day wore on and I took to pacing around and busying myself fussing with the horses. Sometime not long after midnight, I mounted Evelyn and started toward the house. I felt a pang of shame as I rode away. I knew if things went sour and I didn't make it back, Missus Trimble was likely to die tethered to the stunted tree where I left her.

There was a hitching rail near a water trough, a hundred yards or so from the house. I tied Evelyn to it, took the Spencer, and walked on up to the house. The moon was in the first quarter so there was enough light to see by but not so much to where I was likely to be seen easily. I went for the front door because the bunkhouse was only a hundred feet or so off the rear of the place and I didn't want to risk waking the hands if I didn't have to. I stepped onto the front porch and eased myself toward the door, trying to keep my boots quiet on the planking.

The door was bolted from the inside, of course, so I stood there with my heart pounding so hard that I thought it'd leap from my chest, while I considered my choices. Finally, I took a few steps backwards to a window. It wasn't the kind that opened and I wasn't certain what sort of a room it served. I expected a sitting room or the like since it was on the front of the place and so close to the front door. I set the Spencer down, took my shirt off and held it to the window, then picked up the rifle with my other hand and popped the stock of it into the window.

The shirt muffled the noise a little, but not as much as I'd hoped. The window pane shattering wasn't as bad as the glass falling to the wood floor inside. I wasn't going to turn back, so I quickly knocked the rest of the glass from the frame and clambered through. I heard movement and then voices from further in the house. The room was as dark as pitch and I couldn't see a door. I felt along the wall and came upon some sort of cabinet or vanity. I felt my way around it, and just on the other side was the door. The voices were getting louder and I could make out a man and a woman.

"… came from the front…"

"I don't know. It sounded like glass breaking …"

The man sounded Like Michael McBain. I cocked the Spencer and then raised it with my right while I found the door knob with my left. It opened into a hallway and I could see the glow of lamplight coming from somewhere up ahead. I hurried up the hall toward the light and saw it was coming from a cased-opening on the left. I turned and stepped through; it opened into the large drawing room where I'd first met Edward McBain. The light was coming from an oil lamp on the fireplace mantle on the far wall. I caught movement to the left of the fireplace and watched Michael McBain enter into the room through the same hallway Wačhiwi had the day Ed and Michael had degraded her over the dress. Shirtless and bare-foot, he saw me and stopped short, just through the doorway. He held a lantern in one hand and a pistol in the other. The pistol was pointed at the floor. He didn't move to raise it.

An old negro woman in a nightgown and cap came through the door behind him. She saw me and turned on her heels and started back through.

"Come back in here," I said. "Set that pistol on the floor, Michael."

The woman stopped in the doorway but didn't turn.

"You want me to shoot you in the back?" I said.

"No, sir." She turned and stood next to Michael."

"What do you want here, Everett?" Michael said.

I took a step forward. "I'm not going to tell you again. Set that pistol aside or I'll put you down."

He looked as angry as a hornet but this time he did as I said and leaned over and let the pistol drop the last few inches to the floor.

"She's long gone," he said.

I kept the rifle trained on him and moved forward until I was only a few feet away. "Where is she?"

"I don't know. Dead, if there's any justice."

I turned my eyes to the woman. "Where's Wačhiwi—*Rebecca.* Where's Rebecca?"

The woman's eyes darted to Michael.

"Don't look at him. Answer me," I said. Her eyes went to Michael again. He flashed her a stern look before returning his eyes to me.

The woman began to cry. "She took off, sir. She killed the Mister while he was sleeping there in the bedroom."

"That the truth, Michael?"

"It is, you son-of-a-bitch. She waited until he fell asleep one night—couldn't have been more than a week after he saved you from being hanged."

"That the way you see it? Your father saved me?"

"That's the way it was. You stole a horse.... She stuck a kitchen knife in his chest, you know."

"Where's the old man? Peckham?"

"Dead. Not long after you and Rebecca snuck off the first time."

I cocked my head toward the big Chesterfield. "Go sit over there. Both of you."

The woman obeyed but Michael didn't move.

"You're not going to find her. I've had every Texas Ranger and bounty hunter within five hundred miles looking for her the entire summer. Two thousand dollars, dead or alive, Everett. She's either dead or she's made her way back to her red-skinned vermin kin. Now why don't you put your rifle down and ride out of here? No harm—"

I stepped forward, reversing the Spencer at the same time, and hit Michael in the forehead with it. I pulled it slightly at the last second, but he still crumpled to the floor in a heap.

The lamp crashed to the floor along with him and the oil caught fire. The woman took to screaming. I told her to quiet down but she was overwrought and beyond hearing me. I snatched the throw off of the high-back chair nearest me and tossed it on the blaze. It was a fool thing to do, the knitted throw didn't smother it, it only soaked up the oil and caught fire as well. I hurried over to the woman and grabbed her hand and pulled her up from the Chesterfield. She was still wailing, but she didn't resist.

I reached the front door with the woman in tow just as I heard shouts coming from somewhere deeper in the house. The foyer was dark and I'd just come from a lighted room so I had to fumble around for the bolt. I found it, slid it back and threw the door open. The woman took a tumble down the porch steps so I left her where she lay and made a run for Evelyn. It wasn't even a close thing. I made it back to the bluff where Missus Trimble was waiting without any sign of a pursuit.

Wanting to get out of Texas as soon as I could, I headed north and crossed the Red River into Indian Territory once again. After the crossing, I turned east with no real destination in mind. I rode into a decaying town named Paraclifta a week later, tired, despondent, and near penniless.

The tiny town was a cleared spot in an area that was mostly woods. Staggered along its single street were a dozen or so buildings, the largest of which appeared to be a courthouse. The hotel, a resplendent building with an ornately carved sign hanging over the porch reading, *National House,* was only slightly smaller. I located the saloon—an unpainted board building which canted drunkenly to one side—on the far end of town and tethered the horses in front. I took the Spencer out from under my bedroll and went inside. The windowless room had four tables, all empty, and the bar was a wide wood plank set atop stacks of crates. Two men in trapper's furs stood at the bar conversing with the bartender, they were the saloon's only patrons.

All three men nodded at me as I approached. The bartender, a slight man in a white shirt long gone yellow, broke away from the men and sauntered over. He asked what my pleasure was. I ordered whiskey. He took a glass off of the shelf behind the bar and blew some dust out of it and poured.

"Three cents," he said.

I dropped the coin on the bar, thanked him, and took the glass over to the nearest table.

I sipped my whiskey and looked around the room. There was a bulletin board on one wall and something on it caught my eye. I set down my glass and went over. There in the middle, between a Confederate recruitment poster and an 1860 cotton bale price list, was a wanted poster.

It said:

WANTED FOR THE MURDER
OF EDWARD MCBAIN OF SHERMAN TEXAS
INDIAN SQUAW KNOWN ONLY AS REBECCA
$2,000 REWARD DEAD OR ALIVE
IF YOU HAVE INFORMATION ON THIS WOMAN NOTIFY ANY OFFICE OF
THE TEXAS RANGERS or THE SHERMAN TOWN MARSHAL'S OFFICE

The sketch of Wačhiwi was a remarkable likeness. I wondered if Michael McBain's house had burned. I wondered if a likeness had been sketched of me. I pulled the poster from the board, folded it, and put it in my pocket.

"You're not supposed to take those down," the bartender called out to me.

I walked back to the table, downed the rest of the whiskey, picked up the Spencer, and walked out.

I rode west into Oklahoma Territory. I showed the poster to the burly proprietor of a trading post—this would have been in the Choctaw Nation. He told me that for the last two months every mother's son in creation had come in with that poster, asking about the woman.

"I ain't seen her, and I wouldn't tell none of you if I had," he said. "Now do you need something, mister?"

I thanked him and moved on.

I worked my way west through the southern part of the territory, east to west. I stuck mostly to places near known Red River crossings, showing the poster to anyone who would look at it, Indian, or white. Mostly people just shook their heads, but some, like the trading post proprietor, said they'd seen the poster more than once. After a few weeks, the enormity of what I was trying to do became clear. There was so much I didn't know. So many questions I couldn't answer. Did she have help? Had she found someone who, like me, was willing to accompany her? If she struck out on her own, did she have a horse? Supplies? She was an inexperienced rider with no trail know-how. How far could she have gotten? Was she even still alive? And my gnawing regret: why didn't I attempt to free her when I was cut loose from the jail in Sherman? I cursed myself for my fear, my uncertainty, my cowardice.

Defeated, I headed north, intent on Sioux territory. I figured I'd show the poster to everyone I could along the way, and when I got there, I'd scour the country looking for Wačhiwi, Henry, and Standing Elk. It was all I could think of to do, and I had nothing but time, after all.

I was twenty-years-old.

I awoke to pain. Torturous pain in my lower leg, as if it were on fire. I sat up, bleary-eyed and confused, and threw off the blanket. There was an arrow protruding from my left calf. I spun my head around in time to see another arrow ricochet off the ground just behind me. *Indians*, and they were between me and my horses. I always slept with the Spencer by my side so I snatched it up, leapt to my feet and made a limping run for it. I only took a few steps before I realized I was dragging the blanket behind me. The arrow had gone through it before piercing my leg. I turned; four men were rushing at me. I raised the Spencer and shot once and then reached for the blanket and freed it from the shaft of the arrow. Another arrow shot past my head. It was close enough that I felt the air move. I glanced over my shoulder; one of the men was lying on the ground and the three others were nocking arrows, but they'd stopped giving chase. I started running again, though I couldn't tell you where I was going because there was no cover anywhere. Arrows whisked by but none found their target. It gave me confidence the men were poor shooters. I turned and dropped to a knee, intending to cause some casualties and recover the horses; but it was too late. One was running off with the horses and the two others turned and ran after him. I still could have hit one or both of them but I didn't fire. To this day I'm not certain why.

I walked back to my camp, the pain in my leg flaring wickedly with every footfall. They'd left their compatriot behind, lying there in the dust next to where I'd slept. Looking half-starved, he stared up at the sky sightlessly. The bullet had taken him in the left side of his chest. There was a lot of blood. I looked around. They'd left nothing; not my boots, and not the blanket they'd shot me through. They even took my hat. I'd slept fully-clothed, and my father's jackknife and Wačhiwi's neatly-folded wanted poster were in the pocket of the trousers, that was all. I was in about the most barren place they could have left me. I sat down and gazed out at the big emptiness of what is now northwestern Oklahoma: dust, rocks, low mesas, and twisted and stunted scrub, clinging stubbornly to life as if out of spite.

The arrowhead had gone all the way through the meat of my calf and out the other side, which was a small blessing. Things could have been a sight worse if it had imbedded itself in the bone. There wasn't much blood, just a few runnels that had dripped down my calf and onto my foot. I removed my jackknife and grasped the fletched end of the arrow. Touching it sent awful pain all the way up my leg into my groin and down into my foot. I felt light in the head and concentrated on my breathing while I whittled at the arrow shaft as close to my leg as I could. When I'd cut all the way through it, I tossed the end aside, grasped the arrowhead and pulled. It didn't want to come out, and I pulled harder, bellowing in pain and effort. Finally, it slid free, taking some bits of flesh with it. That's when the blood came. In a moment my foot was covered in it. I slid my trouser leg up to my knee and then quickly removed my shirt. I tore off one of the sleeves and tied it as tight as I could around the wound. The shirt sleeve was saturated pretty quickly, but after a while the bleeding slowed.

The air was dry and it was autumn hot as I struck off roughly north. I chose north because I thought my best chance of finding help would be in Kansas or Colorado. My compass went with everything else the Indians took so I couldn't be sure of exactly where I was going to end up. I knew I was in a predicament a great deal worse than when I'd walked away from the Confederate army camp. At least there was water near everywhere in Missouri. In this part of Indian Territory it was hard to come by, and I didn't have anything to carry it in if I did come across some.

By early afternoon my feet hurt as bad as the arrow wound did, so I stopped briefly to cut up the remainder of my shirt to wrap them in. The ground was hot enough to fry bacon and I knew I was going to burn something fierce without my shirt, but I didn't see I had a choice in the matter. My left arm was already as red as a ripe apple on account of the sleeve I tore off for the bandage, so I figured the rest would match up.

I made it to a mesa in the mid-afternoon and stopped and sat in the shadow of its foot on its east side. My calf and my feet ached terribly and I was every bit as sunburned as I thought I'd get.

And I was thirsty.

Damned thirsty.

I decided then that I'd have to start walking at night or else risk being dead in another day or two. I was fortunate in the respect that the moon was still near full and I'd be able to see enough to do it, at least for eight or ten days. My hope was to run into some help before then. I hadn't learned to read stars yet so I memorized my bearing from the position of the sun, so I'd know which way was north after nightfall.

I dozed off until well after sundown and then continued to sit for a while before I decided it was time to get moving. When I finally tried to stand I had considerable trouble. My calf felt like the father of all Charlie-horses had set into it and I couldn't move my foot. The pain was near unbearable—worse than when I was shot—so I lowered myself back down to a sitting position and grabbed my foot and started moving it. After a minute or so I could move the foot without help from my hands so I tried to stand again. I made it up that time, though the pain was still bad.

I didn't find any water that night, and I was far from any cover when the sun first peeked over the eastern horizon. I cursed myself a fool for not stopping a few hours beforehand when I'd passed the crumbled remains of a mesa.

I pushed on, and in the midmorning I spotted what appeared to be a greenbelt in the distance. By that time I was getting too weak to continue, so I walked as far as the next little patch of scrub brush and used the jackknife to cut enough of the rough foliage off to make a sort of cover. Then I used the bones of the brush still planted in the ground for a frame to hold the branches I'd cut off, and I wriggled underneath. It was tight, but it kept most of the sun off. I was asleep in seconds.

It was dark when I awoke and I was addled and couldn't remember where I was. I tried to raise myself into a sitting position but only succeeded in pushing my face into the branches I'd used for shelter. I flailed my arms in a panic and knocked the branches aside, and then squirmed my way out and stood up. Once my weight was on my legs the pain in my injured calf was immediate and intense. It cleared my head some, though. I bent over and retrieved the Spencer and did my best to recall my position to the greenbelt.

From the start I was weaker than the previous night, and walking was becoming more difficult. Along with the pain, I was unsteady on my feet and I weaved to and fro like a man deep in his cups. My tongue was a dry lump of meat in my mouth and I couldn't swallow for the life of me. I tried to focus on the direction of the greenbelt, but I was uncertain.

I fell repeatedly through the night and was crawling when the sun came up. I'd somehow managed to point myself in the right direction and stay on a fairly straight course. The line of trees was less than a mile away when it was light enough to see them. The sight renewed my strength in a way I could never begin to explain. I managed to get to my feet and I moved in this sort of shambling run the rest of the way. I pushed through the brake and found a slow moving, shallow stretch of river, which I later learned was the Cimarron. I staggered down the bank and fell to my knees in a green pool and began to drink greedily. My stomach protested straight away and it all came up in a greenish-yellow gout.

"You gotta drink slower, or else you'll only sick it up again," came a voice from behind me.

I wheeled toward the speaker, glancing at the Spencer, which I'd dropped on the bank before plunging into the water.

"You won't need that, son. I mean you no harm. As a fact, I reckon I can help you."

I must have been a sight, on my knees in the warm, waist-deep pool, staring at him with watery vomit dripping off my chin. But I'm here to tell you that *he* was a sight like I'd never seen. He stood there, looking down at me from where he'd stopped between two cottonwood trees at the top of the bank; a bear of a man, easily the largest human I'd ever seen—seven foot tall if he was one, and his face, outside of his forehead and nose, completely covered in a wild, grizzly-brown beard.

"I got a canteen with better water in it up here," he said. "If you think you can make it."

I nodded and stood and waded a couple of steps upstream where I dunked my head under the water and scrubbed at my face, which felt scratched and sunburn raw. I held my head under as long as I could and then I straightened up. The water running down my body was one of the finest sensations I've ever felt. It was as if my very skin was drinking it.

I picked up the Spencer and started up the bank. I didn't make it far before I was breathing as heavily as if I'd run a sprint. My leg throbbed dully. I started flagging as I neared the top and the man bent and put out a hand and hauled me up as if I weighed nothing more than a feather pillow.

I stood five-ten in those days (I'm a sight shorter now) and was taller than most, but I was staring dead at his chest that day by the river.

"I need to ask you a question before we walk through those trees," he said. "Are you missing a pair of horses?"

I said I was.

"Then I reckon you can tell me what they look like?"

"One's a bay, she has some gray on her muzzle. The other's a buckskin dun.… They're both getting old."

He turned and started off through the trees. "Well, come on, then," he said over his shoulder. "My apologies, but I was too late for the dun. The Indians were butchering it when I came up on 'em. The bay don't seem to be the worse for wear."

We came through the trees and there was Evelyn, tethered to two other horses and a mule with three corpses piled over its back and tied on. I limped over to her and stroked her muzzle a few times before going back to sit against the trunk of a tree.

"My name's Seth Grant," he said. "Not to be confused with the bible fella or the general."

He chuckled as he removed a canteen from his saddle horse. "And who might you be, my unfortunate friend?"

"Everett Ward," I said.

He handed me the canteen. “Only a little now. After a while you’ll be able to stomach more.”

“Thank you.”

“Welcome,” he muttered as he worked to remove two large, leather drawstring sacks from the same horse he’d gotten the canteen from.

I took two small swallows from the canteen. As I was replacing the stopper I noticed that one of the corpses on the mule had my boots on.

Seth walked over with the sacks, opened them, and dumped the contents of both on the ground in front of me.

“This is everything the Indians had with ‘em. I’m going to have to trust you to tell me what’s yours and not claim what isn’t.”

I pointed to the pile. “That’s my hat, those cartridges, both those shirts, those socks, that compass—if you look inside, you’ll see it’s a Drayton—”

“I already looked in there. I can’t say I’m not disappointed, I was partial to keeping that.”

I picked up the compass and held it out to him.

“It’s yours,” I said.

“I’m obliged, Mister Ward.”

“Not near as obliged as I am to you,” I said. “Those pouches of tobacco—you’re welcome to keep one— those matches, that knife, and that pipe.... One of those men is wearing my boots.”

He turned and looked at the bodies. “They’re not going to walk off with ‘em, now are they?” he said and then bellowed laughter. “I was curious why those Apaches had a Cheyenne pipe and a Sioux knife. You smoke the pipe?”

“I do.”

An expression passed over his features as if he'd eaten something sour. It vanished as quickly as it appeared. "Well, to each they're own, I reckon," he said. He pointed at my lower leg. "You got a good sum of blood there."

"One of them shot me with an arrow. I was sleeping at the time."

"Lady luck was on your side then—twice now, on account of I almost didn't come this way...." He rubbed his prodigious beard and shook his head. "I should give up trying to understand the thinking of Indians. I don't know why they didn't slide up on you and cut your throat if they wanted to kill you while you were sleeping.... I reckon it's you who shot the other one?"

"Yes."

He stood. "I'll get your boots. Oh, and there's two canteens over here that aren't mine. I reckon they're yours, and even if they're not, you can take 'em. I can't vouch for the water in 'em, though."

He pulled my boots from the corpses with a grunt and tossed them over.

I nodded toward the dead men. "What are you going to do with them?"

"These boys are wanted in Colorado. They been jumping the border and stealing livestock. I've been after 'em for some time now. The other one—the one you killed—I could have got a reward for him too but coyotes were at his face, and there's nothing much left of it.... I'll leave you some food. I'd invite you along with me but you need to convalesce for a day or two if you're not set on dying. This is about the best place within fifty miles to do it. I can't spare the time to slow down for you, on account of I need these boys to look like who they were when they were living if I'm going to collect my bounty."

"Thank you for everything," I said, lifting the canteen and taking a little more water. I set the canteen aside and removed Wačhiwi's wanted poster from my pocket. I held it out to him. "Have you seen this? Or have you seen her?"

He looked at it, but didn't move to take it. "I've seen the poster," he said. "I've got one myself, or had one, it's been awhile now. I never saw the squaw." He barked a laugh. "If I had, I'd have already collected the reward their offering."

He raised an eyebrow and considered me for a moment. "You don't strike me as the type to be a man-hunter—or in this instance, a woman-hunter. You don't look like no Texas Ranger, either. You don't seem arrogant enough to be in with that lot. If you're either of those, you're new at it."

"I'm not. I'm trying to help her."

"The woman in the poster? Is that a fact?"

"That's right. The man she killed kept her as a slave at his ranch down in Sherman."

"Ed McBain. I know him, though I can't say we're friends. Our paths crossed once and again.... It ain't no matter anyhow, I'm sorry to say. That squaw's long gone, or dead."

I refolded the poster, put it in my pocket and stood.

"Thank you again," I said, as I un-tethered Evelyn from the string.

"Fare-thee-well, Mister Ward. Fare-thee-well."

I headed for Fort Laramie by way of Colorado. Evelyn was none the worse for wear and I wondered why I hadn't taken her on the expedition to find Red Cloud. Old or not, she was a fine horse.

I missed the Drayton compass on the trip, but not having it made me pay more attention to the position of the sun. When my leg was healed enough I picked up work on the Union Pacific, some miles southeast of Denver, laboring with a crew repairing sections of track. It was some of the hardest work I'd ever done but the wage was fair—for me and the six other white men on the crew, anyway. The rest of the men were Chinese, and they made less than half of what we did. I felt sympathy for them, for they were as hardworking as anyone.

After the third week I picked up my pay, which I used to purchase a new bedroll, a wool coat, a rifle scabbard, and some used saddlebags. That same evening, I moved on.

Hoping for some news of Wačhiwi, I telegraphed Calvin Englebright from Denver. I did it knowing full-well there was little chance he'd have any. Telegraphs were expensive at the time and it took almost all of my money, but I was desperate to learn anything I could of her fate. I told him I'd be at Fort Laramie by the end of October, and would receive his reply there, if he was inclined to send one.

The reply was waiting for me when I arrived. It stated simply: *I must see you.*

I was overcome with a flood of conflicting thoughts as I departed the post office. Soon they became so jumbled they were nearly indiscernible from one another. I was still reading those four words over and over as I walked down the steps and started across cross the yard: *I must see you. I must see you,* as if their meaning would become clear to me through repetition. There was a bellowed shout of alarm and I looked up just in time to sidestep and avoid being struck by a hay wagon bound for the cavalry stables.

"Keep yer wits, boy!" the teamster called after me as he passed.

I waved a hand in apology and then shoved the telegram into my pocket. Was it a trick to get me back to Sherman? After all I entered the McBain house by unlawful force, assaulted Michael McBain, and possibly burned the place to the ground. Even if the house hadn't burned, I was surely wanted by the county sheriff. The problem was, the more I chewed on it, the more difficult it became for me to believe Calvin Englebright would be party to such a contrivance. Hadn't he saved me from hanging, after all? So if not that, then what? Did he know of her whereabouts? Had she been arrested? Or worse, hanged?

I mounted the steps to the Sutler's store and walked inside, hoping to purchase a couple of biscuits. Ruby Alden stood behind the counter carefully scooping corn flour from a large sack and then pouring it into a smaller sack which sat atop a scale.

She looked up from her work, her practiced proprietor's smile was friendly but her eyes showed no recognition. As I moved toward the counter the smile faltered and her expression turned to one of astonishment.

"Well if I wasn't a believer in providence, I should be now," she said, setting her flour scoop aside and brushing her hands on her apron before removing a folded sheet of paper from the pocket on the front. "I received this note from a soldier this very morning."

She handed it across the counter to me and I opened it. In inexpert but perfectly legible script, it read:

Mister and Missus Alden,

I am at the Indian camp by the river. I would be obliged if you would give this to Everett Ward if you see him. He was the man who accompanied me last I was in your store.

Respectfully,
Henry.

I read the note twice and was grinning ear-to-ear when I finally lowered it.

"Thank you very much, Missus Alden," I said. "I'll be on my way over there now," I turned for the door.

"Now don't hurry off just yet … please, Mister Ward. Mister Alden and I were worried something may be amiss … otherwise why wouldn't Henry have come himself if he wasn't sick, or injured." She held up a finger. "I put together something, and you can take it to him, if you wouldn't mind. I was going to have one of the boys deliver it when the opportunity arose, or have Frederick do it after we close up for the day, but since you're here … wait, just for a moment."

She disappeared into the opening in the shelving behind the counter. When she returned she was carrying a wrapped bundle. "There's a loaf of bread, some strawberry preserves, and half a chicken in here," she said, holding the bundle out to me.

"I'm sorry, Missus Alden, I don't—"

"There's no charge," she said. "We adore Henry. Will you please let us know how he is?"

I took the bundle. "I'll be happy to," I said. "Just as soon as I'm able. Thank you."

The autumn wind was freshening as I walked from the fort toward the Indian camp, and the dust being picked up from the beaten-down and grazed-out area around the lodges stung my eyes and face. I couldn't help thinking about the dissimilarity here to Red Cloud's camp. The difference was stark and sobering.

I stopped briefly at the perimeter, unsure of where I might find Henry among the seventy or so mixed lodges. A few yards away there were several old women sitting cross-legged in a half-circle around a large bag of flour. There was a line of women and children snaking through the maze of lodges. When they reached the front, they each took two handfuls of the flour from the sack and then moved away. The old women and the whole of the line turned to me as I approached. I stood there, wishing I'd had some money to purchase staples for the camp while I was at the Alden's.

"I'm seeking Henry," I said in Cheyenne, and then again in Sioux, addressing the old women doling out the flour.

They exchanged glances, nodding. One raised a gnarled finger and said, "Nótaxemâhta'sóoma." She stood and gestured for me to follow.

Bent with age, she shuffled slowly but purposefully through the maze of lodges, finally stopping at one located midway through the camp. Staked outside were Harriet and Macklin's horse, Rose. The woman pointed at the hide door and then turned and walked away without a word.

I approached the lodge but manners kept me from entering without an invitation.

"Hello?" I said. "Henry?"

There was only a brief pause and then: "Come ahead, Everett."

A smile broke on my face at the sound of his voice. I lifted the hide and entered the dimly lit lodge. He was there, on the wall to my right, propped up against a pile of skins with his legs splayed out in front of him. The left one was splinted.

"Same leg," I said.

Henry gently patted the splinted leg. "Broke in the same place too. Only it hurts a far sight worse this time. I've been putting it through its paces too soon.... It's good to see you, Everett."

"You as well," I said. "I just got in. Missus Alden, gave me the note. She wanted me to bring you this." I stepped forward and set the package down next to him.

He looked at the package. "She's a kind women."

"Seems that way."

"You can sit," Henry said. "This is one of Chief Big Mouth's lodges. He's allowing me to bunk here and give my leg a rest."

I sat, facing him. "Did Standing Elk find you?"

Henry nodded. "I'll tell you the whole story, if you have time to listen."

"I have the time. And then I have one of my own."

"You want to tell yours first?"

"No. You go ahead. Just tell me if Standing Elk is all right."

"He is. He left yesterday afternoon to visit with Chief Black Kettle.... You know anything about James Beckwourth?"

"Nothing worth telling. I've heard his name a few times, from you and some others. I know he's a scout like you and Bridger."

"Yes, he was."

"Was?" I said.

Henry smiled ruefully. "I'll get to that.... I first met him in sixty-three, scouting for the army up near the Yellowstone River. We were on the same expedition. It was my second time out, and he was the lead scout. He'd been scouting long before I was born; from here to California and back, and he was a half-breed, born a slave like I was. His mother was the slave, his father was her master. That was enough for us to strike up conversation at the beginning, but I can't say I ever took to him ... or him to me, I reckon. We were just different from one another. I kept to myself for the most part, and he was loud and boisterous, and prone to telling stories. He was quick to fight, too. One night drunk, he took on three soldiers on a wager, and whooped all three of them. They were young men, not any older than I was, and I reckon he was near three times my age.

"Anyway, after the expedition, he went his way and I went mine. A year later I was up on the Yellowstone again ... this would have been almost three years back. The army had some business with the Crow Nation, and while they were busy doing it, I rode a few miles from the Crow camp scouting around for a better return route south. I came up on a bend in the river and I heard a woman screaming and men shouting. I picked up my pace and came around the bend and there on the bank a man was dragging a woman down to the water. I heard more shouts and looked up the bank and saw that they were being followed by seven or eight Crow men. The men were hollering but I couldn't tell what their mood was. The man shoved the woman into the water and then stepped on her neck to hold her under. I pulled out my rifle and fired a warning shot and then rode up close. The man was James Beckwourth. He was staring hard up at me and he still had his foot on the woman's neck. By then her struggles were slowing down. I could see his intent was to finish what he started so I pointed the rifle at him. And that convinced him to let her go.

"She didn't move so I told him to pull her out. '"Ride on, Henry,"' he said. '"She's my wife, and she shamed me. This is none of your affair."'

"I told him I'd shoot him if he didn't.

"By this time the Crow men had stopped halfway down the verge. I kept an eye on them but they weren't armed so I didn't expect them to cause me trouble. Beckwourth dragged the woman out and dropped her on the bank. She lay there, not moving. I told him to back up. He was cursing at me and telling me he was going to kill me for interfering with a man and his wife, but he took a few steps back anyway. I got down and checked the woman—she wasn't much more than a girl. She was Crow, and she was dead.

"I'll admit the urge to shoot him was pretty strong, but I just kept the Spencer on him and backed up until I was next to Harriet. I climbed up and rode out of there with him cursing at my back.

"I didn't see him again for a long while, though I heard from time to time that he was set on squaring things up with me—though when he talked about it to folks, he never told them what it was I did to earn his animus. I always reckoned the reason he didn't was because most people wouldn't see what I'd done as wrong. So men like Jim Bridger always wanted me to tell them what there was between us. I didn't see any point in encouraging talk about it, so I kept it to myself.

"Some days after I split with you and Standing Elk, I came across the place where a Crow war party killed a detachment of soldiers. The fight was fresh, maybe only a couple of hours before. The Crow were well out of their territory, so I figured they must have come down to raid Cheyenne camps but ran into the soldiers instead.

"I wasn't being careful enough and I was spotted by some men who must have been a rearguard for the war party. I was wary, but I didn't have a quarrel with them, so I can't say I was overly troubled. I never gave James Beckwourth a thought, though looking back I suppose I should have. He'd lived with the Crow off and again for years, and married into them—several times from people's talk. If I would have thought about those relations, I reckon I would have made a run for it.

"I didn't, and those men rode up on me and recognized me for who I was. I didn't know any of them, but my skin's something of a rarity out here and the scar's a dead giveaway. I don't speak or understand Crow quite as well as Cheyenne, or even Sioux for that matter, but I ken enough, and they spoke of *Bloody Arm,* which was one of the names Beckwourth was known by with them. They didn't give me a choice about going along with them, but in doing so they were polite and didn't put their hands on me. They took my rifle and my pistol and one of them tethered Harriet to his horse with a leader I had on the mule. They left the mule, the horse Macklin loaned you, Standing Elk's army mount and the other two tied to Harriet just as they were and didn't seem interested in stealing the animals or going through any of our belongings. I gave them some tobacco and dried meat anyway. They seemed grateful.

"We caught up with the rest of the war party the next morning. A man named Coyote was leading them and he had me ride beside him the rest of the way.

"The Crow camp was near the foot of the Bighorns, and they brought me straight to Beckwourth's lodge. Coyote went inside and after a moment he came back out with Beckwourth on his heels. Beckwourth wasn't wearing anything but a pair of deer hide trousers, and he was holding a knife the size of your forearm. He didn't say anything, he just stood there, staring at me. I noticed right off that he didn't look much like the man I'd seen drown the woman in the river. He was old when I first met him, more than sixty if I had to surmise, but he'd been hale as anyone a lot of years younger. It was more than age that had been at him the last few years. It was plain he was in ill health. Coyote offered me a knife, but I got my own out of my saddlebags. Beckwourth turned and walked to the edge of the camp to a clearing; it looked like where they had their ceremonies. I followed, and so did most everyone in the camp, but there wasn't much whooping or cheering, and I thought that peculiar. Afterward, I surmised it was because they knew Beckwourth wasn't up to the fight. Either that or he'd fallen out of favor with them.

"Once we were in the clearing he came right at me, swinging that big knife. I could see the same anger in his eyes I saw by the river that day and he was intent on killing me. But there was a weariness on his face as well, and he wasn't steady on his feet. It wasn't a fair fight but I couldn't see any way out of it. It was over not long after it began. He kept coming forward, I stepped back a few times and then dropped low, under one of his swings. I got him under his ribs on his left side. He dropped his knife and lay hold of my neck with both hands. There wasn't much strength in those hands, but I lost my feet and fell backwards. He came down on top of me. I heard my leg break. So did the people looking on. Beckwourth was dead when we hit the ground.

"Two men came up and dragged him off of me and carried him back to the camp. The rest of the folks followed, a handful at a time. Pretty soon it was just me, lying there in the dust and blood. I'd just about set my mind to trying to crawl to where Harriet and the rest of the animals were tied up, when a woman walked from the camp and stood over me. She was thirty-years-old or thereabouts and she had an armful of supplies. She said her name was Small Cloud Woman. She examined me and then put a stick in my mouth and went about setting the leg. It never occurred to me that I may have to endure that twice in my life. I tried to bite down but I let out a wail instead and the stick dropped out of my mouth. She laughed a little at that and went about her work.

"She was near done when Coyote and another man came back and gave me a cottonwood crutch and helped me off to Beckwourth's lodge. Harriet and the others were tied up outside but they'd been unpacked. I didn't have much time to fret over it because they walked me straight inside and everything was there, put up nice and neat off to one side. There were no trappings of Beckwourth's life in the lodge, so I reckoned they'd cleared it out before they unburdened the animals, or it was empty to begin with.

"I thanked them and hobbled on the crutch to the pile of supplies. I dug out three pouches of tobacco and a sack of raisins. I gave Coyote and the other man—his name was Walks In Front—each a pouch and asked Coyote if he'd give a pouch and the sack of raisins to Small Cloud Woman.

"I stayed for three days. Small Cloud Woman looked in on me a couple of times but otherwise I was left to myself. When I felt I could travel I spent most of a morning repacking the mule and Harriet. It was a lesson in patience, as was figuring out how to get on and off of Harriet. That part wasn't as bad as I thought. Small Cloud Woman's splint was good and tight, and as long as I got the leg swung over without hitting it, I was fine. I couldn't ride for more than a few hours, though, or else it swelled up and pained me like fire.

"I rode for Fort Phil Kearny, figuring I owed Colonel Meecham an explanation, though I knew the truth might anger him some. Standing Elk found me about halfway between the Bighorns and the fort. I needn't have worried about Colonel Meecham. He was gone and so was Captain Lange. Word was the colonel went back east and Captain Lange here to Laramie. I sent word to Colonel Carrington but he wasn't inclined to see me, so I turned in the army mule and horses and we rode out. I felt lucky. The way things turned out, Colonel Meecham could have made matters tough for us, had he been inclined that way. I don't expect he'll be seeking us for help again."

"I spoke with both Colonel Meecham and Captain Lange," I said.

"Well, you'll have to tell me how that went. I'm about talked out anyway. We came in night before last and I'm still about as tired as I've ever been."

"Fortuitous we both show back here, days apart," I said. "Missus Alden said it was like providence."

"Standing Elk said you'd be here when we got here. I didn't doubt it. He has a way like that. He was wrong this time, but not far off."

"No. Not far off at all," I said.

I told Henry everything that occurred from the day Standing Elk and I left him, up to that very afternoon at the Indian camp near Fort Laramie. Much of it he already knew from Standing Elk. When I was finished, he said:

"If you don't mind waiting another four or five days, I'll ride down to Texas with you. I want to see that Standing Elk made it down to his people. Mayhap he'll want to come too, though he'd be considered by some to be a renegade on that side of the Red."

"Henry … I'm sorry I didn't go after you with Standing Elk.

"That's not necessary. You did right. I'm sorry things turned out the way they did. Maybe there'll be good news down there."

We set out on October 21st, 1866. Heading southwest to Oklahoma Territory. Henry on Harriet, me on Evelyn, with James Macklin's horse, Rose in tow. We were bound for Black Kettle's camp, south of the Arkansas River. It was more or less on the way to Sherman, and at that point I didn't think another handful of days would make much difference. Truth was, I missed Standing Elk's company. We were riding short days anyhow, on account of Henry's leg. It was healing up but it still pained him fiercely if he was in the saddle too long. During the ride I'd practice Cheyenne with Henry. He was as patient as Standing Elk and I improved more each day. I would have liked to practice more Lakota, but Henry worried he might only muck up what Standing Elk already taught me. In the evenings we'd talk about small things: The past; the future. In the latter we shared something; neither of us had any real notion of what ours might look like.

The short days were probably for the best. We were running slim on supplies as neither of us had any money, so there was plenty of time for me to hunt while Henry rested his leg. The game was scarce at first, then the hunting improved for a while. I shot and dressed a small deer on our fourth day, and a turkey several days later. We rested a day and smoked most of the deer meat. It was a good thing, because the abundance was short lived. Not long after entering what's now Northern Oklahoma, The game all but vanished.

We didn't know exactly where Black Kettle's camp was located, so after we reached the Arkansas we fished around for a couple of days before running across an Arapaho hunting party. They asked us if we'd seen any game. They looked hungrier than we did, and it pained both Henry and I to tell them we hadn't. There were some disappointed murmurs but they all nodded as if they'd expected as much. They explained to us how to get to the Indian Camps along Small Stone Creek. We were only a day's ride away.

The geography surrounding Black Kettle's camp was flat, grassy, mostly treeless and autumn-arid. It wasn't as large as the mixed-nation camp where I'd met Red Cloud and Sitting Bull, but it was a near thing. I judged close to fifteen hundred lodges, packed together tightly near a bend in the creek. The similarities ended there, however. As we rode into camp, I heard no laughter, no pounding and clattering of craft and industry, and I saw few horses. I felt the same despondency and sadness as I'd witnessed at the camp near Fort Laramie.

An old man was sitting with three small girls in the shade of one of the outermost lodges. The girls were crowded around him, listening raptly as he spoke. Perhaps he was telling them a story. Henry put a hand on my shoulder, nodded toward the group, and started over.

"Haáahe, Nótaxemâhta'sóoma," the old man said as Henry approached.

Henry conferred with him for a moment. I wasn't close enough to hear the conversation, but the man's countenance was solemn. Finally, he pointed toward the northeast. Henry gave the man half of what was left of our smoked deer meat.

"Standing Elk is on a hunt with some of the other men," Henry said, rejoining me. "Chief Black Kettle's lodge is up here."

I handed Henry Harriet's reins and we led the three horses up the camp's perimeter. Soon Henry stopped and pointed down a row of lodges. "It should be down that way, near the center," he said.

We walked a short way and Henry stopped in front of one. "Here it is." I didn't notice it to be any different from the other lodges. He paused a few feet from the door.

"Haáahe, Mo'ohtavetoo'o," Henry called out.

There was some rustling from inside the lodge and a moment later an arm appeared and the hide door was pushed aside. A proud-faced man on the border of old age leaned out. He was dressed in a plain white shirt and wool trousers. He smiled and stepped outside, walking past Henry to Harriet, whose neck he stroked while speaking softly to her. He gave her one final pat and then approached Evelyn and looked her over. He nodded with seeming approval and then turned back to the lodge. He pulled aside the hide door and waited. Henry and I quickly staked the horses.

The interior of the lodge smelled strongly of tobacco smoke and was crowded with trunks, crates, and clothing. A narrow path had been left clear and we followed Black Kettle to the far wall where he sat upon a buffalo hide rug and gestured for us to join him.

"Mo'ohnee'ėstse, said that you would come tomorrow," Black Kettle said in Cheyenne.

Henry laughed at this. "Wrong twice now. He's getting old."

Black Kettle smiled broadly. "As I am." He turned to me. "This is Everett Ward?"

"It is," Henry said.

"Haáahe," I said.

Black Kettle nodded. "Mo'ohnee'ėstse told me of you."

Henry unslung the bag holding the last of our deer meat and handed it over to Black Kettle, who pulled the drawstring and looked inside.

"Néá'eše," he said, putting the bag aside. He reached under the edge of the buffalo rug and retrieved an ornately carved pipe and a wooden cigar box. He set the pipe in his lap and opened the box. It was full of tobacco.

"This was all I was given the last time the whites promised food," he said, filling the pipe. "This, and a blanket with holes in it that smelled of death. I buried the blanket out there in the grass, in the white's way." He chuckled and handed the pipe to Henry.

"I didn't see many men here. They're all on the hunt?" Henry said, while searching his pockets. I handed him my box of matches. He struck one and lit the pipe.

"Mo'ohnee'ėstse is leading a hunt with the men who still wish peace," Black Kettle said. "The others—the *Hotamétaneo'o*—are away raiding the whites in the north. They are young and full of hate and will no longer listen to my words. They will bring the anger of the bluecoats upon us again.… Will Mo'ohnee'ėstse go with you to find this Lakota woman?"

At that moment Henry said what I was thinking.

"I can't speak for him, but it seems to me he'd be of more use here."

As we passed the pipe, the conversation turned more cheerful. Henry translated what I couldn't understand as Black Kettle reminisced about when Standing Elk first brought Henry among the Cheyenne. He pointed at Henry and laughed good-naturedly when he spoke of how Henry screamed when his leg was being splinted. He spoke reverently about a time when Henry saved an old woman from a beaver trap left behind from the days of French trappers. Henry told Black Kettle how he'd broken the same leg again in his fight with Bloody Arm Beckwourth.

After some time, a woman entered the lodge. She was perhaps ten years younger than the chief. She walked with a limp similar to Henry's, and a thin scar creased her scalp and left it hairless from just behind her temple all the way to where her skull began to curve to its backside. She greeted Henry warmly and smiled and nodded to me. Black Kettle handed her the sack of deer meat and asked if she would divide it among as many children as she could.

After she left, Black Kettle stood and moved to the door. Henry and I followed suit. The chief held the skin aside for us the same as when we entered. I hadn't noticed coming in, but there was an American flag hung over the inside of the doorway. Black Kettle followed my eyes. "The Great Father Abraham Lincoln gave that to me. It didn't protect me."

He led us to a lodge not far from his and told us we were welcome to use it for as long as we wanted. He nodded as if to take his leave but then he paused, a look passing his features as if he'd forgotten something. Suddenly he lifted a finger and then hurried back to his lodge. When he returned a few moments later, he was carrying a lidless fruit tin. It was full of tobacco. He handed it to Henry with a nod.

I poked my head inside the lodge; it appeared to be used for storing items. There was a battered stage trunk, similar to the ones in Chief Black Kettle's tepee, a wagon wheel, and a pile of hides off to one side.

We moved the horses to our temporary accommodation and unburdened them. Henry fetched bags of water from the creek while I stowed our belongings.

It was only late afternoon but we were both worn-out. We shared out the last of the turkey, which was just this side of being bad, and rolled out our beds. We lay in silence for a time, but finally I had to say what was on my mind.

"I was wondering if we should stay and help out," I said. "I don't even know why Calvin Englebright sent me that telegram. It may not have anything to do with Wačhiwi. Could be that's what I wanted it to be about, so that's what it became in my mind. The truth is, I think she's dead. I suppose it's possible she made it to Indian Territory and got some help, but I've feared her dead for a long time now. Anyway, I believe we could do some good here."

"If that telegram wasn't about Wačhiwi, then what was it about?" Henry said. "Anyhow, there's nothing you or I can do for these people that they can't do better themselves. Black Kettle is only one chief. The men out east have been pushing Indians west into this territory a far sight longer than either of us have been alive. Cherokee, Seminole, Creek, Chickasaw.... Now the same men, or men just like them, are pushing other nations down from the north. The Cheyenne, Arapaho, the Kiowa.... There's too many mouths and the land here can't provide enough to fill them all. If they're caught leaving the territory to hunt, they're considered renegades and can be shot on sight. Black Kettle agreed to bring his people down here because he thought it would save them from being murdered by the army. He knew if he refused, he'd be branded a hostile and the army would finish them anyway. Look around; they're still being murdered, just not by rifles. The men in this camp are better hunters than either one of us, and the woman can find a meal in more plants and insects than you could ever reckon. They don't need our help, Everett. They need their freedom."

"That true about Lincoln giving the chief that flag he has hung inside his tepee?"

"It's the truth. Before Sand Creek he used to hang it on the outside of his lodge. He was proud of it. Lincoln's man told him that as long as he displayed it, he'd be under the protection of the United States. But that wasn't true. Black Kettle waved that damned flag like all-get-out the day the army rode into his camp. They shot him anyway, his wife as well—her nine times.... The rest you already know."

Henry sighed. He may have been weeping.

"The army killed a lot of good people that day," he said. Children included, and for nothing. After that I said I'd never ride for the army again. Like I told you, I wouldn't have done it this time if they didn't have Standing Elk in stockade. I can't think of any vows I wouldn't go back on for him."

Two mornings later, as Henry and I were preparing to ride out for a hunt of our own, we heard a ruckus from the west side of the camp. Curiosity got the better of us and we walked over. The source of the commotion was at the far west end of the camp, at the creek crossing. Black Kettle and twenty or so others were engaged in a shouting match with a group of men on horses. Two of the horsemen were doing the talking: one was a tall and ruddy-faced fellow dressed in a city-style black overcoat, and the other, younger, wore frontier clothing: hide leggings and a tasseled hide shirt. His complexion was dark, and I thought he could be Indian, or perhaps a half-breed. A hundred feet behind these two were twenty or so uniformed soldiers and perhaps close to that many head of the skinniest steers I ever laid my eyes on.

Henry and I kept our distance, away from the dispute but close enough to hear the exchange. The man in the overcoat was speaking earnestly in English while the one in the hide shirt was translating it into Cheyenne for Black Kettle and the others. Hide Shirt's voice sounded strained. What he said to Black Kettle was this: "Your agent, Mister Wynkoop, doesn't have any control over what happens on the trail. We got fifteen head here, and that's all there is. I can't make the rest appear with magic. Some Indians ran off with the other twenty in the night."

Henry and I turned to each other at the same moment.

"That isn't what he said," Henry said, stepping forward.

No one heard.

"That isn't what he said!" Henry shouted.

The cacophony of voices fell to silence in a couple of heartbeats. Everyone turned to face us.

"Pardon?" said the man in the overcoat.

Henry ignored him and walked straight to Black Kettle and another man, whose name I learned later was Ski'o mah—Little Robe. He was also a Cheyenne chief.

Henry pointed at the man in the hide shirt and spoke in Cheyenne. "Edmund Guerrier didn't say what the other one said. The other one said that Mister Wynkoop sends his apologies. He says the Indian Bureau didn't allocate the promised amount of beef to him, so he sent you what he could. He said he's corresponding with the white chiefs and doing his best to get the mistake corrected."

"What is this?" the man in the overcoat said. He turned to the man in the hide shirt. "What is he saying?" he turned back to Henry, "What are you saying?"

"I'm saying that your interpreter said something different than what you said. He said the missing steers were stolen by Indians."

"This isn't any of your affair, Henry," the man in the hide shirt said.

"I don't see it that way, Edmund."

"Why would you say that?" the man in the overcoat asked.

"Because it would be better if they thought other Indians took 'em then having them know the government shorted them again," Edmund said.

"You don't think the chiefs deserve the truth?" Henry said.

"We're on the same side, Henry. And I have more stake in this than you do. I'm only trying to do my part in keeping the peace. Don't you want the same?"

"Mister Guerrier, would you please explain yourself?" the man in the overcoat interjected.

Guerrier stared levelly at Henry. "It's nothing, Mister Pollard. I misspoke. It's fine now."

"Well, then, tell these Indians to go fetch their beef so we can be on our way."

After Guerrier and the agency man and their army escort departed, the whole of the camp busied themselves butchering and preparing some of the steers. Even the children were given tasks. It was the first time I noticed laughter in the camp since Henry and I arrived. The promise of a full belly after a long time of hunger kindled some happiness.

Black Kettle was disappointed, particularly in Edmund Guerrier. Little Robe was plainly angry but spoke little. The promised beef was a long time coming and should have carried them quite a way, had they been given what they were promised. Neither man was particularly surprised. They rarely received anywhere near what was pledged. Black Kettle still found it in himself to be grateful that there was food for his people. He also held high hopes that Standing Elk's hunt would be successful.

Henry and I still rode out for our hunt, though we knew Black Kettle would gladly share the beef. We both wanted to contribute, though, so we figured we'd see what we could find. During the ride Henry told me about Edmund Guerrier.

"Edmund's mother was Cheyenne, and his father was a white trader," Henry said. "He was educated out east—St. Louis, I believe—but he came back west after his father died. His mother passed of the cholera when he was a boy. Black Kettle took Edmund in and he kept a lodge in Black Kettle's camp up north at the same time as me. We got on well enough, though I can't say we became friends. He can speak Cheyenne as well as English and French, so it makes sense the army recruited him for interpreting. I have to admit, I'm a little surprised he agreed to do it. He stayed with Black Kettle when he moved his people to the camp at Big Sandy Creek, and Edmund was there the day the army attacked. He made it out with his life, but many folks he was close to didn't.... I reckon he's just trying his best to make his way with a foot in two worlds, and mayhap I spoke out of turn, but I couldn't abide him not giving the straight of it to Black Kettle, even if his intentions were good ones. These folks have been lied to enough."

We returned from our hunt in the early evening with a turkey and a good-sized rattlesnake. We presented both to Black Kettle and his wife, Medicine Woman Later, and in return we were given generous portions of the beef on spits. When we were finished eating, our stomachs were full for the first time since arriving at the camp.

Standing Elk returned with the hunting party the next day, shortly after noon. The thirty-man hunt produced six small deer, fourteen turkeys, and some small game. It may sound like a lot, but it wasn't, not for the number of people who were in residence at the camp. Buffalo was what they needed, but there were none to be found.

"If we could hunt north of the Arkansas River, we would find buffalo," Standing Elk said. "Black Kettle should never have agreed to come here. A death in war would have more honor. I will travel with you to Texas."

Chapter 6

I was nervous as we approached Sherman, and my innards felt as tight as a banjo string. I had similar feelings in the war, just before a battle. I did my best to keep it to myself, but I have no doubt that Henry and Standing Elk could see it plain on my face.

We passed a couple of wagons and few men on horseback near the outskirts of town. We were given a wide berth by the riders. We must have been quite a sight, the three of us.

About a quarter mile out, I took us off the road and across the scrub to come in behind the Englebright. I offered Standing Elk my spare shirt, thinking if he looked less Indian people might not pay him as much mind. He refused. I should have known.

We tethered the four horses on a rail behind the corral at the back of the Englebright's stable. A man came out, a negro like Henry but probably three times his age. I told him my name and that I had business with Mister Englebright.

"Mister Englebright's in the hotel, sir," he said, and then pointed at Henry. "He can go in with you, but I don't believe the injun'll be allowed inside."

"The *injun* will stay with the horses," Standing Elk said.

"All right, sir. Will you be needing anything? Feed for your horses?"

"No," I said. "Thank you, umm?"

"Clay, sir."

We found Calvin Englebright at his usual place behind the front desk at the hotel. Silus, the bartender and I use to joke behind our hands that it was his favorite place to count his money. An expression of surprise passed over his features when he looked up from his work and saw me. He glanced briefly at Henry and then said, "Come with me."

He turned and led us through the door behind the counter and we followed him down the short hallway to his office.

His office was decorated as ornately as the rest of the Englebright. Oil paintings hung from all four walls, and all of the moldings were of dark, fluted wood. Calvin took a seat behind the desk and gestured for us to sit on the chesterfield against the adjacent wall.

"Here I've summoned you to the very place I suggested you never return to.... You look well, Everett, albeit rather down-at-the-heels, and with a beard.... Who is this with you?"

"This is Henry. He's a friend."

Henry nodded. "Pleased to meet you."

"Likewise," Calvin said. "Well, hopefully you're a *good* friend. Everett may need one.... Everett, the Indian woman is at the McBain ranch. I don't believe she ever left."

He put his hand up to stop me from speaking. "Furthermore," he said, "I believe that Michael McBain was the one who murdered his father, not the woman."

"How do you know Wačhiwi is there?"

Calvin sighed and stood. "I suppose I should have done this to begin with. Come with me."

We followed him up the hallway and through the hotel lobby to the stairs. The Englebright had three floors of guest rooms. He passed the first-floor landing but took the second and followed the long hallway of numbered doors to the room on the very end. He knocked politely.

After several moments the door opened a crack, just enough for an eye to peer out.

"I apologize for the inconvenience, May, but Everett Ward is here. I'd like you to tell him your story."

The door swung open but the occupant stayed behind it. Calvin looked over his shoulder once and quickly entered the room. Henry and I followed and the door swung shut. There stood the old negro woman from the McBain ranch.

This is Maybelle Freeman. She was the McBain's housekeeper for more than ten years, and my mother and father's housekeeper before that. Edward McBain hired her after my father passed. I offered her work here, but she didn't feel comfortable working in a place as busy as the Englebright.... I understand you two have met before, Everett."

"We have," I said.

"Why don't we all sit down," Calvin said.

We sat at the small, round dining table provided with the hotel room. The strictly utilitarian room was as tiny and plain as the rest of the Englebright was spacious and grand. Calvin Englebright kept half a dozen such rooms on the second and third floors, for miners and drovers who needed a break from the camps and could afford the dollar-and-a-half a night.

"I'm sorry I told you lies, Mister Everett. I was afraid," Maybelle said once we were seated.

"Just Everett," I said. "I apologize for handling you so roughly."

"Oh, I was all right. Scraped my arm a little bit. I know you were just trying to get me outta the house. It didn't burn, though it may have been better if it did. Mister Englebright told me the men dowsed it with the kitchen wash pot."

"Maybelle came here that very night, walked all the way," Calvin said. "I've had her sequestered here for her safety ever since. No one knows she's here outside of Rosa and I."

Rosa was the Englebright's head housekeeper and had been with Calvin since he opened the place.

"I didn't know what I was going to do before you wired me, Everett. I was beside myself with all of it, and consequently indecisive. Marshal Flood is a decent man, but he's not a particularly smart man, and he's very close with Michael McBain. And Tom Lowry, the county sheriff, has been in the McBain family pocket since they funded his election campaign against Jonathon Forsythe in sixty-one. I can't trust telling either one of them, so I kept her here and saw to her needs. Then, when I received the wire from you, I didn't even stop to think it over, I just sent one right back. And now here you are, and I don't know what I expected you to do about it … he trailed off.

"Why don't you start with telling me the whole story?" I said. "Everything you know,"

"Of course. Forgive me. Maybelle, tell him everything you told me."

"All right.… Well, sir, I was sleeping one night—back in June this would have been—and I woke to some ruckus from the direction of Rebecca's room. You know, thumping and the like. I poked my head out my bedroom door and looked down the hall and I seen Mister Michael come out of Rebecca's door and hurry off toward the big room. I didn't pay it much mind at the time, but Rebecca poked her head out too. She looked upset. We said goodnight to each other, and no sooner had I shut the door than Mister Michael come knocking. He looked mighty het up, and he told me to get dressed and go wake Old Reg and have him fetch up the wagon and bring it round. He said he wanted me and Reg to ride into town and bring back Marshal Flood. I begun to ask him if something was wrong with Mister Edward, and he told me to hush up and hurry. I shut my door so I could change out of my nightclothes, and I heard him knocking on Rebecca's door … well, bangin' on it, anyhow. After I put on my coat and shoes I walked to Reg's room on the other side of the house, and I woke him and told him to fetch the wagon like Mister Michael asked me to. I waited in the big room while Reg went about hitching the mules. I was settin' there for a minute or two and Mister Michael came in from down the hall where the bedrooms are, and told me to start a pot of water boiling for his bath while I waited for Reg. I didn't notice when he came to my room because there's only one lamp in the hallway, but the big room was lit up and I could see Mister Michael had blood all down the front of his shirt and trousers. Well, he saw that I saw and he said, '"Maybelle, my father's been killed, I tried to help him, but it was too late. Now you run along and do as I asked."' I did what he said. After I started the water, I went out to the porch and Old Reg was along in a minute. We rode into town and woke the marshal. He was none too pleased about being pulled outta sleep, but I told him Mister Edward was dead and he said he'd come along as quick as he could. He said he'd ride his own horse in, so we didn't wait. When we got back to the ranch it was near sunup. Mister Michael was settin' there on the porch in Mister Edward's big rocker. He told us Rebecca was gone and that he 'spected she's the one that killed Mister Edward. He said he'd wait there for the marshal and that me and Old Reg should go and get us a couple hours of shuteye. I can't speak for Old Reg but I was hard put to think Rebecca killed Mister Edward, and it troubled me something awful, but neither me or Reg will see sixty again, and we were dog-tired, so we did just what Mister Michael said."

She paused and stood. "Pardon, I need some water. Would any of you like some?"

"Thank you, ma'am," Henry said. Calvin and I declined. I remember thinking at that moment how I wanted her to hurry up and tell me what she knew about Wačhiwi. I bit back my impatience and kept my mouth closed, though. It was right to let her tell it her way.

She walked over to a small bureau and poured two glasses from a pitcher. When she returned she set a glass in front of Henry and then sat and sipped her own.

"Things went on after that," she continued. "They buried Mister Edward later that week, and it seemed that half the town was there for the service. There wasn't much talk at the house, on account of Mister Michael, but I missed Rebecca's conversation and her help around the place. I know they missed her in the kitchen too, but as I said, there wasn't much talk. I 'spect all the help was thinking the same thing; that Mister Michael done it to his father.

"I found Rebecca some three weeks or a month later. It was by pure chance. There's a room at the west end of the house, down at the end of a hallway coming off the kitchen. Nobody goes down there much, and I don't know why they put it there when they built the place … mayhap for dry storage, because it has a door that goes to the outside as well as the door to the hallway, and there weren't no windows inside. As far back as I remember the outside door was always closed—I can't say whether it was locked or no—but now, the inside door was always open. One of the misters had a couple of the hands put an old sideboard in there a few years back, but other than that it was empty. Well, Alejandro, one of the young men from the kitchen, came to me one mornin' and said that he was moppin' the floor and heard noises from the room. I couldn't ken all of what he was saying, he's from Mexico and don't speak much English, but he was agitated so I thought I should go have a look and see for myself. When I got there the door was closed up tight and it had a hasp and lock like you'd use on an outbuildin'. I never had much cause to go down that hallway, so I can't say how long that lock had been on it. Couldn't have been long.

"Alejandro stood beside me ringin' his hands like he thought a spook was inside. I thought there must be a good reason Mister Michael locked up the room but I knocked just to set Alejandro's mind at ease. I believe we both about jumped from our skin when somethin' moved 'round in there. So I knocked again and said, *Hello?*

'"Maybelle?"' It was no more than a whisper, but I knew straight away it was Rebecca. I asked her what she was doin' in there, and she said Mister Michael put her in there after he killed Mister Edward.

"I was mad as a hornet, and I don't know what came over me but I went straight to Mister Michael. He was working in his study, there at his desk. I stood in the doorway and said, '"Mister Michael, sir, I know Rebecca's locked up back there by the kitchen, and I want you to let her out of there."'

"He set down his pen and stood up and came over and stood before me. He just stood there, staring down at me, just as calm as could be. I saw murder in his eyes right then, and all at once I was more afraid than I've ever been. He said, '"Maybelle, Rebecca stabbed my father with a kitchen knife and then ran off. It was a terrible thing, and if you don't want a terrible thing to happen to you, that's all you'll ever say on the matter."'

"Then he asked me if anyone else knew she was in there. I couldn't speak right off. I just stood, lookin' at the floor. He waited while I gathered myself. After some time I said, Yessir, Mister Michael. Alejandro does, and that was the end of it."

Maybelle lowered her head into her hands and began to sob. To this day I can still hear it. It was singularly wretched.

Calvin reached over and took one of her hands away from her face. He held it in both of his.

She lifted her head. Her wet face looked even more careworn than it had just a moment before.

"I never saw Alejandro again. If Mister Michael did something to him, it was my fault. I was too afraid to lie to him. And I left Rebecca in there. I'd sneak her food sometimes, special things mostly, like a piece of cake or pie if Randall, the new cook, baked something. Then you came that night, and after you run me outside, I left and came here, and here I've been."

I began to weep then. I'm not ashamed of it. Shame was what brought the tears. Both hers and mine. We failed Wačhiwi, but Maybelle was only an old woman. I had no such defense.

"I'm going to kill him," I said, finally.

"Sounds like he deserves nothing more," Henry said. "But it might serve her better if we get the law involved."

"How would that be, Henry?" I said. "Mister Englebright already said he was afraid to go to the law."

"Just Calvin, please, Everett. I'm not your employer anymore. But you're right. I know this woman is important to you, but in the eyes of the law, she's nothing more than an animal. Going up against Michael McBain in a court would be folly."

"If you want to kill this man, then you kill him," Henry said. "But Wačhiwi will still be wanted for the murder of his father. She'll likely be safe in the Sioux nation, if we get her there and she stays there, but you yourself have seen bounty hunters chasing Indians in their own territory. Two thousand dollars is a lot of money."

"Mister Engle—*Calvin,*" I said. "What if we told Marshal Flood the story and convinced him to ride out to the ranch with us to see that room with his own eyes? He'll be compelled to tell the truth, and Maybelle can be a witness in court."

"When Maybelle first came to me, my instinct was to do just that," Calvin said. "Though Maybelle wouldn't be allowed to testify against a white man in a Texas court, Marshal Flood would indeed be compelled to reveal what he witnessed … but can we be certain—*absolutely certain*—that he would? I'd like to believe he'd be truthful. But if he isn't, the Indian girl will be hanged. Are you willing to risk that?"

"No. I suppose not.… I wish I could ask Wačhiwi what *she* wants to do.… What about Maybelle?"

Calvin patted Maybelle's hand. "I've set Maybelle up with an old business associate in Wisconsin, as part of his house help. I wanted to wait until you arrived, or until the time I was fairly certain you were never going to, before I arranged for her transport."

"Maybelle, where is the outside door to the room Wačhiwi was being kept in?" I said.

"It's around the backside of the house. There's an old wind chime hanging from the roof right over it."

"Well, I suppose that's all I need to know, then. I'm obliged to you."

"You'll fetch her out of there?"

"I'm going to try."

Calvin allowed us to spend the rest of the day in the stable.

"I would offer you a room …" he trailed off.

He didn't need to say more. We all knew that Henry was one thing and Standing Elk was another altogether.

He had an afternoon meal of biscuits, ham, and coffee sent out to us and made sure to have the boy who brought it tell us that there was no charge. The three of us sat against the horse hair imbedded plank wall of an empty stall and laid our plans, such as they were.

We holed up until near midnight. Calvin came out around nine to bring us a small bundle of trail food: raisons, peanuts, and some dried beef. He wished us well, and he urged me not to kill Michael McBain, warning that I'd spend my life watching over my shoulder for a hangman if I did. I told him I'd cooled off a bit and was only concerned with finding Wačhiwi. The truth was, I wasn't certain of what I was going to do if I saw Michael McBain.

We took the back route out of town under a sliver of a moon. I was glad to have Macklin's horse, Rose, trailing on a leader behind me. It would make things easier if we found Wačhiwi and had to ride hard.

After some discussion we decided that busying the ranch hands with a calamity would be our wisest move. The bunkhouse was near the back of the big house, and if we had to bust the door down to the room Wačhiwi was being kept in, we'd be sure to wake every single one of them. Most would be simple ranch hands, not gunmen, but it was likely the majority of them would come to the aid of their employer if they thought there was trouble. Better to draw them away.

We rode wide and skirted around to the back side of the ranch and tied the horses to a fence rail at the furthest corral from the house—the number six. We walked the hundred yards or so from there to the cluster of outbuildings that stood behind the main house, on the opposite end from the bunkhouse. The tack house, hay barn, grain storage shed, and tool shed loomed as bulky shadows. We stopped at the tool shed, where I fumbled around in the dark for a crowbar and a sledgehammer, which I found after some searching. Outside, I handed the sledge to Henry, and picked up the Spencer. Together we headed for the back of the main house to look for the door that Maybelle had described to us.

Standing Elk stayed behind to torch the outbuildings.

The waning moon provided scant light, but the wind rarely stops blowing out there below the Red. It was only a puff, barely enough to feel on your neck, but it was enough to make that wind chime Maybelle told us about tinkle softly.

Henry and I stood outside that door and waited until we could hear the hiss and growl of the growing blaze and see its glow emanating from direction of the outbuildings. We both squatted low in the doorway and shouted "*FIRE, FIRE!*" at the top of our voices.

Seconds later I heard shouts from the direction of the bunkhouse and seconds after that men flooded out and ran toward the blaze. The harried men passed us in the dark without a glance, and when it seemed no more were coming, we stood and got to work.

Henry felt around and found the doorknob. "There's a hasp right above the knob with a padlock. Hand me the crowbar."

I handed him the crowbar and he gave me the sledgehammer. He pried the hasp off in a tick and then stood back and kicked the door. It made a cracking noise but stayed closed. He kicked it again and it flew open.

It was dark as a crypt inside. I dropped the sledge and raised the Spencer with one arm.

"Wačhiwi?" I said.

Henry struck a match, handed it to me and then struck another.

The tiny room was empty, save the old china hutch Maybelle had spoken of, standing against one wall. There was no sign anyone had been living in it.

I dropped the guttering match just as it scorched my fingertips. Henry dropped his as well. After the brief moment of light, the darkness seemed even more complete.

"Well?" Henry said from beside me. His voice sounded calm, but I could sense the urgency nonetheless.

"Give me another match," I said.

He struck one and passed it over without a word.

I took the three steps to the door that led into the interior of the house and kicked it just above the knob. The match went out from the motion but the jamb gave way and the door crashed open.

"Let's find Michael McBain," I said.

Henry struck another match and we made our way along the hallway to the kitchen. Once there we quickly looked around and found a shelf with a row of oil lamps. I took two down and Henry lit them with the final match from his box. There was another short L-shaped hallway off the kitchen—the same one I'd followed Michael McBain through my first day at the ranch. I hurried down it and Henry followed. Once we reached the turn in the hall where it opened up into the drawing-room, we could have done without the lanterns. The blaze from the burning outbuildings flickered bright through the windows. Henry drew his pistol, and I set my lantern down and raised the Spencer, this time with both hands.

I nodded toward the opposite side of the drawing-room, where the hallway to the bedrooms began, and at the same time heard more than one pair of running boots coming from the front of the house toward us.

"Mister McBain, Mister McBain!" Someone was shouting.

Michael McBain sprang from the hallway just as two men entered the drawing-room from the opposite side. It was clear he had already heard the ruckus; his boots and trousers were on and he was buttoning up a shirt. Not thinking of anything else other than stopping him from getting outside with the rest of his men, I dropped the Spencer, ran from the hall and leapt over the Chesterfield. I landed good and met him halfway through the room, coming in low and hitting him mid-section like a footballer. We struggled hard on the ground; there was shouting in the room and I remember hearing Henry yell *"STOP!"*

McBain was fighting wildly, and he was damn strong, but I think my hate for the man gave me an edge that night. I was finally able to roll over on my back with his neck snugged up in the crook of my right arm. Once I had him that way, I put some pressure down and cut off his air. He either knew he was beat or losing his ability to draw a breath scared him. He stopped struggling. From my position I could see Henry had his pistol leveled at the two ranch hands. He told them to sit down next to where I was holding McBain. Once they did, Henry said, "You can get up, Everett. If any of you others move, I will shoot you."

I let McBain loose, and nobody seemed inclined to test Henry's resolve, including McBain. I looked down at him and said, "You know why I'm here. Where is she?"

"You're a Goddamn lunatic," McBain said. "I told you last time, she was gone." He glanced toward the rear of the house. The glow coming from the back hall was nearly as bright as daylight. "Are you trying to succeed at burning my house down this time?"

Standing Elk appeared beside me. He handed me my Spencer, which I pointed at Michael McBain. It gave me some satisfaction to see the defiance in his eyes turn to fear.

"Tell me where she is," I said. "Or I swear, I'll shoot you."

"Everett, I—" was as far as he got. As quick as ball lighting, Standing Elk stepped forward and twisted the top of his ear. McBain squealed like a shoat pulled from the tit too soon. Standing Elk twisted a little harder and then let go, but he continued to stand over McBain.

"Christ," McBain said. "She's just a Goddamn Indi—" His eyes darted to Standing Elk before returning to me. Now they were pleading.

"If I tell you where she is, will you give me your word, as a gentleman, not to shoot me? Just take her and go?"

"Where?" I said.

He cocked his head toward the hallway he'd come out of. "Back there. In my room. Down on the right."

I turned and went down the hall. There was only one door on the right. McBain had taken the time to lock it as he rushed out to see what the commotion was about. I kicked it by the knob. It gave way easily.

There was only one small lamp lit in the enormous bedroom. It was on a night-table, beside an equally enormous poster bed. I didn't need the lamp to see, however. On the back wall there was a picture window and the glow from the burning outbuildings shone brightly through the thin linen curtains. Wačhiwi was there, in the far corner, where a narrow mattress had been placed on the floor. She was dressed in a thin housedress, and sitting on her knees; her posture was tense, as if she'd suddenly sprung up from a prone position. I stepped into the room and approached her. When I was close enough to see her eyes, I saw no recognition in them, only wariness. A little closer and the wariness slowly turned to disbelief, and then finally, to joy. At the time, her happiness hardly struck me, because along with her eyes and her smile I saw other things. There was a large yellowing bruise high on her right cheek, and she was chained. The chain ran from a cuff on her ankle to a ring set in the corner of the wall.

Not even in war had I felt the rage I experienced as I turned and walked out of the room. I strode down the hall, raising the Spencer. McBain was turning his head toward me as I re-entered the drawing room. His expression showed that he knew what was coming. He began to say something just as I put pressure on the trigger. The ball took him dead center in his face and went out the back of his head where it also hit one of the men sitting beside him. McBain and the unfortunate ranch hand both collapsed to the floor. McBain, in silence, the hand, wailing. The other man was staring up at me with open fright, his face pasted with blood, bone, and brain.

Henry gave his pistol over to Standing Elk and knelt beside the ranch hand. "Move over," he said to the uninjured hand before taking the wailing man by his face and turning it so he could see his injury. After a bare moment he released the man and stood back up. "It took off half his ear," he said. "It's not grievous."

Standing Elk handed Henry back his pistol. Henry said, "We have to go."

I nodded, and after a long, final look at McBain, I turned and headed back to the bedroom.

"Where's the key?" I said, kneeling in front of Wačhiwi.

She pointed toward the door. "It's there," she said.

And it was, hanging from a small brass hook. I hurried over and snatched it from the wall just as more shouting broke out from the drawing room. I ran back and unlocked the padlock on the ankle cuff. The skin around the roughly-smithed iron was abraded and trickling blood. The rage I'd felt minutes before returned, and I wanted to kill McBain all over again.

"Do you have any other clothes?" I said, taking her hand and helping her to her feet.

"Yes. Across the hall."

"Get what you can … shoes, if you have some. We have to be quick."

She nodded and hurried out. I watched after her as she entered the room across the way. I looked around. There was a leather billfold on the night table by the big bed. I walked over and opened it. Inside was a thick sheaf of bills. These I took without a second thought.

Wačhiwi was back in a minute. She'd changed into a plain brown and white dress and a brown wool coat that was much too large, along with a pair of low-heeled leather boots. She had a small bundle of clothing clutched to her chest.

"Stay behind me," I said.

The shouts from the drawing room had quieted to angry conversation. There was another man sitting on the floor next to the two others and the body of McBain. He was staring defiantly up at Henry and Standing Elk.

"You'll hang for this, nigger—"

His words cut off as he caught our movement from the corner of his eye and turned his attention to Wačhiwi and I.

"I know you," he said. "You're Everett Ward … and her … she's that kitchen squaw. The one who killed old Ed. The law's looking for her. There's a rewar—"

"Shut up," I said.

"What do you want to do, Everett?" Henry said.

Standing Elk raised his pistol and took a step toward the three men. He looked at me expectantly. Wačhiwi brushed passed me and stood over McBain.

"We have to go," I said.

I pointed the Spencer at the man who said he recognized me. He looked vaguely familiar, but I couldn't place a name.

"If any of you follow us, I'll kill every last one of you," I said.

His look of defiance faltered.

I turned to Wačhiwi. She was still staring down at McBain. I saw that she was standing in his blood. "We have to go. *Now*," I said.

She nodded without turning. I took her hand and she allowed me to lead her away. Henry and Standing Elk followed.

I made for the front door, figuring we'd cross the dooryard and circle around the opposite side of the house from the burning outbuildings. It would take us past the bunkhouse, but I was going on the belief it would be empty. Once we were past that, then we could cut across the pasture to where the horses were tied.

I slid the bolt and stopped. The cold night air hit my face. It seemed to me like we'd been inside the house for hours, though it couldn't have been more than five minutes.

"*Wait*," I said, as I turned and started back inside. Henry grabbed my arm before I could get past him.

"It wasn't those men," he said. "You do this, there's no coming back from it."

"He knows me. If he lives to tell his version of what happened here, all of us are going to be hunted for the rest of our lives." I looked over my shoulder at Wačhiwi. "And I can't abide that."

I pulled away from Henry and returned to the drawing room, but the decision to kill—to murder— those three men had been taken from my hands. All three of them were gone. Only Michael McBain remained, crumpled and unnatural looking, his clothes soaked with blood. I stared, mesmerized, at Wačhiwi's tiny maroon boot prints leading away from his body. Finally, I was able to turn away.

Henry, Standing Elk, and Wačhiwi were waiting at the bottom of the porch steps. I stopped on the porch and bent, with my hands on my knees. I was shaking badly and felt as if I was going to vomit. After some time the feeling subsided and I hurried down the steps, past them all, stopping just long enough to steal a look over my shoulder to make certain Wačhiwi was following behind me. I sprinted down the length of the house, and around the back side past the bunkhouse and the number three corral. Off to our right, at the other side of the house, the tack house collapsed with a thunderous *Whoom.* I stopped for a moment behind one the corral gates. The tack house was a pile of burning rubble and the other buildings were all fully engulfed. The hay barn was an inferno. The glow from the flames illuminated the chaos as a score of men ran around, shouting, a handful throwing buckets of water on the back side of the big house and on its roof so it wouldn't catch. Others stood in small groups, still others seemed to be wandering aimlessly. There was no bucket line for the outbuildings. Most of the ranch's buckets were in the burning tool shed. I knew the men from the house must be out there, raising the alarm. I took Wačhiwi's hand and made for the horses.

Riding in silence, Standing Elk led us north to the Red River. We made the crossing, followed it northwest for a bit, and then crossed back over two more times during the next couple of hours. Finally, when the purple glow in the east allowed us to see more than just shadows, we halted.

"Time for us to part company," Henry said.

I shifted in my saddle. "I've put you in an unfair situation," I said.

"I don't see how else things could have gone. We did right, though it won't look that way to some.... However things come out, I'm glad you didn't kill those men."

"Where are you going to go?"

"Mexico, for now. Thought I might look for an old friend down there."

I turned to Standing Elk. "What about you?"

"I'll go to Mexico."

"I'm sorry," Wačhiwi said. "I've put you all in danger."

"You have done nothing," Standing Elk said.

I divided what food we had and then fished the sheaf of bills from my pocket, divided it roughly in half, and held half out to Henry.

"I took this from Michael McBain's room. It makes me a thief, but I'm not going to say I feel ashamed. It might make your journey a little easier."

He took the money. "Good luck to you ... to both of you. Stay in the rough, and avoid towns as much as you can."

"I'll do that. I'm more troubled about you and Standing Elk riding through Texas."

"We'll stay out of Texas. I've been thinking we'll keep northeast and circle back down to the Rio Grande. I've never seen it, but I've heard it's quite a sight.... What are you going to do after you get her there?"

"I don't know. I haven't had the time to give it much thought."

"Well, you'll have it now. You take care."

"You too.... Standing Elk, I know you're not much for goodbyes, but farewell anyway. Hopefully our paths will cross again."

Standing Elk nodded once, pivoted his horse, and rode off.

Wačhiwi and I watched Henry and Standing Elk melt into the shadows before turning north. It had been more than a year since the night we'd left Sherman together under the cover of darkness. Now we rode out together again, this time as the sun rose.

"I'm sorry it took me so long," I said.

"Many times I dreamed you'd come, but I lost hope.… What I did that day at the jail … I thought you would forget me.… I did what I did to save you."

"I know."

"After you were shot, more men came in the night. They argued over killing you. They chose to let you suffer and die alone.… They took everything, even your blanket, but still you lived. How?"

"A man and woman found me—Indians. A father and daughter, I thought. They cared for me for … weeks, I suppose, but I can't be certain how long it was."

Wačhiwi nodded. "Their medicine must have been strong."

"I reckon it was.… Will you tell me what happened after I saw you at the jail?"

She was silent for a time, and I began thinking that she wasn't going to answer. I remembered when we'd been together before, and how she'd hardly said two words to me until I was gunshot and delirious from fever.

Finally, she spoke.

"When Michael became old enough, he began coming to me at night. Most times he would have to wait until Edward was finished with me, and I returned to my room. Sometimes he would hurt me, mostly where you couldn't see, but sometimes on my face. I would lie to Edward, and Mister Peckham, and Maybelle about where the marks came from. Not long before you first arrived, Edward discovered us. He told me that I should have resisted Michael. He said I was an Indian whore, and that he would kill me if I lay with Michael again. Edward and Michael argued, and then Michael stopped coming for a while. After I saw you at the jail, Michael came to me again. This time I did resist … I bit him. He cried out, and he hit me, and I struggled with him. Edward was awakened, and he came into the room. He was very angry, and he shouted at Michael. Then Michael walked out, but he came back … he killed Edward with a knife from the kitchen.

"The days were better with Edward. I was allowed to work, and I had a room. Mister Peckham taught me to read, and Maybelle taught me things she knew about white medicine. After Edward was gone, Michael put me in a room near the kitchen. He chained me, like how you found me. I spent all of my days alone, and there was no light except for what came under the doors. He told me he would kill me if I made noise or cried out to anyone. I could hear the people working in the kitchen, and the men working outside, and the cattle dogs, and sometimes a horse. Michael brought me food late at night. He would watch me eat, and then he would want to lay with me, and he would hurt me. He liked to hurt me more than he liked the other.… I was in the room alone for so long that I began to await the moment he would come, even though I hated him. Then Maybelle found me and Michael moved me to his room.... And then you came, Iníla Ská Wičháša"

"Quiet White Man," I said.

She'd kept her eyes forward the whole time she'd been speaking, but she turned to me then; her eyes were wet and she smiled the most tortuous smile I've ever seen on a human face. I could live another hundred years and still not understand the complexity of that smile, but I can picture the way it looked on her face as if it were yesterday.

We pushed on through the day and late into the night. I knew the county sheriff would have trouble finding any local men with the sand to give chase into Indian Territory at any price, and it would likely take days to bring in outside bounty men. But I couldn't be certain that there weren't some qualified men in the McBain's employ who would quickly shift their allegiance from their lost McBain salary to the county's per diem. The previous year Edward McBain had had trackers on the trail of Wačhiwi and I only hours after we'd left Sherman. I had to surmise Michael McBain still had some of these men on the payroll and that Sheriff Lowry or the Texas Rangers would try to make use of them.

We finally made camp in the cover of a deep, dry wash. That part of Oklahoma was a tinder-box that time of year and there was a fair breeze, so it was the only place I felt safe setting even a small fire. I wasn't worried about the smoke; it was probably three a.m. and I didn't plan to make enough of it to be seen even if there was a soul in the area not asleep. I only had the one bedroll, and I gave it to Wačhiwi. I figured I'd keep a watch while she got some rest. There was a trading post I knew of in the Chickasaw Nation, near the Washita River. I'd come across it when I'd been searching for her after Michael McBain lied to me about her killing Ed McBain. But going there was risky. Anyone who saw us, from the McBain's ranch to the Dakota Territory, could help give us away to anyone searching for us. We needed food and bedding, though. The less hunting I had to do, the more miles we could cover.

Wačhiwi was up with the sun without any prompting from me. The morning was cold. There was ice from the north on the wind, and I wished for hot coffee while we ate some of the peanuts and raisins. I packed up the bedroll and kicked around the charred remnants of the night's fire. It was enough to hide it from a casual glance, but it wouldn't fool a good tracker.

"You should trade me coats," I said, holding out the reins to Rose. "This one's new."

She shook her head, ignoring the reins and looking at something over my shoulder. "I'm not cold," she said, as she walked over to the chin-high bank.

"Suit yourself," I said, watching after her.

She reached up to the top of the bank and began picking some plants with white, lacy blooms.

"What's that?"

"I don't know the English word. We call it tȟaópi pȟežúta. It's good medicine."

I dug around in my saddle bags and brought out a small drawstring sack.

"You can put it in this," I said, walking over. "Standing Elk taught me a little about plants, but he didn't show me this one."

"My mother and father were … healers. Like your white doctors. My brother and I would help them gather plants like this."

"Your mother is alive," I said. "I'm sorry. I should have told you last night."

She stopped picking flowers and turned to me. Her eyes searched my face and I was ashamed for not telling her sooner.

"You've seen her?"

"I have. I spoke with her. She's with other Lakota—with Red Cloud, a great chief—up near the Powder River. It's where we're going."

She began stuffing the flowers (yarrow, I learned later) into the sack. "I know of Red Cloud, from before, when I was a young girl. How long before we arrive there?"

"Three or four weeks, if all goes well."

Wačhiwi considered this. "That's not so long.… Will there be men following us?"

"I don't know. Probably. But they won't catch us so easily this time."

"Thank you. You've put yourself in danger for me again."

"Only because I didn't do it right the first time. You would have been back with your people a long time ago if I'd been more careful.… Everything you told me, all of your suffering over the last year, it's my fault, and for that I'm sorry."

"You're not to blame. It wasn't for you to choose for those men."

I searched her eyes. Finally, I nodded. "Well, we should get moving."

We reached the trading post just before sunset that evening. The low, ramshackle, sod-roofed log building was set in a cleared spot in the middle of a cottonwood grove. There were two horses tied to a rail in front of a water trough. One of them was sickly and so impossibly thin that its ribs appeared ready to cut through its skin. The water didn't look so good, but it smelled all right, so we tied Evelyn and Rose up next to the others.

The interior was near empty, save two tables fashioned from wood crates and an ancient-looking pile of dirty canvas tarps. It was dimly lit and smelled of dust and unwashed bodies. The proprietor was the same man as before: thin, ill-tempered, and rapidly approaching old age. He was wearing a red shirt—the same red shirt he'd previously worn—faded to a dusty pink, along with a pair of equally faded red suspenders. I shaved my beard that morning with the hope that if it *was* the same proprietor, he wouldn't recognize me, and in turn he wouldn't remember the wanted poster I'd showed him with Wačhiwi's likeness on it.

When we entered, he immediately complained that he was closing up for the day and we'd have to hurry our business.

"I don't take customers after sundown as a rule," he said, eyeing my Spencer from where he stood behind the makeshift split-log counter, punching holes in a square of hide with an awl. I didn't see any recognition in his face, only irritation and narrow suspicion. "And I don't have any use for her, if you're looking to trade. So don't waste your time offering. Squaw whores are ten for a dollar around here."

There was a chuckle to my left. A second man was sitting in a rocker in the corner. His long hair was matted and it fell around his ears in wet-looking clumps. The portion of his face that wasn't covered in beard was streaked with dirt. He had a shotgun in his lap and was regarding me with a thin smile.

"You'll want to keep that rifle pointed at the floor, friend" he said.

"I don't see a reason I'll have to do anything but."

"Well, that's just fine."

We approached the counter and looked over the plank shelves that had been constructed a few feet behind it. They were half bare, and what *was* there was mostly whiskey and something in Mason jars that could have been pickled eggs.

"We're a little low on stock," the proprietor said, following my gaze. "Some Creeks from up north robbed me last month. That's why I hired Mister Plemons over there. I haven't had a resupply since. Filthy bastards. First time I've had any trouble with the Indians in ten years of trading here."

"They let you live," the man in the rocker said.

"Well, they didn't do me any favors there."

"What do you have in the way of food, aside from what's on there on the shelf?" I said. "We need canned or dried."

The proprietor set down his leatherwork, walked over, and stood across the counter from us.

"I'm all out of beef. I've got some salt pork, and some dried persimmons. Some biscuit flour...."

"All right," I said. "We'll take twenty pounds of the pork, ten of the persimmons, and ten of the flour.... five pounds of salt, three blankets—new, and clean—and that iron frying pan hanging there, if it's for sale. Do you have a lid for it?"

"I'll sell it to you, but there's no lid."

"I'll take it anyway. Coffee?"

"I have some, but it's mine, and it'll come dear."

"How dear?"

"Fifty cents a pound … and you can take it or leave it. It's roasted."

"We'll take a pound."

"Sugar?" Wačhiwi said, putting a hand on my shoulder.

"You have sugar?" I said.

"I've got some back there."

"We'll take some of that, then. Say, a half-pound? Do you have any tobacco?"

"No tobacco. Creeks took it all. That it?"

I turned to Wačhiwi. She nodded.

"Yes."

"It'll take me a minute to gather it up, and I need to see your coin first.… Do I know you from somewhere?"

I set a five-dollar bill on the splintered counter. "No."

He nodded as if he'd expected my answer, but his expression was doubtful. The look made me uneasy.

"I'll need another dollar," he said, gazing at me stonily.

I set one on top of the five.

"That should cover it," he said, making the five disappear. He stood there a few seconds longer, staring at me from across the counter, before he finally turned away and disappeared into a narrow passageway in the shelving.

"Funny how much Indians like sugar," the man in the rocker said. "I never met a one that wouldn't just about fall

all over themselves to get some. I see your squaw even knows the word."

I set the Spencer on the counter and turned to him but didn't speak.

"I was just making conversation," he said. His words were penitent, his expression was not.

Wačhiwi and I stood in silence at the counter for another ten minutes before the proprietor returned with a wood crate filled with our purchases, the two rolled up blankets teetering on the top. He set it on the counter in front of us.

"Are you sure you aren't mistaken? I'd swear we've met before."

I picked up the crate, Wačhiwi lifted the blankets from the top. "Thank you for the goods," I said, turning away and heading for the door.

"You two take care, now," the man in the rocker said.

I didn't reply.

Once we were outside, I packed the horses in a hurry. I tossed the empty crate up onto the store's porch and gave Wačhiwi a hand up onto Rose. I had a dark feeling and wanted to get as far from the trading post as I could, as quickly as I could.

Wačhiwi glanced warily up at the store.

"That was the same man I showed your wanted poster to when I was here before," I said.

I'd shown the poster to Wačhiwi that morning. She marveled over the accuracy of the likeness.

"He knew you," she said, wheeling Rose around. "Even without the hair on your face."

"You're right, he did."

It was full dark before we made five miles and the feeling of foreboding I had only worsened as we rode. The terrain was flat and grassy, so that was all right, but Wačhiwi was an inexperienced rider and there still wasn't much of a moon to speak of. I resigned myself to a third night with no sleep, something I'd done many times during the war. I hoped Wačhiwi would have the grit to ride with me through the night.

I needn't have worried. She rode all night and, outside of a rest and water stop for the horses, all through that next day. We'd come to an area of buttes and mesas—in what is now northern Oklahoma—and in the late afternoon I began searching for a place to camp that would provide sufficient cover and give us a good view of anyone approaching. Luck came to us in the form of a shallow cave that was mostly obscured by several massive chunks of broken-away mesa.

I strung a rope across the opening of the cave and tethered Evelyn and Rose to it. While I unpacked them, Wačhiwi tended to the wound on her ankle left by the iron shackle. She crushed some of the yarrow in the frying pan, mixed it with a few drops of water, and then sat against the wall of the cave and smeared it all over the wound.

After a meal of dried persimmons, we agreed we'd sleep in shifts. I took the first watch as the sun dropped below the horizon in the west. Even with the concern of being tracked, it was all I could do to keep my eyes open past midnight. I smoked my pipe until my throat was raw, just trying to stay awake. Finally, around one a.m. I caught myself dozing and woke Wačhiwi. I showed her how to work the Spencer and told her to shoot anything that appeared this side of the horses.

I must have been asleep before my head was all the way down on the spare shirt I used as a pillow, and it seemed I'd just lay down when I was shaken awake.

"It's past dawn," Wačhiwi said, kneeling over me. "There's coffee. I lit a small fire, only enough to boil the water and cook some of the pork."

"Coffee sounds good," I said, sitting up. From the quality of the light coming into the cave, I figured it was well past dawn.

"Sugar?"

"Yes, thank you."

She walked over near the cave entrance where she'd set her fire and poured coffee into my only tin cup. She pinched some sugar out of the small sack and dropped it in, seemed to consider briefly, and then dropped in another pinch. The frying pan was sitting on a rock near the fire; she carried both it and the cup of coffee back over and sat beside me. She sipped at the coffee and smiled. "It's good," she said, passing me the cup.

While I slept she'd braided her hair and changed into a pair of wool trousers and a blue cotton button-up shirt. Even with the yellowing bruise on her face, she was beyond beautiful.

We shared the coffee and then ate the small pieces of the salt pork she'd fried up. Afterward we repacked Evelyn and Rose and were on our way.

As the weeks passed, my fear of pursuit gradually faded. The days became routine: we were up with the sun, shared coffee, and ate a small breakfast before saddling the horses and moving out. We practiced Lakota while we rode, hers was rusty, but it improved quickly and she taught me a great deal that I hadn't learned from my time with Standing

Elk. We'd start looking for a suitable place to camp in the late afternoon and would have it set by nightfall. Some evenings I'd put out snares and we'd get rabbit or ground squirrel for breakfast. We made it to Powder River country without incident, and by then my mind was sitting easy.

The camp by the lake had been abandoned—the only sign anyone was ever there were the remnants of a stone fish trap jutting out into the blue water. It was easy enough for me to follow the movement of over two thousand souls, though, and on the gray and snowy afternoon of December 7, 1866, we were escorted by a party of Lakota warriors to Red Cloud's new camp on the Tongue River.

Sentries had spotted us about three miles from the camp. We stopped the horses and waited as the large group of riders came at us at a hard gallop. When they reached us, we were encircled. No one raised a weapon. They were painted as if for battle, as were their horses. One man moved forward and reined in his mount directly in front of us. His hair was streaked with gray and his face paint didn't hide the rope-like scar that ran from his temple all the way down to his neck and then disappeared under his deer hide war shirt. I couldn't help but to think of Henry. Wačhiwi began to speak quickly, in halting Lakota. He listened patiently, his expression going from guarded and suspicious to one of glad astonishment as she gave him a very abridged account of who she was and where she'd been. His name was Mathósapa—Black Bear. He was Oglala Lakota.

We were led immediately to Red Cloud's lodge where the chief welcomed us warmly. We were brought smoked buffalo meat and some peppery greens and ate by the fire while someone fetched Wačhiwi's mother, Zitkala-ša—Red Bird.

Zitkala-ša screamed in delight and ran to the daughter she'd not seen in over ten years, the daughter she'd believed dead. The reunion was moving. There were perhaps a dozen people inside the lodge, and there wasn't a dry eye among them, myself included.

As hospitable as Red Cloud was, it was apparent that he was distracted. After Wačhiwi told her story, judiciously leaving out most of the details of her suffering at the hands of the McBain's, Red Cloud passed a pipe and spoke of war.

"Little White Chief Carrington and his bluecoats continue to build their forts," he said in Lakota. "With the soldiers' help, more whites are coming. They come with their wagons and their tools to take the yellow metal from the mountains and rivers. They kill our game and trade whiskey to some numbers of us who do not know better. We are no longer standing aside while the whites take whatever they want. The white commissioners lie, and the Great Father's ears are deaf to us. I am Red Cloud, and I will not allow my people to become beggars to the whites. We are at war with the whites, and we will defeat them. Tomorrow I leave with our warriors to attack the bluecoats and finally drive them away from our land, but for today, you are here with a great gift, and I am glad.

"A long time ago, I was friends with white men. Men who traded fairly and did not try to take what was not for sale or given as gifts. But those men are no longer, and another kind of white man comes. These are not good men. You are as the white men of my youth. You have returned this woman, Wačhiwi, to us, and I see that you are a friend. For this you will have a lodge among our people. This is my word. You are welcome to stay here if it is what you desire."

That afternoon Red Cloud gave me a lodge, an unadorned deer hide shirt, winter leggings, and four buffalo hides. The significance of the gifts wasn't lost to me, though a part of me knew I didn't deserve them. As much as I respected and admired Red Cloud, I didn't do what I did for him, or the Lakota people. I did it for Wačhiwi. And I did it for me. I loved her, and love can be selfish. I proved that, some time later.

I had just finished unpacking Evelyn and Rose—Wačhiwi had said goodbye and walked the quarter mile downriver to her mother's lodge. I was unsuccessfully trying to figure out how to work the lodge's smoke flaps when Black Bear walked up. He stood there with his arms folded, watching me while I struggled with the two fifteen-foot lodge poles that acted as arms to open and close the smoke flaps. A fire ring had previously been constructed in the lodge and a supply of wood was stacked outside, so I'd started a fire before unburdening the horses. It turned out the smoke flaps were closed, and the lodge filled with smoke before I knew it. I turned to Black Bear and he was smiling wryly.

"Let me show you," he said in Lakota, as he stepped forward and took control of one of the poles.

He leaned into his work and planted one end of the lodge pole firmly in the ground so that it ran up to the smoke flap at a severe angle. Then he did the same with the other one. When he was finished, he pulled them both up and closed the flaps again. He stepped aside.

"Now you," he said.

I did it the way he showed me. It was remarkably easy and I felt the fool for not figuring it out on my own. He smiled and nodded. "Red Cloud seeks your companionship," he said in Lakota.

I followed him back to Red Cloud's lodge, and three men and two women were there, sitting around the low fire along with Red Cloud. I recognized one of them as Tȟatȟáŋka Íyotake—Sitting Bull, and one of the women had been present both times I'd visited Red Cloud's lodge. She was around Red Cloud's age and kindly of face. I learned later that she was Red Cloud's wife, Wínyan Hinhán—Owl Woman.

Red Cloud smiled and bid Black Bear and I sit. Owl Woman leaned over the fire and lit a bundle of what I learned later was dried sage. She stood and held the smoldering bundle in front of Red Cloud's chest. He held a feather—a hawk tail feather. The quill was wrapped in a thin hide thong. He let the smoke drift over the feather as he turned it slowly above the bundle. He then used the feather to wave the smoke toward him. As the smoke haloed his face and hair, he closed his eyes and softly mumbled some words I couldn't quite hear. He passed the feather to Sitting Bull, who was seated on his right, and Owl Woman moved the bundle of sage in front him. Sitting Bull used the feather to direct the smoke over him as Red Cloud did. The process was repeated, and I did as the others when the feather and bundle reached me. The sage smoke was oddly comforting, and to this day I place it as one of the most wonderful smells on Earth. I wish I could smell it right now, but I lost the honor and privilege of smudging long ago.

When the circle was completed, Owl Woman handed the hawk feather back to Red Cloud and placed what was left of the still smoking bundle of sage in a small bone bowl at the edge of the fire. Red Cloud held the feather in front of his face and looked at it closely.

"This feather came to me the day that you and Standing Elk of the Cheyenne departed," he said in Lakota. "I knew that the Great Spirit sent this feather for you, and I knew at that moment you were Wačhiwi's protector in this world, and that you would return her to us."

He the leaned forward and held the feather out to me. Its tiger-looking stripes glowed in the firelight. "Piláymaya," I said, taking the gift.

He signed *good* and smiled at me in a fatherly way that made me think of my own father. Sitting Bull made eye contact with me. He didn't smile, but he gave me a short nod. I might have appreciated it more if I'd known him better. Sitting Bull's hatred for all things white ran deep, and the simple nod meant a great deal.

After the smudging and being presented with the gift of the hawk feather, the entire Lakota camp, along with the nearby Cheyenne and Arapaho people, celebrated Wačhiwi's return. Neither the cold nor the cloud of ongoing war with the United States dampened the revelry. There were huge bonfires spaced along the river from one end of the miles-long camp to the other. There was buffalo, deer, and fish, and some bitter but somehow delicious roots, and singing and dancing; more dancing than I'd ever seen.

For most of the celebration, I sat, leaning against my lodge by the open entrance. I ate my fill and worked on smoking the last of my tobacco—I'd given most of what I had left to Red Cloud. Wachiwi sat with me for a time. She looked beautiful in her happiness, her face glowing in the gold firelight emanating from the inside of the lodge. She admired the hawk feather. She told me I should display it.

“Where?” I said.

“Here” She touched the hair behind my right ear.

I handed her the feather. She took it and tied it into my hair by the length of hide thong wrapped around the quill. I reached up and felt it. She’d tied the feather to match the length of my hair, which was nearing my shoulders at the time.

She leaned back and admired her work. “You look *strong*,” she said playfully.

At that moment her mother, Red Bird, arrived and took her hand, insisting that she go with her to meet some people. Red Bird glanced at me. She smiled but looked troubled. Wačhiwi let herself be led away. I picked up my pipe, dug a match from my pocket and struck it. I smoked slowly and watched the celebration. After some time, Black Bear arrived. He was carrying a wood bowl with a large pile of smoked fish chunks in it. He squatted and held the bowl out. I was already full, but I took several pieces of the offered food. It was delicious. We sat and ate in silence—something I appreciated about him right away—and then I shared the last of my tobacco with him.

The next morning I awoke, satisfyingly warm under a buffalo hide, although I’d let the fire burn out in the night. I dressed, and then stirred up the coals from where they slumbered under a few inches of ash. I threw some dried prairie grass on them and rekindled the fire, adding a few twigs, and then some pieces of broken lodge pole. I poked at the growing blaze with a stick, trying to shed the troubled dreams of Henry and Standing Elk that had come to me in the night. I felt morose and out of sorts as I prepared coffee. I missed my friends, and was ashamed that I'd most likely turned them both into wanted posters. And Henry being a negro, and having that scar, wouldn't be very hard to pick out just about anywhere he ended up. At the same time, I felt fortunate to have had them there with me at the McBain ranch. I didn't believe I would have succeeded in freeing Wačhiwi without them. And after all the years I've lived and all the miles I've traveled, I still don't.

With some difficulty I convinced myself to set it aside. It was done. Even at twenty, I knew I couldn't go back.

My thoughts drifted to Wačhiwi. Now that she was where she belonged, was there more for her and I, or had I finished playing my part in her life?

When the coffee was done, I poured a cup. It had never been usual for me to take sugar before I met Wačhiwi, but I'd acquired a taste for it and so I added a pinch. I set the sack of coffee and the sack of sugar aside, thinking I'd give them both to her later. I sat by the fire and sipped the coffee, missing sharing the morning cup with her. I looked around the lodge and wondered what I should do. I'd spent the last year and some months in the saddle; on a quest, so to speak. Now, for the first time since landing in Sherman after the war, I wondered what was next. Red Cloud said that I was welcome to stay, and I believed he meant it, but I wondered what that would look like. I wasn't Indian, and even after my time with Standing Elk, their ways were mostly a mystery to me.

I heard a sound from behind me and I turned. The hide door to the lodge was shaking.

"Thimá hiyú wo," I said—*Come in.*

Black Bear pushed back the hide and entered. I invited him to sit and then offered him my coffee. He accepted the cup and sipped at it. He smiled and nodded and handed it back to me. He sat there for a long moment, plainly discomfited. Finally, he spoke.

"Red Cloud bid me speak with you," he said in Lakota. "There is talk among some of the men … and a few of the women. You were right to bring Wačhiwi to us, but some question her life among the whites. Red Cloud and some of the other elders would not have this talk, but people will do as they will. They talk because it is shameful to the Lakota for a woman to … lay with a man, without the marriage ceremony—"

"None of you can know what happened, or didn't happen to Wačhiwi while she was with the … the whites," I said, a little too defensively. "She was taken as a child and kept a prisoner."

Black Bear put up his hands. "It is not my wish, or Red Cloud's, to anger you, but we would have you understand. We do not know the ways of whites in these matters, and it is not for us to say what is right or wrong for them and their women, but these are old ways for the Lakota.… If she were to marry, all would soon be forgotten, but there may be no suitors among the men who are ready, and some may even have the desire to send her from here. You came to us first as a messenger of the Great Father, yet now you are here as a friend. Red Cloud believes you to be the one who should marry Wačhiwi.… Do you have any more horses?"

"He thinks Wačhiwi and I should marry?" I said, trying to contain my excitement.

Black Bear smiled. "Yes. I said this. Do you have more horses?"

"No. Just one. The other one doesn't belong to me."

"It is as Red Cloud feared. You are poor. We will need to find another way. For the Lakota, a man who has many horses, or has been successful against his enemy, or is a great hunter—this is a man who is suitable to marry. Once, your influence with the whites would have been enough for you to be seen as worthy to marry a Lakota woman, but no more. We no longer care about friendship with the whites, or their gifts."

"I'm a good hunter," I said, enamored with the thought of marrying Wačhiwi. "Better than most."

"I'm certain that is true, but that has not been proven among us," he said.

"What if she doesn't want to marry me?"

He laughed at this. "Wačhiwi's father no longer walks in this world. If you are an acceptable suitor, the decision will be Red Cloud's, but he will agree with Red Bird's thoughts. Her medicine is strong and her word is valued."

"I'd still want to speak with her first," I said.

"You should not speak with her until you are ready to offer her a marriage token, and provide gifts to her family. We closed our eyes last night, because you do not yet know our ways. Red Bird has spoken to Wačhiwi of this. She should have known but has been living the ways of the whites for too many winters."

"What is a marriage token?"

He reached down his shirt and pulled out a beaded necklace.

"This was given to me by my wife, before our marriage, but it can be something else."

"Like a wedding ring," I said as much to myself as to Black Bear.

He waved his hand and continued. "If you offer her a token, and she accepts it, and gives you one in return, then she has accepted your offer of marriage. But, if Red Bird and Red Cloud do not approve, then you still cannot marry."

Black Bear stood, nodded to me, and started away.

"What am I supposed to do?" I said.

"With this I can't help you," he said, and disappeared through the door.

I stared after him, bewildered. A moment later his face reappeared in the doorway.

"Perhaps if you rode toward the setting sun, Wakan Tanka will show you the way …" He smiled an odd, dry smile, and then was gone.

I stayed there by the fire for some time, drinking coffee, while I fried up a piece of the salt pork. I thought about what Black Bear said, and came to the conclusion that it was a riddle; his way of helping me without helping me. I surmised there was probably good hunting to the west, maybe even a buffalo herd was wintering in the area and Black Bear knew about it. Either that or he was making sport of me, and I didn't get the sense that was what he was doing. So, I thought if I could make some good kills, and offer the meat and hides to Red Bird, then my proposal might be accepted by her and Red Cloud. Afterward, it was a matter of Wačhiwi accepting—or rejecting—my wedding token, whatever that turned out to be. I wasn't much of an artisan.

The prospect of marriage aside—if she would even have me—the thought of *doing* something, something I understood, was appealing. Suddenly the uncertain feeling I'd had earlier in the morning was gone. For the moment, at least, I had a purpose.

I began packing Evelyn and Rose immediately after eating my breakfast. I divided what was left of the salt pork in two—Wačhiwi and I had eaten all of the persimmons and flour—and put half of it aside with the remaining coffee and sugar. I'd miss the coffee in the mornings, but I wanted Wačhiwi to have it, and I'd done without many times before. I thought about giving her some salt, but thought I may need it to preserve meat. When I was finished, I went searching for Black Bear.

The lodges were staggered along the river. My nearest neighbor was sixty feet or so upstream. I started there. No one was about so I moved on, working my way upstream on foot. The camp seemed strangely empty, and I realized I'd slept through the departure of the war party. *War Party.* The term sat heavy with me and memories of the war between the states—*my war*—and the hollowness of it, invaded my thoughts as I walked.

The war was all but over when what was left of our company was marching south to a village named Newtonia, where we were to meet up with General Thomson's brigade. One morning before breaking camp, our commanding officer sent a dozen of us out to forage. We'd shoot game if we could find any, but mostly we'd become proficient at taking from poor Missourians who didn't have much to begin with. All in the name of the Confederacy, of course.

About a mile from the camp we came upon a dense pawpaw thicket. We worked our way through, stopping here and there to scavenge any fruit that had been missed by the animals. There wasn't much, and what was there was overripe. For men half-starved it was still a blessing.

Finally, the thicket gave way to a clearing, and the first few of us to walk out into the open found ourselves staring down the rifle barrels of a company of Union soldiers perhaps forty strong. They'd heard us in the thicket and had readied themselves in an infantry line, about thirty feet away. It was close enough to see they weren't fresh. Thin and haggard, their uniforms soiled, these men didn't look much better than we did. Haggard or not, though, they had us cold. We dropped our rifles and waited to find out whether we'd be taken as prisoners, or be shot.

"Tell the rest of your boys to come out," a man wearing captain's bars said.

The rest of our men stepped out, arms raised.

"Is that all of you?"

No one answered, so I did. "Yes, sir."

"You have any food?"

"Nothing to speak of," I said. "We have some pawpaw."

"We ate so much of that last night, we had a man shat himself," the captain said.

"It'll do it," I agreed.

"Are you boys spoiling for a fight?"

We all looked at each other, and then shook our heads. "No, sir," I said.

"Well that's fine," he said, lowering his rifle. "I think we've all seen enough of it." He turned to the man on his left and nodded westward.

'Let's go," the man said to the others. The soldiers slowly lowered their rifles.

All save one.

"These men are the enemy, sir," he said, keeping his rifle sighted on us.

"Then you stay and fight your war, Nichols," the captain said.

The other men had already turned and walked away, heads down, many shambling like weary Dickension ghosts. The captain fell in with them. From what I saw, none of them looked back.

The lone rifleman stood there for a moment longer, then dropped his rifle, as if it had suddenly become too heavy. He was beardless and his face was smeared with dirt. He stared across the clearing at us with his shoulders hunched and his arms dangling at his sides. I couldn't be certain but I thought he was weeping. He turned and followed the others, leaving the rifle where it lay.

We stared after them, too shaken to speak, and watched them disappear into the woods on the other side of the clearing.

We all agreed not to speak of the encounter with the other men, and as far as I know, none did.

I found Black Bear an hour later near a sharp bend in the river, at the northeast end of the camp. There was a corral, fashioned from lodge poles which had been fastened with rope to some trees that by chance had grown in a rough circle. The corral held a hundred or more horses. Black Bear was there with forty or so other men, preparing to leave, it appeared.

"Leaving?" I said in Lakota.

"We have been left to protect the camp. Other men circled and watched during the night. Now they must rest."

"I'm also leaving. I'll be riding westward."

Black Bear smiled and signed, *Good.*

I held out the small sacks of coffee, sugar, and salt pork. "Would you give these to Wačhiwi?"

He nodded and took the sacks. I nodded in return and started away.

"HínyankÁ!" he said, then "*Wait*!"

I turned, eyebrows raised.

"I know some white man words," he said, striding forward and handing me a coil of rope. It looked to be fifty or sixty feet.

"Piláymaya ..." I said. "... I have nothing to give you."

He waved his free hand and smiled while shaking his head. It was clear he thought what I'd said was foolish.

Chapter 7

It was early afternoon when I rode out of the camp. The sky was the color of lead, and there was a light snow falling, adding to the few inches of powder already dusting the high prairie. It was cold, but not cold enough that I felt the need to turn up my coat collar.

Evelyn trotted easily and Rose kept in time, trailing behind on a leader. I kept my eyes moving, searching for sign, but I saw none in the immediate vicinity of the camp. Several miles out, I came across a trail left by a small group of doe, but I didn't think a few deer were what I was looking for.

I camped the first night in a copse of trees. It offered some protection from the wind, which had come up in the late afternoon. I remember that damned wind seemed intent on blowing snow into every breach in my clothing. I started a fire and wrapped myself in one of the two buffalo hides I'd packed. Sitting as close to the flames as I could, while eating a supper of salt pork, I wished for some tobacco and a good book.

The next morning dawned clear and the temperature had dropped considerably. I cut a two-foot-long thong from the buffalo hide I'd slept under and then cut some holes near where the animal's neck would have been. I wrapped the hide around me and threaded the thong through the holes so I could tie it like a cloak. I forwent breakfast and got moving before the sun was much more than two fingers over the eastern horizon.

I saw them before they saw me; two people sitting under a close-set pair of trees a quarter mile off. The sun was at my back at around ten o'clock. As I got closer, one of them—a man—lifted his head and put a hand up to shade his eyes. The other didn't move. I removed the Spencer from its scabbard and laid it across my lap.

"Háu," I said as I approached, thinking he was likely Lakota.

The man stood. He was sickly and thin. I put him in his thirties. He was dressed in a well-worn, plain hide shirt and equally worn hide trousers. He was shoeless, and he was shivering violently. The other, an old woman, was unquestionably dead. Out of reflex, I looked back the way I had come. I had to have traveled at least thirty miles from Red Cloud's camp. I wondered if there was another Indian camp nearby.

His look was both wary and hopeful. "Háu," he said in return.

He didn't appear armed, so I dismounted but held onto the Spencer.

"Do you need help?" I said in Lakota.

"I'm cold and hungry."

I cocked my head toward the woman.

"She is my mother," he said. "She walks in the Spirit World."

"What is your name?"

His eyes kept darting to the Spencer. "Zičáȟota," he said. I reached for the word and it came—*Squirrel.*

"I'm Everett Ward," I said.... "A friend."

After a moment of thought, I slid the Spencer back in the scabbard. I didn't have much salt pork left, but I got into my saddlebags and cut him a small portion anyway. I handed it over and he returned to sit by his mother, where she sat propped against one of the trees, her legs splayed out in front of her as if she were taking a rest. I wondered briefly if she'd died sitting there that way. While he ate the pork I went about untying the second buffalo hide from Rose. When I had it free, I walked it over and dropped it at his feet. He looked at it and then back at me.

"It's yours," I said. "Don't leave, I'll be back with more food."

I rode back the way I'd come because I'd spotted more fresh deer sign not a half hour before. There were quite a few sets of tracks, and I thought I had a fair chance finding something.

I followed the first trail I came to for a mile or so, but soon saw sign that the deer had been frightened by something and had lit out at a gallop. I doubled back and rode a little further east where I came upon other tracks. I followed them north, and after a couple of miles I spotted a glimmer of water in the distance. There were no trees nearby but I found a healthy growth of scrub to tether the horses to. I took the Spencer and headed toward the glimmer. As I got closer I could see it was a creek or small river.

Fortune was on my side. When I was about a hundred yards from the stream, I could see ten or twelve deer grazing near the bank, their tan hides distinct against the whiteness of the snow. They'd spotted me, but didn't run. They only watched. I slowly raised the Spencer and picked out the closest one. It was a clean shot and she dropped and didn't move. The rest were gone before I could lower the rifle.

I walked back and retrieved the horses, then dragged the doe a little ways upstream to a medium-sized cottonwood that had a low enough branch for me to hang her from. I suspended her by her hind legs and let her bleed out for a while before throwing her over Rose and tying her on. It didn't take long to ride back to where I'd found Squirrel. He was right where I left him, sitting against the tree by his mother.

I dismounted and began untying the doe.

"Do you have a knife?" I said.

He nodded and picked up a small bundle that sat on the ground between him and his mother. He removed a wood-handled knife, stood, and and held it up.

"Good," I said.

I dropped the doe to the ground and then cut off one of the haunches with my own knife. He hurried over and took the doe's front legs and dragged her a few feet away. He began the process of skinning her.

I wiped off my blade and pointed it at the doe. "That should keep you for a while. I can take you to the Lakota camp when I come back through."

He looked up from his work and shook his head vehemently.

I was bemused.

"Where did you come from?" I said. "Were you with Red Cloud?"

He returned his attention to the doe but nodded. I began to have the sense that he might be a bit simple.

I considered pressing further but decided not to. I'd extend the offer again if he was still by the tree when I returned. I looked around and didn't see any evidence of a campfire. I shook several matches from my box, made certain I had his attention, and then struck one. It appeared to me he knew what they were, so I stepped over and set them on the little bundle he'd been storing his knife in. This took me near his mother, who smelled of corruption even in the cold. He stood up fast, as if he might need to protect her, but I backed away with my hands up. This seemed to satisfy him. I picked up the haunch I'd cut from the doe, tied it to Rose and continued on west.

I was four days out—some hundred miles from the Lakota camp—when my fortune changed. I was in an area of low, rolling hills. The sky had been spitting snow off and on since the night before and there was six inches on the ground. I ascended a hill, and when I reached the crest, I could see a swath of prairie a quarter-mile wide, where the snow had been chewed up, exposing the grass and mud beneath. The trail ran north to south. My first thought was buffalo, but when I reached the bottom of the hill, I discovered it was horses. More than two hundred of them, from the look.

I followed the trail south for two days. On the third I caught up with the herd.

Mustangs.

I'd just come up a rise when I spotted them below, maybe a mile-and-a-half out. I backed down the side of the hill so I could get out of the wind and stay out of sight. Now a wild horse is as skittish as any other animal that isn't accustomed to the company of humans, and the last thing I wanted to do was scare them off. They can't see as well as we can, and the winds were coming from the southeast, which was helpful, but I kept my distance anyway.

Even at twenty-one, I knew horses. I had a natural feel for them. But I'd never tried to capture any wild ones. I didn't have the means to build a corral and trap them, and both Evelyn and Rose were too old to give chase so I couldn't rope any. In the end I decided to follow them and study their movements.

Their course remained steady to the south, but there was no consistency to how far they traveled each day. That first day they moved about five miles, the second, two. On the third they didn't move at all. On the afternoon of the fifth day, they arrived at the confluence of the Bighorn and Little Bighorn rivers. It was there I worked out a tack.

The water was high and the confluence was both wide and deep. Just how deep, I couldn't tell from a distance, but I could see it was deep enough that a horse couldn't cross it at a run.

The herd was bunched up on the east side of the river, drinking their fill and grazing in the grassy crook made by the two rivers. My plan was simple enough: startle the horses and run them into the water, where they'd be slower and easier to rope. I thought that if all went well and I was a little bit lucky, I could get two or three of them roped, led to the bank, and tied off to a tree, before they all got across or turned back the way they'd come. Doing it without getting killed would be the trick. I'd never witnessed a stampede of two hundred frightened and angry mustangs, but I knew the lightest of them weighed somewhere around seven hundred pounds, and I'd been bitten, charged, kicked, and thrown enough times to know that even a single horse can be as dangerous as all-get-out, under the right circumstances.

I removed all of my gear from Evelyn, save my rope and saddle, and put it on Rose, who I tethered a half mile downstream of the confluence, where I felt comfortable she'd be well away from trouble. I circled back around to the east and then charged Evelyn toward them, shouting a war-cry and firing the Spencer in the air. The move worked and most of the horses plunged into the water and started across. Some panicked and headed towards me, and others galloped off upstream, but they were the minority. As we neared the river I slid the Spencer back into the scabbard and grabbed up one of the lengths of rope I'd prepared; I'd cut the rope Black Bear had given me into three pieces, and I had two good lengths of my own. Evelyn slowed slightly before she hit the water in order to avoid a horse that had gone over and was working to right itself. Despite the water being breast deep on her, she responded to my commands in the way you'd expect from an experienced stock horse, and we managed to avoid being swept into the fray. I roped the first horse—a good-sized chestnut—from only a few feet away. Strangely, it didn't fight much—not as much as I expected, anyway. I pulled the rope tight and pivoted Evelyn around, working her back up the low bank to a tree I'd marked in my mind as a hitching post. As soon as I reached it, I leapt from Evelyn and quickly tethered the chestnut. I remounted and saw the lead horses were already climbing the bank on the other side of the river. There were still plenty in the water, though, and still more charging in to follow the leaders. We pounded back to the water and I spotted a gray and white paint about twenty feet out and directed Evelyn toward it. We caught the paint a third of the way across and I roped it on my second try. It tried to shake off the rope and lost its footing. It went part of the way down and nearly took us with it, but Evelyn held her feet and backed a step to give some slack. The paint gained its feet and Evelyn moved steadily toward the bank. With some effort she made it with the paint still in tow. We got it up alongside the chestnut, I tied it off and Evelyn and I headed back. We weren't to get anymore horses that day, though.

Half the herd was already up the far bank and galloping off west, but there were still forty or more horses in the water. The rest had scattered to all possible points on the east side of the river. We hit the water again; Evelyn was almost belly-deep when a horse came from behind and stumbled into her flank. She almost kept her balance—*almost*. She lost the fight when another horse ran into the first one. We went down and the first horse went down on top of us. I grabbed Evelyn's mane and managed to stay with her. Stars exploded in my head as the offending horse kicked me in its frenzy to stand. Evelyn struggled up and dragged me with her as she made for the bank in a near panic. I got her stopped fifty feet or so downstream. I could feel a goose-egg rising from my skull, and I was soaked to the bone and half frozen, but otherwise I was all right. It didn't even enter my mind to try for another one of the mustangs.

Five minutes later it was over, and outside of the whispered babble of the river, silence once again prevailed. Two drowned horses lay in the water. I felt regret about that. I found my hat a hundred feet downstream, caught up in the branches of a fallen tree.

I fetched Rose and set camp a few yards from where the new horses were tethered. The two mustangs stamped and chuffed nervously while testing the strength of the ropes, with frequent attempts to back away from the tree. They were both mares, and they both seemed healthy, so that was good. I tethered both Evelyn and Rose close by and this seem to calm them a bit.

I spent the next several days camped there by the Bighorn. Wanting to give Evelyn a good rest, I used Rose to drag the drowned horses from the water and take them a mile from the camp, where I left them for the wolves. I spent the remainder of the time working the new horses. It was a dangerous business, having no corral to contain them. I settled for tying myself on. I knew then it was foolish, but so was the whole affair. Young men do foolish things. I was fortunate, and neither of them went down. The paint ran flat-out for at least ten miles the first time I rode her, though. This was after she figured-out she couldn't throw me off.

On December 21, 1866, sore and bruised, I broke camp and moved out with the two new mares in tow. I couldn't know it at the time, but on that very day Red Cloud and his Lakota, along with a confederation of Cheyenne and Arapaho chiefs and warriors, was making good on his promise to attack white soldiers.

As I worked my way east, back toward the Lakota camp, I hunted. Two days out of my camp by the Bighorn River, I shot an elk. The small herd was all I saw of elk on that journey, but there were plenty of deer. By the time I reached the tree where I'd first found Squirrel, I had over five hundred pounds of butchered and salted meat. I figured I'd share some of the meat with him and ask him to accompany me back to the Lakota camp on the Tongue, but he was gone.

It was the first time I saw a burial tree.

Squirrel had used his knife to cut down some wrist-thick branches and then lashed them between the two trees to make the supports for an elevated platform. It looked like a suspended travois. It was about eight feet from the ground. He'd cut some strips from the buffalo hide I'd left him and used them for the lashing. Then he'd taken smaller branches and laid them crossways and lashed them to the larger branches. Afterward, he'd somehow managed to hoist his mother up onto it. He'd covered her with the remainder of the buffalo hide. I studied the ground and saw his tracks heading off north. I gave him the buffalo hide with the hope he would make some shoes from a piece of it, but his tracks showed he was still barefoot. I decided to follow and try to convince him to come with me. It was unlikely he'd survive much longer out on his own.

I found him five miles to the north, face-down in the shallow snow. He'd been dead at least a day.

Now I wasn't a religious man, and I'm still not. It was rarer in those days, but my mother and father didn't attend church, and never spoke much of God or the depth of their belief. The most Clyde and I ever heard of it from either of them was through the occasional holiday grace. Most of what I learned about religion, I learned during the war. And I knew almost nothing of Indian religion. Not then, anyway. Standing Elk spoke of the Spirit and his visions now and then, but that was about it.

I mention it, because I was at a loss of what to do with Squirrel. I wouldn't leave him there in the snow, but after seeing what he did with his mother, I wondered if it would be some sort of sacrilege to bury him. I thought about taking him back to the Lakota camp, but I was concerned about breaking a Lakota convention I knew nothing of.

I stood over him for quite some time before the obvious occurred to me. I decided to place him with his mother. Hopefully, it's what he would have wanted.

I learned later that Squirrel was the one who broke convention by putting his mother's remains on a scaffold in the first place; a ritual that was reserved for men. He must have loved her very much.

I camped in a thicket of scrub that night, a few miles east of Squirrel and his mother's burial tree. In the early morning hours a storm rolled in, and the snow came with an earnestness I hadn't experienced in some time. The day dawned a near white-out, so I dug in and stayed put. The following morning it was still stormy, but it had lightened up enough so I could see where I was going. I rode out wrapped tightly in my buffalo hide and hunched over in the saddle.

Under normal conditions, I would have made it back to the Lakota camp in one long day's ride. Tired from travel and a lack of sleep, with two feet of snow on the ground, the remainder of the journey took me three. On that third day, the storm broke and the sun shone so bright its reflection off the new snow was almost blinding. I rode into the camp shortly after noon, and headed straight for Wačhiwi's mother's lodge.

It appeared that most of the men were still away, but I drew the eyes of curious women and children, and not a few old men, as I made my way up the river through the lodges. I tethered the new horses, along with their burden of meat, to the post outside of Red Bird's lodge. I didn't wait to see if anyone was inside.

Afterward, I went to my lodge. I unloaded Evelyn and Rose, stowed the fresh meat Rose had been carrying in the snow outside, and then lit a fire. I laid down beside it, and was asleep in moments.

I slept straight through to the next morning. When I awoke, I rekindled the fire, melted some snow in my cookpot, and cleaned myself. Before washing my hair, I carefully removed the hawk feather. I looked it over and was happy to see it hadn't been damaged from my swim in the Bighorn. After dressing, I spitted and cooked some elk meat while I thought about what to do next.

I stayed at the lodge through the morning, screwing up my courage. I tooled around, brushing out my coat and organizing my few possessions. Finally, I took the feather and walked up river to Wačhiwi's mother's lodge. I didn't go right up to it, I just loitered nearby on the riverbank. The two horses were still tethered to the post, but they had been unloaded.

Over the next two hours, as I paced around and skipped stones in the river, I began to notice that quite a few people from the camp had sauntered up and were milling about the area. Again, they were mostly women, and they were pointedly not looking my way.

I was half-heartedly whittling on a piece of driftwood with my father's jackknife when I caught movement from Red Bird's lodge. Wačhiwi had come out. Her hair was in two braids and she was wearing a beaded hide dress with calf-high winter boots. She was beautiful beyond words.

The way the lodges were staged-out caused the open space between them and the river to be a weave-work of paths. She walked toward the river on one that would take her past where I was sitting. She glanced my way, briefly, and then stopped to talk to a group of women, who I now thought of as onlookers. As I pretended not to watch them, I could see Black Bear standing near a lodge upriver. I hadn't noticed him there before. He was speaking with an old man, but his eyes were on me.

Wačhiwi broke away from the group and continued down the path. When she neared, I dropped the piece of driftwood, pocketed my knife, and then stood and waited.

She stopped in front of me, looking expectant. She wore a tiny smile that just touched the corner of her mouth.

I removed the hawk feather from my coat pocket.

Her eyes darted to the feather and her face clouded with a look of alarm. She held my eyes and shook her head almost imperceptivity.

I slid it back in my pocket and thought frantically. After several awkward seconds I did the only thing I could think of to do: I removed my father's jackknife from my trouser pocket and held it out to her.

Her smile returned. This time it wasn't contained to just the corner of her mouth. She took the knife, turning it over slowly, examining it. This made me smile, because she'd seen the knife, and even used it herself, on more than one occasion. "Piláymaya," she said, and then dropped it into a hide sack she had tied to the waist of her dress. After that, her smile faltered, and her expression turned to one of diffidence. She reached around her back, and from somewhere produced a simple four-tiered bone and bead necklace.

"I made this," she said. The bones were polished but unpainted, the beads were jet black. There were no other adornments. It was striking and beautiful in its simplicity, and it still is. It's hanging from the lamp on my desktop, directly over my father's jackknife. I'm looking at it as I write this.

"Thank you. It's beautiful," I said, taking the token.

She nodded demurely, turned, and walked back the way she'd come. I watched her rejoin the group of women standing nearby. There was laughter and a great deal of stolen glances in my direction.

I started back toward my lodge. A small handful of the men—the few who weren't on lookout at the outskirts of the camp—had been watching from a distance. They approached and patted me on the back and wished me well. Black Bear met me and walked with me for a ways.

"They're good horses," he said in Lakota.

"How did you know they'd be there?"

"They are always there."

"Do you want your rope back?"

"No," he said. "You will need it."

"What happens next?"

"We will wait for Red Cloud."

"I found a man out there. His name was Squirrel. Did he come from here?"

Black Bear stopped, and turned to me. "Yes."

"He was with his mother. She had … passed on. I found him by some trees, sitting in the snow with her. I fed him and gave him a skin, but after I returned from the hunt, he had also passed."

"He stole a horse, and he was sent away. His mother could not bear to be without him."

"He was sent out there to die?"

"Whether he lived or died was not up to us. I've been told that whites hang men who steal horses. Is this not the truth?"

"Yes," I said, inwardly conceding his point.

He shrugged once, and began walking again. "Why only two horses?"

The next morning when I went outside, I found a pile of gifts stacked against the lodge. There was a pair of fur-lined winter boots, leggings, one buffalo hide, a wool blanket, some dried meat and fish, a length of rope, and a small pouch of tobacco.

I stowed everything but the boots—these I put on and found they fit reasonably well, if a little tight. I saddled Evelyn and, with Rose in tow, rode through the camp intent on finding an un-grazed area upriver to let the mares forage. As I passed, everyone I saw made a point to smile and wave.

I chose upriver as opposed to down because it would take me past Red Bird's lodge, where I hoped to get a glimpse of Wačhiwi.

I wasn't disappointed. She and Red Bird were sitting on a buffalo hide in front of the lodge braiding horse tail hair into rope. The two new mares were tethered a few feet away and appeared a little thinner in the tail than they had previously. Wačhiwi smiled and waved. Red Bird nodded as well, and as she did, she smiled in a reassuring way.

As far as smiles go, I wore one like a stone fool for the rest of the day. The almost festive atmosphere of the camp didn't last, however. The following day, Red Cloud returned with nearly one thousand Lakota warriors. There were forty-one casualties among them. Eleven had died on the journey back to the camp, the others' injuries ranged from minor to grave.

Red Bird was a Pȟežúta wíŋyaŋ—a great healer—among her people, and she went to work straightaway. Wačhiwi assisted her as she made her rounds to the lodges of the injured.

In addition to the Lakota, Little Horse of the Cheyenne and some hundreds of other Cheyenne and Arapaho warriors had also returned to their camp just downriver, and they too were bearing injured. One of their healers had been lost in battle, and Red Bird and Wačhiwi were summoned to give aid there as well.

Over the coming days I learned of what happened, and later learned a great deal more.

In their continued effort to drive the U.S. soldiers out of the Powder River country, the mixed-nation army of warriors had been harrying an army woodcutting wagon train on the Bozeman Road near Fort Phil Kearny. Somehow Colonel Carrington got word while it was in progress and dispatched a detail of some eighty infantry and cavalry to assist. The attack on the wagon train turned out to be a ruse planned by two Lakota warriors named Canku Wakátuya and Tȟašúŋke Witkó—High Backbone, and Crazy Horse. Most likely you've heard of the latter, if not the former. The trick worked and the warriors killed every single one of the soldiers. Red Cloud named it the *Battle of the Hundred-in-the-Hand.* The newspapers, and later the history books, called it the *Fetterman Massacre*.

I felt regret about the deaths on both sides. I knew that most of the U.S soldiers who were actually doing the fighting, were young men who either joined or were conscripted by the military during the war. That, or they were poor young men with no money and little or no skills, who were looking for a way to improve their situation after the war ended. Men—especially young men—are easily manipulated into hating who they're told to hate by their leaders. I witnessed it first-hand in that idiot war. I was never able to hate the men I was fighting against, but I killed them on orders just the same. That made me a murderer long before I killed Michael McBain. Anyway, in this fight the Indians had right on their side. That's the way I saw it then, and the way I see it now. The Indians were fighting invaders in their country. Over the last sixty years I've heard or read every argument to the contrary; arguments justifying what the U.S. government did then, and is still doing, to some degree. I'm not going to entertain those here. I have a story to tell and don't want to get caught making an argument that a hundred years from now still won't have a consensus.

I wanted to help in any way I could, but at the time, I didn't know what my place was in the Lakota community. The people were more than welcoming, but I was still an outsider. I sought out Black Bear and he suggested that I make use of my rifle and hunt to help supply meat for the injured men and their families.

So that's what I did.

I was in and out of the camp over the next week. The weather held out, clear and cold, and the deer hunting was good about fifteen miles to the northwest. I left the meat outside the lodges of the injured warriors, making sure I saved back enough to provide for Wačhiwi and her mother. I saw very little of Wačhiwi during that time. On the occasions I did, it was a brief passing; hardly long enough to exchange a glance, and she appeared beleaguered.

Some ten days after the return of the war party, Red Cloud visited me at my lodge. It was early evening and I was sitting outside on a section of log I'd cut and then dragged up to the lodge to use as a sort of bench. I was smoking the pipe Standing Elk had given me while I watched the sunset. I was a little taken aback at the sight of him. With the absence of his typical entourage, he appeared … ordinary.

I stood, and he put up his hand.

"May I sit?"

"Please," I said, sitting back down on the log.

He gazed silently at the sunset while I repacked the pipe. I passed it over and lit it for him with a match from my rapidly dwindling supply.

"This is good tobacco," he said, relishing the smoke.... "You are white. Perhaps you can tell me why whites always want what does not belong to them. They have their cities, and their riches. All we have is the land. We were born here. We were here long ago when the whites lived far over the great waters. Now here they are, wanting us to give up our land so that they can have even more riches. Why do they desire more than they need?"

"I wish I could answer that question." I said.

He turned to me and passed me the pipe. "Though you are not all this way." It wasn't a question.

"No."

"I'm told you wish to marry Wačhiwi."

"Yes, I do."

"There was a time I would have thought this marriage good for the friendship between the whites and the Lakota. I no longer care about this. Wačhiwi was away for a very long time. You will be good for her, perhaps better than a Lakota husband, in some ways. This is what is important."

Red Cloud stood. "You will be married in the Hard Moon. Black Bear will see to it."

With Red Bird and Red Cloud's approval of the marriage, it was acceptable for Wačhiwi and I to go about the camp together. It was difficult at first, because she was still occupied with the recovery of the wounded men. She made what time she could, however, mostly in the evenings. We'd walk along the river and she would tell me about her day tending to the wounded men, and she'd ask after mine, which was usually spent hunting.

"Two warriors moved on to the Spirit World today," she said one evening. We spoke English, more often than not when we were alone together. It wasn't anything calculated, it was simply more natural for both of us.

"The others will live," she continued. My mother is as great a healer as my father was. Perhaps I will learn enough to be one also."

"Black Bear tells me you're already becoming one."

She flushed. "I'm learning … and what of you, great hunter? You're making a good Lakota."

"It's not so much," I said. "I have a rifle."

"Some of the other men have rifles …"

"You're partisan," I said.

"What does that mean?"

"It means you're partial to me over others."

"That's true."

She stopped then, and turned to me. She stood on her toes, put her hand to the back of my neck and pulled me toward her. It was our first kiss—my first kiss. It was warm, and brief, and wonderful beyond words, but when she pulled back, her eyes were welling with tears.

"There was a child," she said. "Not with Edward, he was careful not to … it was Michael. The child was a boy. They took him the day he was born, and I never saw him again."

She began to weep then. She turned away and moved up the path toward the lodges. I started after her but she put up a hand without turning around. I could only watch her go.

The incident passed and wasn't repeated. We kissed, discreetly, when we could, and Wačhiwi seemed happy. I tried to broach the subject of the child, once. We were sitting on a buffalo hide near her lodge, eating a midday meal of smoked buffalo and dried berries before she needed to return to her doctoring.

"We don't need to speak about it," she said, matter-of-factly. "I wanted you to know, and you do."

I waited for more, but there wasn't any. I never brought it up again.

We were married on January, 23, 1867. It snowed lightly, off and on, but that didn't stop the Lakota people from celebrating. It was quite an event. Everyone dressed in their fanciest clothes, and it went on through the entire day. There was food; a bounty of it, considering the time of year. The women and children performed a special dance, and Black Bear acted as the Lakota equivalent of a Master of Ceremonies. There were no vows, or any of the somber formalities you'd expect from a Christian wedding. It was an altogether gay affair.

Later, as we lay by the fire amongst the piles of gifts we'd received, Wačhiwi, with her head on my chest, running her finger over the scar from my bullet wound, said, "I love you, Quiet White Man. Strangely (as I see it now) it was the first time either of us had said those words.

"I love you too, Dancing Girl," I said, and then kissed her.

I'm uncertain how I should tell this next part. I want to be respectful; to Wačhiwi, and anyone else who may read this.... I'll just say that the love came then, or we began, anyway. But she started to cry; terrible, hurt sobs. My heart broke from the sound. So I stopped. After that I held her close, and like the subject of the child, I didn't bring it up again.

We settled into our life together over the coming months. My first order of business—by Wačhiwi's request—was to move her mother's lodge nearer to ours, which I did happily. Had I of known we were to move the entire camp further up the Powder a few days later, though, I would have waited.

Breaking down the camp only took half a day. The Lakota were accustomed to relocating, so it was no great undertaking for them. The move put Red Cloud closer to the Bozeman, and the forts there. With his recent victories, and the fact that the combined numbers of the Lakota, Cheyenne, and Arapaho had grown to nearly twice what they were the previous year, he was no longer overly concerned with hiding his whereabouts.

Once re-settled, Red Bird gave Wačhiwi and I the two mares I'd captured at the Bighorn as wedding gifts, claiming she had no use for horses. I was grateful, as Evelyn was beginning to show her age, and Rose didn't belong to me.

Wačhiwi continued her work as a Pȟežúta wíŋyaŋ, and was becoming a highly respected citizen of the nation. There were some who looked down on her; ten years with the whites, and then marrying one, was cause for some to distrust her. These were the same people who were wary and, in a rare instance, openly unfriendly to me. Mostly, however, these people were few and reticent.

As 1867 wore on, there were more skirmishes between the Lakota and U.S. soldiers on the Bozeman, more run-ins with gold seekers bound for the Montana fields, and conflicts with ongoing railroad construction on hunting lands in what is now Nebraska. President Johnson sent men of war like General Sherman and William Harney out west as peace commissioners, which resulted in varied outcomes. There was also discord brewing between different bands of Lakota: Spotted Tail—a Brulé Lakota chief—and some others thought acquiescence was the appropriate way to deal with the white leaders, while Red Cloud, Sitting Bull, and younger men like Crazy Horse were for nothing short of completely expelling whites from their lands. With Red Cloud's recent victory, he was confident that the Lakota would succeed in just that, and he ignored multiple requests to meet with peace commissioners.

Though I listened closely to the news, I wasn't Lakota, and was therefore unaffected by it, for the most part. It's true I was married into the nation, but I was still only a guest. Camp life went on. I built a smokehouse that first spring, but mostly I hunted. On occasion, Black Bear would accompany me, but mostly I went out alone. Once, during one of his stays at the camp, Sitting Bull joined us and brought along a few of the younger men he always seemed to have at his heels. He claimed he wanted to see for himself if I was the hunter everyone said I was.

We came across a small herd of buffalo on that outing. Sitting Bull shot one with the Henry rifle he carried back then. He was too close, and it wasn't a clean shot. The animal turned and charged him. The buffalo made a glancing blow to his horse's flank, and Sitting Bull was knocked off and then trampled by it as the wooly lumbered off and collapsed nearby. Black Bear laughed and pointed while he hurried over to assist, but Sitting Bull got up, bruised and bloody and missing a chunk of his scalp the size of a three-cent piece, and simply brushed himself off. After that, he retrieved his horse and continued on as if nothing happened. We finished our hunt over three days and ended up with five buffalo; bled, skinned and butchered. I found out later he'd broken a rib and two fingers in the mishap. I don't curse often, but that man was about the toughest son-of-a-bitch I ever met.

There was a lot of game in the region then, though that was to change quickly over the coming years. There was always surplus meat, so I kept what Wačhiwi and Red Bird and I needed, and hung the rest out to share with others as was the common practice with the Lakota. No one went without.

Wačhiwi and I rode in the north country together as often as we could, and over time she became a skilled rider. I accompanied her on her herb forages, and even learned a little lore from her along the way. It was on one of these outings, in the fall of 1867, that we finally consummated our near one-year-old marriage. I was hunkered down on the bank of a creek a few miles east of the camp, filling our waterskin, when her shadow appeared over me. I turned to look up at her, the sun was at her back so I had to squint to see. I already said I'm not religious, but if there are angels, she was the picture of one that day, standing there, silhouetted against the sun. It was one of the best days of my life.

Red Bird died on the morning of November 3, 1867. She'd been carrying an armload of firewood from the stack I'd put up between our two lodges when she collapsed. She was already dead when I found her lying on the ground among the scattered lengths of wood. Her body was still warm, so it hadn't been very long. I picked her up and carried her to her lodge. After that Wačhiwi and some other women prepared her for her Lakota burial— which isn't a burial at all. Red Bird's body was wrapped in skins from her lodge and dragged a mile northeast of the camp by Wačhiwi and a large procession of other women, where it was left on the prairie. Afterwards, when all of the women save Wačhiwi returned to t, they disassembled Red Bird's lodge and burned it. Wačhiwi returned two days later, worn-out and hungry. She'd cut her hair short with a hunting knife; it was a Lakota sign of mourning.

A government agent arrived in April, escorted by Chief Big Mouth and three other chiefs. They carried a message for Red Cloud from the U.S. government's peace commission. The message—delivered verbally by Big Mouth—stated that the Great Father (President Johnson) no longer wished to be at war with the Indians and that a new treaty had been written that favored the Lakota. The agent pointed out that other chiefs had already agreed to sign the new treaty. Red Cloud stood firm on his demands and said he would sign nothing until the whites vacated Indian land. The agent departed unsatisfied and Red Cloud prepared for more war. There was talk of moving the camp again, but it didn't occur while I was there.

Wačhiwi's monthlies stopped in April of 1868, and by May she was certain she was carrying our child. It was around that time that I began acknowledging my restlessness, which I see in retrospect, had been steadily growing for over a year.

It was a good life, living with the Lakota, but it wasn't the life I'd envisioned for myself. When I was growing up, I thought eventually I'd have a place of my own, and possibly raise livestock. Later, after I discovered a love for horses, I'd daydreamed about my own ranch, possibly a smaller version of James Macklin's place in Kansas. Wačhiwi and I married, two or three children …

I approached her near the end of May about moving on.

We were sitting on a log by the river and I was reading out of Walden to her. She could read; we'd practiced often over the previous year. She liked to hear me read Thoreau's words, though, and I enjoyed doing it.

I stopped at the end of a passage and set the book aside. "I was wondering if you'd consider living in Missouri with me," I said. "I thought I'd breed saddle horses. The land isn't ideal for it, but it will do for a start. We could rebuild the house I grew up in, start raising our children … and we can visit here. It's not so far. Not for us, anyway."

She turned away and gazed out at the horizon. After a moment she slid her hand over and took mine in hers.

"I've expected this day," she said. "You don't belong here, and often I feel as though I don't belong here. I'm Lakota, but I lost something … some of what it is to be Lakota. I don't believe it will ever return." She turned to me then. "I'll go where you go."

Red Cloud was away with the warriors, keeping eyes on the Bozeman forts, but he returned a week later. This time Black Bear had gone with him. I waited a few days for them to settle back in and then sought out Black Bear. He listened patiently to what I had to say, but disagreed with the part about me not belonging. Afterward we went to see Red Cloud.

"Few whites are contented with Indian life," he said in Lakota, as we sat around the circle of his fire, passing a pipe. "We live poor and simple compared to how the whites live. That's why we look as animals to them." He raised his hand as he saw I was about to protest. "You do not see us this way. I have known others like you, though few. Still, even they possessed this spirit as the beaver. This spirit I see in you.… Wačhiwi accepts this decision?"

"Yes," I said.

"She will be missed once again. More now, as she has strong medicine. We will be in this land of our father's should you choose to return. You will be welcomed as one of us.… I know the whites do not prefer our horses, but I wish you to take five of mine, perhaps you can trade them for something useful."

"Thank you for all you've done for me," I said.

We lingered for two more months. Wačhiwi was caring for an elderly man who was nearing the end of his life. They'd developed a bond and she didn't want to pass him off to one of the other Lakota healers. I spent the time preparing for the coming journey; first to Kansas, to return Rose to James Macklin, and from there on to Missouri.

Red Cloud picked five horses from his impressive string. Two studs and three mares. They were fine examples of mustangs: young, well broke, and experienced. I thought I could get twenty dollars each for them, and that was high for mustangs at the time.

Near the end of July, Chief Itȟáŋka—Chief Big Mouth—arrived at the camp again. This time he was bearing other news: The Great Father had finally agreed to abandon the forts on the Bozeman Road. All bluecoat soldiers and miners had been ordered to leave the territory immediately. Red Cloud departed with Black Bear and others the very next day. They found that Fort C. F. Smith had indeed been abandoned. Red Cloud ordered it burned to the ground.

Red Cloud and the alliance of Lakota, Cheyenne, and Arapaho had somehow beaten the United States government. I wished Henry and Standing Elk were there to hear the news.

Before he left, Big Mouth visited me at my lodge and asked after Henry. I had nothing I could tell him.

We departed the Powder River Country bound for Kansas in August of 1868. I rode Evelyn and Wačhiwi rode the painted mustang mare, which she named Red Bird, after her mother. It was slow going, with Wačhiwi being three months along and with six horses in tow. We weren't in a hurry anyway. We had plenty of food.

We passed through a small Indian village in what is now Northern Nebraska. The village was surrounded by cultivated land—mostly corn and squash—and was scattered with dome-shaped earth and wood lodges. We were greeted warily, though not threateningly, by a group of fifty or so men, women, and children. I learned much later that they were Ponca, and the reason for their caution was our Lakota clothing.

Communication was limited to sign, as they spoke in a language that was different from both Lakota and the

Cheyenne. One elder spoke some broken English, but I couldn't make out most of it. I did understand the word *meat,* and we ended up trading some of our salted venison and buffalo for corn, which was a much-appreciated change to our diet of salted meat and dried berries.

Once out of Indian Territory we stowed our hide garments and changed into what I can only refer to as our *white* clothes. Though it had been two years, and Lawrence, Kansas was a long way from Sherman, Texas, the affair at the McBain ranch was in the back of my mind, so I left my hair long and shaved everything from my face save a moustache. I had no way of knowing it then, but the combination made me look a little like George Custer, only without his close-set eyes.

On the morning of September 2, we arrived at the Macklin ranch. He'd built on quite a lot since I'd been there: two new corrals and another barn, from what I could see. Most of the hands must have been on a drive, because the place was quiet. The hands that were around paused whatever work they were doing to watch us pass.

We stopped at the corral I'd previously worked horses in, dismounted and began tethering the horses to the rail. The corral was empty of animals but a man was inside, shoveling manure into a wheelbarrow. He stopped and tossed the shovel into the barrow. "Help you, Mister?" he said, walking toward us. He glanced at Wačhiwi. His look was one of open suspicion.

I did my best not to appear put off. "I'm here to see James Macklin, but I'll settle for Oliver Belle, if he's around."

"Mister Belle's out with the herd. Mister Macklin's up at the house. Who can I tell him is calling?"

"Everett Ward," I said. "This is my wife, Wačhiwi. You don't need to trouble yourself. We'll walk up. That roan there belongs to him, if you want to separate her and give her a stall."

Not waiting for a reply, I offered my arm to Wačhiwi. She took it and we started up to the big house.

"Did you used to work horses here?" the man called from behind me.

"I did," I said.

"I heard a lot about you."

I nodded, not knowing what to say.

I knocked on the door of the big house and waited. After a moment I heard footsteps from the inside and then a latch sliding free. The door swung open; James Macklin stood there, looking quite a bit older than I remembered him and puzzled to boot.

"You folks need someth—" he began, before recognition dawned on his face.

He smiled. "Well, I'll be … Everett."

"Hello, Mister Macklin," I said.

"I think we're beyond that, son. Just Red, from now on." He turned to Wačhiwi. "And who might this young lady be?"

"This is my wife, Wačhiwi."

"I was hoping you'd say that. It's a pleasure to meet you."

"I'm pleased to meet you, Mister Macklin," Wačhiwi said.

"Confound it, my manners flew out the window … come in," he said, moving aside so we could enter. "It's been so long, I suppose I got to where I didn't expect to see you again."

"I wanted to return your horse," I said.

He regarded at me for a moment, and then reached out and put a hand on my shoulder. "Well, it's good to know I had you figured right from the start. Come on. You and the missus take a seat in the dining room. I'll put on some coffee."

"Where's June," I said.

His face clouded. "June passed on this last winter. She came down with a fever … it went to her lungs and she died three weeks later."

"I'm sorry to hear it."

"Yes, well, I haven't been able to find it in myself to replace her, so I cook my own meals and make my own coffee."

Wačhiwi and I took a seat next to each other at the big table while Macklin proceeded deeper into the house. It seemed like a lifetime had passed since the night I'd first met Colonel Meecham and ate supper at that very table.

"He's kind," Wačhiwi said.

"Yes, he is."

Macklin returned carrying a tray laden with an enamel coffee pot, creamer, sugar bowl, and three ceramic mugs. He set everything out and began pouring coffee into the cups. I noticed then that his knuckles were swollen and his fingers had begun twisting with arthritis.

"Cream and sugar?"

"Both please," Wačhiwi and I said at once.

After passing us our cups he sat down in his usual chair at the head of the table. He took a sip of his coffee and looked at us in turn. "Where do we start?"

"This coffee is wonderful," Wačhiwi said.

He laughed. "That's as good a place as any."

I nodded my agreement. "It's the first we've had in a long time."

For Wačhiwi's sake and for his own, I gave him the abridged version of the events of the previous two years, saying only that I had to break into the McBain's place to rescue Wačhiwi, when it came to that part of the story. Red Macklin was a smart man. I'm certain he deduced most of what I left out. I asked him if he'd seen any wanted posters with my name and likeness on it, and he said he hadn't. The whole tale still took two hours and three pots of coffee.

"I hope Henry shows up here like you have," he said when I was finished. "He's a good man, and I'm partial to him. He's endured more hardship in his young years than most men do in a lifetime."

"I hope to see him again," I said.

"I can't imagine you have much money. You'll need a stake if you're going to start a horse ranch. And you have to put up a new house before you can do anything, and it's getting late in the season. Why don't you stay on and work here for a while? I'll pay you a foreman's wage. You might find you're happy here and want to stay ..." He glanced at Wačhiwi "... now that you've accomplished what you set out to do."

"I have five mustangs I was intending to sell to get started. I figured that would pay for the lumber for the house, with a little leftover."

"Mustangs, huh? I have a few men who prefer to ride them when they're roping. There isn't much money in them. Are they good ones?"

"Fine examples," I said.

"Well, I'm not one to tell you your business, but I've been at this for a long time, and from where I sit, the math doesn't add up. In the end, that's what it's all about; numbers.... I tell you what: I need another man with a good head on his shoulders, so as I said, I'll pay you foreman's wage. You'll oversee the equestrian end of things alongside Oliver Belle. Of course, I'll want you to continue breaking horses, at least until you get someone taught to do it as well as you do. I'll buy your five mustangs. You can use the money to find a place for you and Wačhiwi. I know where there's some small spreads west of here that went under in the fifties. Some folks just couldn't make a go of it, and others got scared and run out after that ruckus with Sheriff Jones. Washington Hadley down at the National Bank owns them all now, along with half of everything else in town. Oliver's been leasing one since he got married last fall. It's working out well for him. All the buildings need some repairing, but there's some good ones out there. I could speak to Washington on your behalf. And then come spring, if you still want to move on and go ahead with your plans in Missouri, you'll have some going money, and I'll stake you with fifty head of my stock on top of it. That would get you started and we can work out the repayment terms later."

I turned to Wačhiwi. "What do you think?"

She took my hand and squeezed it. "We should be grateful."

"Well, then, we accept," I said.

"Then it's settled, and I'll put you up here until other arrangements are worked out."

Chapter 8

There were three small ranches, all within fifteen miles of Macklin's place. Wačhiwi and I looked at all three of them. The first had burned down, and from the look, it happened more recently than the burnings during the war. Apparently no one had seen the smoke, or bothered to report it if they did. Washington Hadley was apologetic for taking up our time with it. The second was a fair-sized house with three rooms and a barn out behind it. The house had a stone fireplace, and there was a cast iron stove in the small kitchen that had some surface rust but was otherwise in fine working order. Part the roof had blown off and there was some damage to the floor inside because of the weather getting in, but all things considered, it was in pretty good shape. It also had a good well. The third house needed the least repair, but it was only two rooms, and they were small.

The simple choice was the second one, so we leased it, along with the fifty acres it sat on, from Washington Hadley's bank (with an option to buy) for five dollars a month. The lease price was set with the provision I performed the necessary repairs to make it habitable or hired someone to do it.

I worked four days a week at Macklin's ranch, and three at the house, repairing the roof, the floor, three busted windows. Wačhiwi took some of the money from the sale of the mustangs—thirty dollars a head, a sight more than they were worth—and ordered bedding, fabrics for curtains, baby clothes, and the like, through a mail-order catalog. By the middle of October the house was starting to look like a home.

At the time, the people of Lawrence were a little more enlightened than folks were in some other places in the west, but nonetheless James Macklin and Oliver Belle thought it prudent to put together a list of businesses they thought that Wačhiwi and I should avoid.

I showed it to her one night over supper on our new dining table—well, new to us. I'd purchased the simple oak table, along with four chairs, used, from the Saturday open market in town that very morning. I hauled it home on a buckboard I'd borrowed from James Macklin.

"I shouldn't go to town at all," she said, sliding the sheet of paper across the table toward me.

"There's only a handful of businesses on it," I said. "Run by small-minded people who don't deserve our patronage." I tapped the paper with my finger. "Look; two of the places are saloons, and one is a newspaper. I don't imagine us needing those anyway."

The following Saturday I convinced her to accompany me to the open market, which was held in a vacant lot at the end of town. There were several such lots scattered about Lawrence, leftovers from William Quantrill's raid on the town in 1863. A good portion of the town's buildings had been burned. Some were never rebuilt.

I still had Macklin's buckboard, and we started off around nine a.m. Wačhiwi was mostly silent during the seven-mile ride. It could have been simple apprehensiveness; it *was* her first time going into town, after all. But, as long as we'd been married she'd been prone to passing bouts of detachment. I made a few attempts at conversation; they were met with stilted responses.

"It looks like it's going to be a nice day, not too hot."

"Yes."

"After the market, I thought I'd visit the hardware store and get a pound of nails."

"All right."

Finally, I gave up and concentrated on minding the horses, and like most of her silences, it passed.

Once we arrived at the market and I'd secured the wagon, her demeanor changed. She went about confidently, with her head up, smiling and nodding as we passed other people. We received one or two odd looks and a few pairs of averted eyes, but by and large most folks were polite and friendly.

I led her straight to a row of vendors near the center of the lot, and was happy to see it was still there, sitting atop a plank table: a pinewood crib, painted white, with carved balusters.

"Well, you're back," the woman from behind the table said.

"Yes, ma'am," I said. "This is my wife, Wačhiwi."

"It's a pleasure to meet you, Wačhiwi. Your husband …?"

"Everett," I said.

"Yes, Everett; my apologies. Everett was admiring this crib. He thought you might like it."

"It's beautiful," Wačhiwi said.

"Isn't it just? My husband—he was a woodworker, you see—built it for our son when we lived in Ohio. We hauled it all the way out here thinking we'd have another child, but it wasn't to be. My husband's three years in his grave now, and our son's working for a senator in Washington and hasn't been back here in eight years. I thought it was high time I let someone else get some use out of it."

I turned to Wačhiwi. "Should we buy it?"

She ran her hand over the crib's railing. "Yes," she said.

I paid the women her asking price of two-dollars without a haggle and carried it back to the wagon.

The first time I'd ridden into town, some three days after we first arrived at James Macklin's, I considered buying Wačhiwi some new clothes. After some consideration, I discarded the idea, figuring she'd enjoy picking out her own. I decided to wait and surprise her when I finally got her to go into town.

After I secured the crib to the wagon, I drove straight to *Heywood's,* one of the two local clothiers.

"You said you wanted to purchase nails," Wačhiwi said, as I maneuvered the wagon into a space between two others.

"I thought you may like to look around in here first."

She leaned over and quickly brushed my cheek with a kiss. "I would like that very much," she said.

Suits and dresses were hanging in the red velvet-lined window display that fronted the shop. A small bell tinkled over the door as we entered. More suits and dresses—along with work clothes, children's clothes, and hats— were displayed on the walls. Still more were hanging from wood racks spanning the length of the building.

There was an elderly man sitting at a sewing machine in the corner. He didn't hear the bell over the clatter of the machine and so remained bent over his work. Wačhiwi saw something straight away; she took my arm and led me over to a cornflower blue dress with a white flower print. She ran her hand lightly over the fabric.

"That's a fine dress," a woman's voice came from behind us. Wačhiwi and I both turned, startled. She was about the same age as the man at the sewing machine. Her careworn face appeared severe, but her tone was friendly.

"If you don't mind me saying so, it may be a few months before you'd fit into that one properly. I have some skirts over here that might be more comfortable for the time being, and they'll still be suitable … after."

"Thank you," Wačhiwi said. "I'd like to see them."

I dropped away to leave them to it and began looking at a few items for myself. It must have been a banner day for the shop; in the end, we purchased the blue dress, two skirts, two blouses, two pairs of shoes for Wačhiwi, and two sets of shirts and trousers for me.

A few days later, when I was preparing to leave for the Macklin ranch, Wačhiwi handed me a small canning jar containing what I first took to be bacon drippings.

"Give this to Mister Macklin," she said. "He should rub it into his hands and fingers before he goes to sleep at night. It's for the twist. I wanted to prepare it sooner, but I couldn't find any caŋȟlóġaŋ hu caŋ swúla uŋ he tukťėkťel yuke, and it doesn't work very well without it.

"Please be careful foraging when I'm away," I said.

"Yes, Quiet White Man."

The ointment worked wonders for James Macklin.

A week later he walked up to the corral I was working in, just as I was finishing up with a horse. Oliver Belle was out east with his wife, meeting her family, so I was on my own. I tethered the animal and joined him at the fence.

"Afternoon, Red," I said.

He held a hand up and open and closed it several times.

"You see that?" he said. "That concoction Wačhiwi sent over is short of a miracle, though not by much. And it works a whole lot better than what Doctor Stadlehoffer's been giving me. I have to confess, I wasn't very keen on putting that foul-smelling muck on my hands, but the pain was bad enough last night that the smell didn't matter so much. When I woke up this morning, my knuckles felt more like they did when this cursed thing first started setting in, two winters back."

"She'll be glad to hear it," I said.

"You be sure to send my thanks, and tell her she ought to bottle it and sell it."

"I'll do that."

"How is she, anyway?"

"She's doing well. She's excited about the child. She's already talking about another one."

"How's the town been?"

"Real pleasant, for the most part. She's only been there three times. Once, some kids yelled *Indian lover* and *redskin* from across the street and then ran off. Other than that, people have been pleasant."

"That's good. Lawrence is a good place.... I better let you get back to it."

I wrote a letter to Calvin Englebright in early October. I let him know things were all right, and that Wačhiwi and I had a child on the way. To err on the side of caution, I wrote the name Edmund Waldon over the return address. Three weeks later I received a reply. Calvin wrote that Edward McBain's sister sold the ranch the previous year to some cattle speculators out of the very state I was in. He also wrote that a ranch hand had come forward after the incident out there and named me as Michael McBain's killer. An arrest warrant was sent out for me and Wačhiwi—who they figured had been with me since she murdered Edward McBain and disappeared—and an unnamed negro with a scar on his face, and an Indian. Calvin closed the letter with an encouraging word: *That storm has long since passed and provided you stay where you are, all should be well. Yours truly, Calvin.*

We corresponded fairly regular. I wrote him on December 15, to let him know that two days prior—December 13, 1868—Wačhiwi gave birth to a boy, who we named William Ward, after my father. We also named him Takóda, which is Lakota for *Friend To Everyone.* That's who we hoped he'd be.

Wačhiwi acted as her own midwife, and I, her assistant. It was wondrous and affecting. I'd taken leave from the Macklin ranch for the entire month of December to be certain I'd be there when the labor began; the time gave me a chance to get some work done around the home place and make certain we were prepared to be three. There were no complications for Wačhiwi or the boy. He came out near purple and as silent as midnight, and then a second later he began to wail like a frightened coyote, and his skin transmogrified to a healthy pink.

He was as beautiful as his mother.

Also in December of 1868, I learned of Chief Black Kettle's death. The story in the newspaper was titled: *Custer's Cavalry Defeats Hostiles in Battle Near Washita River.* The story was as short as it was vague. Having not been there, I can't speak to the details of what actually occurred. I was told later by another scout—a man named Ben Clark—that Black Kettle and his wife were both shot in the back, and that more than half of the hundred or so killed were women and children. I didn't know him very well, but he struck me as an honest man. George Custer later gave his own account to the newspapers, which was quite a bit different than Clark's.

Wačhiwi's pain ointment became as popular as a summer thundershower that following spring. James Macklin used all she'd given him and asked me to ask her if she could make more.

"I only have a little caŋȟlóġaŋ hu caŋ swúla uŋ he tukt'ėkt'el yuke," she said when I brought it up after work one day. "It's not enough to make more. You could go out to find some."

I translated the Lakota in my head to something like: *small weed that grows here and there,* but it didn't help me any. "What does it look like?" I said.

She was sitting at the kitchen table shelling some winter peas we'd purchased at the Saturday market. William was in her lap, contentedly gumming a pea pod. "Take him," she said, standing and holding him out to me.

He grumbled at first but I walked him around the room, bouncing him while I did it. Wačhiwi went to the kitchen area and rummaged on a shelf. She returned a moment later with a folded sheet from one of the Lawrence newspapers. She opened it up and there were a few woody-looking stems, about as long as a stove-length and a single, dried, purple flower.

"I know this plant," I said.

"There wasn't any near here," she said. "I rode for two hours to find this."

"North?"

William started squirming, like he usually did when I was holding him and Wačhiwi was close.

"Yes. Give him to me," she said, setting the newspaper on the table and then holding her arms out. She held him close, and he nestled his head in her neck.

"There won't be any flowers," she said. "But that doesn't matter. The stems and roots are what I need."

It was an off day for me, so I rode out on Evelyn early the next morning, bundled up tight against the cold. I found the plant—people call it skeleton weed now—about thirty miles northeast of our place. It started as a small patch growing on the downside of a gentle slope and it spread out from there.

I let Evelyn graze while I took the small garden spade I'd purchased for the house and began digging up the spindly plants. I stuffed a twenty-pound flour sack full, figuring it would be enough to keep James Macklin in ointment into the next century. When I got back to the house that afternoon, William was napping and Wačhiwi was busy in the kitchen, preparing the other ingredients for the ointment.

She glanced at the flour sack I was holding and nodded her approval. "I'll need more jars," she said.

I purchased a flat of half-quart jars; she filled them all and still had to use a few of the quart jars we had in the pantry. The next week I brought two quarts to James

Macklin. He was overjoyed and wanted to give me five dollars to bring to Wačhiwi.

"She won't want your money, Red. That isn't why she made it."

"Is that right? Well then, how about you take the day off work Friday and the two of you come to supper."

Friday came and we rode out to the ranch around three o'clock. We took it slow because I was carrying William on my back in a Lakota-style cradleboard I'd built under Wačhiwi's instruction. After James Macklin was finished fawning over William, we sat down to a meal of roasted chicken and potatoes, which he'd prepared himself. Soon, he got down to business.

"Wačhiwi, I took the liberty of giving some of that remarkable ointment you made to Doctor Stadlehoffer. Now, being a studied man of medicine, he was rightfully doubtful at first, but he indulged me and gave some to another one of his patients who also suffers this accursed condition. Both the doctor and his patient were astounded by the results. Doctor Stadlehoffer would like to buy the recipe—he's offering a hundred dollars—or barring that, he'd be interested in purchasing a regular supply of it, if you're willing to continue making it. If I were you, I'd choose the latter; it could really improve your financial solvency, over time."

Wačhiwi was holding William in her lap, feeding him bits of her food. She gave him a bite of smashed peas and set the spoon aside. "Thank you, she said. "I'll give the doctor the recipe, and I have some made that he can have for his patients."

"Magnificent. Why don't you decide how much you want for what you have already prepared, and I'll relay it to Doctor Stadlehoffer."

"I don't want any money."

"Can I ask why?"

"If it helps people who need it, then that's payment enough."

"Well, that's very kind, but consider that you could be helping people and earning some money for your future at the same time."

"I'll send it over with Everett," she said, returning her attention to William.

A look of bemusement passed over James Macklin's face, but vanished as quickly as it arrived. He sipped his wine and then nodded almost imperceptibly. "I apologize; to both of you," he said. "Money should never be the most important consideration, especially with something like this. I'll let Doctor Stadlehoffer know your wish to make this available free of charge.... Now, who's for seconds?"

James Macklin was one of the kindliest men I've ever known, but he was still a business man. I think he had difficulty not viewing situations like the one with Wačhiwi's arthritis ointment as an opportunity to make money, even if it wasn't for him.

The doctor had given credit where credit was due, and over the coming months Wačhiwi was treated somewhat differently in town. It was a subtle change; people who before had only smiled politely as we passed, would sometimes stop and ask after William or comment on the weather. People who had once averted their eyes, often smiled and nodded a greeting. There was still the occasional whisper, the muttered insult, or the shout from an open window or alleyway, but the instances were very few, and very far between. The veiled questions as to why we didn't attend church were more commonplace than anything concerning Wačhiwi being an Indian.

It was the happiest time of my life, and at the time, I thought it was hers too. Possibly it was. There's no way for me to know for certain. There was laughter in our home, and we had enough money. Wačhiwi planted a sizeable summer garden, all on her own, while William crawled around and foraged for insects or napped in the shade of the hackberry tree that grew beside the barn. We attended the Saturday market regularly, and often ate supper with Oliver Belle and his wife, Margaret. They had a little girl of about William's age and we'd all sit around and watch the two play together. James Macklin invited us over frequently as well. He never did replace June, and I got the sense he was lonely. I also thought that she was perhaps more to him than a maid.

As contented as Wačhiwi appeared outwardly, what I began to think of as her melancholia episodes began to come more frequently as 1869 wore on. On more than one occasion I returned home from my workday to find her at the dining table, crying. I'd ask what was the matter and she'd reply with something like: *I closed my finger in the cabinet drawer* or *I struck my knee on the bedpost.*

Once, I asked her if she was happy, and she replied, *of course I am,* and kissed me on the forehead.

A telegram I received from Calvin Englebright on November 10, 1869, changed everything. It read as follows:

Sender: Calvin Englebright

To: Everett Ward

Henry captured. Circuit judge three weeks out. Perhaps less.

The telegram was a day old when I received it. Wačhiwi was in her garden, harvesting the last of the fall crop. The carrier, a boy of about fourteen, found me in the barn after fruitlessly knocking on the door to the house. As to the untimeliness of the delivery, he explained that the local office had two carriers, and one was out with a broken arm he'd received after taking a tumble from his horse. I read the telegram over and over, as if I thought the words would change if I willed them to.

"Sir?" the boy said, after some time.

I lowered the telegram. "Thank you. I don't have a reply."

He nodded, and took his leave. I closed the stall I'd been freshening and walked out to the garden. Wačhiwi was sitting on her stool, carefully brushing dirt from a displeased and squirming William.

"I have to go to Sherman," I said, handing her the telegram. I picked up William and finished brushing off the garden soil he'd collected on his person.

Much like I had, she stared at the telegram for some time. Finally, she looked up. She didn't say anything, she only nodded, her expression both unhappy and resigned. I kissed William, and then Wačhiwi. We stood there in the garden, embracing, with our son between us. The tears came then: hers, mine, and soon, as if commiserating with our distress, William's.

I rode out that very afternoon on Red Bird, with Evelyn in tow, who was packed with everything but the rifle.

I made the journey in eight days.

Like I had with Henry and Standing Elk before, I entered Sherman from the northeast, where I could approach the back side of Calvin Englebright's stables and enter the town unseen. I kept my scarf wrapped around the lower part of my face—it was November, and cold, so I didn't think it would draw any attention. No one appeared to be about, so I led the tired horses inside the big stable and picked out two empty stalls that were side-by-side.

I was unpacking Evelyn when a familiar voice came from behind me.

"I expected you yesterday," Standing Elk said in English.

I turned. He looked the same, save perhaps a few more gray streaks in his hair.

He stepped forward and put a hand on my shoulder. His eyes were an ardent storm. "You and I must rescue Henry." It was one of only a handful of times I heard him use Henry's English name.

"We will," I said. "Where's Calvin?"

"He comes here many times a day, looking for you. He'll come soon, or Clay."

I resumed unpacking Evelyn. "What happened?"

"There was too much trouble for us in Mexico, and I wished to return to my people in the north. We stopped and camped near Santa Fe. In the morning, Nótaxemâhta'sóoma rode into the village alone to get food and tobacco. I stayed behind with the two mules we'd traded for in Mexico. He never returned. That night I set the mules free and rode to Santa Fe. I was told by two white men with metal stars on their shirts that I was not welcome. I left and searched outside the village for three days. On the third day, I found Harriet's tracks—she has trodden the earth strangely since she was shot in the battle with the white colonel Picton. I saw that there were four horses and three riders. I was too late. Had I not passed over the sign the first day, I would have caught the riders and killed them before they reached here. I followed their trail, but I demanded too much of my horse and she could not go on so. I came to this place and your friend, Calvin told me they arrived two days before. I have been waiting for you here."

"What sort of trouble in Mexico?" I said.

He waved a hand. "That is unimportant."

Standing Elk's horse had injured her knee. Clay, Calvin Englebright's groom, had attended to it but she was finished as a saddle horse. Standing Elk was lucky she carried him all the way to Sherman.

I was rubbing down Evelyn and Standing Elk was helping by doing the same to Red Bird. He admired the painted mare, and commented that she was *a good, Indian horse.*

Calvin arrived in the late afternoon. He stood in the doorway for a moment, a silhouette with the setting sun at his back.

I removed the telegram from my pocket and held it up. "Sending this could have put you in danger," I said. "But I'm grateful you did."

He stepped inside the stable. He'd lost weight and appeared unwell.

"Were I to have a choice. Standing Elk insisted, and I expect I'll live to regret it. I fear your being here will only end with your child being fatherless, and the woman you risked so much for being husbandless. As for me, there was no danger. Frank Lawson has allowed me to send my own telegrams since the line was erected in fifty-nine."

He extended his hand. "It's good to see you."

I took his hand in mine; his grip was weak and there was a slight tremor. He saw my concern and pulled his hand away. "The doctor doesn't know what it is," he said. "Let's not fuss over it. Now that you're here, we have more important matters at hand than worrying over my soundness. One being the mob that has been assembling every day since they brought Henry in. They've been growing in numbers, and there's been talk of storming the jail and lynching him. Marshal Flood couldn't risk deputizing anyone from town, so he called on the county sheriff to send deputies. There's six or eight of them in there with Henry around the clock. Word made it to the circuit judge and he's postponed some of his stops. He'll be here sooner than was first anticipated; perhaps as early as next week."

"Who brought Henry here?" I said.

"Two bounty men. Milton Watt's shiftless nephew told me they're staying for the trial, and that they have rooms at the Sundown."

The Sundown Hotel was Sherman's only other hotel after the Englebright. It was larger than the Englebright and not nearly as nice. It serviced drovers, miners, and salesmen, for the most part.

"Do these men have names?" I said.

"I'm certain they do, but I don't know them. Is that important right now?"

"No. I suppose not."

"What are you going to do? You can't show your face around here—him either," Calvin added, nodding toward

Standing Elk, who was sitting silently on a stall rail. "Sending for you was a horrible mistake."

"I could turn myself over to the marshal. Henry and I might have a better chance of bringing the truth to light for a jury if we stood together. Besides, I'm the one who shot Michael McBain, not Henry."

"Even if they believed you, you'd still both be hanged. That ranch hand put you both there that night. And honestly, Everett, Henry is a negro. With or without your confession, what justice do you think he'll receive in Sherman?"

I turned to Standing Elk. "What about the Cheyenne. Can we go for some help?"

"When I first arrived here, Calvin gave me a horse to ride to Black Kettle's village. I found that he and many others had been murdered by Long Hair Custer and his white soldiers. There were no warriors there to help … there are no fighters left south of the Arkansas River. Only men who are broken, like these horses, and men who were young when my father was young. Those Hotamétaneo'o that are left have all traveled north to fight the railroad builders and the white ranchers, or to join the Cheyenne at the Powder River."

"Well, we'll have to devise something ourselves," I said.

"Perhaps we could hire some men … Highwaymen," Calvin said.

At that moment I began to appreciate the hopelessness of the situation. Any rescue attempt would involve me risking my life and, as Calvin Englebright had said, likely leaving Wačhiwi and William alone. I looked at Standing Elk; I wouldn't be the only one risking my life.

The jail was only five hundred feet away, and on the opposite side of the street from the Englebright. I asked Calvin if he could give me a room upstairs so I could keep eyes on it, and possibly come up with some sort of tactic to gain Henry's release, either through legal means or force.

He gave me a room; it was on the corner of the building and commanded a clear sightline to the jailhouse. Standing Elk stayed at the stable.

I sat in a chair and watched through the window as the evening waned to dark. Sherman had grown considerably since I'd last been there. In '65 it had been a town in recovery; now it looked prosperous. Calvin hadn't exaggerated when he said there was a mob by the jail. The men had stationed themselves across the street. They milled around the boardwalk in front of a land office. Every so often one or another would shout toward the jail, *"Send him out, Marshal!"* or *"We demand justice!"* I judged them at thirty men strong, or slightly better, and they were armed. They made me anxious, like watching a simpleton handle a powder keg with a lit cigarette in his mouth. The law was predictable; it would take its course when the district judge arrived. There would be a trial, the jury would almost certainly find Henry guilty, and they would set a date—likely the next day—and hang him. But men find courage in numbers, particularly when they're convinced their cause is righteous. These men might just try something.

As far as the men in the jail were concerned, I reckoned there were five at any given time. Throughout the evening men would come and go. Some carried rifles, all wore sidearms. The men from the mob would shout more of the same at the lawmen coming and going from the jail. Mostly they were ignored.

The mob broke up gradually, between midnight and one a.m. The men walked off, or untied their horses from the rail at the street, in ones and twos, until there was only one remaining. He sat alone on the steps smoking for fifteen minutes before he stood and strode up the street eastward. As I undressed and pulled back the bedcovers, I decided I'd watch through the next day and night. If the men went off home at around the same time, then Standing Elk and I would make our attempt at around three a.m. the morning after that, if Standing Elk agreed. As I lay there listening to the creaks and groans of the hotel, I came to the conclusion that surprise and arms were the only chance we had of saving Henry.

The next morning, not long after sunup, there was a knock at the door. It was Calvin. He was holding a tray with a tin coffee pot, two tin cups, and a medium-sized muslin bundle on it. He brushed past me and set the tray on the sitting table in the corner.

"Since you're here, I thought you could bring Standing Elk his breakfast and save me the frigid trip to the stable."

"Happy to," I said.… "And thank you, for everything."

"Don't thank me, Everett. I neither want, nor deserve it."

"You were right to wire me. Make no mistake."

He walked to the door and stood there with his back to me. "I don't know what right is anymore," he said, before stepping into the hall and pulling the door shut behind him.

I ate breakfast in the stable with Standing Elk: coffee, biscuits and ham. Afterward, we walked the horses in the corral. The distraction seemed to help Standing Elk's restlessness. He'd been cooped up in the stable for days, worrying over his friend.

There was a small stack of books waiting for me on the table when I returned to the room. I smiled to myself, thanking Calvin for his thoughtfulness. I selected one at random; *The Mill on the Floss,* by George Eliot. I learned much later that the author's true name was actually, Mary Ann Evans.

I sat by the window with the book on my lap. It was midmorning, and the mob was about the same size it was the previous evening. I wondered that there could be so many men willing to set aside their work and businesses to fixate on a jailed man awaiting trial.

After some time, I opened the book and began reading. I'm not certain how much time had passed—two hours, about—when I heard shouting break out. I peered out the window; there were three armed men in the street, faced-off with the mob. One of them was Marshal Flood. There was a lone gunshot, and then a second later the sporadic crackle of more. One of the two men with Marshal Flood fell to the street, and then the mob surged forward, knocking both the marshal and the other man down as they charged for the jail.

I dropped the book to the floor, snatched up my saddle bags from the foot of the bed, and stormed from the room and down the stairs, pushing startled hotel patrons out of my way as I went. Once in the vestibule, I turned and ran through the kitchen and out the back door, which led directly to the stable. Standing Elk was already saddling Evelyn when I arrived.

"I'll finish her," I said, "Saddle the paint."

Standing Elk nodded and snatched Red Bird's saddle from the stall rail. I finished tightening the flank cinch around

Evelyn and then retrieved the Spencer from where it was propped in the corner, checked the loads, and then slid it into its scabbard.

We hit the street at a gallop and could see the mob gathered at what passed for a town square in Sherman. It was an open, grassy area, a hundred feet or so up the street from the jailhouse. In its center was a huge pecan tree. My stomach lurched as Evelyn pounded up the now crowded street and onto the common. I reined in and pulled out the Spencer as I was entering the circle of men. The scene was chaotic and men were hooting and shouting and firing their pistols and rifles. Suddenly I saw Henry being lifted above the crowd from a rope around his neck. He was shirtless and covered in blood. The rope had been thrown over a branch of the old pecan tree, and a man on a horse had the end of it wrapped around the horn of his saddle and was guiding the horse away. I took aim and fired, just as someone grabbed onto my leg. The shot went wide, and I was nearly pulled from Evelyn, but she shied away at just the right moment and I was free. Now men were advancing on me, and I heard the high-pitched whine of a ball fly past my ear. There was no chance of staying still long enough to try another shot. I was just wheeling to charge to Henry so I could attempt to cut him loose, when Standing Elk rode past me and through the throng of men to where Henry was hanging. Henry was too high, and Standing Elk couldn't even touch his feet, which were kicking wildly. One of his boots flew off and disappeared into the crowd. The mob surrounded Standing Elk and tried to pull him from the saddle. Red Bird was an inexperienced horse and she began to spook. She reared, and almost threw him. I urged Evelyn forward, one-handed, and swung the Spencer like a club. Standing Elk was shot in the face; I saw the blood fly from his cheek as the ball exited. He lost his grip on the reins and fell, rolling away as Red Bird bucked and kicked, and then ran off back toward town. I pulled up short and began shooting men nearly pointblank as they fell on Standing Elk. It was enough to gain Standing Elk the instant he needed to leap to his feet and pull himself up behind me on Evelyn. Men ran at us from all sides, striking and grasping and shooting. As I pivoted Evelyn, I was shot. The hit took my wind and I was nearly pulled from the saddle by another man who had my leg. Standing Elk kicked him in the face, and I succeeded in holding on as Evelyn charged away. I craned my neck around; Henry wasn't moving. My eyes fixed on his one bootless foot. For me, the indignity of his death was summed by it.

How I hoped he saw us there.

I hoped he knew his friends were with him at the end.

We rode out of Sherman as fast as Evelyn could carry the two of us. We were pursued by a lone rider; probably the one who hanged Henry. He was the only one there on horseback besides us, that I saw. I considered turning around long enough to kill him. I didn't, though. Standing Elk was shot three times, and I was once. We needed to put as much distance between us and Sherman as we could, as quickly as we could. Evelyn was getting old, and carrying twice the weight she was accustomed to. Whoever it was, they gave up after five miles or so.

What was left of Black Kettle's camp was only thirty miles from Sherman and, after an hour-long stop a few miles north of the Red River to field-dress our wounds, we made for it. The ball that hit Standing Elk's face entered just above his jaw, about an inch from the corner of his mouth, and exited just below his cheekbone on the other side. He'd lost several teeth, but the bleeding had stopped on its own. The second wound was in his chest, but it wasn't deep. The chunk of lead was imbedded just under the skin, in the lower part of his breast. I dug it out with the tip of my knife. He was also shot through his leg, about midway between his knee and his hip. Like the one in his face, it had traveled all the way through, but he'd lost a lot of blood from it. I knew at the time that if any of his wounds were mortal, it was that one. He was pale, but lucid.

"The whites have been trying to hang Henry for years," he said. "I stopped them, once."

"I know," I said, as I wrapped his leg.

"I knew in my heart they would succeed this time. The Great Father proclaimed that Henry was a free man; the whites never saw him as such. Most judged his value by the color of his skin, but his worth was that of a thousand of them."

"It was my fault. It should've been me."

He waved his hand, as he did so often. "This is not true."

I left it alone.

My wound was superficial. I was fortunate, because if it was a little lower, it might have hit my liver, and I probably wouldn't be writing this. The ball hit my lowest rib; it broke my skin, but it wasn't imbedded. I found it down the front of my trousers. I surmised that the shot must have come from outside the confines of the town square.

That evening, I reluctantly left Standing Elk near the Washita River, in the care of a woman named,

Ameohtsehe'e—Walking Woman. Standing Elk claimed she'd lived through more than a hundred winters, and that she'd been treating gunshot wounds since whites first appeared on Indian land intent on taking it for themselves. She appeared to me to be every year of one hundred, and I hoped she was up to the task. I wanted to take him to Wačhiwi, but I knew he was unlikely to survive the long ride to Lawrence, if Evelyn could even make the journey carrying two riders.

"I hope to see you again," I said, as I prepared to leave.

"I will stay in this world for some time yet, and you will linger here long after I, and all who you've known have passed on."

He was right, of course.

I arrived home, worn-out and hungry, four days before William's first birthday. The journey home took me twice as long as it did to ride to Sherman. This was by design: I knew the local law and the Texas Rangers were unlikely to pursue us, even if they suspected who we were. A mob had torn Henry from the jailhouse; I figured the attention would be on that, not on whoever may or may not have tried to intervene. That left bounty men. Calvin Englebright was told the men who brought in Henry were still in Sherman. If they were able to puzzle out the events, then they may have tracked us. They'd easily follow our trail to Indian land, but they'd find no help there. When I left Standing Elk, I headed northeast, toward Colorado, instead of north toward Lawrence, Kansas. I used every device I knew to confound any possible pursuers. It was hard on Evelyn, but as always, she weathered it without complaint. She was the best horse I ever had the privilege to know.

When I walked through the door, there were tears—Wačhiwi's and mine—but they were the good kind of tears. She insisted on poulticing my wound, though it was mostly healed by then. I didn't mind. I held William while she did it. I don't know how it was possible, but that boy felt ten pounds heavier than when I'd left. Wačhiwi told me James Macklin sent Oliver Belle over when I didn't show at the ranch for two days. She told him about the telegram.

I rode out at first light the next morning and went into Lawrence to buy a wagon. It was smaller than the one I borrowed from him from time to time, but it was all we needed and could be pulled by a single horse for most undertakings. I was in a hurry, so I didn't haggle the price. The purchase took a good portion of the money we had saved but I wanted to be able to take Wačhiwi and William with me wherever I went, at least until I was certain no one had managed to track me from Sherman. We drove out to James Macklin's the day after William's birthday; I tendered my apology and gave him the news about Henry. He was about heartbroken, and fought tears while he retold the story of how he'd found Henry cradling his wife's dead body on the side of the road back in Missouri. "If there's a Lord in Heaven, Henry's with his wife now," he said.

I asked him if he could do without me until after the new year. He asked me why, and I told him I needed to be with Wačhiwi and William for a while. He said he'd see me January 2.

A week after my return from Sherman, I was startled awake to a cacophony of shouts and wails. I heard Wačhiwi crying out my name as I opened my eyes. The first I saw as things came into focus, was the business end of a Colt Navy revolver just inches from my forehead. I turned my head to look for Wačhiwi; she was standing by the chest of drawers near her side of the bed. There was a man behind her with his chin on her shoulder, his face right next to hers. He had one arm around her neck, and was wielding a short-barreled side-by-side shotgun with the other. The shotgun was aimed at me. Wačhiwi wasn't looking my way, her eyes were on William, who was in his crib at the foot of the bed. He was holding himself up by the rail and wailing at her.

"Keep still or I'll have to kill you, and I'd just as soon not," the man with the pistol said. He was nearly shouting to be heard above William. His free hand held a lamp. He raised it and held it near my face. "It's him," he said, without taking his eyes off of me.

I recognized him then, and the rage that filled me was beyond reckoning. He was Seth Grant—*not to be confused with the bible fella, or the general who'd just become the eighteenth president of the United States*—the man who had once saved my life beside a stagnant stream in Oklahoma Territory.

"I can see what you're thinking, friend, and I can't say I blame you, but if you let it get hold of you, this won't end well for you, or her."

"What do you want?" I said.

"I have a legal arrest warrant for you and the squaw, out of Grayson County, Texas.... That's dead or alive, you understand? Now where's your clothes?"

"On the table behind you."

He set the lamp on the floor, and then picked up my trousers and shirt from where I kept them on the bedside table. "Hers?" he said.

In that chest of drawers behind her.

"Your coats?"

"Hanging on the back of the door."

He walked over to the open door and reached behind it, never taking the pistol off of me. He pulled his arm back holding both of our coats. He held them up, and after a moment's deliberation, deftly tossed mine to me and Wačhiwi's onto the bed next to where she stood.

"Let her get her clothes," he said.

The other man released Wačhiwi and turned the shotgun on her.

"Take a good look at this," he said. "If you come out of them drawers with anything but your clothes, I'll put you all over this room. And hurry it up, that nit's caterwauling is paining me."

She selected her deer-hide trousers and pulled them on underneath her nightgown. Keeping her back to the men, she stayed close to the chest of drawers and slipped the nightgown over her head. She quickly took out a blue button-up shirt and put it on.

"Mighty proper for an Injun woman," the man with the shotgun said. "You ain't got nothing I ain't already seen." He barked a laugh. "It's a long way to Texas, *Missus Proper Squaw*. Might be I'll see it all before we get there."

Wačhiwi turned to the man and nodded past him. "My shoes," she said.

He took a step back and kicked her boots toward her.

Grant tapped my shoulder with the barrel of his pistol. "Put your boots on, then get on the floor and lie on your back. I'm going to bind your hands, then the four of us are going to go out to your barn and saddle the horse I see you've got in there. Then we'll ride back down to Sherman where I'll turn you over to either the county sheriff, if he's in town, or the town marshal if he isn't. Now I'm going to back away; you do as I told you."

"I remember you," I said. "You helped me, down in Oklahoma Territory."

"I remember," he said. "Helping another man in need is never wrong, but situations change. Now I'm not going to ask you again. Down on the floor."

I wanted to charge them and tear their throats out, but I knew I had no chance—that we'd have no chance, unless I waited for an opportunity to show itself. I lowered myself to the floor. "Take me, and leave her and the boy," I said. "I can pay you whatever reward you'd be getting for her."

"Is that right?" the second man said from across the room. "Where might I find this money?"

"At the bottom of a tin of beans. In a cabinet in the kitchen."

Grant kneeled down on my neck. He put enough of his weight on it to make it difficult for me to draw breath. He wasn't gentle, and he tied my wrists so tightly that I lost feeling in them almost immediately. When he was finished, he hoisted me to my feet as if I weighed no more than an infant.

"Sit down there on the bed," he said, then walked around the foot of the bed. He gave William a strange look as he passed the crib. It was somewhere between pity and revulsion. To this day I can see that expression as clear as I could that night.

I watched as he tied Wačhiwi's hands, towering over her, his head nearly touching the ceiling. When he was finished, the other man hurried toward the door. "I'm going to see if that money's where he says it is." Suddenly he also looked familiar to me, but I couldn't place him. Not then.

"Now I want you both to walk through the door. Keep it slow and stay close to each other," Grant said.

Wačhiwi went straight to William. She leaned over the crib and his cries subsided to hitching gasps at once. Grant leveled the pistol at her with one hand and shoved her backwards toward the door with the other. William let out a scream of dejection and fury. Out of instinct I leapt up and started toward Grant. He turned the pistol on me and I stopped short.

"I'm getting the idea you aren't going to make it to stand trial," he said.

"What about our boy?"

"That's not for you to worry over anymore. We'll see to him."

We stood a few feet apart, I held his eyes for a moment, but I knew there was nothing for it. And he knew I knew it. I turned and nodded to Wačhiwi. She shook her head vehemently, but after a moment she lowered her head and walked through the door into the shadowy sitting room. The predawn light coming through the windows was scant, but I could see the second man rummaging through our kitchen cabinets.

"Watch them," Grant said.

"There's only seventy dollars in here," the other man said. "Where's the rest?"

“I can get more,” I said.

“Forget about that,” Grant said. “Watch them.”

The man picked up his shotgun from where he’d set it on our butcher board and sauntered over. Grant disappeared back into the bedroom and shut the door.

Wačhiwi screamed just as William’s cries were cut off with a sound I won’t describe here. I can tell you that it was terrible. We both threw ourselves at the door. I hit it with my shoulder hard enough to hear the jamb crack, but it held fast. That’s all I can remember.

I awoke lying in the dooryard, in a thin duff of snow. My head felt as if it were filled with shattered glass, and the world spun for several seconds before slowing and then coming to a stop. Seth Grant wasn’t there, but the second man was standing over me, smiling thinly. He kicked my leg. “You awake?” he said. He had his shotgun in one hand and my Spencer in the other. I recognized him then. He was the man in the rocking chair at the trading post; the one the post’s proprietor said he’d hired after getting robbed by Indians. His name was Plemons—at least that’s what the proprietor said his name was.

“If it was up to me, I’da shot you both, instead of only clockin’ you one in the skull. Dead or alive means dead is easier. Get up. We’re quittin’ this place.”

I went into some sort of fit, then. The pain and rage consumed me, and I began to shake and thrash, and scream. I screamed until I thought my head would split open. I rolled over on my side, retching, and vomited thick, yellow bile on the snow. It passed, leaving me shaken and weak. Plemons chuckled and asked if I was finished. When I didn’t reply he bent and took me up by the shirt and helped haul me to my feet.

He followed me to the barn. Wačhiwi was sitting on the chestnut mustang she'd named Taté-iyòhiwin—Reaches For The Wind. She was hunched over in the saddle with her face in the animal's mane. Evelyn was saddled and standing next to her. Seth Grant was holding the leaders to both of them, and there were two other horses tied to a stall rail nearby.

"Help him up on that other horse," Grant said.

I didn't wait for Plemons. I walked over and hooked my bound hands over the saddle horn, put a foot in the stirrup and pulled myself up.

"Wačhiwi?" I said.

She lifted her head, slowly, and turned to me with a look so full of sorrow I began to weep. Plemons found this amusing, apparently, and he mocked me:

"Wooohoo hoo," he said. "Sounds like a little girl, don't he?"

"Now there isn't any call for that," Grant said. He turned to Wačhiwi and me. "I don't want you speaking to one another. If you do, I'll stuff a kerchief in your mouth. You understand?" He didn't wait for a reply. "Let's get moving."

We rode south/southwest single file: Grant led, then Wačhiwi, Plemons, and me. They'd tied our hands to our saddle-horns and then strung leaders connecting all four horses.

It was evident from the start that Grant's arrangement with Plemons was one of business and not friendship. Plemons rambled incessantly about how many men he'd killed and how many women he'd bedded. Grant would grunt something or other in the right places, mostly, but occasionally he'd reach the end of what he was willing to tolerate and tell Plemons to shut his trap for a while.

"You always kill Indians straightaway. I don't know why you're insisting on keeping this one alive. Same money either direction," Plemons said.

"You let me handle the particulars, Jacob. That's the arrangement."

"Just seems strange to me, is all."

I stared at their backs, puzzling an escape and plotting all sorts of revenge. Wačhiwi watched the horizon, mourning William, I'm certain. Through that entire first day, she never once looked back at me—at least that I saw.

The cold winter sun had already dropped below the horizon in the west when we finally halted. Grant chose a shallow lowland that sustained a sizable mixed-wood thicket. Wačhiwi faltered and fell to her knees in the boot-deep snow when Plemons attempted to get her down from Reaches For The Wind. We'd been allowed off the horses only once the entire day, to do our necessaries. Her muscles probably stiffened up on her. Plemons yanked her up roughly by her coat collar.

Plemons held his shotgun on us while Grant tied us to opposite sides of a three-foot thick tree, with our arms behind us and our backs to each other. Doing it that way required untying our hands, and it was a relief. I'd long since lost all feeling in the ring and little fingers of my left hand.

The ground was frozen and the cold set in right away. Grant and Plemons went about setting up camp several feet from us. It was far enough that no heat reached us from their campfire. Like most of the day, Plemons mumbled and grumbled about this and that, while Grant remained mostly silent. While I watched them, I discovered that if I stretched my fingers out far enough, I could just touch Wačhiwi's forearm. She moved it back and forth slightly; it was the closest thing to a caress we could give each other.

I awoke to Wačhiwi's voice. It was sometime in the early morning hours, perhaps three a.m. One of our captors was snoring noisily by the near-dead campfire. My lips were beginning to crack, and I was trembling from the cold. Wačhiwi was speaking softly in Lakota.

"… I no longer believe there's a Spirit World," she said. "There must be only darkness.… This is a world of suffering. How could I not carry it with me into the next, and in turn walk forever in a world that's only a reflection of this one?"

I tried to reach her with my fingers, but they were too stiff to straighten.

"I'll find a way to get us out of this," I said, not believing it.

"I don't want you to. I'm ready for the darkness, Everett—my love; my Quiet White Man.… I've been ready for a long while. Avenge William, if you're able. Our son was innocent."

"So are you. I'm the one who's guilty."

"You're a good man. Try to sleep."

Those were the last words she ever said to me.

Sleep did return, albeit fitfully. I was awakened at dawn by a kick to my legs. Clouds had moved in and it was a bit warmer than it had been during the night. Plemons pointed his shotgun at us while Grant began untying his complicated bonds. The moment Wačhiwi was free, she leapt up and threw herself at him. His balance faltered and he took several steps back, cursing in surprise, but he didn't lose his feet.

Wačhiwi was like a mountain lion: screaming and clawing and biting. I struggled to free my hands but the ropes held them fast.

Plemons turned the shotgun toward them and was shouting, "Get offa him! Get offa him!" but he couldn't shoot Wačhiwi without hitting Grant. I struggled against my bonds and gained enough slack in the rope to allow me to shimmy my back up the trunk until I was standing. The rope leading off my wrists was still wrapped around the tree, but the end that had secured Wačhiwi was loose, so I started frantically working it around. Grant let out a bellow of pain and fury, and I turned to see him throw Wačhiwi to the ground. Blood was pouring from his neck and down the front of his shirt. I redoubled my efforts, and Plemons, who had been facing away from me, suddenly wheeled around. He hesitated just long enough for me to watch Grant pull a big skinning knife from his boot and begin wildly stabbing Wačhiwi as she tried to get to her feet. I lunged forward and the rope pulled free. Foolishly, Plemons fired both barrels of the side-by-side. His aim was off the mark and the shot took me in the left arm, shoulder, and chest. He broke the shotgun and began fumbling on his person for shells. The shot wasn't enough to knock me down, and I ran past him and made for Wačhiwi. Grant was standing over her, the knife dangling loosely in his hand, the other was pressed to his neck. Blood was running freely through his fingers. I stopped short; Wačhiwi was on her back, her eyes half-open and sightless. There was blood smeared across her mouth. It looked like war-paint. He lowered the hand he'd been holding to his neck wound and raised the one with the knife. I met his eyes; Hell was in them. I hope he saw the same in mine. I ran for the thicket a heartbeat before the shotgun roared a second time.

Chapter 9

I ran southwest, choosing that direction for no other reason than it seemed the path of least resistance through the thicket. My instinct told me to hide; my head told me to run. I intended to live to see both of those men die, so I ran hard. They didn't pursue me, at least not straightaway. If they had, they would have caught me inside of an hour no matter how fast and far I ran. The thicket couldn't have been more than a hundred acres, and beyond that, at all points of the compass, was empty prairie as far as one could see. Grant's neck wound must have been grievous indeed for them to allow me to escape.

Plemons missed me clean with his second shot, but I was bleeding considerably from the first one. The wounds themselves seemed shallower than his distance from me could account for. The only conclusion I could come to is that he'd chambered bad loads—wets, possibly. It's hard to say, the report seemed as loud as it should have been. It's just another thing I'll never know for certain.

Regardless of the condition of the shells, the wounds they inflicted weren't mortal in and of themselves, and I wasn't going to bleed out. The problem was that I had no way to dig out the shot, or treat the wounds.

How far I ran, I don't know. A mile through the thicket and another mile on the prairie, I'd surmise. I finally caught my boot in a rodent hole and went down face first. I struck my knee on a rock and bit my tongue hard enough for it to bleed. After that I just lay there, breathing in ragged gasps and dripping blood on the snow. Once I caught my breath and had a moment for events to set in, I wept. I wept for Wačhiwi, and I wept for William. But mostly I wept for Wačhiwi. I'm ashamed that I lamented the loss of her more than I did our boy, but there it is. My heart was broken. I couldn't save her. Even back when I thought I had, I really hadn't. Haunted by a life of tragedy and anguish, she was always just beyond my reach. Henry, Standing Elk, and I may have freed her, but it had been far too late to save her.

The cloud cover cleared off that afternoon and the temperature dropped below freezing. I kept south, more or less, throughout the day, watching my backtrail for signs of Grant and Plemons. I wanted to turn around and head for home so I could bury my son, but my instinct told me that going back to Lawrence would be a mistake. I didn't know what else to do, so I decided to make for the Cheyenne camp where I'd left Standing Elk.

I found no water that day, so I ate little bits of snow. When I stopped at sundown, too pained and tired to take another step, there wasn't a tree, shrub, or wash in sight. I kicked a spot clear of snow and lay down in the dormant grass and curled up like an infant, right there out in the open. I dozed a little, but it was too cold to get any real sleep. The sun rose without warmth or relief, but there were storm clouds in the north and they were moving south. I hoped for snow; it would cover my tracks and there was a good chance the temperature would go up some.

It took some effort to stand; it seemed like every part of me hurt. I noticed that the little finger and ring finger on my left hand had begun to turn black at the tips, fading down to a dusky purple below the first knuckles. There was no feeling in either one, outside of a dull ache in my hand below them.

The snow never came. A few clouds rolled over in the early afternoon, just enough to dampen what little heat the sun was providing. They didn't accumulate, and by evening they were gone.

An hour before sunset I came to a deep wash that was cut roughly east to west. There was a trickle of partially frozen water in the middle of it, but most of the bed was dry. I lowered myself down the five-foot bank and drank some of the water before huddling up against a cut in the north side bank. I took off my coat and my shirt and examined the shotgun wounds in my arm and chest. Each spot where a pellet had entered was raised to a peak and angry red. Most of them—I counted thirteen—were weeping pus. I set to squeezing them and four popped right out. The rest were too deep. I thought about trying to break a rock and possibly get a sharp shard out of it, but I decided against it. I figured I could take such measures if they got worse.

I slept a little better that night, but in the morning I was feverish. One minute I felt as if I'd burn up, regardless of the cold, and the next I'd be shivering so hard I couldn't stop my teeth from chattering. My fingers were worse, as well. Both of them were black nearly all the way to my hand. I got moving as soon as the sun was up, and if things didn't appear bad enough, about a mile out of the wash, the wind came up from the north, bitter cold and blowing a gale. There was no shelter to be had so I continued walking, hunched over to make myself as small as possible. I alternated between holding my hands over my ears to keep the icy wind out, and shoving them into my coat pockets to warm them back up. Finally I tore off my right shirt sleeve to tie around my ears. It was a tough operation; I had to sit on my coat so it wouldn't be carried away, and the wind kept trying to rip the sleeve from my hands while I tied it in place. It was worth the effort, though.

The wind let up a bit around noon and then died almost completely an hour later. An hour or so after that, I happened on a road. I didn't want to believe my eyes at first, but as I got closer there was no denying it.

I followed it west, and in the late afternoon a calvary company bound for Fort Larned overtook me.

I may have been walking in my sleep, or more likely, a stupor. I can't recall whether I heard the horses first, or felt them, but something alerted me, and I turned to see the single-file company coming from the southeast. I sat down at the edge of the road and waited. The officer leading the column wore a captain's uniform. He was round-faced with a neatly trimmed moustache. He raised his hand and called a halt as they drew close.

"Are you in trouble?" he said.

I struggled to my feet. "Yes, I am."

He looked all around, as if for a horse, or possibly other people, before turning back to me.

"Where did you come from?"

"Lawrence," I said.

"No one should be travelling this road alone.... You're injured. Were you attacked?"

"Do you have any water?"

"Sergeant!" he called out without taking his eyes from me. "Bring up a mount and a canteen."

He eyed me speculatively for several moments. When the sergeant arrived with a saddled horse in tow, the captain thanked him and took control of the animal.

"Can you ride?" he said

"I can ride."

"Well, you can ride alongside me, then, and you can tell me who you are and how you came to be out here. We'll pick up the Santa Fe by nightfall and arrive at Fort Larned by midnight. There's a doctor. He can tend to you, and we'll get this sorted out."

The captain's name was Parker. He told me with clear discontent that he was the *sometime* commanding officer of Fort Larned, and that currently he was the second-in-command. He didn't elaborate.

Captain Parker had a calm and comforting nature. Something about him reminded me of James Macklin. When he pressed me to explain who I was and why I was sitting on the side of the road in the middle of Indian Territory with rope-burned wrists, frost-blackened fingers, cracked lips, and blood on my hands and face, I chose to tell him everything.

I wept when I spoke of Wačhiwi, and he showed compassion in my indignity. We were leading the line, and with a kindly glance, he urged his horse forward to increase the distance between us and the nearest soldier.

"That's quite a story," he said, when I was finished. "And I'm inclined to believe it, though whether I believe it or not won't make any difference in a Texas court. Nonetheless, my good sense tells me this is worth looking into. These soldiers need rest, but I'll send a fresh detachment out at first light to look for these men you say abducted you, so I can question them. Hopefully my men can recover … your wife. I've never met Colonel Meecham, but Captain Lange and I have been acquainted. I'll send a courier out to Laramie tomorrow, and we'll find out if he'll corroborate at least a portion your story. It may not help you in the end, but I'll see it through that far."

It was well into the early morning hours when we rode into Fort Larned. Captain Parker left me with a corporal, who led me to the tiny, foul-smelling infirmary. The room was full, save two beds. I sat on the edge of one and listened to the sleep sounds of the men occupying the others while I waited for the doctor to be awakened. Some thirty minutes later, he strode in, bald and bespectacled, with his shirt only partially tucked into his trousers and his suspenders hanging. He held a lantern in each hand and set one on each side of the bed on the small night tables before introducing himself as Doctor Leonard Myers. He stated no rank so I assumed him a civilian.

"How about putting those lamps out," a man from the next bed said.

"Go to sleep, Private," the doctor said without turning. Then, to me, he said, "Take off your coat and shirt and let me see what shape you're in."

I did as he asked; he picked up the lamp nearest him and held close to me.

He whistled. "These don't look very good. How long ago was it?"

"Two days," I said.

He put a hand to my forehead. "You're fevered, too.... Let me see that hand."

I raised my left hand.

"I'm going to have to take these two fingers off, but I'm not attempting that without a few more hours sleep. I'll go get my bag, and I'll pick the shot out of you and clean up the wounds. In the morning we'll deal with your fingers."

The next morning he returned and, after a large dose of laudanum, cut off the little finger and ring finger of my left hand. I don't remember much about the procedure, except that he was whistling Camptown Races while he was preparing to operate. I came around some two hours later with a bandaged hand that felt as if it had caught fire.

"What happened to you, anyway?" the man who'd complained about the lamps said. "Injuns get you?"

"No." I said. "It wasn't Indians."

I convalesced in the infirmary for three days without going out. It was as long as I could stomach the sickroom. Most of the men were being treated for some sort of intestinal ailment and the place reeked of vomit and feces. The men on either side of me tried to make conversation but gave it up when they found I wasn't very well-disposed to the idea. Doctor Myers loaned me a book of poetry and another with short stories about mariners. I passed the time with them while I tried not to think about Wačhiwi and William. My shot wounds were healing nicely, and Doctor Myers said that my hand looked like it was doing well. I'd been given a hospital nightgown by a private, who acted as the doctor's orderly on the morning my fingers were taken. He'd carried off my clothes and returned them the following day, laundered and folded neatly. He set them on the end of the bed without a word. My coat and shirt were both peppered with holes, but the laundering had faded the blood stains more than I would have expected.

I stepped outside to a clear and cold morning. I brought one of the doctor's books with me in the event I felt like reading. The fort appeared as if it had recently undergone renovations. Most of the long, rectangular buildings—including the infirmary—were new. They were constructed of sandstone and built in a rough square, with a few wood outbuildings for livestock. A porch ran the entire length of the infirmary, with wood benches lined along the wall.

I took a seat and watched the goings on. The parade ground was empty, save for a few inches of snow and the flag pole. The stars and stripes hung limply in the still air. Soldiers moved about; carrying tool crates and water buckets. Some were leading horses or steers. A few nodded or lifted a hand as they passed but most minded their business.

Breakfast was brought around not long after I sat down. I laid the unopened book about seafaring men aside and took mine right there. Like the previous two days it was coffee and some sort of watery porridge. They did put a sprinkle of sugar on it, though, which went a long way in making it palatable, and they'd topped it with a hunk of salted pork belly.

Captain Parker had visited me a few hours after Doctor Myers amputated my fingers. He said he sent a detachment to follow my backtrail.

"I attached the duty to a regular patrol," he said. "I told them to look around, and then make a standard circuit. That would put them back here in a fortnight or thereabouts. They have orders to return straightaway if they find your wife, but going on what you've told me, I find that outcome doubtful. I also sent a dispatch to Captain Lange, just to satisfy my curiosity, if nothing else. It could take some time to get word back. Meanwhile I'll put you up here. It'll be a cot in a storeroom once the doctor tells me you're well enough to leave the hospital. It's either that, or the barracks, or the lockup, and you're not a soldier, and you're not under arrest. With that said, you're free to leave, if you'd rather."

"I'll wait. And I'm grateful, Captain," I said.

"You're welcome. I can't say whether or not I'm doing what's right. The post commander didn't want to hear anything about it—or any other business, for that matter. He's being moved back east in two weeks, and in his mind, he's already departed." He barked a short laugh. It sounded rueful. "The command will fall to me again anyway, at least until they send someone else who outranks me.... I'll be happy when I hear back from Robert—Captain Lange. The way I see it, if that part of your story is true, then the rest probably is, and I won't feel I was wrong for taking you in, no matter how things end up for you."

So I sat on the porch, and I watched. I had a clear view of the Pawnee river crossing, and past that, the Santa Fe trail as it disappeared around a bend on its way into the northeast. Captain Parker's detachment would be coming from that direction when they returned. I intended to wait for them, and for whoever the courier was who'd been sent to Fort Laramie. The former because I had faint hope that somehow the detachment would return with Wačhiwi, and the latter out of courtesy to Captain Parker. After that, I had other matters to attend to.

I whiled away the entire day there on that porch, finally going back inside when the sun went down and with it, the temperature. The next morning I did the same thing, only that afternoon the detachment returned.

They were approaching the crossing when I spotted them. I tried to keep my seat and wait, but I couldn't. I got up and hurried across the parade grounds and paced around near the building closest to the crossing until they arrived. It looked to be about twenty mounted soldiers, and at the rear, one of them was pulling a travois. As they got closer, I could see Plemons' hulking frame riding his dun horse, and a canvas wrapped body hanging stiffly over the back of Evelyn. I waited until they were across the river and then I charged at the convoy, ignoring the confused shouts as I sprinted past the cavalrymen. It was too late when Plemons realized it was me running at him, and he hauled hard on his reins just as I leapt up and grabbed onto the collar of his coat. I tried to pull him backward off of his mount but he held tight. It caused his horse to lose its balance and the animal squatted and went down. Plemons rolled off before the horse could pin him, narrowly escaping being trampled both by it, and the horse and rider who'd been in the column behind him, towing the travois.

I landed on my feet but off-balance; I backpedaled several steps but couldn't regain it and fell. Both of my hands went out to break my fall before I could think better of using the left one. Bright pain exploded in my hand and shot all the way up my arm to the elbow. I got right to my feet, but Plemons was already on his knees, aiming his shotgun at me. The soldier's shouts turned to warnings and sidearms were drawn. The horseman nearest Plemons said:

"Lower your weapon or I'll shoot you."

Plemons was disarmed and we were marched to Captain Parker's office. Plemons ejaculated loudly on the walk over, claiming the soldiers were interfering with a sworn officer of the court. A sergeant and two privates ushered us into the office and stood by while the captain was located.

The office overlooked the parade grounds and was sparsely furnished, housing only a simple desk and several chairs. There was a lithograph of President Grant, and another of a woman—presumably Missus Parker—on the wall on either side of the large picture window. The sergeant moved two of the chairs in front of the desk, then thought better of how closely he placed them, and moved them apart.

"Take a seat, and don't speak," he said.

Plemons managed to keep his mouth shut. He just sat there, glaring at me and breathing so hard through his mouth that I could smell the rotted meat stench of his breath from four feet away. I wished he could see my thoughts at that moment; the suffering I was envisioning for him.

Captain Parker arrived some twenty minutes later. His face and head were bright red with anger. He took the chair behind the desk and stared across it at us.

"You can stand outside the door, Sergeant," he said without looking up.

When the door snicked shut, he laid his hands flat on the blotter, leaned forward, and peered over the desk. "You're dripping blood on my floor, Mister Ward. Doctor Myers might take offence to the way you're mistreating his work."

He sat back and gazed at Plemons. "And you're Jacob Plemons." It wasn't a question.

"I am," Plemons said before turning to me. "And this here is my—"

"I know who this man is," Captain Parker interrupted. "I'm told your … partner, Grant, may not live."

"That's right," Plemons said. "The squaw took a chunk outta his throat. He about bled to death … would have if your boys hadn't found us."

"Sergeant Smith?" Captain Parker said.

The door opened and the sergeant stepped in.

"Take Mister Ward out to identify his wife, his horses, and anything else these men were carrying that may belong to him."

"Now, wait a minute," Plemons said, shoving his chair back and standing. "I have a legal warrant for him and the squaw. They committed two murders in the state of Texas—"

"Sit down, Mister Plemons. Before I have you shackled."

Plemons grumbled something under his breath but retrieved his chair and sat. "I don't care about his effects," he said petulantly. "But until I get to Texas, both him and that dead squaw are my charges."

"The way I see it, they're my charges, if they're anyone's."

"The law says you have to ex … extra …"

"Extradite?"

"Yes. That's just right," Plemons said, pointing at the captain. "You have to extradite him—and the squaw—to Texas, and I'm here to take them."

Captain Parker appeared to be losing his patience. "You'd be correct," he said, "if this were a state, but it's not a state; it's a territory, Mister Plemons, and it's under the control of the federal government. *I* am representing the federal government, and I'm telling you that I have neither the obligation nor inclination to involve the federal government in a state criminal affair.… Sergeant Smith. Please take Mister Ward out—*now*."

"I don't have nothin' but his rifle, and I only took that so he couldn't arm himself. Now you don't let him go pawing through my personals—"

"Sergeant Smith will be sure to oversee matters." Captain Parker said dismissively.

"What about the money you took from my kitchen?" I said.

"You're a goddamn liar."

Choosing not to pursue it, I stood. I looked at Plemons, marking him. There was no fear in his eyes. It didn't matter. I nodded to Captain Parker and followed the sergeant out.

The horses were tied to a rail on the side of the blockhouse. Sergeant Smith was polite enough to stand away while I struggled to move Wačhiwi's canvas-wrapped body from Evelyn to Reaches For The Wind. He came and stood by while I retrieved my Spencer and the box of cartridges Plemons had taken from the house. I patted his horse's cheek and apologized for tipping her over. I didn't look for anything else. I had what I needed.

"Follow me," he said. "Bring everything."

Leading the two horses, I tailed him across the way to the adjacent building. It was a little smaller than the infirmary but was identical otherwise. I tethered the horses near the steps and then followed him inside. He led me to a small room that was empty save a stack of flour sacks on the far wall.

"Captain Parker will be with you when he's finished with the other one."

He turned and started for the doorway, but he stopped before he reached it and turned back to me.

"Did you do all of what that other fella said you did?"

I shrugged. "Yes. But not how he tells it."

Rubbing at his beard, he seemed to consider this for a moment. He appeared as if he would say more, but instead he nodded once, turned, and walked out.

I pulled the book about mariners from the waistband of my trousers, mildly surprised it was still there, and then muscled a pair of the fifty-pound flour sacks off of the top of the stack—careful to use only the forearm of my left—and set them on the floor against the stack to make a seat. I tried to read from the book but it was no use. I set it aside, and wept instead. Feeling Wačhiwi as dead weight … the permanence of all of it occurred to me then in a way it hadn't before. She was gone forever, along with the beautiful boy who'd been born of her.

That was when I realized that what Standing Elk had said about me lingering after everyone I loved was gone was not just a meaningless prophecy, but a curse. A curse I'd been carrying with me since the day I coaxed Clyde into joining up to fight a war with me that meant nothing to either of us. I walked away from every battlefield, every fight, every precarious predicament I got myself into, most often after dragging others into with me. Something—or someone—always showed up in the nick of time to pull me out while everyone around me fell.

Less than an hour passed, and the private who worked in the infirmary arrived with a medical bag and fresh bandages.

"The doctor is busy with the big fella they brought in," he said apologetically. "He asked me to look and see if you tore your stiches out."

"Is he going to live?" I said.

"I really can't say."

He kneeled down in front of me and I put my hand out so he could remove the blood-soaked bandages.

"You popped these two on the end," he said, tossing the old bandages aside. "I'm not a doctor, but I can stitch these back up, if it's all right with you."

"I'd be grateful," I said.

"I don't have any laudanum."

"You go ahead."

The private left after he rebandaged my hand. He said that outside of the broken stiches, the wounds looked fine as paint.

Not long after, Captain Parker walked in. He tossed a bundle of cotton bandages to me.

The doctor says if you can keep from fighting and keep your bandages clean, you should heal without any further help from him.… You can sleep in here tonight, I'll have some bedding sent over. Sergeant Smith is pulling a week's worth of supplies for you. I want you to leave in the morning, first light. I don't regret helping you—at least not yet. I suppose I can reassess that if I'm court-martialed. Regardless, Fort Larned is a military post, and this has gotten out of hand. I sent Mister Plemons on his way with a six-man detachment, to see him past the Indian camps and to be sure he doesn't decide to skulk around and lie in wait for you somewhere. He wanted to go south—to Texas, I'd wager. I'm advising you to go north. You can go in any direction you want, of course, except south. Sergeant Smith and five men will ride with you until you're well away from here. If you want to turn south and seek your revenge after that, my hands won't be stained from it"

"I figured I'd wait for you to get word from Captain Lange."

"There's no need for that. What he says won't help you any, and I already know he'll corroborate what you told me. If he doesn't, then I'm the bigger fool."

"Everything I told you was the truth."

Captain Parker nodded. "If I were you, I'd think about changing my name, make for California or Oregon. If you don't, sooner or later someone like Plemons, or Grant, is going to catch up with you, and you may not be so fortunate."

I appreciate what you've done for me, but I don't feel very fortunate.... Is Grant going to live?"

"What difference does it make?"

"I'd feel better if I knew Wačhiwi killed him."

"I don't think you're going to be so fortunate there, either. Goodbye, Mister Ward."

A week later I arrived at the Cheyenne camp near the Washita River. It had been moved a few miles north, and there weren't nearly as many lodges as there had been when I'd left Standing Elk in the care of Walking Woman. I counted sixty, scattered in what first appeared to be a haphazard fashion, but on closer inspection I could see the circular depressions where not as much snow had built up. These were where other lodges had been, not long before. I dismounted and walked through the maze of them. All of the people I saw were too thin. There weren't many men about, and the ones that were there were old or infirm in some way. Children played buffalo hunter, chasing the one chosen to be the buffalo while waving sticks above their heads. Several dropped their sticks and followed me; some of the older ones running up and looking curiously at Wačhiwi's wrapped body. I turned and shook my head. It was enough. Three women were repairing a section of a lodge and paused their work as I approached.

"Mo'ohnee'ėstse?" I said.

All three pointed toward the creek. "Tóxeo'hé'e," one said.

I nodded, said, "Néá'eše," and led the horses toward the creek. The waterway was narrow, not more than twelve feet across, and the edges, where it was shallowest, were frozen over.

Standing Elk was there, knee-deep in the frigid water, stacking rocks for a fish trap. His back was to me, but he turned long before he could have heard me. He nodded, as if he'd been expecting me, then bent back to his work. He placed a few more rocks and then waded to the bank.

Like the others, he was gaunt. His face wasn't as bad as I'd expected, though the geography had changed some. His left cheek, where the ball had exited, was the worst. He'd lost most of his top teeth, and likely some bone on that side, so his face had sort of a sunken look on that side. The new scar was as big and round as a silver dollar and still pink, darkening to an angry-looking red at its center. The right side of his face where the ball had entered wasn't so bad: A nickel-sized entrance wound that was completely healed.

He gazed long at Reaches For The Wind before turning back to me. "Wačhiwi?"

I couldn't answer, so I nodded.

"There's still no men here?" I said in English.

"Much as they were.... Some are hunting in the north on the Canadian River to get food for the village, though they will be shot by the white soldiers if they are discovered. Others have joined the Hotamétaneo'o. They have gone to fight a war they cannot win; these men would prefer death than to be crushed under the foot of the whites any longer."

"What about you?"

"I was waiting for you."

I nodded my head back toward the camp. "What about them?"

"Many would not stay here. Black Kettle was wrong to bring them. Some say he was enchanted by the white's gifts, but that is untrue. He was old and afraid. Not afraid for himself, he was afraid for The People and what the whites would do if he did not obey. Little Robe is now chief and many have followed him, two miles up the Washita. I will take the ones who would go, back to the Powder River where they can live as Indians—as *Tsêhéstáno*—not dogs for the Great Father and his soldiers to kick. Black Kettle thought if he befriended the whites, they would let his people live in peace, but the more he gave them, the more they took, pointing their overfed fingers here and there as they told him to go further and further away from the land of our fathers, to this place of suffering. Then Long Hair Custer and his men killed him anyway."

"I was heading that way, myself," I said. "After a stop in Lawrence. My boy was killed as well, and I need to get him. I'm going to take him and Wačhiwi to Lakota land and bury them. Then I'm going after the men who did it."

"We will travel together, and you will tell me of this. It will be dangerous; most of those who come will be on foot, and the white soldiers are everywhere now. So are the wood houses and fences of white settlers. We must remain watchful."

"If the Indian agent assigned here finds out people are leaving, he's certain to sound the alarm," I said. "If that happens, we'll be caught by U.S. cavalry, and all of these people will be considered renegades. We can't hide the sort of trail we'll be leaving, so we'll just have to hope no one comes across it.... When do you want to leave?"

"When the men return. Perhaps today, or tomorrow."

It was a long, difficult journey. Scarce game, below freezing temperatures at night, only slightly above during the day, old age and illness, were all contributors. The group was stoic, however, particularly the women. They'd been through so much hardship over the last several years: the murder of loved ones by Colonel Chivington's men at Sand Creek in '64, and Custer's at Washita in '68, constant displacement, and always near starvation. But they weathered it all, and with quiet dignity.

We began with fifty-four souls: thirty-seven Cheyenne including Standing Elk, sixteen Arapaho from a nearby camp, and myself. Sadly, there were only fifteen horses, including Evelyn and Reaches For The Wind. Standing Elk said there had been ten other mounts in the camp, but they'd been butchered for their meat some weeks prior when the winter allotment of beef promised in the last government treaty never arrived. Several old men and women needed to be towed by travois, and on the third day out a boy of about ten stepped in a prairie dog hole that had been concealed by snow and broke his ankle. Standing Elk splinted him and then we tied him onto a stack of lodge skins that was being towed by one of the more robust horses.

There were five men of young age and good health, and they did most of the hunting, along with Standing Elk and I. Two of the men carried old Springfield rifles, the others, bows. Some evenings all seven of us would return empty-handed to whatever camp we'd set, but most times we brought in just enough to ensure no one went completely without. We stayed on Indian land as long as we could: Chickasaw, Creek, Seminole, though not by their leave. Neither the Cheyenne nor Arapaho were at war with any of these nations, but since more and more Indians were being pushed out of their homelands and into the Oklahoma territory, competition for already scarce game often caused tension when one was found hunting on another's land.

Standing Elk solemnly helped me lift Wačhiwi's frozen body off of Reaches For The Wind every afternoon when we set camp, and lift it back every morning when we broke. For me, it was a fresh broken heart twice every day, and I often wished—selfishly—that I'd buried her out on the prairie after I left Fort Larned. I needed to grieve but didn't know how to start with her body there with me day in and day out. It was a constant reminder of how I failed her.

I minded my wounds and changed my bandages every day. My hand looked better each time. As the pain subsided it began to itch terribly. The itch was almost worse than the pain.

On January 1, 1870, an old Cheyenne man by the name of Runs Far died in the night. It was a sad occasion. He'd been full of hope and had spoken of how he was looking forward to returning to his birthplace, where he could live out his days in this world on the same land he'd been born onto. He was survived by his only remaining daughter, who was rapidly approaching old age herself. Standing Elk oversaw the building of a scaffold out of spare lodge poles, and Runs Far's body was placed upon it along with an ancient bow and some other of his belongings. A short ceremony was held and then we moved on.

We parted company a week later, about midway between Fort Dodge (what is now Dodge City) and Wichita. I headed northeast toward Lawrence, and the group continued on northwest toward the Platte River, and beyond that, the Powder River. The intent was for me to catch up to them somewhere on the Platte, once I retrieved William.

On January 23, I arrived back home. William wasn't inside, but there was a handwritten note on a single sheet of paper, propped up against the oil lamp on our dining table. It read:

Oliver Belle and I took the liberty of burying William. He's in your garden. I'm praying for you.

It was signed, James Macklin.

The note was written in pencil and Macklin had left the pencil lying on the table. I turned the paper over, took up the pencil and wrote:

Mr. Hadley:

Please accept my sincerest apology for leaving your house and property in such a state. Regretfully, I will not be returning.

Respectfully,
Everett Ward

I went back into the bedroom, took a knee, and pulled out the bottom drawer of Wačhiwi's chest. Once it was open, I could smell her. I lifted a nightgown and held it to my face, breathing deeply. I began to weep uncontrollably then, and I curled up with the nightgown on the tiny carpet beside our bed and continued for some time. Later I awoke, shivering. It was mid-afternoon by the quality of light coming through the window curtains. It hadn't even been noon when I arrived. I laid Wačhiwi's nightgown up on the bed and turned back to the drawer. There was a small drawstring sack at the bottom, underneath Wačhiwi's clothes. I opened it and removed a small sheaf of bills; money she'd been saving for William. There was fifteen-dollars all together. I dropped the sack to the floor and separated five dollars out. The rest I shoved into the pocket of my trousers. I left the five dollars next to the note on the dining table. I figured Mister Hadley could use it to pay someone to clear out the place.

Next, I went through the house, gathering up essentials: clothes and blankets, cooking utensils, coffee, and what food there was. I took the necklace Wačhiwi had made for me as a marriage token, my father's jackknife, and the hawk feather. After I repacked the horses I went out to the garden and dug up William's body. They didn't put up a marker, but Red Macklin and Oliver Belle had done right by my son. They'd either built or purchased a simple, wood box to put him in, and they'd wrapped him up in a quilt. They even included his little crib pillow. I couldn't help unwrapping him. Weeping again, I set him on the soil next to the remnants of Wačhiwi's winter peas. The cold had preserved him, for the most part. Mercifully his eyes were closed, but his skin was blue and his neck was broken, leaving his head cocked at an unnatural angle. Seeing him in that state caused me to fly into a rage. I ripped up what was left of the garden and destroyed the rail fence I'd built around it. When it was over, I had no more tears and no more anger. The anger would return, but for the moment I was empty. I wrapped William back up in the quilt, carried him over to Reaches For The Wind, and tied him onto her with his mother.

I caught up with Standing Elk and the others about fifty miles southeast of Fort Laramie, on the North Platte River. The following day we abandoned the Platte and headed due north. The hunting improved as we traveled and deer, elk, and rabbit became plentiful. The mood of the pilgrimage turned from somber to jovial in just a few days. A week later one of the young Cheyenne men discovered a small buffalo herd. Standing Elk and I stayed behind while the other men followed the trail. They made a kill, and that night they celebrated. It was a good thing we had a surplus of meat, because the weather turned south over the next few days and got steadily worse until it was a blizzard. We holed up in a low pass between two hills for three days and huddled close together for warmth while the storm blew over. Once the weather cleared we moved northwest. The snow was deep and slowed us down, but no one was hungry.

When we neared the Powder, Standing Elk and I scouted around. We found an Arapaho camp and were able to learn where Red Cloud was as well as the Cheyenne chief, Vóóhéhéve—Morning Star, who Standing Elk believed would take in his relatives. We parted company the next morning. Standing Elk agreed to meet me at Red Cloud's camp in a few days.

I rode north to where the camp had been located when Wačhiwi and I lived there. From there I located roughly where her mother had been left on the prairie. I tied the horses to some scrub and unpacked the pickaxe and shovel from Reaches For The Wind. The ground was frozen, and it took me half a day to dig the grave, alternating between busting up the frozen soil with the pickaxe and then scooping it out with the shovel. When I was finished, I lowered Wačhiwi into it, and then put William—Takóda—next to her. After a moment's consideration I dropped the hawk feather Red Cloud had given me into the grave with them. I didn't protect them, so I didn't deserve it. The feather see-sawed down and landed in the bottom next to Wačhiwi's head. I noticed a strand of her hair had escaped the canvas. I thought about climbing down there and tucking it back in, but decided against it. Possibly it was right, having a part of her touching the earth.

I filled in the grave and spent the rest of the day collecting rocks to put over it so the animals couldn't get at it. It wasn't how the Lakota would do it, but I wasn't Lakota, Wačhiwi was. I couldn't abide the thought of her being scavenged like her mother must have been. I stood over the grave for a while. I didn't say any words, except that I loved her and William, and that I was sorry for being the man I was, and I was sorry for taking her away from her people. And regardless of what she'd said to me that last night, I hoped that somewhere inside her, Wačhiwi left this world believing in another, better one.

There was a foot of snow on the ground but the skies were clear as I rode toward the Red Cloud's camp a day later.

The smoke from the lodges and meat drying fires warned me I was near. The sprawling camp was set among a vein-work of creeks between the North Platte and the Powder River. I began to feel apprehensive and wondered if I shouldn't simply cut south, and ride on. I couldn't be certain that what I was doing was right. Could be I wouldn't be welcome any longer.

I sought out Black Bear straightaway and felt fortunate when I found he was in camp. He and several other men were raising a new lodge for a forthcoming wedding. When I approached, they were setting up the lodge poles for the framework. One of the men noticed me approaching and tapped Black Bear on the shoulder. He turned and smiled and started toward me.

"Háu," he said.

"Háu."

I climbed down from Evelyn—the horse I'd once thought too old to travel distances—and met him.

"Wačhiwi and our son Takóda were killed," I said. "I'm being hunted."

He bowed his head. After a long moment he raised it. "You will stay here with us now," he said. "We must speak with Red Cloud."

Chief Red Cloud was away from the camp, shooting his new rifle. According to Black Bear, Red Cloud had traveled east with a delegation of other Sioux chiefs and dignitaries during the warm moons of summer to speak with the Great Father, President Grant. He and the other delegates were given many gifts by the emissaries in Washington, but no rifles or powder. When he returned, Red Cloud traded some of the white man's clothing and other trinkets he'd been given to a white trader for a Winchester and fifty rounds of ammunition. Black Bear also said that Red Cloud had been complaining that he had been promised a hundred rifles and ammunition for them by the new Indian agent but had received none.

I was invited to Red Cloud's lodge that evening. He and Owl Woman wore matching linen shirts and winter skin trousers. The shirts looked new.

It was unusual that there was only four of us; Red Cloud was typically surrounded by people. But there was only Red Cloud, Owl Woman, Black Bear, and myself. They were being respectful of my grief, and I was grateful for their thoughtfulness. We smoked, and I told them everything that happened since Wačhiwi and I left, all the way up to her dying at the hands of Seth Grant.

"This world is full of blood," Red Cloud said. "Since the whites came, there has been rivers of it, and it floods the land and stains the grass. If you and Wačhiwi would only have stayed here with us...." He waved his hand. "It would have pleased me for your child to have known the ways of the Lakota."

Later we ate buffalo meat while Red Cloud told me of his journey to Washington and his long meetings with U.S. officials and his short one with President Grant. He showed me a magazine that depicted him and President Grant on the cover, shaking hands. In the drawing, Red Cloud was shirtless.

"Even the white man's papers lie," he said, pinching the front of his shirt between his fingers and giving it a shake. "I was wearing this shirt, when I met the Great Father."

I looked at the cover for a moment and then handed the magazine back to him. "The newspapers said that you signed a new treaty," I said. "And that the army has abandoned the forts on the Bozeman Road."

"It is true they left the forts, and we burned them after. But they will return. Treaties are meaningless. The men the Great Father sends to make them are liars and cheats, and they know we cannot read them anyway. Still, they ask for land, we give them land. They promise to send beef and goods in exchange but then tell us that most of it was stolen on the road and we receive almost nothing. The Great Father and his little chief's intention is for us to give up our ways and raise stock, and farm crops on the tiny pieces of land that whites do not want for themselves. But we will not. They want us to become whites like them, but not as men like them. They wish us to remain as their children; to obey them as children. We were here long before they came. We have shared with them and given them room to grow, but we have given all we will. The Great Spirit put me here and told me to keep this land."

As he spoke, I noticed that something had changed in him since we'd last spoken. It was if he were carrying a sense of foreboding that hadn't been there before. His words were as strong as they'd ever been, but his countenance seemed less sure. Looking back on it, I think the trip to Washington, and the subsequent meetings with the Indian agents and other officials assigned to the Red Cloud agency, caused him to realize the true might and will of the U.S. government.

I was a guest in Black Bear's lodge that night. It was just he and I. His wife had died the previous winter. Their only son had been killed in a fight with U.S. soldiers in 1865. He asked me if I was going to stay; I told him I didn't know. I lay awake, listening to Black Bear's soft snores and the sounds of the night winds on the prairie until the early hours of the morning. My plan had been to bury Wačhiwi and William on Lakota land, and then hunt down and kill Seth Grant—if he'd survived Wačhiwi's attack—and Jacob Plemons, but since I'd left Wačhiwi and William in their unmarked grave out on the prairie, I was beginning to wonder how I was going to accomplish that objective. It was coming into the hardest part of winter, where tracking a man in the open would be the toughest. I was wanted for murder, and would need to be asking questions at every trading post, Indian agency, ranch and township from the Texas border to Nebraska—which by then had become a state—if I was going to locate them.

The lodge was empty when I awoke. The night's fire had been rekindled, but Black Bear was gone. I stood and went to my little pile of belongings, retrieved my cookpot, and walked out away from the lodges and scooped up some undisturbed snow to melt for coffee. When it was ready, I drank a cup while preparing Evelyn. I left the remainder on a rock near the fire to keep warm for Black Bear, should he return.

The morning was crisp, clear, and cold as I rode Evelyn northwest. I arrived at the Cheyenne camp at midday, hoping Standing Elk hadn't chosen that morning to ride out to meet me at the Lakota camp.

He hadn't. After some inquiries, I found him, busy as always, working in a circle with a group of men and women fashioning winter leggings. He nodded to me as I walked up leading Evelyn, and then he picked a pair of the leggings from the small pile next to him and tossed them to me.

"Where are we going?" he said in Cheyenne.

"I thought I'd ask you that question."

He studied me from where he sat for quite some time. Finally, he said in English, "Perhaps you and I should go on a hunt, if you can bear the cold. You can work to improve your Cheyenne. It is …" he shook his head reproachfully.

"I believe a hunt may do me good," I said. "Tomorrow?"

"Héehe'e."

When I returned to Black Bear's lodge that evening, Sitting Bull was there, standing beside Reaches For The Wind.

"This is a good horse," he said in Lakota, running his hand down her neck.

"That she is," I said.

He patted the horse's flank and then walked around her and stood facing me. His eyes were narrow and black, like two pieces of flint. "Wačhiwi belonged here. She is no longer, yet here you are."

"I'm leaving tomorrow."

"To return to the whites?"

"I'm going hunting. After that, I don't know."

"You would do well to stay here. Red Cloud and Black Bear believe you are as we are."

"And what do you believe?"

He seemed to consider his answer. "I believe that you are not my enemy," he said. "But Wačhiwi and your son would still be walking in this world if you would have stayed among us." He moved over and stood between Evelyn and Reaches For The Wind. "These are good horses," he said, then turned and strode away.

I said my farewell to Red Cloud and a few others that night, and to Black Bear in the morning over cups of coffee. It was snowing lightly as I rode away from the camp.

"Your revenge will come later, when your spirit is ready," Standing Elk said as we sat smoking by the fire of our first camp, which we'd set against the south side of a low butte. I'd thought about bringing up the subject several times that day, but was enjoying talking of simple things and didn't want to spoil it for either of us.

"I feel as though I'm betraying Wačhiwi and William by waiting," I said.

"Often it is better to wait until your enemy believes you are sleeping, and perhaps these white manhunters from Texas will forget you, in time. For now, we will hunt, and live peacefully, as the Great Spirit intended. There is time to go back to war. I've had many dreams … there will be much more fighting. I've also dreamed of Nótaxemâhta'sóoma … he rides a horse the color of the grass in the Cool Moon, and holds his hand up to me from the distance, as if he still walks in this world."

We spent the next year wandering the north country, which still mostly belonged to the Indians then. It was one of the most peaceful times of my life.

There was a letter waiting for me at the Lakota camp when I returned in April of 1871. Red Cloud was holding it for me. Chief Big Mouth and five men from his band had escorted a small party of soldiers to the camp two months prior to deliver it. The unaddressed envelope contained a single sheet of paper. Written on it in a barely legible scrawl was this:

Mister Ward,

I hope this finds you in good health. William Meecham, (Colonel, Retired.) would like to discuss matters of some import with you. For now, I can say that your entanglements in Texas have been successfully resolved in your favor, but there is more to be discussed. You will find either Mister Meecham or myself at Fort Laramie through the remainder of the spring.

Yours, Respectfully and Sincerely,
Captain Robert Lange

"He wrote it there beside the fire," Red Cloud said. "We shared a smoke, and he used all the right words, but I didn't trust him. He was there, at one of the Great Father's meetings at the fort on the Platte River. This was before we started fighting over the forts in the north. It was the first time General Sherman told me he wanted us to move to the Missouri. I have told them many times since, that if the Great Father likes the Missouri so much, he should live there himself."

Red Cloud was too polite to ask what was in the letter, so I read it to him.

"This means the whites no longer hunt you?"

"That's right. At least that's what he's saying."

"Beware. Soldiers of the Great Father are seldom truthful."

"Standing Elk is going with me."

"This is good. Standing Elk of the Tsêhéstáno has traveled far from his people, but he will be good medicine for you."

Standing Elk and I departed for Fort Laramie that very day. On our way, we delivered somewhere around four hundred pounds of meat to the Cheyenne and Lakota camps, though neither greatly needed it. There was still plenty of deer, elk, and buffalo in the spring of 1871, and all of the Indian camps in the Bighorn, Powder, and Tongue River region were well supplied and living as they always had. We saved close to another six hundred pounds for the Indians camped near Fort Laramie, who would almost certainly need it more.

We arrived at Fort Laramie the first week of May. The outlying Indian camps—mostly Cheyenne, Sioux, and Arapaho—were indeed in need of the meat we carried. Standing Elk called them *agency Indians*, though he said this without rancor. He said that all Indians who'd capitulated to the U.S. government and relied on same, ended up living in poverty and beggary.

Nearer the fort I noticed a great deal more traders than there had been previously. They were spread out for miles. Many were operating out of the backs of wagons, or shoddily-constructed lean-tos. They sold everything from canned food, to clothing, to tobacco. Most sold spirits in one form or another and drunken Indians loitered about many of them. A pair of such men waylaid Standing Elk and I as we passed, aggressively asking for money. Standing Elk said something to them that I didn't quite hear, and the men went off on a tirade about him being a slave to the whites.

When we arrived at the fort, we weren't allowed to enter because Standing Elk was an Indian and I refused to ride in without him. I showed the sentries the letter from Captain Lange, and they bid me wait. After some twenty minutes, one of them returned and escorted Standing Elk and I to the quartermaster's office. Captain Lange was seated behind the tiny desk.

"That'll be all, Corporal," he said to our escort.

Once the soldier was gone and the door closed behind him, Captain Lange said, "Trouble seems to follow you wherever you go, Everett." He shot a glance at Standing Elk. "You three are as thick as thieves. Too bad your negro friend's locked up down in Huntsville; this would be a regular reunion."

Standing Elk and I exchanged a glance.

"Is this supposed to be humorous, Captain?" I said. "Because I don't find it so. Not at all."

Captain Lange sighed, rubbed his hand over his beard, and then patted his hand on a stack of paper on his desk. "I'm not fooling about. I don't have the time for it. I have forty pages of notes on this mire. A lot of it's third-hand news, but I'll tell you what I know.... Henry was taken from the jail and lynched by town men in Sherman after they killed a deputy sheriff in the street. There was a fight over it—no doubt you two were the men involved." He pointed at Standing Elk. "Probably where you took that ball through your face; isn't that right? Well, the sheriff arrived with his deputies and some armed volunteers, but by then most of the fight had been taken out of the men doing the lynching. It seems seven of them were killed by the two men who intended to stop their doings."

He looked pointedly at us before he continued.

"Henry was lying on the ground when the sheriff arrived, the rope still around his neck. A doctor showed up, but he busied himself with the wounded town men. It was the sheriff who finally took a look at Henry and saw he was breathing. They hauled him right back to the jail and there he lay. Looks like they left it up to God whether he lived or died. The doctor went to see him two days later, but there wasn't much he could do by then but salve the rope wound on his neck. After that, they waited for the circuit judge. When he got there, he held a trial. He listened to everyone's account, and then found Henry guilty of accessory to murder. Normally, he'd have been hanged—probably that very afternoon—but the judge felt sympathetic to the fact that he'd already been hanged, and sentenced him to thirty years hard labor down in Huntsville Penitentiary instead.... You know the rest. Captain Parker came across you out on the Santa Fe and sent me a dispatch telling me what you told him. I wired Colonel Meecham, who in turn wired the governor of Texas. Eventually the charges against you were dropped. From what the colonel told me before he was called back to Washington, Governor Davis sent one of his best lawyers from Austin up to Sherman to interview witnesses. A man who owned a hotel there ..." He began shuffling through his notes.

"Calvin Englebright?" I said.

"That's right. Englebright. Englebright said there was a maid who could corroborate your story. It took some time, because she was out east, but they sent for her and she did just that. A cowpuncher who worked at the ranch came forward as well, said there'd been talk amongst the hands of a women being kept captive in a room there by the younger McBain. The maid was a negro so her story might not have held much water if it weren't for the cowpuncher. Governor

Davis's man reported back to him down in Austin, and not long after, they dropped the whole affair. Henry was pardoned just last week, months after you, but the wheels turn slowly, don't they? Especially when it comes to releasing a convicted negro from prison. But they'll be releasing him soon. Any questions before I move on?"

Still trying to make sense of what I was just told, I shook my head. Standing Elk remained silent.

"Good. Now I'd just as soon have Colonel Meecham explain all this, but since he's not here, it falls to me.... The colonel's been tasked by a certain group of Senators and Congressmen to report on the Indian situation here in the west. These politicians feel that the Bureau of Indian Affairs, as well as the War Department, have been mishandling the—"

Standing Elk made a *hhmmff* sound—not quite a laugh—but Captain Lange ignored it and pressed on.

"This isn't the first time there's been a government committee assembled to investigate the goings on out here. The Doolittle Committee ordered a similar report a few years ago. There were accusations of profiteering, and fraud, and mistreatment of Indians, but in the end it didn't make one damn bit of difference in regards to Indian policy on the frontier.

"Colonel Meecham was a very respected attorney in New York before the war. He handled government affairs and the like, and has close ties to the men assembling this new committee. He retired from the military, so these friends of his thought he'd be perfect for the job of documenting whatever it is they want him to find. Me and some of my men have been charged with acting as his escort while he canvases the Indian agents, and contractors, and settlers, and soldiers

… and Indians. I can't say it's a duty I want to draw, given the choice, but I wasn't asked my opinion. Anyhow, this is where you come in, Everett. We need scouts who know the country, speak the languages, and are still on friendly terms with the Indians—particularly Sioux and Cheyenne. Unfortunately, most of the old guard has retired or died. Jim Bridger returned east, and from the rumors, James Beckwourth is dead. So's Frank Cole and Frank Tisdale. Fort Supply won't give up Richard Curtis—I heard his leg's bad anyway—or Ben Clark, and Edmund Guerrier's lost trust with some of his own. That leaves you, and, I presume, your Cheyenne friend here, if he can do his job without stealing livestock or letting his politics influence his judgement.

"What about Henry?" I said.

"I didn't recommend him, to be frank. As you may or may not know, Henry and I have history, and I don't trust him."

"But you trust me?"

"As a matter of fact. Call it intuition. Both myself and Colonel Meecham believe you're of good character—the colonel took a particular shine to you from the start. My only hope is that you're not as impressionable as you were when our paths first crossed."

"Henry's of good character," I said.

"His character is irrelevant." His eyes darted to Standing Elk. "Your negro friend is a crusader, and because of that, I don't trust him, or his motivations. We're paying a scout, to scout—which means to find us the swiftest way from one place to another, and to keep us out of the path of hostiles and interpret when required—that's all. If you're prepared to do that, then we want you. The pay will be as a private contractor; eighty dollars a month. I'll give you a little context; my salary is one hundred fifty-three dollars, and I have ten years of service and three hundred men under my command. As I've said, it's no secret that good scouts are in short supply, and Chief Big Mouth says you've learned to speak Sioux like you were born to it—"

"Standing Elk taught me. Cheyenne, as well, though I can't say I'm as easy with it as I should be.... How long would you need us? And if he and I agree, He'll need to draw the same wage I do."

"We'd contract you for a year. That's so you don't decide to abandon us in the middle of it all. If it doesn't take that long, you'll still be paid the full amount. As far as his wage, that decision is Colonel Meecham's. Paying an Indian a white man's wage isn't regular, but, under the circumstances, I don't expect he'll balk."

"We'll need to talk it over," I said.

"Take as much time as you want. The way this has been going, it'll be next spring before we get moving on it anyway. Any questions?"

"Were you with Colonel Chivington when he murdered my wife and my people?" Standing Elk said.

If Captain Lange was ruffled by the question, he didn't show it.

"No, I was not. Anything else? … Corporal?"

The door opened. "Yes, sir?"

"Escort these men back to their horses."

Standing Elk and I stood. I nodded to the captain and started toward the corporal who was standing in the doorway.

"Everett?" Captain Lange said.

I turned.

"I'm sorry about your wife and son. That was a terrible thing. If you don't accept our offer, go back to

Kansas, make a life, and forget everything else. You escaped a noose, don't put your neck in another one. You might not be as fortunate as Henry."

"I'll consider that, Captain. Thank you."

Standing Elk and I set our camp about four miles downriver from the fort, away from the Indian camps and traders. Our first thought was to ride to Huntsville, to see Henry alive and free with our own eyes. But Huntsville was over a thousand miles away, in unfamiliar territory, and we had no way of knowing when he would be released, if he hadn't been already.

For me, the scouting money would be helpful in going after Seth Grant and Jacob Plemons, but pushing that down the road for another year or longer didn't appeal to me. I was afraid one of them would find death before I got to him. It was a deadly business they were in, and I didn't want to be cheated out of my retribution. I still couldn't be certain Grant even survived the wounds Wačhiwi gave him, but my heart told me he did.

Standing Elk said he would stay with me, whatever I decided, though this wasn't the first time he'd been asked to act as a scout and interpreter for the army. In the past he'd always said no out of hand. He saw it as being a traitor; only helping whites take more from his people.

Finally, I decided I'd go back to Kansas, figuring I'd work a few weeks for James Macklin to earn money for the trail—that was if he'd still have me. I hadn't proved to be a very reliable hand. Even if he wouldn't, I owed him a debt of thanks and an explanation. It had been weighing on me for a long time, and he deserved that at the least.

There was also the possibility Henry may show there for work. I could leave a message for him.

Standing Elk stayed in camp while I returned to the fort the next day to give Captain Lange the news.

I was led to the officer's mess by a sergeant. Captain Lange was seated alone at one of the five tables, drinking coffee and reading what was probably a week-old newspaper.

"Pour yourself a cup," he said, cocking his head toward the corner of the room where there stood a large cast-iron stove with a coffee pot sitting atop the brass hot plate. I nodded, walked over, and helped myself to a tin cup from the table beside the stove.

I took a seat across from Captain Lange and tried the coffee. It was strong and good.

"I'm going to venture to say that you're not interested."

"I'm grateful for everything you and Colonel Meecham have done, but I have something I need to do."

"Your life. You have to live it how you see fit."

"That's a fact."

"And I can appreciate it, but I still wish you'd reconsider. You'd be doing your country a service, and helping out your Indian friends in the bargain."

"With all respect, I'm not looking to be a service to anyone, and my Indian friends don't need me to take care of them. Thank you for the coffee, and give my regards to Colonel Meecham."

James "Red" Macklin had been thrown from his horse the previous year. The fall broke his neck. I was told by the new foreman at his spread that he lived in a world of pain for nine days before finally succumbing to his injuries. His ranch had been purchased in its entirety by one of his competitors.

Oliver Belle still lived at the same place he'd shared with his wife Margaret, on the outskirts of Lawrence. Standing Elk and I rode out there after stopping by the cemetery so I could pay my respects to the man who'd done so much for me. Oliver had taken work at the General Mercantile in Lawrence. He didn't volunteer an explanation as to why he wasn't kept on by the new owner of the Macklin ranch and I didn't ask. He told us we could stay in the barn as long as we needed to, but he asked if Standing Elk wouldn't mind wearing some regular clothes as to draw less attention to himself. Standing Elk agreed, grudgingly, and I handed over some of mine, though they were a little tight on him. I must say he looked a sight different in brown wool trousers and a blue cotton shirt. I wished Henry would have been there to see him.

That first night, over an awkward supper of beef and peas—Oliver's daughter stared at Standing Elk's scarred face through the entire meal—Oliver told me he'd cleared out the house Wačhiwi and I had been renting.

"Mister Hadley paid me five dollars to do it," he said. "I sold all of your things, including the extra saddle and tack in the barn." He produced a small, leather drawstring sack from inside his shirt—Margaret frowned at this—and tossed it across the table to me. Inside was forty-three dollars.

"Not exactly a fortune," he said, apologetically.

"It is right now," I said.

I separated ten dollars from the thin sheaf of bills, returned it to the sack and handed it back to him.

"You didn't have to do that," he said.

"I think I did. Thank you."

"You're welcome."

We ate in silence for a while, but Margaret finally broke it:

"We're so sorry about Wačhiwi," she said.

I nodded and said, "Thank you," as soon as I felt I could say it without a crack in my voice.

We stayed two more days, but it was clear that both Oliver and Margaret were ill at ease having us there. I asked Oliver for a sheet of paper and use of his pen, and I wrote a note for Henry.

Henry,

I hope that if this finds you, it finds you well. I cannot be certain of how much you know, but Wačhiwi was killed and so was our son. I'm off to search for their murderers. They are Seth Grant and Jacob Plemons, and I will travel wherever their trail may lead. Standing Elk is with me.

Your friend,
Everett Ward

I left the note with Oliver, who promised to give it to Henry, should Henry seek him out. Standing Elk and I rode into Lawrence and purchased food, along with a red cotton shirt, brown canvas trousers and a wide-brimmed felt hat for

Standing Elk. He drew attention even in the new clothes; not just because he was an Indian, but because the angry red scars on his face stood out like lighthouse beacons. I'd traded at the store when Wačhiwi was alive, and I introduced Standing Elk as her grandfather. Chet Traynor, the shopkeeper had nodded noncommittedly at that, but was polite enough not to ask questions, and he did offer his condolences for the loss of Wačhiwi and William.

"Do I look like a white man?" Standing Elk said in English, once he'd donned the entire ensemble.

"You walked right past a mirror. It's over there," I said. He walked over and stood in front of it. After a moment, he shook his head, turned around, and walked out of the shop. I paid for our purchases and bid Mister Traynor a good day.

"You want to get a holster for that?" I said, when I saw Standing Elk atop his horse with his pistol hung from his neck.

He waved his hand, "Hová'áháne."

"Suit yourself," I said.

Chapter 10

We made our way toward Oklahoma Territory. I figured the trading post in the Chickasaw nation where I'd first encountered Jacob Plemons would be a likely enough place to start. Standing Elk changed back into his buckskins as soon as we were out of Kansas, saying he'd wear them when we were near white towns. We stopped along the way to look in on the handful of his people who were still on the southern reservation. As was usual with him, he made certain we brought meat. The hunting had been pretty fair along the way and we'd taken several day-long breaks on the trail to smoke what we'd killed.

We were disappointed when we reached the trading post. Half the roof was caved in and it appeared as if it had been some time since anyone had been there. There was a wood plank nailed over the lintel—the door itself was lying inside on the floor—on which was scrawled **Gone To Cherokee Agency** in charcoal letters.

The Cherokee reservation wasn't far, and when we arrived we made our first stop at the handful of plank and earth buildings surrounding the bustling Indian agency.

Two soldiers sauntered up while we were tying the horses to a rail in front of the largest of the buildings. They were both privates, and both unkempt and surly-looking in their soiled uniforms.

"What's your business here?" One of them said, eyeing us up and down.

"We're looking for a man who used to have a trading post over in the Chickasaw nation," I said.

"What do you want with him?"

"We've done some trading in the past."

"Is that right?"

The one who hadn't spoken yet moved closer to Standing Elk and began examining his face."

"What happened to you, Red?" he said.

Standing Elk stared down at the shorter man with distaste. Finally, he turned away and began attending to his horse.

"Gonna cost you two bits," the first man said. "Otherwise, you two can ride on. Both of you look like trouble in spades to me anyway."

I fished the money from my pocket and held it out to him.

"Where's the tribal police?" I said.

The two men looked at each other and shared almost identical looks of contempt.

"We are the tribal police," the first man said, and then nodded toward one of the plank buildings. "His name's Frank Blackwell. He's in there."

"I'll stay with the horses," Standing Elk said, looking around at the twenty or so men—mostly Indians—loitering about.

The mostly earthen store was in better shape than the one Blackwell had done his business in previously, but not by much. The inside was just as dim, and the smell was the same blend of woodsmoke, dust, and sour sweat. He did have a good deal more stock set out, mostly blankets and clothing, but it all looked to be used and of poor quality. It was easy to recognize him; he was wearing the same faded red shirt and suspenders he'd been dressed in the previous two times I'd seen him. He was standing behind a counter which ran the entire length of the building, speaking loudly to an Indian woman who was holding a baby. I stood just inside the door, waiting.

"I don't know how many times I have to tell you, this ain't a church and I don't give charity." He pointed toward the door and made a shooing motion with his hands. The woman lowered her head and hurried past me and out the door.

He turned his attention to me, appearing impatient. Recognition dawned on his face and it quickly transfigured into a mixture of fear and suspicion. "What do *you* want?" he said.

"Jacob Plemons."

"I haven't seen him in months." He reached under the counter and came up with a shotgun, which he set down on the counter in front of him. He moved his hands away from it, but not far. "I didn't have anything to do with him going after you. That business is between you and him."

I took a step forward. "I don't believe that, but if I was here for you, I would have walked in shooting. If you tell me where I can find him, you'll never see me again. Otherwise, I'm going to walk out of here, and the next time I come, you'll be dead before you see me."

He put his hands back on the shotgun, but didn't pick it up.

I stood there and waited to find out if he was going to use it. I didn't think he was, but one can never be certain what another will do when they feel threatened.

He picked up the shotgun and I steeled myself. I wasn't in killing range, but it would be a near thing if he managed a head-shot. As it turns out, I needn't have worried; he stowed the scattergun back where it had been and strode down the length of the counter to the corner, where he retrieved a sheet of paper from somewhere underneath. He returned to where he'd been and silently held out the paper, his lips pursed tightly. I walked up and took it from him; it was a handbill, and it read:

BOUNTY OFFERED

The Great Northern Cattlemen and Railroad Company Will Pay $25.00
Cash Money For Each and Every Indian Found And Killed While Residing, Hunting, Or Otherwise Loitering On Land Not Designated To Them By
The Treaty Of Fort Laramie Signed 1868
Bounties Paid At The Great Northern Office, Cheyenne.
No Questions Asked.

I stared at the handbill in disbelief.

"You'll find him up there. Nebraska, more likely than not. The other one too."

"Grant?"

"Ayuh."

"Can I keep this?"

"You go right ahead, but I'd as soon not see you again."

"I'm also looking for a negro named Henry. He has a scar on his face you couldn't miss."

"You gonna kill him too?"

"He's a friend. Have you seen him?"

"We don't get too many niggers in here …"

"Have you seen him or not?"

"I ain't seen him."

Outside, I held the handbill up to Standing Elk, who was kneeling beside our horses, handing out strips of smoked meat to a growing crowd of clamoring children. He handed the last few pieces out and then raised his hands to the children to show they were empty. He stood. "Read it," he said in English, which I did.

Standing Elk unwound the tether and carefully climbed on his horse, avoiding the children who still crowded around him. He held my gaze, and opened his mouth as if he was going to say something. Instead, he shook his head and began backing the animal away from the children. I folded the handbill, stuffed it in my pocket, and followed.

Cheyenne wasn't exactly bustling in 1871, but for a frontier town, it was sizeable. I'd estimate around fifteen hundred souls, if I was put to it. Standing Elk stayed south, in the rough, while I rode into town to look for some field glasses. I stopped at the general store, and they had a new pair for twenty-two dollars, but that was well above what I had to spend. The woman working the store suggested I go to a place at the end of town that sold second-hand goods.

The shop was a three-walled plank structure with a sod roof. Cracked and rotted tack hung from one of the walls and dusty kitchen items, canvas tarps, and broken chairs were stacked haphazardly everywhere. Plank shelves piled with goods took up most of the back wall and I found what I was looking for in a pair of battered field glasses with one cracked glass and fraying cloth wrap. There was a curtained-off section in one corner and the proprietor appeared from there while I was browsing. He was the fattest man I've ever seen. I asked him the price of the glasses and he said one dollar. At that price, I thought they would suit. I asked him if he could direct me to the Great Northern Cattlemen and Railroad Office, and he barked a hearty laugh and said, "Pardon, that hits me in the belly every time … an office, no less.… The place you're looking for is northeast of town, four miles. You a scalp hunter?"

"Just a ranch hand."

"As you say.… Can I interest you in some corn liquor? There ain't better for miles. Bargain price, too."

"No. Thank you. Just the glasses."

We found the small spread where the man said it would be. The reason for his laughter was apparent right away; it wasn't much more than a cabin with a single small barn, an outhouse, and a fenced corral that housed five horses. We posted ourselves on a nearby bluff—the nearest high ground—and it was just close enough so we could see riders come and go through the field glasses. Even so, I was dubious as to whether we'd be close enough to actually identify anyone.

"We should burn it," Standing Elk said after he'd looked through the glasses.

"I agree with you. Can we wait until we find out if this will help us find Grant and Plemons?"

He handed me the field glasses. "Héehe'e," he said.

We watched the place, taking our turns with the glasses. There were five men: one was old enough that all of his hair was gray. I put him as the leader, not only because of his age, but because he was the only one who ever went outside without a rifle. The others could have been anywhere from fifteen to fifty, it was difficult to tell from the distance.

On the fourth day a buckboard with a two-horse team rolled in trailing a cloud of dust behind it. Three of the men came out of the cabin, unloaded some crates, and the driver was on his way.

On the seventh day three riders arrived in the early afternoon. It was what we'd been waiting for, though from their sizes, I was confident none of them were Grant or Plemons. They tethered their horses on a rail below the porch. I could see what was almost certainly scalps hanging from the side of the saddle of a light gray horse. Long, black hair, like some hideously misplaced tail hung down the horse's flank.

I handed off the glasses to Standing Elk. He watched for a long time. By the time he lowered them, the men had already gone inside. He carefully set the glasses down on a rock, and then ran a hand through his hair. I don't think he was even aware of the motion.

"Did you see them?" I said. "The scalps?"

"I saw them. Perhaps twenty."

"I think we should follow right after they leave. Chances are they'll go into Cheyenne to spend some of their money. They might even stay awhile."

Standing Elk nodded. "We'll follow. If they stay in the town, you stay to watch them. When they depart, you follow, I'll come here and burn the house while the men inside sleep, then find you on the trail."

"I'll get the horses ready.'

The three men departed less than thirty minutes later. They headed back in the direction of Cheyenne. We waited until they were out of sight and then dropped down the south side of the bluff and circled up to pick up their trail, well off the road and well out of sight of the Great Northern Cattlemen and Railroad Company's 'office.'

As we suspected they would, the riders went into Cheyenne. I followed them in, while Standing Elk headed out to the draw he'd holed up in when we first arrived.

I milled around outside, fiddling with Evelyn's saddle and repacking her several times while the men visited the general store and then the saloon. The town was busy, and no one seemed to pay me any mind. Around five o'clock, they made their way down to the hotel. I was disappointed to see it. I didn't have money for a room and, busy or not, eventually I'd draw attention loitering around the street.

An hour later they sauntered out of the hotel—apparently they'd only taken a meal—and lingered on the boardwalk, smoking. After a time they mounted their horses and walked them, easy, eastward up the street. Something in the way these men carried themselves, sure, and seemingly careless, sparked a hot fury in me. I was glad Standing Elk wasn't there to see them.

Once I'd watched them pass the edge of town, I rode out to give the news to Standing Elk. It was a thirty-minute ride to the draw; Standing Elk was gutting a rabbit when I arrived.

"The three of them took the road east out of town," I said. "I don't know how long they'll keep to it. I'll leave some sign if we go rough. I'll take Reaches For The Wind with me, it'll give you the freedom to ride hard if you need to."

"I'll find you tomorrow."

"You certain you want to do this?"

"Héehe'e." He held up the rabbit with a questioning look.

I shook my head. "I better get a move on. I'll eat dried tonight."

He caught up with me twenty miles northeast of Cheyenne the following day. The sun was at my back and I easily spotted him coming. I stopped and waited for him.

"The men were poor warriors," he said in Cheyenne.

I was perplexed, as I thought he'd said something about them being lizard warriors.

A look of exasperation passed over his face. "They were poor warriors," he repeated in English. "You need to speak the language of the Tsêhéstáno more. You have forgotten what should be simple."

"I suppose you're right," I said in English, not feeling up to practicing my Cheyenne.

He let it go, and began searching the ground. After a moment he urged his horse forward, in the direction the three men were travelling. I followed and Evelyn fell into step with his horse.

"Before morning I set fires near the door," he said. "Four of the men ran out with their rifles. They looked all about, as if they were still sleeping. I shot all of them.... I waited but the old man never came out."

"Nothing more than they deserved," I said.

Five days later we crossed into Nebraska—into true buffalo country, and treaty designated hunting lands for several Indian nations.

Their tracks led us toward a cluster of mesas. Not wanting to expose ourselves, we waited out the day and moved in closer after dark. There was only a sliver of a moon and that was helpful. About a half-mile out, we tied the horses to some scrub and continued on foot. The camp was on the north side of the westernmost mesa, on a wide, low cleft. There was only one way to get up on it, and it was just high enough—probably twenty-feet—to give them an advantage in a fight. Their cook fire was cunningly concealed, but they lost all covertness with their loud, drunken-sounding voices.

It was clear the three men had met up with others. We couldn't see their horses, so it was impossible to be certain how many there were all told. We thought at least fifteen, possibly as many as twenty-five, and they were bound to have lookouts so we didn't want to move in too close. Knowing we had as much knowledge as we were likely to get, we worked our way back to our horses and rode south for a mile and found a safe place to sleep.

We doubled back in the morning; the men had broken camp and ridden east—eighteen of them, with four pack horses. There were more tracks, though. They came in from the north, and then left again the same way they'd come.

Standing Elk dismounted and studied the tracks. "Sixty horses … soldier's horses."

"Is that a fact?"

He looked up at me curiously. He did that often when I said something he thought was a waste of words.

We followed the men east, though we weren't certain what we were going to do. We only had one rifle, so an ambush would likely be suicide. Regardless, we didn't want to lose them, so we continued on, but at an easy pace.

We came into the absolute flats; the prairie grass was high and brown, with only faint hints of green leftover from the recent spring. The scalp hunter's horses cut a clear path, meandering like the trail of a giant snake. As we rode, I decided to ask Standing Elk a question that had been troubling my mind for some time.

"Why did you choose to continue on with me all this time, instead of staying with your people?"

He seemed to consider this carefully. Finally, he said:

"I mourn when I am with them. I mourn my wife, and I mourn our ways, which are slowly dying like this grass. I cannot live by the commands of the white men in the east, or the soldiers they send to break us like horses. I cannot sit and grow old with my hand out to them for their leavings while they grow fat from our despair. We are free, you and I, and now we have a purpose together; to hunt these men who murder Indians for metal and paper."

Knowing we couldn't lose their trail on the prairie, we stopped for an entire day and hunted, hoping to replenish our dwindling meat supply. There was no game to be found, so we continued on the next morning.

That afternoon we came upon a place where seven of the riders had suddenly veered south. Another path—made by people on foot—trailed away to the north. Eleven of the horses had gone in that direction but then returned and followed the others south. Standing Elk and I followed them, and the next morning we came upon eight bodies. They were lying strewn in a circle of trampled prairie: one woman and seven children. We judged the children to be from six to thirteen years. The woman was stripped naked, there was blood between her legs. All of them were scalped. Standing Elk said they were Pawnee.

The scalp hunters rode northeast from the killing field, presumably to resume their previous path. I mounted Evelyn and started in that direction. Standing Elk didn't move to follow. I stopped and waited. He shook his head and then nodded toward the direction we'd come from.

"There were others," he said.

I looked at the bodies, then at him.

"All right."

We returned to the place where the men had first discovered the Pawnee woman and children. Standing Elk dismounted, I did the same and followed him as he walked his horse on the foot-path that led away to the north. The sign told us that four women and fifteen children had been walking south. The scalp hunters had spotted them from a distance, but the women must have also seen the riders. For some reason the group split up; the dead woman and children ran south, the others turned back the way they'd come, and had somehow managed to elude the eleven riders who'd pursued them.

We found the three women and eight children that afternoon. They were camped in the shade of a tree, on the grassy bank of an almost dry pothole lake to the northeast of where they'd been discovered by the scalp hunters.

The women took a defensive position around the children as we rode up. One of them held a knife.

Standing Elk reached into one of the two grain sacks he kept tied together with a hank of rope and slung over his horse's flanks. When he withdrew his hand, it was holding a bundle of our dried meat. He said something to the women in a language I didn't understand, and then slowly dismounted and took a few steps toward the group. Pausing while he was still ten feet away, he said something else, and held up the meat. One of the women hurried forward, took the bundle, and then stepped back just as quickly. Standing Elk turned to me and cocked his head. I dismounted, minding I did it slowly. He sat down cross-legged without moving any closer to them. I sat next to him in the same fashion. He spoke some more words and the women seemed to relax. They all sat as well, and the woman who'd taken the meat distributed it amongst them. They ate greedily, as if it had been some time since they'd had anything. Standing Elk remained silent while they ate. When they were finished, he said something else. The women looked at each other, and a few words passed between them. They all nodded in some sort of agreement and the women who'd wielded the knife began to speak. Standing Elk translated.

"Our men were hunting to the north of here. Our village was to the south. When they didn't return, some of us went searching for them." She pointed to two of the women. "Her and her, and another who we lost when the white men found us. We found our husbands; they were killed by Lakota warriors. When we returned to our village, we discovered that the Lakota had attacked there also. Our grandfathers and mothers and some women and children were killed, but some," —she pointed to the other woman, and then swept her hand in front of the children— "hid themselves. We walked south to find our relatives' village. That's when the white men found us. Iírikis and her children ran to the south, while we ran to the north. We called after her but she did not hear. We ran and ran, and then there were Lakota men on horses—perhaps twenty. We ran east while the white men and Lakota faced each other from a distance. I don't know what came of it. Neither pursued us."

Standing Elk turned to me. "We must find these Lakota men. They can help us kill the scalp hunters."

A boy of about eleven stood and walked over to me then, ignoring the admonishment from one of the women. He pointed at the kerchief I was wearing around my neck. It had been blue, once, but it was faded to an almost gray, and lines of permanent sweat stains ran across it in the places where it had been folded. I took it off and handed it over. He ran back to the other children waving it in the air triumphantly.

"What about them?" I said, nodding toward the children. "Shouldn't we see them to wherever their other relations are?"

"We cannot help them. The Cheyenne are the enemies of the Pawnee. Their warriors would kill us."

My mouth must have been hanging agape because Standing Elk held up his hand.

"I know what you would say, but it is not for me to decide peace."

"If Indians would have chosen peace with each oth—" I cut myself off. "Never mind," I said. "It's not my place to speak." I turned my head to the sky. There was a single wispy cloud floating slowly to the southeast. It was a beautiful image. I stared at it and wondered what was wrong with men that we could turn the world into such an awful place.

We left the women with half of what was left of meat—it wasn't much—and departed to track the Lakota men. We found them thirty miles to the southeast, some twenty miles north of the Platte River. Once we spotted them, we followed them slowly until one of them finally looked back and noticed us. They stopped and readied their weapons, but didn't mount an attack.

As we approached, Standing Elk recognized someone. He pointed and said, "Pawnee Killer," in English. We stopped our horses some feet away and faced the eighteen Lakota men. Standing Elk greeted the leader and introduced me. The man said he knew of me as a friend to the Lakota.

He nodded gravely as Standing Elk told him of the scalp hunters. Afterward, he agreed to help us kill them.

It turned out Pawnee Killer was actually his name. It's likely that wasn't his original name—unlike whites, Indians often change theirs due to feats or events. He was middle-aged and severe of features, but he smiled easily and was friendly enough. As we rode together over the next two days, I had a difficult time reconciling this with the fact that he was the same man who led his men to murder other Indian women and children.

The scalp hunters weren't completely foolish, they'd set a watch, but there was no high ground for them to camp on and the grass was waist high. We waited until around three in the morning. We left the horses tethered a mile back and walked half the distance. Then we crawled until we were within a hundred feet of the camp. We approached from downwind. The wind blowing through the grass masked any noise we made moving through it but carried sound to us from the camp. I could hear a man whistling softly, likely their watchman.

It was agreed that Pawnee Killer would lead. He had a Henry repeating rifle, and two of his men had Springfields. The rest carried bows and war clubs. When there was just enough of a glow in the east to see shapes, Pawnee Killer let out a cry and charged. The rest of us leapt up and followed. The whistling ceased and the scalp hunter's watchman screamed *Indians* at the top of his voice. I stopped at about thirty feet and took a knee and started shooting. I shot two men who were just getting blearily to their feet, before

Standing Elk and the Lakota men hit the camp and I couldn't tell who was who anymore. Shouts and war cries, screams of pain, and rifle and pistol reports all mingled in a confused disharmony. I stood and ran into the fray, picking targets once I got close enough to see who I was shooting at. It was over in minutes. Every one of the scalp hunters lay dead or dying. Two Lakota men were killed and one gravely injured. Some of the Lakota men moved through the camp and cut the throats of the wounded scalp hunters. The warriors began gathering whatever they wanted from the belongings of the dead. Standing Elk took a Sharps rifle from one of them. I walked through and looked for Seth Grant and Jacob Plemons. Even in the dim I saw with disappointment that they were not among the dead. As the sun rose, I could see money the Lakota men had either missed or ignored, trapped and fluttering in patches of untrampled grass on the downwind side of the camp. I went around and collected all I could find.

We parted with Pawnee Killer and his men less than an hour after we attacked. They scattered to all points, in order to throw off pursuit. We made a couple of circles for the same reason and then rode south. We didn't decide on that direction, we just broke out of our ever-widening circle and rode. Neither of us knew what to do next.

"I wish we would have thought twice about burning that place outside of Cheyenne down.... I feel the fool. We could have used it to find more of these men, and Grant and Plemons—"

"More Indians would have been killed while we watched and waited. The head has been cut from the snake. For a time."

I felt ashamed when he put it that way. He was right, after all.

"Perhaps we should go to Fort Laramie, to look for Henry, then back to Cheyenne. We still may find something there."

"Nótaxemâhta'sóoma has gone back to Mexico. I first believed he would not, but I've dreamed of his crossing the great river."

"What's in Mexico?"

"A woman."

"Are you going to tell me what went on down there?"

"Someday."

I could only shake my head.

We turned west, with no particular destination agreed upon. A full circle.

Two days later, we spotted riders coming fast from the northeast; easily seventy, possibly more.

"Army," I said.

Standing Elk nodded. "They want to know who killed their friends."

I thought about the signs of army horses at the camp of the scalp hunters. "We should hope that's not it," I said.

We kept riding as we were, clutching the dim possibility that the arrival of the cavalry was mere coincidence. When they overtook us, we halted, and they immediately surrounded us. At least sixty soldiers, three white men in civilian clothes, and a half-dozen Indians, likely Crow or Arikara.

A man in a colonel's uniform urged his horse forward until he was facing us. "What is your business here, sir?" he said, addressing me. He gazed curiously at Standing Elk for a moment before turning his attention back to me. I was struck by the familiarity of his face. It was much like my own, only his eyes were more close set and his nose was larger. My beard was fully grown in by then, but I'd worn a similar moustache as the one on his face some time before. He pushed his horse so close that its nose was right up to Evelyn's. I could smell some sort of a spice, cinnamon perhaps, and I wasn't certain whether it was coming off of him or his horse.

"I'll have an answer," he said.

"We're heading to Fort Laramie. We've been asked to do some scouting for Colonel Meecham and Captain Lange."

The colonel removed his hat and fussed with his hair. The motion was one of practiced familiarity, and wholly feminine. He didn't seem to be aware he was doing it.

"Is that a fact, Mister …?" he said finally, returning his hat to his head.

"Ward. Everett Ward. This man is Standing Elk, of the Cheyenne."

He nodded. "Ward, yes … Captain Lange asked if I'd keep an eye out for you." He waved his hand vaguely behind him; "This was some time ago, of course.… Apparently, Colonel Meecham has aspirations of becoming a senator." He shot another quick look at Standing Elk. "We were tracking the murdering variety of the noble Indian when we came across your trail. You saw the carnage?"

"Yes. The fight couldn't have been more than a few hours old when we happened by. I wondered what they'd been doing out here. There wasn't any sign they'd been hunting."

A look I'll never forget flashed across Custer's features then. He knew precisely what they were up to. The look passed as quickly as it came, but I couldn't unsee it.

"What, indeed," is what he said. "Tragic."

Something caught my eye just then, a flutter of blue-gray from the rear rigging of a soldier's saddle, just behind Colonel Custer.

"Where did you get that?" I said.

Custer turned to see who I was addressing. The soldier, a corporal, appeared confused.

"That kerchief, on your saddle. Where did you get it?"

"I took it off an Indian pup, if it's any affair of yours," he said.

I handed the reins to Standing Elk, dismounted and walked over and faced the corporal. "Did you kill him?"

"Killing Indians has become the seventh cavalry's business, Mister Ward. Not by my choice, but by the Indians' own," Custer said from behind me.

I reached up and untied the kerchief. The corporal didn't move to stop me.

"This is mine," I said. "I gave it to that boy.... Did you kill him?"

The corporal didn't answer. He turned his head away and stared out at the prairie. It was answer enough for me. I stuffed the kerchief in my pocket and walked back to Evelyn.

"It appears Colonel Meecham found just the right man to assist him on his errand," Custer said. "I considered a run for office, once, before I found my true calling. Farewell, Mister Ward."

He turned to Standing Elk. "That is a remarkable wound. Do you mind if I ask where you received it?"

Standing Elk met Custer's eyes for a moment, and then turned his horse and pushed her through the line of soldiers. He waited for me outside of the circle. Custer watched after him and then muttered, something under his breath. After a moment, he said, "Corporal Meyers, we'll be riding north to rendezvous with the rest of the men. Give the orders."

Later that afternoon, after being even more silent and pensive than usual, Standing Elk said this:

"When I was a young man, my father taught me to hunt on this land. There were times then, that we would roam for days and not see another. Even after he passed to the Spirit World, I would come here, sometimes with other hunters, and sometimes alone, and I would walk without fear. That time is over. This land is vast, but it is not vast enough."

We arrived back at Fort Laramie two weeks later. I couldn't get the picture of the Pawnee boy exuberantly waving my kerchief in the air out of my mind. My son was dead, Wačhiwi was dead, and nothing was going to bring them back. In the end I realized my revenge was far less important than the lives of Indian children who already had the deck stacked against them simply because they were born. If Colonel Meecham's friends in Washington wanted to know the truth of what was happening, and that truth might save some of those children, then I wanted to help him learn just what that truth was; starting with the scalp hunters. Standing Elk didn't require any convincing; he was as lost as I was.

As always, we brought smoked meat to give out, but we discovered there weren't nearly as many Indians camped nearby as there usually was. Some of the traders had moved out as well. There were still more stomachs than the food we'd brought would fill, but a great many Indians had gone elsewhere, nonetheless. After canvassing several people, an

Arapaho elder who was missing half of his left foot told Standing Elk that most of the Lakota had gone to live near the new Red Cloud agency and more Cheyenne had been pushed south by the army. As we handed out the meat, I recalled how I'd once wondered why the Indians around the fort didn't just leave, and go where the hunting was good. With my mind's eye I saw the scalped women and children lying dead on the trampled and blood-stained prairie grass.

I'd been as green as Captain Lange said I was.

There was a ruckus at one of the small camps nearest the fort; several Lakota women and one old man were being held by four soldiers at rifle-point. A fifth soldier was holding up what appeared to be an animal leg bone and was shouting at the terrified group about a stolen dog. I was about to intervene when a soldier in a lieutenant's uniform rode up and put a stop to the interrogation and sent his grumbling men back to the fort.

We waited underneath the fort's lookout while the sentries sent for someone in authority. The someone turned out to be the duty sergeant, who told us that Captain Lange was away and that Colonel Meecham had also departed to an unknown destination a week prior. We left word for Captain Lange—the sergeant was unsure of when he'd be returning—and then I went inside to visit the Alden's store for supplies, while Standing Elk rode downriver to set us a camp.

Captain Lange sent for me a week later. He left instructions for me not to bring Standing Elk. Specifically, the handwritten note said, *Do not bring the Indian.* We met in the mess again.

"Your change of heart came too late," he said, after we'd exchanged pleasantries. I didn't need to ask why he didn't want Standing Elk there because I'd already deduced that the previous offer had been retracted. Captain Lange didn't like Indians, and for some reason he particularly didn't like Standing Elk. If I could no longer be of service to him, then he was no longer obligated to tolerate the company of Standing Elk. It was a testament to how narrow of mind Captain Lange was. Standing Elk was the real scout, and one who spoke four Native languages.

"Is that so?" I said

"It is. William Belknap wasn't happy when he discovered his army was being used to investigate itself—"

"Who's William Belknap?" I said.

He shook his head, looking exasperated. "Do you know who the president is?"

"Grant," I said.

"Well at least you're not completely ignorant. William Belknap is the Secretary of War, and he leveraged his pal Grant and had the plug pulled on this whole affair—which was as fine as paint with me. Too bad for you two. If you would have taken the job at the beginning, I would have had to honor an entire year's pay for you both."

"Well, then," I said, standing. "Thank you for your time, Captain."

"Everett, I already spoke with my commanding officer. He'd said I could put you on the payroll here. We're always in need of good scouts. The offer doesn't extend to the Indian, though."

"You know his name, Captain."

He nodded as much to himself as to me. "Yes, I do. You look after yourself."

"Goodbye, Captain."

I felt unsettled as I rode back to our camp. I suddenly understood that my life was meaningless. Even if I found and killed Grant and Plemons, then what? What was next for me? I'd been so fixated on tasks, that along the way I'd slowly lost the unshakeable—though often unrealistic—sense of hope that young people almost always possess, without being aware it was happening. My view of the world had gone dark and cynical as slyly as a cancer eats away at a man's innards. My life had been one of blood and death and loss since before I'd shaved the first whisps of stubble from my face, and I was no longer able to envision it ever being more than that. Part of me wanted to go look for Henry in Mexico, if that's where he was. I knew Standing Elk believed in his dreams and visions, but I didn't. If Henry was really down there, and he'd found a woman, then the best I could do for him was leave him be. Standing Elk wouldn't say anything about what had gone on when they were in Mexico, but he didn't seem in too much of a hurry to find Henry either. He played things pretty close to the vest, but I got the sense that he probably felt the same as I did.

Back at camp, Standing Elk and I sat by the fire and smoked. We didn't speak much; I think we were both lost in our own thoughts.

"I suppose I'm going to continue looking for Grant and Plemons," I said.

He nodded as if he'd been waiting for this. "I'll go to the southern agency to look in on them," he said. "You will need to linger in towns where I am not welcome and would not wish to be. The white man's clothes do not suit me anyway."

I was inclined to argue, but I knew he was right. I'd picked up over a hundred and seventy-five dollars of the scalp hunter's money. I could ride from town to town and use it to buy information. Standing Elk would be left waiting in the rough, more often than not, purely because he had been born an Indian.

The next morning I divided the money, walked over to where Standing Elk was packing his horse and held out half of it. He stared at it in my outstretched hand and then turned without a word and resumed his work.

"You know there's no game down there anymore. At least with this you can buy what you need from a trader until I finish this business. After that, I'll meet up with you and we'll go hunt woolies up north."

He turned then, and the look of sadness on his face broke my heart. But I knew it wasn't sadness for our parting. It was because he knew he had no home; that he would never have a home again, and that the freedom he'd spoken of when we were on the plains was nothing more than words. How can someone be free in a world that is no longer theirs?

He took the money and put it in his tobacco sack, then he nodded once, mounted his horse, and rode away.

I rode south to Fort Collins, Colorado. It's where I began drinking, though it would be some time before it began to take its toll. The town wasn't much of anything then, but there was a boarding house and a saloon. I paid for two days at the boarding house; it was the first time I'd slept in a bed since my last night at home with Wačhiwi, unless you count the metal rack with the hay-filled mattress on top of it at the hospital in Fort Larned.

The first night, I had a bath with hot water—something else I'd not enjoyed in some time—and had a bottle of beer filled at the saloon, which I took to my room and drank while I read a week-old copy of a Denver newspaper. The act reminded me of my days at the boarding house in Sherman. I spent most of the following day in the saloon, where I bought drinks and asked just about everyone, from drifters, to drovers, to the bartender, to the town sot, if they'd heard of or knew Seth Grant or Jacob Plemons. No one had.

So I moved on.

I rode south, stopping briefly in Denver, and after that, to what is now Colorado Springs, though it wasn't much more than the surviving remnants of the Pikes Peak gold rush back then. I arrived at midday and the sky was clear and it was promising to be hot. I bought a mason jar of some sort of grain liquor from a man selling from the back of a wagon. I asked him if he knew of Grant or Plemons; he said he didn't. I sat beside the creek to drink the liquor and read out of one of the two books I'd purchased in Denver.

"Everett Ward?" came a familiar voice from behind me.

I turned to see Colonel Meecham. He was dressed neatly, in a blue cotton shirt and brown trousers with brown suspenders. His face was clean-shaven, and he wore a brown flat-brimmed hat. His face was more careworn, and he was thinner than when we'd first met, but it was him.

"This is fortuitous," he said.

I stood. "Colonel," I said. And as an afterthought, I held out the mason jar. He looked at it, considering for a moment, and then took the jar.

"No telling what he makes this with," he said, before tipping the jar and taking a taste. He handed it back. "Thank you."

"You're welcome. Would you like to sit?"

"If you have some time, I have a tent just over there with a pair of folding chairs in it." He pointed upstream. I could see a white canvas officer's tent set high on the bank. I untethered Evelyn and Reaches For The Wind and followed him over.

"Is this your wagon?" I said, nodding at a buckboard parked alongside the tent.

"Yes, it is."

I tied the horses to the back.

The tent was furnished with two folding chairs, a small folding table, and a folding army cot. There were three leather suit cases off to one side and he walked over to these as soon as we entered. "Take a chair," he offered.

He returned from the suit cases with a small humidor. "The cigar I was unable to offer you the last time we met."

I took one and thanked him. He struck a match, lit mine, and then one for himself, before sitting in the chair across from me.

He puffed on his cigar and exhaled appreciatively. "I understood you were travelling with Standing Elk…."

"He decided to spend some time on the Southern Cheyenne reservation."

"He should be careful. If the Indian agent there puts him on the rolls, he'll have trouble coming and going as he pleases."

"He'll manage.… I haven't been able to thank you for what you did for me … so, thank you."

"Please don't. I'm not deserving of your thanks. In fact, I want to ask for your forgiveness. I told you I would make inquiries for you and I never did—that is until I needed your assistance. For that, I'm truly sorry. I had every intention of writing a letter to the local sheriff after you came to Fort Phil Kearny, but another event overshadowed everything else, and I forgot.

It took a moment for me to grasp what I was just told, and then all of the possible outcomes began to flood my mind. I'd always assumed he'd written his inquiry, and that it had likely been ignored by Sheriff Flood. Learning he'd never looked into it at all took my breath away.

He leaned forward. His expression was pained, earnest. "Mister Ward—Everett," he said. "I received a dispatch the very morning you returned to Fort Phil Kearny to give me the news of your meeting with Chief Red Cloud. The letter informed me of my wife's death, but it gave no cause. I departed for New York the next day. My wife's brother met me at the train station. He told me she was a … a suicide. She'd shot herself with our son's revolver, which had been delivered to our home the previous day, along with his uniform and a folded American flag. She did it in the bedroom we'd shared for twenty-two years. Our son had been killed more than eight months before, but as you know the United States Army moves slowly on most matters. I think receiving that parcel was too much for her. He was our only child. He was your age—"

"Stop talking, please," I said. I was light in the head. I was breathing, but I felt as if I wasn't getting air, and I couldn't think. I set the cigar in the hammered copper ashtray on the table and put my head down. After several minutes the feeling began to pass. I lifted my head; he was gazing at me with an expression of concern. I wanted to be angry. I wanted to hate him. But I couldn't. Everything happened the way it happened and nothing could change that. I thought of the boy waving my kerchief in the air. I might have been able to save that boy, and I didn't try.

"I'm sorry about your wife, and your son," I said. "It's understandable you forgot about …" I trailed off.

"And I'm sorry about yours. I truly am. Captain Lange told me everything. I'd ask you not to fault him for that.… There's more.… Not long after I returned west, General Sheridan ordered me and my men to clear out a renegade camp of Cheyenne Dog Soldiers on the south Platte River. We found the camp, right where it was supposed to be. I rode ahead with the scouts to have a look, and we discovered it was inhabited almost entirely by women and children. There were a few old men, but there were no warriors. After four days of watching the comings and goings, I sent word to the general that his reconnaissance was incorrect. If there had been warriors there, they were gone. We camped several miles away and waited for orders to come back. Colonel Custer arrived with his seventh, eight days later. He very loudly relieved me of my command, per General Sheridan's orders. I left that afternoon. The next morning at dawn, he attacked the camp and killed every soul. Afterward, I resigned my commission and returned to New York. I spent months reflecting on my morality and how my indifference to the suffering and displacement … and murder of these people must appear in the eyes of God. Do you know for most of my life, I never considered Indians at all, and when I was first sent west, I didn't think of them much differently than I did animals. I wonder if I'm damned for that. I decided I couldn't live with what I learned out here, so I wrote to friends, and a handful of acquaintances in congress, and I convinced them to assemble a committee to investigate how the War Department, through the Department of the Interior, is treating Indians in this region. One of my closest friends, who I'll not name, risked a great deal to make it possible. He was understandably reluctant; there was another such committee a few years ago. They failed to influence any changes. When all was said and done it didn't matter anyway. The War Department got wind of this new effort and it was silently shut down."

"Captain Lange told me some of it," I said. "What are you doing now?"

"I'm writing a book. Eventually every acre of this land will belong to the United States and there's nothing anyone can do to stop it. I knew that before I was first sent west, but I was indifferent to it. God and country, after all.

"I've come believe that most of us will ignore even the most egregious atrocities if it doesn't affect our lives directly, and further, I believe that far too many of us will readily commit them, if it will enrich us, and we can do so from afar. Now that I've come to my senses, I'm also aware that I can't help them. My intention is to document what's happening so that someday the history books can tell the truth of it."

He smashed his cigar in the ashtray. I'm waiting here for some men interested in hiring on to be my escorts and interpreters. I'd rather have you. You were my first choice to begin with. I can pay you seventy-five dollars a week."

"This all from your own purse?"

"Yes, it is."

"Would you mind if I ask why me, Colonel? You don't know me other than that treaty affair I helped botch."

"I'd say that was nothing more than a first experience for both of us. I didn't know how to navigate the water I was in any better than you did. If you'll call me William—or Bill, instead of Colonel, I'll tell you why. There's not much to it."

"All right.… William was my son's name."

"Well, you reminded me of *my* son, from the very first. He'd only been in the grave a short time when I met you. You don't look much like him, but at the time your manner was enough like his that it was unsettling. You're different now, of course. The years have hardened you. I can still see a similarity, however, just not like it was. His name was William, also.

"Captain Lange, though we're about as different as two men can be, took a liking to you from the start as well. He kept his ear to the ground about you."

I considered his offer, and didn't see that it was any different than the one we'd returned to Fort Laramie to accept. I thought about Grant and Plemons, and I thought of Standing Elk. I thought I could let Grant and Plemons go awhile longer. I'd been intending to anyway.

"I'd want Standing Elk with me," I said.

"I thought you might. Will he do it?"

"I believe he will."

The men William Meecham had been waiting for arrived five days later. He thanked them for riding all the way down from Denver and then paid them each seventy-five dollars for their trouble. I didn't know how he came to make their acquaintance and I didn't ask. Collectively, their manner seemed churlish and shifty to me, and I thought I'd do well to keep an eye on our backtrail for a while.

I suggested that he sell the wagon—though he'd only just purchased it—and buy two pack horses instead. It would be easier travelling and we wouldn't look as appealing—or easy—to those who may want to take what we had. He agreed, and we departed two days later, bound for Oklahoma Territory.

We found Standing Elk at one of the several Cheyenne camps scattered in between Fort Cobb and Fort Reno. The military presence in the area was heavy and we were stopped twice on the journey and asked about our business. William handled the inquiries with patience and diplomacy, and he used the inconveniences of the stops as opportunities to ask questions of the soldiers. We were left both times with the admonishment to watch out for Indians, as they had been robbing travelers through the nations.

Standing Elk seemed both angry and despondent when we found him sitting on the ground, angrily ripping the feathers from a small turkey. His horse was standing next to him. He had a length of rope tied to the mare's hackamore with the other end tied around his wrist.

He looked up as we approached. As usual he didn't appear to be surprised to see me. He glanced at William Meecham and afforded him a short nod before turning back to me. He held up the skinny turkey and gave it a shake. "This is all I found in four days. There are hunters hiding behind every rock as far as you can see, but nothing to hunt. I have to keep my horse near so that others don't steal her and eat her. The rations we receive are not suitable for dogs, when they arrive at all. Now the army and the agents sent by the Great Father Grant tell my people to move from place to place whenever they choose and the land of the Tsêhéstáno grows smaller."

He finished plucking the bird, stood, and carried it over to an old woman tending to an enamel pot over a cookfire. He handed it over without a word. She smiled a nearly toothless smile; he returned the smile and then strode over and stood before us. "Do you have money?"

"Yes," I said, reaching into my pocket and removing the folded bills. I held the money out to him. "It's around sixty-dollars."

"There are traders near Fort Reno. I will get as much food as I can with this—a little from each one so that they will not question where the money came from. After, I will bring the food here. Then I will go with you."

I looked at William; he nodded. "We'll go with you," I said.

Chapter 11

For the next six years, William Meecham, Standing Elk, and myself, traveled the west: Colorado, Kansas, South Dakota, Nebraska, North Texas, and what is now Wyoming, Montana and Oklahoma, while William filled his seemingly endless supply of blank books with words written with dozens upon dozens of pencils. The things we saw … I don't know where to begin; so much of it was unspeakable. And if I tried to tell it all, it would fill volumes, so I'm going to tell the parts that marked me the most. I was pretty well numb by the time William returned to New York in 1877 with the hundreds—possibly thousands—of pages of notes he'd taken. As time and events passed, I drank more and more, and so did William. Standing Elk wouldn't touch it. For William and I, the liquor helped mute the reality of the time. Standing Elk endured what he saw, but it took its toll. By 1876, he couldn't abide the life we were living any longer. He packed his things one morning and left William and I near the foot of the Black Hills without so much as an au revoir. Six months later, having spent a considerable portion of his family fortune, William declared he had all he needed for his book. He caught a train east from Kansas City.

He did say goodbye. There's that.

William never wasted time. He interviewed Standing Elk and the elders on the reservation before we departed to purchase food for the camp as Standing Elk wanted. Near Fort Reno, he interviewed the Indian agent appointed to the southern Cheyenne reservation at the time—I can't recall his name now, but I remember he was a distasteful man who had a habit of digging in his ear with his forefinger while he spoke. The agent didn't want to talk to William at first, but William changed his mind with his convincing manner and a twenty-dollar piece—one of hundreds of such payments I witnessed him make over the coming years.

We rode north, intent on visiting Red Cloud. Along the way, we stopped at ranches and homesteads located near unceded Indian Territory in Nebraska and what is now Wyoming. William spoke to anyone who was willing.

Of the settlers in the area who would talk, most had low opinions of Indians, claiming that they periodically had livestock stolen by Sioux, Cheyenne, and Arapaho raiders. Many spoke of living in fear, and of neighbors who'd been run off, burned out, and in a handful of instances, murdered. Some were distrustful of Standing Elk, and others flat-out wouldn't have him on their property. Often he and I would stay back somewhere nearby, while William interviewed people. Then, on more evenings than not, he or I, and later Standing Elk, would read the notes he'd taken that day, aloud. On the nights we didn't read from his notes, we'd read from a book or a newspaper.

Standing Elk became interested in learning to read, and William soon embraced teaching him. In turn, Standing Elk began teaching William Cheyenne. I can't say they ever became friends; for some reason there always seemed to be a barrier of caution between them. But there was a sort of kinship between the two men nonetheless.

As for William and I, there was friendship, though it was different from the bond Standing Elk and I had. Willian lost his son, and I lost my father. Both deaths occurred long before the sort of relationship fathers and sons share in their later years could develop. We filled a void for each other.

One man William spoke with directed us to a nearby ranch with a half-finished split-rail fence and the charred and leaning skeletons of a house and barn. A hand-painted sign had been driven into the ground of the dooryard. It read:

Andrew Goodall
Mary Goodall
Zackary Goodall
Hope Goodall
Murdered By Indians
In The Year of Our Lord 1871

Local militias had been assembled and they patrolled each other's land, claiming the army wasn't doing all it should to protect their property. Even the people who sympathized with the Indians' *predicament*, often seemed to fear them.

As we traveled, and I observed him, I could see that William Meecham was suited to the task he'd undertaken. His years as an attorney served him well. He asked intelligent questions, never leading ones, and he was astute at separating wheat from chaff.

At the Lakota camp, Red Cloud seemed distracted, and since last I'd spoken with him, his attitude had changed from one of outright defiance to one of reluctant acquiescence. He complained of his loss of influence with some of the younger Lakota men.

"The whites withhold rations because of these young men, and I fear they will soon provoke the bluecoats into more bloodshed. We triumphed over the bluecoats once, but may not again. There are soldiers everywhere now. They are as many as the grasses. They make the rifles and we have few. They make the ammunition and we have none. These young Lakota men drink the white's drink and do foolish things. They raid white farms and steal horses and beef. I was once a great warrior of my people, but I fear I am no more. I would have peace."

Red Cloud also told me that Black Bear had moved on to the Spirit World. He hadn't been killed in battle, but of some unknown fever. It was sad news.

Other chiefs: Sioux, Cheyenne, Arapaho, Crow, and even Pawnee, who most often allied themselves with the army, had similar complaints about the U.S. government not upholding treaty promises. Rations of food and blankets being short, or not arriving at all, were the most common. Hunger was rampant. White traders trading liquor to young men was another problem most chiefs brought up. Many felt as if they were losing these young men to the white's drink.

We visited the Ponca village that Wačhiwi and I had traveled through years before. The once thriving village appeared neglected, the people downtrodden and gaunt. Their chief was named Standing Bear. He was as kind as he was striking in appearance, with his piercing, set eyes and downturned mouth. Standing Bear explained to us that their land had somehow been deeded to the Sioux in the treaty of 1868, and that the Sioux had been coming to their village and demanding tribute ever since. In spite of hardships, the Ponca chief welcomed William and Standing Elk and I, and fed us a meal of deer meat, corn and squash.

In 1878, the U.S. government forced the small nation of peaceable Ponca farmers to move from their homeland to an arid reservation in the south. The imposed march took some two months and it killed many of them, including Standing Bear's daughter. More died once they arrived—hunger, pneumonia, malaria. It was one of the sadder tragedies in an era filled with them.

Evelyn died in the fall of 1872. She developed a cough over a period of weeks. Reaches For The Wind was small and had become accustomed to being a pack horse, so I purchased a four-year-old grullo mare from a dealer near Fort Laramie. I relieved Evelyn of all burden, in hopes she'd overcome whatever was ailing her. She didn't. One morning when I awoke, she was lying on the ground and wouldn't get up. We stayed put that day, and she died silently in the night. My heart ached. I'd never thought such grief could be felt for an animal. I named the new horse Shadow and she became a good one, although she was never quite the horse Evelyn was. Evelyn was the horse I measured all others by for the rest of my life.

Chapter 12

I found Jacob Plemons in July of 1873. It was entirely by chance. We were in southwest Nebraska. William was documenting the massive buffalo kill. That entire summer the thick stench of death on the plains was almost unbearable as thousands of buffalo killers—I never thought of them as hunters—descended upon the plains to shoot the animals. They skinned the woolies for the three-dollars apiece the hides would bring. Some would cut out the tongue to eat, but the remainder of the carcass was left on the prairie to rot. The army was in it as well, only not for the money. One day early that spring we spotted a battalion-sized group of soldiers, who were spread out along a low ridge, east to west, as far as the eye could see in either direction. They were shooting into a massive herd of the beasts. Standing Elk and I stayed behind while William rode up and spoke to some of them, though we already knew why they were doing it. The army had been killing buffalo whenever the opportunity arose for some time. *Every buffalo dead, is an Indian gone,* was the maxim within the military stationed on the plains. We surveyed the killing field after the soldiers departed; hundreds of the woolies lay dead or dying. Not for the first time, Standing Elk lamented the wasted meat and spoke of butchering and smoking as much as we could carry so we could give it to the people at the southern Cheyenne reservation. William wasn't ready to leave Nebraska yet, but promised Standing Elk we'd do just that in the fall.

And we did.

In mid-September, we followed a group of skinners and when they were finished with their evil work, we went in and butchered and smoked well over two thousand pounds of meat. William Meecham vomited the entire contents of his stomach during the first hour, but admirably, he stayed with it and worked through the night right beside Standing Elk and I. A group of Pawnee came through the next morning and began rolling some of the carcasses over to get to the meat that was the least fly and sun tainted before beginning to butcher their own. What they were doing was dangerous, as they were off treaty-designated hunting grounds and likely to be shot by soldiers or skinner gangs if they were discovered. For them, though, the risk was considerably less than the possibility of being killed by Sioux on the already-depleted north grounds.

It was July seventh when we rode into a skinner's camp looking to either purchase or trade for some matches. The camp was the most revolting place I've ever been: huge, bloated flies buzzed thick in the air, the ground was littered with bones, wagon parts, food tins, broken glass, and pieces of putrefying hide. Fires burned here and there, and cooking meat mingling with the scent of corruption and human excrement caused my stomach to lurch. I turned to Standing Elk, his look of distaste puckered his already disfigured features. Hundreds of men meandered about the maze of tents and lean-tos. Some were frontier-hardened men, but most looked fresh from the east and as green as river grass.

There was a sprawling tent the size of a small house midway through the camp, and we headed for it, figuring the vendors would be housed there. Just before we reached it, I saw him—Plemons—big as life, sitting on a plank bench beside several other men. They appeared to be tossing dice onto a scrap of canvas. They all looked up as we walked our horses by, wearing the same look of judicious curiosity afforded us by most of the others. Plemons' eyes passed over me, but there was no recognition in them. It didn't surprise me. I'd always figured him a dull-wit.

When we reached the pavilion, I told William and Standing Elk that Plemons was in the camp. I also told them he wasn't leaving with his life. William blanched visibly at this, but he didn't argue. I asked them to ride northeast ten miles and wait for me. I didn't want William or his work associated with what I was going to do.

I asked Standing Elk for his pistol. "Perhaps I should stay with you," he said.

"I don't think you should be remembered for this any more than William," I said. I nodded at his face. "You already have a face that's hard to forget. If all goes well, I'll catch him alone and no one will be the wiser. Now go, please. I'll get our matches."

He handed over the pistol.

"You could let it go," William said, knowing I could do no such thing.

"I'll see you tonight," I said.

I tethered Shadow to the bridge-rope hitching rail outside the pavilion tent and purchased matches and three cheap cigars from one of the sellers inside. After that, I led Shadow to an inconspicuous place that was still within view of Plemons, and I sat and smoked and watched, taking occasional sips from the silver hip flask I'd begun to carry not long before.

The dice game broke up a short time later and the men went their separate ways. Plemons and another man walked toward the five massive piles of buffalo hides that loomed over the south edge of the camp like a small mountain range. Plemons appeared to be unarmed, the other man carried a sidearm in a military holster. They moved around one end of the hides, opposite the camp. It wasn't ideal; I had no quarrel with the other man, but I figured it might be the best opportunity I got, so I took it. I got up and walked Shadow to the edge of the camp. Once there I mounted her and followed.

Plemons was squatting over a hole with his trousers down around his ankles. The other man was a few feet away pissing on one of the piles of hides. Both watched me approach. When I was within range, I drew the pistol.

"You'll leave your pistol be if you know what's good for you," I said, addressing the pissing man. He raised his hands until they were even with his head, and turned all the way around so he was facing me. I glanced at Plemons, who was still squatting over the hole, staring at me fearfully.

I returned my attention to his friend. "Put your pecker away, unfasten your holster and let it fall. Then step away from it." He nodded and did as I said.

"I know you," Plemons said. "Ward."

"That's right," I said, flicking my eyes to him "Stand up, and pull up your trousers."

"I didn't do nothin', Mister," the other man said.

"My quarrel's not with you," I said. "But I can't let you sound any alarms, so you'll have to come along with us for a bit. If you don't cause any trouble, I'll let you go."

I dismounted, keeping Standing Elk's pistol trained on him. "Now step over there next to him," I said. He walked over and stood next to Plemons, never lowering his hands. I picked up his pistol holster and returned to Shadow and climbed up.

"Now start walking south," I said. I chose south because it would keep the mountains of hides between us and the camp. Plemons wasn't so dim that he couldn't recognize where this was leading. He started screaming "*HELP*" at the top of his voice as he took off at a run, moving parallel with the piles of hides in an attempt to move around to the camp side where he could be seen. I urged Shadow after him, the other man seized the opportunity and ran in the opposite direction. I shot Plemons in the back long before he made it to the end of the row of piles.

I walked Shadow up to him where he lay in the stinking mud with his back arched, sobbing and squirming in pain. He looked up at me, eyes wide with terror. "Grant killed both of them," he said. "It wasn't me. You saw it wasn't me."

I shot him in his face, and then I shot him again, just to be certain.

I dropped the other man's pistol and holster on the ground and then rode south until I was far out of sight of the camp. I turned east and then north to find Standing Elk and William. As far as I know, I was never followed. There was no real law out there, and men like Jacob Plemons rarely have friends so close they're willing to avenge them.

By the middle of 1874 the U.S. government had dropped any pretense of upholding the treaties they'd made with the Indian nations of the great plains. For me it marked the final chapter of the way of life they'd known before the first whites arrived there. Custer led his seventh cavalry on an expedition into the Black Hills of what is now South Dakota that year. In Lakota the Black Hills are the *Pahá Sápa*, and in Cheyenne, the

Mo'ôhta-vo'honáaeva. It had been a sacred place to Indians for as long as their history and was included in the Fort Laramie Treaty of 1868 as part of The Great Sioux Reservation. According to the treaty, the Black Hills were supposed to belong to the Sioux, *Forever.*

Custer's expedition, conducted without the consent of the Lakota people, discovered gold—likely the intent of the foray in the first place—and another gold rush was started. Whites flooded into the area, unchecked by the army, and more bloodshed ensued. Like Red Cloud before him, Sitting Bull began to make a name for himself as a leader. He refused reservation life, and many of the young men who had once followed Red Cloud allied themselves with him. Two years later, with the help of Crazy Horse, Two Moon, and others, he defeated Custer and his seventh at Little Bighorn.

Of course, everyone knows about that one.

What everyone may not know, is that the punitive damages inflicted by the U.S. army were swift and severe. No Indian from Montana territory, east to the Black Hills, and south to the Oklahoma Territory was safe from its wrath. If you were an Indian, and you were off of your designated reservation, man, woman, or child, you were more likely than not to be shot on sight. William Meecham, Standing Elk and myself, came across more Indian corpses than I'd ever care to count, lying dead on the plains between 1874 and 1877 when William finally called it quits.

I still wonder sometimes if he had any inkling of how bad things would get. I know Standing Elk did. He'd always known how things would end.

Chapter 13

At thirty-two-years-old I found myself alone and aimless. It was four years since I killed Jacob Plemons behind the stinking piles of buffalo hides, and after all I'd seen in the interim, seeking out Seth Grant to kill him made no sense to me. Wačhiwi and William were long dead; at the time, I could hardly recall their faces. Vengeance is a word that can only mean something to someone who experiences loss, grief, anger. I'd lost the ability to feel anything at all. I was hollowed-out, empty. In many ways, I still am.

I drifted down to Kansas. I didn't even stop at Oliver Belle's to inquire about he and his family's welfare, or to find out if he'd seen Henry. I ended up in Dodge City—formerly Fort Dodge. I suppose it was the perfect town for someone like me. There couldn't have been more than twelve hundred residents but there were more saloons and brothels than a porcupine has quills, and rough men like me were so commonplace that it was easy to disappear among them.

I had plenty of money: five thousand dollars that William convinced me to deposit in the First Bank of Omaha in 1876, rather than continue to carry it on my person, and just under two-thousand in a tobacco sack I kept down my shirt. I secured a room at the Dodge House hotel and set to drinking away as much money as I could.

I kept to myself at first, spending most of my time in my room with a book and a bottle. I had my meals brought in. After a while I began going to the saloon that was attached to the hotel, where I'd sit and play poker with the drovers and gamblers and whores. I met Emily there. She wasn't a whore, though I wouldn't have held it against her if she was. Life for unwed women was tough then, and it still is. Who am I to judge what someone does to survive.

Emily's husband had owned one of the liveries there in Dodge. He'd been murdered the previous year for a horse that wasn't even his and the eight dollars he'd had in his pocket. He'd been shot through the liver and bled out in their dooryard long before anyone figured out where the shot had come from. Emily told me he hadn't been a gentle man, but she said he'd been a good provider, for whatever that was worth.

She's never caught pregnant, so there were no children. A month after his murder, her late husband's brother arrived on a stagecoach and laid claim to the livery business as his rightful inheritance. He sold the place and left town directly after. The affair left Emily homeless, as their tiny house had been attached to the livery office and was part of the sale. She had fifty-seven dollars to her name when she moved into the Dodge House and began working there as a kitchen and bar maid.

She was older than me by nine years, and she was different than Wačhiwi in most every aspect. Her hair was straw-colored, much like my own was then, and she was full in both hips and bosom. She wasn't soft-spoken or refined in language, but she was kind to her bones. Things started off innocent enough; she'd stop and talk with me for a moment when she delivered a beer or a shot to the table I was playing cards at. Soon after, she began bringing my meals to my room, though she'd never done it before I started frequenting the saloon. One evening there was the usual knock at the door. I set whatever book I'd been reading at the time aside and answered it. She gave me a curt smile and brushed past me, setting the tray she was carrying on the room's small table with a loud clang. She turned to face me then, and I moved toward the night table to get the fifty-cents I'd been giving her every evening when she brought supper.

"I don't *want* your fifty-cents," she said, "I want you to notice me."

I stopped; arm outstretched for the coins on the night table. "I noticed you," I said, turning to her.

She was wearing a white dress with blue flower print. She brushed her hands down the front of it primly. "You haven't said so much."

"Well, I suppose I'm not accustomed to … this."

"You could start by inviting me for a drink."

So I did, and we started keeping company regularly.

She wasn't much of a drinker, when it came to it, but she didn't say anything to me about mine. When she wasn't working we'd take Shadow and Reaches For The Wind out riding, or have supper at one of the handful of places that served food there in town. She was curious about my life before I came to Dodge, and I told her what I could. She was from Topeka and had married the first boy who courted her. When her father died, they took the small inheritance and moved to Dodge City on the advice of the husband's brother—the same brother who eventually laid claim to the livery business Emily and her husband built.

I have to appreciate that she never asked me for more than I had to give. There was no talk of settling down or marriage. Outwardly she seemed content with the way things were, and for the most part, so was I, though I think the loud bustle and raucousness of Dodge was beginning to wear on me. It was never quiet, not even in the earliest hours, when most of the night animals had already bedded down. I wondered often, while I was in Dodge, why I hadn't stayed with the Lakota when Wačhiwi had been alive. It was a good life; a quiet life. It was painful in a way I can't explain, to miss the life we had there, knowing that I was the one who wanted to leave, and knowing what the outcome of that choice was.

I'd been in town for eight months when Seth Grant showed up in the Dodge House saloon. He looked much different than when I last saw him. He'd traded the beard for a thick moustache, he was grayer, and he had a thick knot of scars on his neck where no hair would ever grow again. Wačhiwi had seen to that.

I didn't even notice him in the saloon, though I should have, as big as he was. I'm not sure how long he'd been in there, but he noticed me, and he recognized me.

I was playing poker—I remember I'd been doing pretty well that evening, and wasn't quite drunk yet, though it was a near thing. Emily was working the evening shift and would have finished up around ten. I caught him out of the corner of my eye when he was still a few steps from the table. I lifted my head from my cards just as he moved in between me and the player to my right. I slid around in that direction so I could look up at him. He loomed over me. I wasn't afraid.

"A while back, it didn't seem I could go anywhere without folks telling me you were looking for me. Well, here I am, standing before you. Question is, are you still looking? Because if you're not, I'm willing to go about my business as if we've never met."

I gazed into his flat eyes and knew I couldn't do that. I remembered the last words Wačhiwi spoke to me: *Avenge William, if you're able. Our son was innocent,* and all at once

I could see her face again, and I could see William's face again. He nodded his head as if I'd given him an answer aloud. The town ordinance stated that you couldn't carry a firearm on the north side of the railroad tracks, and the Dodge House was just to the north of the east/west tracks, otherwise shooting may have started right then and there. Instead, Grant backed up a few steps, bent, and removed a knife from his boot. The same skinning knife he killed Wačhiwi with. The poker table cleared out with that, a couple of them knocking their chairs over in their hurry to move away. The saloon went silent for a moment before erupting into a disharmony of excited shouts. I scooped up my money from the table and stood.

"You won't need that, son," Grant said over the din. The context was different, but he'd said the same thing to me when he found me by the stagnant creek in Oklahoma Territory, years before.

I stuffed the money in my pocket. "Outside," I said, moving past him toward the back door, which led to a sort of blind alley made by the Dodge House and its outbuildings. I pulled my knife and walked about twenty feet and turned. He was right behind me, and a flood of shouting and cheering and jeering saloon patrons were squeezing through the door behind him.

He stopped a few feet away, the skinning knife dangling loosely from his right hand. "I heard you got Jacob Plemons up there in Nebraska. Shot him in the back, they said."

"That's right."

"Cowardly, if you ask me. I'm glad you never got the chance to do me that way. Particularly after I saved your life." He cocked his head. "Let's get to it."

Grant was a giant, near a foot-and-a-half taller than I was and probably three times my weight. It was never my intent to engage him in a knife fight. I had something else in mind.

He came at me then, and he came fast, swinging his knife in an upward arc. I sidestepped, and he swung a haymaker with his left as he realized the knife was missing its mark. I could have ducked the blow, but I took it, and let it send me reeling backward where I fell over a water trough that was pushed against the side of the building. I reached over the trough, between it and the building, and brought out the Spencer and swung it around. He was almost on top of me by then, and his eyes widened in surprise when he saw what was about to happen.

The shot took off the top of Seth Grant's head. If it had been an inch higher I would have missed, and almost certainly would have been the one laid out on a wood plank that night. But I didn't miss. He made a strangled sound and fell atop me, breaking three of my ribs in the process.

There was utter silence as I struggled out from under Grant's body. Then, as I was getting to my feet there came a woman's scream—Emily. A second later, a voice from behind me said, "Hey!" I wheeled to see a rifle stock coming toward me. Then the world went black.

I awoke on my back, on a floor. There were voices. I turned my head; men were sitting against the wall, their legs splayed. They were laughing at something one of them said. I turned my head the other way; there was a steel cot hung from the wall. There was a man lying in it, either sleeping or dead. There was a pile of yellow vomit on the plank floor beside him.

My head was pounding and every breath caused bright pain on my left side. I realized then that I was breathing through my mouth. My nose was completely plugged. I raised a hand and felt it, gingerly. It was swollen and I thought it was broken. My fingers came away sticky with blood. I got to my feet. It took some effort.

"Hey, Marshall, he's awake," one of the men sitting against the wall called out.

Feeling out-of-temper, I shot him an angry glance.

"Well, he asked me to tell him," he said, truculently.

I walked to bars. The cell I was in was the first of three, set in a row down a narrow corridor. The other cells were to my left, to my right was a doorway. There was a barred door, but it stood open to the adjoining room. A gun case attached to the wall was all I could see through the opening.

I stood with my arms through the bars. The men sitting against the wall had fallen silent. Finally, one said, "You really shoot that big fella?"

I didn't answer. I heard the sound of a chair being slid across the floor and then footsteps. The man's shadow preceded him through the doorway. He stepped through; it was the man who'd clocked me with the rifle stock. He was tall and slight of build, and dressed in black. He stood in front of me and eyed me as if I was a particularly interesting insect.

"Emily Watkins tells me your name is Everett Ward. That right?" he said.

"It is."

"Well, Mister Ward, my name's Wyatt Earp, I'm a deputy marshal, and you've been arrested on the suspicion of murder."

"I shot him defending myself. You can't jail me for that."

"I can jail you for anything I please. At the very least, you broke a town ordinance by not checking-in your rifle. If you want to be a hardcase, we can go that way. Otherwise, Marshal Masterson is down at the Dodge House questioning the witnesses, and if they say it was self-defense, then you'll be free to go … after you pay the fine for the rifle." He looked me up and down. "You need the doctor?"

"It can wait," I said.

Two hours later I was freed by Ed Masterson. He questioned me as to why I had my rifle hidden behind the hotel. I told him I always kept it there so I had access to it if I needed it in a hurry. It was the truth of it, and he seemed satisfied. He returned my Spencer to me after I paid a twenty-five dollar fine, then he said, "You're not welcome here anymore. You understand?" I said I did.

He struck me as a decent man. I read that he was shot and killed by a drunk, not long after that night.

From the jail I went straight to my room and gathered up my things, then took them down to the stable where I'd been renting stalls for both Shadow and Reaches For The Wind. I settled up with the stableman after waking him—it was past midnight by then—and then I packed up Reaches For The Wind, saddled Shadow, and rode out of town. I never said goodbye to Emily. I'm ashamed of that.

I rode up to Omaha so I could draw some money from the bank. After I told him my name, the man working the counter summoned the bank manager. The manager, Benjamin

Clutterbuck, a cadaverous man with a pencil-thin moustache and weak chin, asked if I would accompany him to his office. Once there, he removed an envelope from his desk and handed it to me. The envelope was addressed to **Mister Everett Ward C/O First Bank of Omaha** with the return being: **Treagle and Waterman, Attorneys at Law.**

I opened the letter, and written in small, neat script, was:

Dearest Mister Ward:

As attorney for William Meecham, it is my sad and solemn duty to inform you that William Meecham was murdered in his home on Manhattan Island on December the Twenty-Third, Eighteen and Seventy-Seven by an unknown assailant. I was told that he was shot in his sleep and that he did not suffer. As stated in William's undisputed Last Will and Testament, you are the sole beneficiary of his estate, which, per his instructions, has been liquidated into cash by this firm. Said cash has been deposited in your name, to your account at the First Bank of Omaha, in the amount of One Hundred, Thirty Thousand, Four Hundred, Sixty-Two Dollars.

Yours Truly, and Respectfully,
Jonathan Treagle

I thanked the bank manager and exited the office feeling unsettled. He followed me to the door, asking if I intended to stay in Omaha, and if I were interested in investment opportunities there. I told him I'd consider the possibility.

There was a hotel with a stable a few doors down from the bank. I checked in and inquired about a telegraph office. The clerk informed me that the hotel housed a telegraph office right off of the lobby. I thanked him and walked over.

The telegraph operator was a severe-looking woman of middle-age who pointed to the forms on the edge of her desk without looking up from her newspaper. I took a pencil from the box and wrote this:

Dear Mister Treagle:

I received your correspondence and offer you my sincerest thanks. I would like to know if you can tell me if William's book was published prior to his death. I will wait here in Omaha for your reply.

Yours,
Everett Ward

I received a reply the very next day. It read:

Mister Ward:

Sadly, William's manuscript was not among his belongings. I didn't wish to burden you previously, but your inquiry is intriguing. Curiously, and, I might add, suspiciously, the publishing house William contracted for the printing and distribution of his work was burned to the ground along with half of a city block just days after his death.

Yours Truly, and Respectfully,
Jonathon Treagle

I read the telegram over and over in my room that evening. Several glasses of whiskey couldn't quell my anger. My thoughts went back to nights in camp with William and Standing Elk, and how most often William or I read aloud from his book of notes, whatever he'd taken down that day. I hadn't considered it much at the time, but there were many times he didn't read from his notes, or offer to have me do it. And in retrospect, a few of those times had been after he'd interviewed an army officer or an Indian agent. Had he learned something that he was killed for? It's a question that plagues me to this day, though I know it will never be answered.

I withdrew three thousand dollars from the bank—the manager was clearly relieved I was leaving the bulk of the money in his care—and I re-outfitted myself for the trail. I bought three colt M1878s and two holsters from a grateful gun dealer on the edge of town, along with six boxes of .45 caliber cartridges. I figured I'd give the pistol without the holster to Standing Elk because he'd never use one anyway, and one with a holster to Henry, if I ever saw him again.

I rode south in no particular hurry. When I reached Lawrence I stopped to look in on Oliver Belle. He was gone, and there was another family living in the house. The man there told me Oliver had pulled up stakes and moved to California back in '73.

I made my way down to Oklahoma Territory and found Standing Elk at the Cheyenne reservation. He'd taken a wife, and she'd given birth to a child a few months before. For that I was happy, but the conditions on the reservation hadn't improved any from the last time I'd been there. I gave him the pistol and one thousand dollars. He knew to spend the money a little at a time. An Indian with cash aroused suspicion.

We sat and smoked in front of his lodge and I told him about William, and about Seth Grant.

"Do you ever miss the trail?" I said.

"No," he said in English. "I miss the north country, and the way it was when my father's father still walked in this world. And I miss hunting. There is nothing here but snakes."

"What do you think Henry's doing? Do you think he's alive?"

"He's alive, but like you and I, death is all around him."

I spent the next dozen years roaming. I still don't know exactly why. I had plenty of money to buy a ranch and settle down, but whenever I considered it with any real vigor, it ended up seeming absurd. I think, at the time, I was tired of living, but not quite prepared to die. That may not make sense to some, but I believe that's the truth of it.

I caught up with Captain Lange in the spring of 1880—just a year before he retired and returned east—and started scouting for the army. My only condition was that I stayed off of their roles and didn't have to sign any contracts. There weren't many men with more experience than me at the time; we were on our way to being extinct. So, officers who needed someone like me found ways to make it work, often fudging expenses or dipping into their own pockets to pay me. I didn't need the money, of course..

Mostly I just drank, did my job, and kept to myself. When there was no scouting work, I'd run dispatches, guide civilians, or guard trains and stages. I even did a bit of marshalling, though I discovered I didn't have the temperament for it. Once, I made my way down to Texas, thinking I'd visit Calvin Englebright. As it turned out he'd died years before, not long after helping clear my name. I never thanked him for that. Another regret in a life filled with them.

Sometimes I'd head up through Montana and cross the border and do some hunting. If I did well, I'd smoke the meat and take it, along with my wages, to one Indian reservation or another like Standing Elk and I used to do. Once, I bought fifty head of beef and hired a couple of men to help me drive them south to the Cheyenne reservation. Everything was fine until I left. Standing Elk told me later that some men associated with the Indian agent rode in the very next day, armed with rifles and claimed half the steers. I took it up with the Indian agent when I found out about it, and he claimed Standing Elk and the others who corroborated his story were liars. No surprise there.

The conditions on all of the reservations were terrible. Sickness and hunger were unchecked, and mass graves were commonplace.

I visited Red Cloud at the Pine Ridge Agency in what is now South Dakota several times over the years. The last time I saw him was in 1888. By that time the once-great warrior and leader was growing dim of sight and frail of body. Seeing him that way was a hard thing to witness. He said the young men thought of him as a puppet to the whites and poked fun at him. He also said that the same young men were the first in line when the whites were handing out their rotten blankets and moth-eaten clothes.

"The whites took the last of our land," he said, as we sat on the porch of the Indian agent's office and watched the sun sink in the west. "Now we are nothing more than prisoners here."

"I know," I said, feeling like I should say more.

The previous year the U.S. government had enacted what they named the Dawes Act. In essence, the law broke up Indian land, allotted small parcels to each Indian family on the tribal roles, and claimed what land was left—tens of millions of acres—as excess and sold it to whites for next to nothing. For Red Cloud and others like him, it was the final humiliation.

"They said they wanted us to be farmers. We're not farmers. Nothing grows very good here anyway. When we are lucky enough to get beef from the agent, the young men will put one in the horse corral and chase it around before they kill it, as if they are on a hunt. This saddens me, and yet makes me grateful for living in the time when we were free to roam the land and hunt as we pleased."

I saw Sitting Bull a few times after he finally gave up and turned himself in to the Standing Rock Agency—also in what is now South Dakota—but he mostly feigned he didn't know me. I did speak to him once, just a few months before he was killed by tribal police at his home on the reservation. I'd just delivered a handful of dispatches to James McLaughlin, who was the Indian agent at Standing Rock at the time. There's been a small handful of men in my life who gave me an uncomfortable feeling for no outward reason, and he was one of them.

I was just climbing up on Shadow when Sitting Bull strode up behind me. I lowered myself back down and turned to face him.

"Háu," I said.

He nodded and then glanced up at the agent's office. McLaughlin was standing in the window, gazing at us.

"I am always under his watchful eye," Sitting Bull said in Lakota. "Do you remember when we hunted, and the bull buffalo charged me?"

I smiled at the memory. "I do," I said.

He nodded again. "Those were good days."

That was all. He turned and walked away.

During that same year, the Lakota had been performing what was named the Ghost Dance. The dance had been introduced to them by a Paiute man named Wovoka. The belief was that the dance would spur the return of Indians from the Spirit World, and invoke a new beginning for all Indians. Whites would be covered with earth and new grass, and the buffalo would return to the plains.

The dance gave them hope, and it came to where it was being performed at all of the Sioux agencies regularly. The dance made the Indian agents anxious; James McLaughlin most particularly. He feared it signified an Indian uprising, though myself and others told him different. Regardless, tension was building, and between October and December of 1890, I never left the area. I ran as many as fifteen dispatches a week between the Sioux agencies and army posts.

Sitting Bull had been allowing the Ghost Dance to be performed near his small wood house at the Standing Rock Agency. McLaughlin ordered him to stop the dance, not only near his home, but everywhere at Standing Rock. Whether Sitting Bull wouldn't or couldn't, I can't say, but the dances went on. On December 14, McLaughlin ordered Sitting Bull's arrest. The following day, a man named Bull Head—going by the name, Henry Bullhead—a lieutenant in the tribal police, and four other men rode out to carry-out that order. There was an argument in Sitting Bull's dooryard between Bull Head and a group of men loyal to Sitting Bull. One of the men pulled a rifle and shot Bull Head. Curiously, Bull Head turned his gun on Sitting Bull instead of his assailant and shot the aging chief in the chest. Immediately, one of the men Bull Head had brought with him, shot Sitting Bull in the head, killing him.

A short time later, Bull Head and his men were hunted down and killed by Sitting Bull's son and some other men.

I wasn't there to witness what happened that day, but I've always figured it was never James McLaughlin's intention for Sitting Bull to make it to the jail alive. Even if it was, he would have been better off leaving Sitting Bull be. Barring a few misguided young men who thought that if they acted white, then whites would treat them as equals, Sitting Bull was a hero among the Lakota. Eventually the tension caused by the Ghost Dance—and likely the Ghost Dance itself—would have blown over. Instead, things on the entire Sioux reservation became more strained than ever. The army presence grew. The talk among the soldiers was all about the pending uprising. To me, the idea was laughable. This wasn't 1866, or 1876. By 1890 the Indian warrior was nothing more than a shadow, a rumor, the Ghost Dance nothing more than a desperate plea for help from an oppressed and broken people. Perhaps one day there will be a phoenix for the Indians, but it wasn't then, and it isn't now. That week a paranoiac war department started rounding up influential Indians and containing them tightly near the agencies. At the same time, many Lakota who lived on the Standing Rock Agency were secretly fleeing to outlying camps or to the Pine Ridge Agency.

On December 28, I was at the Pine Ridge Agency. I was sent to find and deliver a dispatch to Major Whitside with the Seventh Cavalry, who'd been ordered by the war department to arrest Chief Big Foot, another Lakota chief the Indian agents and the war department considered an instigator. I caught up with them just before nightfall, at a camp they'd set near Wounded Knee Creek. Whitside and the seventh found the chief and some three hundred fifty Lakota men, women, and children several miles away at Cherry Creek. Apparently they were on their way to the Pine Ridge Agency to seek council from Red Cloud. Instead of arresting only Big Foot, who was sick with pneumonia, and hardly able to walk, Major Whitside arrested the entire group and marched them from Cherry Creek to Wounded Knee Creek. I delivered my dispatch and then set my own camp some hundred yards outside the perimeter of the military's camp, as I'd learned to do from Henry so many years before. To be clear, there were two camps side-by-side at Wounded Knee: One for the army, and one for the Indians.

As usual, I set to drinking in my tent and didn't pay much attention to the going's on nearby.

Sometime in the night, Colonel Forsyth, the commander of the seventh, arrived with more troops, and two more Hotchkiss guns to add to the two Major Whitside and his men had already been carrying. That would have brought the troop strength in the camp to around five hundred.

When I awoke in the morning, I stuck my head out of my tent. I could see the Hotchkiss guns had been set up on a low rise to face the circular area the Indians were camped in. Now, these Hotchkiss guns were made for warfare. They're as big as cannons and capable of firing close to seventy rounds a minute. I thought it curious that the guns had actually been deployed, considering that the hundred or so half-starved and sickly Lakota men couldn't have had more than a dozen old rifles between them, and most would be single-shot muzzle-loaders at that.

I'd slept in my clothes that night, the ground was frozen and it was South Dakota cold. I slipped on my boots and started up to the hill to have a look at the guns. The two in the center were manned, the other two sat alone. Halfway up the hill I glanced down below and saw that cavalry riders had circled the Lakota camp. I stopped and watched; other soldiers armed with rifles or sidearms were walking through the camp, forcing people to sit on the ground and then going into the Indians' tents and lodges. Some of the soldiers kicked the lodges over after they came out. I continued up the hill, one of the soldiers manning a Hotchkiss, gave me a nod. Suddenly there was a single report from down the hill. Just as I turned, screams erupted, and then a rapid staccato of rifle and pistol shots. All at once it was chaos; I stared, dumbfounded, hardly believing my own eyes. The soldiers surrounding the camp were firing on the Indians, but they were in a circle around the camp. So they'd created a crossfire and were shooting each other in the process.

Thunder roared from the top of the hill. The soldiers were firing the two Hotchkiss guns. I stood motionless as Lakota women and children were shot down trying to break through the line of soldiers to escape. Some made it through and were shot while running away. I saw two Lakota men carrying rifles running toward the line of soldiers, both were cut down. I turned to the soldiers on the Hotchkiss guns, and then looked at the unmanned one nearest me. I had a vision of running up to it and turning it on the soldiers, just as several more of them hurried up from the opposite side of the hill and dispersed to the two unmanned guns. A soldier in a Captain's uniform was among them, likely the battery officer. He shouted something to his men, then he saw me and angrily waved me away. I ignored him. I was well out of their line of fire. More shots erupted from the two previously mute Hotchkiss guns. I looked back down the hill, but I couldn't see anything through the powder smoke.

When it was over, hundreds lay dead or dying; most women and children from what I could see. Wounded soldiers were being tended to but no one was seeing to the injured Indians. When I tried to get closer to see if I could help, Colonel Forsyth, who'd been walking back and forth barking orders at his bewildered-looking soldiers, shouted to a sergeant who was a few feet away from me.

The colonel's words were: "Remove that Indian lover or shoot him. I don't care which."

I camped nearby and went back early the next morning, barely ahead of an incoming storm. The dead Lakota had been left there on the ground. Chief Big Foot was among them; an old man in a weathered wool coat and a knitted kerchief to protect his head and ears from the cold. His arms were in the air as if he were clutching at something. It occurred to me I'd never spoken to him in life.

Along with the body of the chief there were perhaps eighty men and more than a hundred women and children—some infants—scattered among the tattered remnants of the camp. I found more bodies in a shallow ravine nearby. It appeared as if they'd fled, and were either chased there or found afterward. They'd all been shot.

I made my way to the Pine Ridge Agency. Fifty or so wounded Lakota had been loaded into wagons hours after the massacre. A man I knew named Left Hand told me that they were left in wagons unattended for several more hours before they were finally moved into the church.

The sky was the color of gunmetal and snow had just begun to fall as I rode west from the Pine Ridge Agency. I've never been back.

I don't know what sparked the shooting that day, or who fired the first shot. Accounts from people who were there—and from many who weren't—have been in conflict since the question was first asked. The question I want to ask is this: Does it matter? I don't think so. Even if every armed Lakota man in that camp opened fire on those soldiers, it could never excuse what was done that day; not in all the ages of the Earth.

In the spring of 1891 I purchased the ranch that had previously belonged to James "Red" Macklin for the sum of thirteen thousand dollars from the same bank Wačhiwi and I had rented from so many years before. The ranch had gone belly-up the previous summer and had sat vacant through the fall and winter. I held onto an additional twenty thousand and gave the rest of the considerable fortune William Meecham left me to the National Indian Defense Association. The transaction was handled through a befuddled Jonathon Treagle, and I never had any direct contact with the organization. I don't pretend to think it did much to help Indians; hopefully it fed some people.

I named the ranch The Dancing Girl, and I raised horses there until I turned seventy and sold the place and moved to California. It's strange, where I ended up. It's a small railroad town named Portola, and it's located not far from the Nevada border. What makes it strange is that James Beckwourth lived here for a time in the 1850s, not two miles from where I now sit. His cabin is still there. I walked through it, once. If Henry were still alive, he'd chuckle over that one.

I suppose I can't finish this story without telling you what became of Henry and Standing Elk.

Henry showed up at my door on January 5, 1893 in the middle of storm. He'd lived in Mexico for some time, and then later Texas and California. I don't have enough paper to tell his stories. Suffice to say, Henry lived an interesting life. He stayed at the ranch with me in Kansas until his death in 1911. One night after supper he said he wasn't feeling well and he retired early. The next morning, when he didn't come to breakfast, I looked in on him. He was there, in his bed, just like he was sleeping. I suppose it was a good way to go.

Standing Elk showed up in the summer of 1894. I'd written him, shortly after purchasing the ranch, to let him know he was welcome. I addressed the letter to him care of the Cheyenne Agency. I never really believed he'd get it.

There was a hammering on the door well after midnight. It was just me and Henry in the house and I didn't keep a bunkhouse. I had three men that worked the place regular, but they all lived in town. I reached the door just after Henry, who'd already opened it, and there in the foyer was Standing Elk.

Standing Elk's son was killed by a rattlesnake bite in 1885. His wife sickened and died seven years later. In 1893, in its effort to force assimilation and live up to its *Kill the Indian, Not the Man*, rhetoric, the U.S. government, in a partnership with a Christian organization, opened a boarding school some seventy miles from the reservation. The reservation's children between the ages of six and sixteen were required to attend and live there. If the parent refused, then rations and other subsidies would be cut off to that family. The children were taken to the school, their hair was cut, and they were no longer allowed to speak their own language. They studied English, the bible, and white history. Standing Elk was outraged and he stormed the place one night with the pistol I'd given him—he'd turned in his other one in 1889 when the army 'disarmed' the Cheyenne reservation. He killed every adult on the premises, men and women alike, loaded the children into the school's wagon, and made his way back to the reservation with them.

After I retired to my room, Standing Elk's story played over and over in my mind. It had been years since I slept well. Every black episode of my life came creeping back in the watches of the night, and though I didn't drink like I had before, a glass of whiskey or three after dark usually afforded me at least some sleep. Not that night, though. Not a wink.

He had to have known there'd be repercussions. Two weeks later, I read in the newspaper that two of the children's fathers had been hanged for the crime. I never told Standing Elk, neither did Henry. And neither of us told him that the school was rebuilt in a different location just a year later.

Standing Elk lived there on the ranch with me for the rest of his life. He died a very old man in 1915, outliving Henry by four years.

And here I am. Through all the long years I knew Standing Elk, his prophecies proved wrong far more often than they were right. But he was dead-on in what he said to me some sixty ago; I've outlived everyone I've ever known.

I'm tired, though.

To my very bones.

I'm also afraid.

I've come to believe that a man's life can be measured—and judged—as much by what he doesn't do, as by what he does. Standing Elk was the only one of the three of us who truly believed in an afterlife. He believed it all the way to his deathbed. I hope he was wrong about that. With every breath I take, I hope he was wrong.

Thank you for reading. Please take a moment to leave a short review or rate this title on Amazon, Goodreads or both.

Special acknowledgment and thanks to Andy Marr, Jeffrey Keeten, and Sarah Pearce.
Without their input, this book in its present form would not have been possible.

Made in the USA
Coppell, TX
12 October 2024